**It was a movie kiss, the one in the rain,
the reunion in the desert.**

That first humiliating fumble all those months ago was finally erased by this most perfect melding of mouths.

He pulled back, breathless, before she could get busy with her hands. A helpless little sound, part lust, part disappointment, emerged involuntarily from her throat. She wasn't proud of it.

"Jules, I've seen you with the Cheerio hair accessories and that Manchester United shirt so ragged you should burn it. Sometimes you look like you just fell out of bed and your hair hasn't seen a brush in forever. All it does is remind me that your focus is your kid and that you're the most unselfish person I've ever met. Seeing you, the real you, turns me on big time. So don't tell me how I feel."

She swallowed, absorbing into her bloodstream what taste she could savor from his lips and those heart-stopping words. Holding on to that taste for dear life.

HOT AND
BOTHERED

Also by Kate Meader

Feel the Heat
All Fired Up

HOT AND BOTHERED

Kate Meader

FOREVER

NEW YORK BOSTON

Forever

Hachette Book Group

1290 Avenue of the Americas

New York, NY 10104

HachetteBookGroup.com

Twitter.com/foreverromance

Originally published as an ebook

First mass market edition: January 2015

10 9 8 7 6 5 4 3 2 1

OPM

Forever is an imprint of Grand Central Publishing.

The Forever name and logo are trademarks of Hachette Book Group, Inc.

The publisher is not responsible for websites (or their content) that are not owned by the publisher.

The Hachette Speakers Bureau provides a wide range of authors for speaking events. To find out more, go to www.hachettespeakersbureau.com or call (866) 376-6591.

*To my sexy hero—thanks for taking
this crazy ride with me.*

Acknowledgments

Thanks to my amazing beta readers, Amber Lin and Monique Headley, for your insight and support. To the team at Grand Central for your faith in me and for my sizzling hot covers. And to everyone who has embraced my sexy chefs and the DeLucas, happy reading and *buon appetito*!

HOT AND BOTHERED

In the beginning...

Lying half-naked and spread-eagled with a hot hunk whispering encouraging words in your ear might be the fantasy of millions of women, but this particular variation was not doing the trick for Jules Kilroy.

"I need to bleedin' push!"

"Not yet," Dr. Harper said firmly. Her tough-as-old-boots OB must have been a sergeant major in a previous life.

Push, don't push, deep breaths, shallow breaths... agh! Jules was trying not to act like she was the first woman to give birth, but it was *her* first time and blimey, the pain was excruciating.

"It's not called labor for nothing," the man at her side added, a knowing smile in his deep rumble of a voice. Usually that voice worked gangbusters to get her through the rough times, not to mention fueling a few luridly inappropriate fantasies, but today she just wanted to drop-kick Tad

DeLuca's beautiful face into the middle of the next millennium.

Instead of losing the plot, she made a conscious decision to breathe herself to serenity. From time immemorial, the entirety of womankind had endured the pain of childbirth, so she needed to stop being such a trauma queen. The sucking-in-air part she could manage. *Slow, deep breaths.* Around her, the low hum of hospital equipment and the professional, almost balletic movements of Team "Get Demon Out of Jules" focused her mind on the task ahead.

Bloody hell, she was having a baby!

Pain, sharper than before, lanced through her. She clasped Tad's hand so hard she half expected to see diamonds pop out.

He didn't flinch, but then he never did.

Tad had been her rock since she showed up in Chicago five months ago, straight off a flight from London with a bun in the oven. Those broad shoulders, indecently covered with drip-dry fabrics ready to absorb her weepfests, had borne the weight of her weary head more times than she cared to count. He was the first person she confided in about her dyslexia, the last person who comforted her through every piddling panic. She had her brother, former celebrity chef Jack Kilroy, and an amazing extended family in the DeLucas, her brother's in-laws, but Tad was the guy who made her feel like she was part of something bigger. He made her feel special.

A rolling wave of pain caught her by surprise—surprising because she had passed the point where the contractions let up and gave her breaks. For the last hour, they had been blurring into each other, shifting like tectonic plates heralding an earthquake of suffering.

"Demon wants out," she muttered, tears rolling down her cheeks.

"Of course he does." Tad thumbed at the corners of her eyes, swiping her leaking emotion away. "He's dying to meet you. And we're all dying to meet him."

Him. That she was having a boy was bloody typical. The male of the species had been nothing but trouble since that first moment on a London school playground when she realized the anatomical differences between boys and girls were worthy of further exploration. Curiosity, every woman's downfall.

"Now's the time to push," Doc Harper barked.

Jules bore down, trying to remember how to do something that was supposedly innate and natural. She had to be getting it all wrong, like she always did.

Tad squeezed her hand, much more gently than she had squeezed his. "Hold it for ten seconds, just like we practiced in the classes." With an empathetic held breath of his own, his shoulders lifted, inflating his already immense chest. The scrubs he wore should have been loose-fitting, but they molded to his muscles on that inhale, a fact she should not be noticing now, of all times. Think of the fortune this deliciously distracting man could make hiring that face, bod, and voice out to birthing mothers everywhere.

"That's good. Now relax, don't push," Dr. Harper said, her professional eye on the fetal monitor. Its steady beeps reassured everyone in the delivery room that the baby was okay even if Jules felt like an alien was about to explode from her hoo-ha.

"Maybe you should take some of that dope they offered so liberally a while back," Tad said, in clear violation of her instructions.

No matter what happens, don't let me take any drugs.

There had been other instructions to Tad as well: *refrain*

from flirting with the pretty nurses and *under no circumstances are you to look down there!* But mostly, the "just say no to drugs" was rule numero uno.

Though she had always been open to the idea of an epidural, in the end she had elected to stick with a natural childbirth. Not because she was an earthy-crunchy, tree-hugging hippie type. She had a sneaking suspicion that if she got high, she'd get chatty and might reveal a few unfortunate home truths to the man at her side.

Such as how he made her tingly in troublesome places and that she had a whopping mega crush on him.

"Too late for that," Doc cut in, eliminating the need to make a decision.

"So the window for legalized narcotics has passed," Tad said. "But that's okay because *I'm* here. I'm your drug, baby. Just look at me and tell me you're not addicted to my shocking good looks."

"Arsehole," she muttered, annoyed that he had the audacity to read her mind while she was at her lowest point. Shocking good looks weren't far off the mark, though. Taddeo DeLuca was a Prada commercial come to life. The hard bod, the piercing blue eyes, the dark, wavy hair that framed his face like a wimple of sin. In his banged-up jeans and motorcycle leathers, he was sex-on-Italian-legs.

He smiled brazen and wide, passing over her ill humor like a true friend. That smile was killer. "If my hotness is not enough to distract you, let's talk about all the things you're going to do once you offload this basketball."

For months, she had been whining constantly about everything she missed while pregnant, so even in her addled state, the list reeled off her tongue smoothly.

"First up, spicy tuna rolls."

"I've got Aiko's on speed dial," he said, referring to their favorite sushi place in Wicker Park, the north side neighborhood where they both lived. "Just say the word."

"A double gin and tonic." As soon as the words escaped her lips, her mouth watered like she was Pavlov's dog. "Just one, though, because I'll be breastfeeding."

Tad's dark brows lifted and his gaze dropped to her breasts, covered by a hospital gown. They'd ballooned to a point where they could be seen from the International Space Station. There was the Great Wall of China, then her massive boobs.

"The miracle of life," he murmured dreamily.

She thumped him in the arm. "Perv."

"Well, they already look fantastic, but I'm all on board with them getting bigger when your milk comes in." Tad had devoured all the pregnancy books in the name of supporting her as they approached the big day and he knew more than the average male on the topic. He mimicked cupping zeppelin-sized breasts. "What are we talking here? Double Ds, Double Fs?"

"You're impossible," she said, feeling dangerously tender toward him right this minute.

He raised her clasped hand to his lips and brushed his soft mouth across her knuckles. "What else are you looking forward to, *mia bella*?"

Mia bella. My beautiful. She loved when he called her that, especially when she was feeling less than beautiful.

"Seeing my feet again." Also on the MIA list were unmentionable body parts, such as the overgrown forest between her legs that machetes might have trouble hacking through. Jules had set up an appointment for a bikini wax about ten minutes after her waters broke seven hours ago.

"Cute shoes. My feet have puffed to marshmallows and

my shoe collection misses me terribly." She'd sequestered
them in the back of her closet along with her most fashionable threads—the ones single girls on the pull wore as their
armor—because the sight of them every time she opened the
closet door gouged her fashion-loving soul.

Most of all she missed feeling sexy, and all research
pointed to the disturbing conclusion that it might be a while
before she got there again. Demon was going to be a real
crimp in her love life for sure.

As if the little bugger heard her negative thoughts about
him, he made a break for the border.

"I have to push," she said with authority, desperately trying to sound like she had some control over this frightening
situation. It was a biological need to propel this baby into
the world, but also a psychological grasp at the tethers. Her
entire life had been spent ducking and diving from the hard
decisions. Fleeing when it got tough, shutting down when
the situation demanded she step up.

Five months ago, she'd made the best choice for her baby
when she left London and all the pain behind. Finding the
strength to admit she needed help by mending fences with
her brother had brought her to Chicago. To a new life and a
ready-made family.

"Not yet," Doc ordered.

"Yes." Jules disagreed because it felt right.

Demon applied the screws again, determined to rip her
open in his push to embrace daylight. The pain. Oh, God, the
pain. She screamed, terrified and thrilled to be finally taking
charge of her life.

"Okay, push," the doctor said as if this baby wasn't running the show.

"Come on, *mia bella*." Tad wiped his rough, callused
palm across her sweaty hair-matted forehead. *Do I look*

beautiful now, you bastard? "You can do this. You can do anything."

And in that moment, she believed him. He was a man, so lying was ingrained in his DNA and one of his penis people had got her into this mess. But he was also her friend, and she believed him.

Forty seconds of the most agonizing torture she had ever experienced and it was over. Her eyes registered a blur of red, a ball of raw meat, really, before the doc whisked him away to be examined and prodded.

"Is he all right?" She turned to Tad, whose face was frozen in a mix of wonder and fear. "Tad, is he all right?"

A baby—*her baby*—let out a wail that must have reached the waiting room where she knew her brother was likely wearing a groove in the floor. Choosing Tad to be her birthing partner had pissed Jack off in the extreme and set them back a few steps in their relationship rehab. But her brother needed to recognize that having her own agency in this, in all aspects of her life, was paramount.

"Fuck, he's got a set of lungs on him," Tad said, awe deepening his voice. "Sounds just like his mouthy mom."

Jules raised a weak hand to smack him, only to let it fall away. She had nothing left to give.

Or, so she thought until she saw *him.*

Her fresh-born baby, out in the world, wrapped in a blanket and looking oh-so-innocent. The pretty nurse Tad had not flirted with placed the child against Jules's chest and her jellied arms locked naturally in place to cradle the helpless bundle. Predictably, her stupid heart melted into a puddle of love and hormones while protectiveness pounded in an unrelenting build through her bloodstream.

A big head, no neck or hair, distended torso, wrinkled skin—alien and yet instantly recognizable as her flesh and blood. Large, soft blue eyes stared at her, seeking connection, making no apologies.

Oh, he was his father's son, all right.

Pushing that evidence down deep, she re-focused on the new, beating heart in her arms as he found a rhythm with the one inside her chest.

"Thanks, Jules," she heard beside her. *Tad.* She'd almost forgotten he was there.

Her son blinked the biggest eyes Jules had ever seen and tried to shift his gaze to the source of the voice. Tad met him halfway, with his face hovering close, giving the little guy his first taste of Italian perfection. Lost in each other, her two guys forged a bond she hoped would last a lifetime.

"Thanks for what?" she managed to husk out.

"For letting me be a part of this." The reverence in Tad's tone caught her off guard. Leaning in, he kissed her sweaty forehead with warm, firm lips, then dropped a gentle kiss on the soft crown of her baby boy's head.

The pleasure was all hers, though the way her vision blurred seemed to contradict that. Demon's fist shot out and grabbed at her hair in vain.

"He's going to be a great pitcher for the Cubs," Tad said with a chuckle, ghosting over the serious moment from a few seconds before.

"Footie, Tad. You'll have to teach him the sport of his ancestors."

"I'll teach him everything he needs to know. How to score with girls, how to appreciate the finest wines—"

At her raised eyebrow, he laughed. "In moderation and not until he's at least fifteen. Hey, he's part of the Italian culture now. And if he's got Jack riding him hard, he's going to need a cool uncle."

Uncle. And that's all Tad would or could ever be. She

had spent twenty-three years on planet Earth wishing for a family to love and accept her, hoping she might one day be the center of someone's world. Reconnecting with Jack and finding acceptance in the bosom of the DeLucas was the best thing to ever happen to her.

Well, the second best thing. Her gaze fell to her bonny baby boy and she let go of a happy sigh.

Acting on this inconvenient attraction to Tad would only put her newfound stability at risk. She had responsibilities now and they trumped her treacherous hormones. Men would come and go, but *this*—she looked down at her new focus, the precious heart beating outside her body—this was the love of a lifetime.

CHAPTER ONE

Wine, women and tobacco
reduces one to ashes.

—Italian proverb

Tad DeLuca ground his teeth so hard he risked bone dust shooting out of his ears.

"It needs a part," came the latest utterance from under the hood of the pizza oven. Four little words that signaled a screwing over of the major variety was about to take place. Compounding the insult, the speaker, complete with abundant ass cleavage and just-for-show tool belt, crawled out from behind the oven, butt first, and adjusted his waistband.

Too late, dude; you're already the clichéd repair guy who can't seem to find a pair of jeans—or a belt—to fit him.

"That's what you said last week," Tad said patiently. Really patiently. "You installed the..."

"Temperature regulator."

"Temperature regulator, and said that should be it."

Over the oven guy's head, the pizza oven loomed, mocking Tad's foray into the world of business ownership. Flatbreads were one of the cornerstones of his new wine bar menu—or had been—and now he was thinking about his back-up plan. The nonexistent one. The joys of being his own boss.

"It's not the regulator this time. There's a—" He said something incomprehensible and Tad tuned out. Three semesters of engineering coursework under his belt didn't really qualify him to talk pizza oven repair shop, but maybe if he'd stuck around college longer, he'd be on more of a conversational footing here. Unfortunately, thinking about his college days inevitably led to thinking about how they'd ended, conjuring memories that scorched him fresh to this day.

"How long?"

Still in an ungainly squat, Oven Guy rubbed the back of his neck while he caught his serrated breath. "A week. More like two."

God *damn it*. The man's eyebrow shot up as if Tad had spoken that aloud. He hadn't, but the pulverized bone dust blasting from his ears might have given anyone pause.

In less than a week, he was slated to open Vivi's in trendier-by-the-second Wicker Park, just a stone's throw from his family's restaurant, DeLuca's. Going from bartender to bar owner had seemed like a logical progression, but fate hadn't been on speaking terms with logic for a while. His first location choice had burned to the ground before he signed the lease. He had been outbid on the second. Not to mention his chef had up and quit, leaving Tad without someone capable of cooking the spectacular tasting menu he had planned. But he couldn't dwell on the roadblocks; now it was all systems go.

It had taken him a while to get here. Years of dwelling on his mistakes and making excuses had held him back.

Letting people down was second nature to him, but *this*— he looked around at the gleaming, polished surfaces of his new kitchen—would be his way back in. Making Vivi proud might get him there.

A menu of delicious snacks would definitely help.

"Penny for 'em, babe," Tad heard softly in his ear. "Or should I just *tell* you what's going on in that charming head of yours?"

Smiling away his irritation at how shitty the day had gone so far, Tad turned to greet the girl-next-door blonde who could make it all better. Hair in a topknot, dark circles under her green-gold eyes, her shirt shapeless and wrinkled over baggy desert camo pants rolled to just below her knees. If it were anyone else, he would guess she had just tumbled from a warm bed where she had been well and truly serviced. But this was Jules Kilroy, his best girl who, as far as he knew, had never been on a date—or anything more—in the two years he had known her.

The smart upturn of her lips couldn't disguise how tired she looked. Neither did it detract from her pale, fragile beauty, which had him itching to wrap his body around her and gather her tight to his chest.

Instead of focusing on all the reasons why he wanted to protect her, which inevitably led to the reasons why that was a terrible idea, he moved his gaze back to the safer territory of that smirk. When Jules wore that look, it was easy to remember why they had become friends in the first place. They had connected the moment she showed up in his family's restaurant, knocked up, beat down, and in need of a pal.

Some pal he had been. He jerked his brain away from that thought and dialed up a friendly grin.

"You don't want to know what's going on in my head. It's

a whirling cesspit of debauchery that would make your hair curl."

She gave a discreet nod to Oven Guy, who had once more descended to all-fours to poke around the appliance mechanics.

"You're thinking there's nothing more attractive than the sight of a generous arse peeking out of denim."

He'd always liked that word. *Arse*. Or really he liked the way Jules's lips shaped it. Her British singsong accent hadn't diminished one iota in the time she had lived in the States. It wasn't one of those regal voices that sounded like her mouth was filled with plums, either; it was a good-time girl voice. A little husky, the kind of rasp you might get from screaming above the boom-boom bass at a club the night before.

Up until her baby bump had made her self-conscious about shaking her booty on the boards, they had been quite the team on the dance floor. Now she had her hands full with her eighteen-month old, Evan. The kid was adorable but those circles under Jules's eyes confirmed he was also a handful.

His phone buzzed and he checked it discreetly, unable to hide his frown at the number of the last person in the world he wanted to talk to. When he looked back at Jules, there was no missing the blatant curiosity on her face.

"How's the washed-up ballerina?"

Usually there was a more engaging proposition on the other end of the line and Jules liked to tease him about his flavor of the month.

"Retired Olympic gymnast," he corrected, referring to the gamine hottie he had been seeing the week before and who had now been relegated to Tad's past tense.

"Still pulling out all the stops on the floor exercise?"

That drew a laugh from deep in his gut. Jules and her cheeky mouth.

"It didn't work out," he said sadly.

"Oh, the poor thing. Marked down by the Italian judge." A slender finger touched her lips. "Or maybe not as flexible in her old age. What was she? Eighteen, fifteen?"

"Twenty-two. She just looked young."

"Taddeo DeLuca, when are you going to settle down with a nice-ah plump girl and make-ah da bambinos?" she sang in a terrible stage Italian accent. For good measure, she pinched his cheek, an unapologetic nod to his aunt Sylvia, who devoted her non-Mass time to matchmaking for her un-attached nieces and nephews.

In his head, the answer to the rhetorical question rang clear as a bell. No one compared to the fair, green-eyed beauty standing before him. On his lips, something more flippant hovered. Maybe a joke about how his Facebook fan base would never stand for it, but she had already redirected her attention.

At Oven Guy, who had pulled himself to a lumbering stand and was writing up his chit of can't-help-you-a-damn.

"Hi, there." Her bright grin became impossibly wider.

Visibly startled, the repairman ran thick fingers through his untidy hair.

"Uh, hello," he offered cautiously.

"Looks like hard work," Jules said, her eyelashes flutter-ing. That's right, fluttering.

Juliet Kilroy did not have a flirty bone in her body. Not once had he seen her even talk to a guy with any intention beyond ordering a Sprite in a bar. Of course, as long as he'd known her, she was either pregnant or mom to a rambunc-tious kid, so flirting was fairly low on her list.

But it sure looked like she was flirting now.

With Oven Guy.

"So two weeks to get that part?" She loosed a breathy sigh and chewed on her bottom lip. Oven Guy's cheeks flushed and he stood up a little straighter, and damn if Tad didn't blame him. That lip snag thing was very cute. And very sexy.

Defenseless in the face of Jules's charm assault, the man's hands fell into a distinct caress of his tool belt.

Jules looked down at the belt with wide-eyed innocence, as if the notion of belt-stroking and all it implied had only just occurred to her. Slowly, she returned her gaze with a slide up Oven Guy's body.

"What are you doing?" Tad asked her and then wished he hadn't, because his voice registered more peevish than curious.

"Practicing," she said without taking her eyes off the non-repair guy. "You don't know how much we'd appreciate it if you could get that part sooner. The pizza needs of the masses must be appeased." Was it Tad's imagination or did her accent sound a little posher than usual?

"Practicing what?" Tad asked, no longer caring how put out he sounded.

Ignoring him, she kept her green-gold gaze trained on her target.

"I could probably put in a special order," Oven Guy said, his blush now saturating his hairline. "Have it in a couple days."

"Lovely man," she said with a fire-bright smile.

Lovely Man returned a shy grin and backed out of the kitchen, muttering something about calling with an update the next day.

"Sorted," Jules said, rubbing her hands together in satisfaction.

"What in the hell was that?" Tad asked.

"It's a well-known fact that honey gets the bee. Do you want your special part or not?"

If it meant he had to witness that display again, that would probably be a whopping great negative.

"Thanks," he said, trying not to sound like a curmudgeon and failing.

"You're welcome." She folded her arms beneath her breasts, an action that molded the shapeless material to her figure in a way he should not be noticing. "Where's Long Face?"

That was the nickname she had given to Jordie the chef, who usually wore the lugubrious expression of a man with the weight of the world on his reedy shoulders. The bastard hadn't sounded all that sad when he called to quit this morning. Tad filled her in on his tale of woe, glad for the distraction and gratified when she made sympathetic noises in all the right places.

Moving her gaze around the room, she rocked that look where she wanted to say something, usually some criticism about how he was mistreating his latest woman or the fact that he drove too damn fast on his Harley. As well as being one of his closest friends, she was unafraid of playing annoying sister and nagging mother hen.

"Out with it," he said, eager to hear what she had to say. Her smart-mouthed take on his occasionally imperfect decision-making was often the highlight of his day.

"No working pizza oven, no vittles, and a dining room about to be filled with the harshest critics known to man. You're in deep doo-doo, mate."

Shit. In all the excitement, he had forgotten to cancel the trial tasting of his now nonexistent small plates menu. Luckily, the impatient herd about to descend on his fledgling bar was his family and not Chicago's rapacious food cognoscenti.

He had planned trendy accompaniments to go with the extensive wine list. Duck rillettes. Porcini and shallot flat bread. The expected selection of artisanal cheese and charcuterie. Items that didn't require too much effort and absorbed healthy mark-ups. He might expand the menu later but he didn't want to overextend himself starting out. For now, it was all about the wine—especially today when there was no hot food to offer.

At least there were cold cuts. He strode over to the prep station and uncovered a couple of platters.

"Here, make yourself useful, wench," he said to Jules. "Take this out to the horde."

* * *

"What do you mean he quit?"

Jules lifted her head at her brother's sharp tone. Jack was going with the dark and disapproving thing he used to great effect, and laying it on even thicker because he also happened to be an investor in Tad's business. She knew Tad would have preferred to go it alone, but it was either bring Jack on board or wait another three years to accumulate enough seed money. Sometimes dreams involved compromises.

Her brother, Jack Kilroy, was one of those incredibly successful restaurateurs with a household name even Pygmy tribes in New Guinea had heard of. In the last couple of years, he'd scaled back his multinational food empire and eliminated his TV commitments to focus on his grand passions: his Chicago restaurant, Sarriette, the go-to foodie destination in the West Loop and his wife, Lili, who was Tad's cousin.

"He was offered a job on a cruise ship," Tad was saying about Longface, the AWOL chef. "The *idiota* wants to see the world. I hoped you could spare Derry for a few weeks while I work on getting someone else in."

Jack's forehead crimped. Lending Sarriette's sous chef to Tad for a month was not trivial. While Jules suspected her brother wouldn't even cross the street to piss on her friend if he were on fire, she also knew Jack would do what he needed to make sure his investment succeeded. There had always been tension between them, most of it stemming from her brother's disapproval of her closeness to Tad.

"We'll sort something out," Jack said after a long beat. "So we're not eating, but what are we drinking?"

Tad twisted the bottle in his hand to face the rest of his audience—Lili, her sister Cara, and Cara's Irish husband Shane Doyle, who was also Jack's half-brother on their father's side. Long story.

"Doggie!" Evan struggled in Jules's arms, reaching for the bottle with a picture of a friendly overgrown terrier on the label. Her precious boy, the center of her world, was a touch obsessed with dogs lately. The label's letters leapfrogged over each other, making little sense to Jules's literacy-challenged brain. Dyslexia could be a real pain in the arse.

Tad launched into his wine spiel. "This is a Chilean Pinot. Plummy, lashings of fruit, full-bodied. Goes well with zin-braised short rib flatbread." He met Jack's pointed stare. "Or it will when we have someone to cook it."

Tad poured tasting samples of the purple-red wine into stemware and passed them around. A small smile shaded his lips as he took a seat on the plush, chocolate velvet sofa, just one of three sofas ringing a low-to-the-ground stone table near the entrance. He had been planning this place for so long that Jules knew he couldn't help himself. His pride at how the bar had turned out was clear. It was beautiful.

The flickering votive lights sitting on the window ledges bathed the room in an ethereal glow, casting a shine over the cherrywood furniture. On the exposed brick walls, Lili's beautifully tasteful nude photos with nods to wine culture— models holding bunches of grapes in provocative poses, others with slashes of terracotta mud on their skin—were like a love letter from Mother Nature. Sun, earth, life. The kicker was the glass-walled wine cellar, which brooded behind the bar, a window onto the world of wine. Or at least that was the sales shtick the guy who built it had given Tad when trying to convince him to go with that design. Jules was glad he had. The shock of floor-to-ceiling glass staved off that air of pretension that often shrouded these types of places. There was an accessibility about being able to see right into the cellar from out here.

He caught her looking around and shared the secret smile with her. It was his dream, but he had talked about it for so long that she felt a small measure of ownership over it as well. He was unafraid of seeking her opinion and she was unafraid of giving it. Usually about the ~~skank~~ supermodel he was dating and how she didn't much like that (lilac) shirt he was wearing and *damn it, Tad, could you not walk into every room like a herd of African elephants? I've got a kid trying to sleep here!*

Underneath the sarcastic quips and snarky comments, the deep affection was unmistakable. Simpatico, that's what they were. It had been like that from the beginning.

Cara leaned in and sniffed Shane's glass, her hand falling naturally to her swollen belly. Five months gone with twins and already big as a house. She should have looked tired and worn, but this was Cara, who always managed to project disgustingly radiant.

"God, I miss this," Cara said, burying her nose below the lip of the glass.

Shane snatched it away and took a healthy slurp before pulling his wife close for a hearty kiss.

"Don't say I never do anything for you, Mrs. DeLuca-Doyle," he murmured against his wife's lips, the pleasure in his voice at being able to claim her as wife impossible to disguise. Jules turned Evan in her arms and lay his fussy head against her shoulder so she could take a sip of the wine. Yes, she was a terrible mother.

"What do you think, Jules?" Tad asked as the aroma of berries filled her nostrils.

"Warm, a bit spicy." *Like your lips.*

No, no, no. Where the hell had that come from? She had been getting along just dandy, planting her head in her life as a busy mom, and trying not to dwell on that horrible night a year ago when she had almost destroyed her friendship with Tad. One kiss, three seconds of horror, a year of regret. She had harbored illicit hopes fueled by a lack of sleep and new mom hormones, but he shot her down. The right decision, she acknowledged now. Thankfully, they had recovered and got back on the friendship track, but every now and then a stray, wanton thought popped in to say "hello" courtesy of her inner bad girl trying to front a saucy charge.

Now, now, Good Girl Jules admonished.

Bad Girl Jules giggled naughtily.

Within seconds, she felt the telltale signs of baby drool on her shoulder. Excellent. There was nothing like a cut to the reality of motherhood to remind her of her obvious unsexiness.

She had left the house in a hurry. Nothing new there. People had told her that once she had a child, getting out the door would be the biggest challenge, between the need to remember everything and the last-minute tantrums of your kidlet. There was no time to take a shower or put on any make-up. People had told her that, too. Forget about running a comb through your hair. All that is secondary to the needs of your child.

Usually she didn't mind, but since she had moved to her own place the burdens of motherhood had started to weigh more heavily. For the last two years, she had been living a blessed existence in her brother's town house, with all the human and financial support she needed. Early on, Jack had shared the childcare duties, getting up in the middle of the night no matter how late he trailed in from the restaurant, and feeding Evan from the milk supply she had pumped earlier. When the blues came to visit, her sister-in-law Lili was there for her, listening to her griping and moaning. She had the best extended family in the DeLucas that any girl could ask for. She knew she was lucky.

She also knew she was lonely.

It sounded so ridiculous, this need to have a man's arms to hold her. Hairy, tanned, muscle-corded arms...

She was ensorcelled by Tad's forearms again. Her friend's forearms.

Could she help it if they were the model for the forearms she imagined cradling her as she slept? That when she thought of a line of ropy muscle and brawny sinew banded beneath her breasts while she stood at the sink washing out Evan's milk bottles, these were the ones that shot to the top of the list? Maybe it wasn't the sexiest fantasy—a man taking you while you tried to scrub that tough stain off the pot—but boy, a nice set of forearms could spice up the dreariest of tasks. But did they have to be her friend's arms?

So what if her circle in Chicago was small; it was large where it mattered. Her family had no problem jumping in to babysit when she headed to the gym (for a smoothie) or picked up pin money while catering for one of Cara and Shane's special events, but meeting people—meeting men— was nowhere near as easy as it had been in London. Back then, she had been single, child-free, and up for most anything after a couple of G and Ts. She didn't miss those days, but she did long for the chance to feel sexy, desired, wanted. Frankly, she didn't know a lot of unattached men, except for Tad.

And unattached was how he liked it.

Tad made a living out of blowing through women like he was in a race. Some of the stories he told her made her hair stand on end. Other body parts, too. She encouraged his sexy confidences, partly because they turned her on, and partly because Tad fascinated her. He was the kindest, funniest guy she knew—and he treated women like conveniences until they became inconveniences. She shuddered to think what it would be like to have Tad's special kind of inattention.

But she'd never met anyone who cared so much about his family and friends. After all she'd been through, family like Tad and the DeLucas was worth its weight in gelato, and no way did she want to risk screwing that up.

In the kitchen, they had joked around and it was good to be back to the easy vibe between them. Their friendship was precious, and that she felt comfortable teasing him about his vigorous love life again was a good sign. They were firmly ensconced in the F-zone—the friend zone—once more, and all was right with the world. And the occasional hormonal brain fart where she started fantasizing about his forearms, of all things, was just that. Occasional and hormonal.

He crinkled his eyes in a "You okay?" kind of way, and she battled to lose whatever frowny/befuddled/horny look she wore. Really, she needed to get a shot of Botox so her expressions around Tad could become unreadable.

Her efforts to blank her features failed miserably. Tad stood and held out his arms, concern bracketing his mouth.

"Let me take him, honey. You relax and have a drink." He scooped Evan up and settled him into those strong, fantasy-inducing forearms. Thick as oak branches, they held her son safe and summoned up different, yet just as dangerous, fantasies.

"What's that?" Tad was saying to Evan, listening intently as if his baby babble was as important as a State of the Union speech. "Wine? Cheese? Oh, a cracker. I hear you, buddy."

Tad sent a questioning look Jules's way. When she nodded her approval, he picked up one of the crackers from the cheese platter and placed it in Evan's chubby little fist. *Sigh.* The sight of the two of them together busted her heart wide open.

Coming back to earth, she plastered on a smile for her family. Less than ten minutes in, and Jack and Shane were ribbing each other about who had the better palate. You could set a clock by the rhythm of their playful teasing.

"Your taste buds are ruined from all that sugar," Jack said. "You probably can't even detect salt anymore."

"Taste buds deteriorate with age," Shane shot back, instantly defensive of his pastry chef credentials. Jack was nine years older than Shane and they had only recently connected, but the bond between them had been instantaneous. It was as though they understood the meaning of family on some cellular level. Each passing day only strengthened the brothers' relationship and while Jules was crazy about Shane, she couldn't help a pinch of envy at how natural it was between them. Especially when she and Jack always seemed to be teetering on the edge of a sibling meltdown.

"Jealousy is so unattractive, little bruv. Don't forget whose name is in bigger letters on the book cover," Jack said, referring to their joint collaboration on a cookbook that had shot straight to number one on the *New York Times* bestseller list when it was released last year.

"Big-headed limey prick," Shane muttered affectionately as he threw a thumbnail-sized wedge of gouda at Jack. Her brother caught it easily and popped it in his mouth with a grin.

"Now, now, you're both pretty," Lili said, snagging Jules's eye with a *men* headshake. Like a magpie distracted by something shiny, Jack ran a hand through his wife's hair, a look of boundless love for her softening his rugged features.

Jules checked her sigh. Her brothers—and their wives—were such talented buggers that it was bloody difficult to feel anything less than a complete loser around them. Coming from a family of rock stars sharpened her feelings of inadequacy to barbed points.

There had been a moment back in the kitchen as Tad recounted Long Face's departure story when she thought: *I can do that!*

Common sense had punched it back down where it belonged. She was an amateur among gilded professionals. Her small-time efforts making pizzas, preserving lemons, and futzing about in her organic vegetable garden were hardly the stellar credits needed to work in a real restaurant kitchen. Shane and Jack had been cooking since before they could walk. They had years of training under their belts. With her dyslexia, she could barely read the recipes, and then there was the hassle of finding childcare for Evan.

No, she was lucky. Filled with needs and desires, but incredibly lucky.

"So, we have some good news," Cara said, all efficiency. She wasn't one for lazy afternoons of shooting the shit with the clan, preferring to keep everyone on task. "Shane and I got the Daniels wedding in May next year."

Everyone made noises of congratulations and raised their glasses. DeLuca Doyle Special Events had become the hottest party planning company in Chicago since its inception just over eight months ago. Getting the wedding of the mayor's son was huge, but then Cara never did anything by half.

"By that time, the babies should be a few months old," Jules said, unable to keep the awe out of her voice at the idea of Cara as Supermom. She'd always had a bit of a girl crush on the dazzling blonde who exuded sophistication and frightening competence. "How are you going to manage?"

Cara gave one of her knowing smiles. "This event will be big enough that we won't need to take on as many clients for the next year, but we'll probably hire someone to help with the business."

"Yeah, we will." Shane's expression was filled with loving concern. Cara was a whirling dervish when it came to work, and pregnancy hadn't slowed her down, much to Shane's chagrin.

Jules adored how they complimented each other. Having a partner like that at her side, who loved her despite her many faults and adored her son as his own, was a dream Jules could barely fathom in her current situation.

Her son had no shortage of strong male role models, but she had to admit a small part of her longed for the dream of co-parenting. Discussing how your child was doing in school, whether he had an aptitude for footie or baseball, does he have a crush on that girl in eighth-grade English. The idea of having to do this alone had been the one thing that terrified her from the beginning. It was why she had sought out Jack after her ratfink ex, Simon, left her low and dry.

Her gaze slid to Tad and Evan, deep in serious conversation about the color differences between gouda and cheddar. They had a special bond, those two. Pity the man never once looked at her with a fraction of that adoration.

All this talent and go-getting and love…Tears pricked at the backs of her eyelids. The good-natured poking ebbed and flowed around her, threatening to pull her under if she stayed here one more second. Quietly, she slipped away to the restroom.

No one noticed.

The evidence in the mirror was as plain as the pimply skin on her face. She had stopped breastfeeding a couple of months ago, so her skin was starting to clear up, but there was no doubt why she would be kryptonite to any healthy man's libido. No wonder Tad had recoiled in horror when she made a move on him. Hells bells, she looked like a teenage nightmare.

"Hey, are you okay?"

Muscling in on her reflection was her gorgeous, curvy sister-in-law Lili, who with her unblemished olive skin and mane of dark hair looked like a young Sophia Loren. Fortunately, she was as beautiful inside as she was out, so Jules couldn't find a single reason to hate her.

"Yeah, just taking a break."

"We can be a bit much," Lili acknowledged with a sympathetic smile. "Must be great to have some peace and quiet at your own place. Though I'm not sure I've forgiven you for leaving me alone to absorb all your brother's attention."

"You love it," Jules said, knowing that her sister-in-law was being nice but that she craved privacy with Jack while they tried for a baby. Ten months married, her brother was antsy about Lili not being pregnant yet and especially competitive because his brother and sister-in-law were expecting twins. If Jules could facilitate more spontaneous sexy times by not being around, then she was happy to help.

If she could find her place in the meantime, all the better.

The door flew open and in stomped Cara in a whirlwind of barely boxed energy. She stood with hands fanning her hips, drawing all eyes to her huge baby bump.

"So, what's eating at you?" she asked Jules. Not known for her subtlety, Cara was fond of striking to the heart of the issue, and for once, Jules appreciated it.

It was time to make things happen.

Getting a place of her own was step one, and Jules had taken care of that a month ago when she'd moved into Shane's old flat above DeLuca's. The thought of what she needed to do next scared her silly, but she had to step up. And she was going to need the support of her friends and family, starting with the women before her.

She sucked in a bolstering breath and pushed it out quickly.

"I'm going to start dating."

Cara's sapphire blue eyes widened and her mouth dropped open. "That's fantastic! Any help you need, I'm your woman. Seriously."

"This is going to be so much fun, girl," Lili added with a sly smile.

Jules sighed in relief. She had known that they would be supportive, but hearing it spoken aloud warmed her heart.

Cara was already tapping on her phone. "There are so many options. We'll just set up a few online profiles and watch them come begging."

"You'll need a photo. A glamour shot." Lili squared off her fingers, lining Jules up in her imaginary viewfinder. "We're gonna make you look so fine."

This was moving faster than she expected but it felt so good to be doing something. How long had it been since she felt anything remotely close to glamorous? Or proactive? It was time to stop being a coward and grab life by the balls, preferably ones that were attached to a hot guy who would treat her the way she deserved.

The girls chattered on about what needed to be done to get Jules ready for liftoff. Salon appointments, shopping excursions, her "requirements in a mate" list. Jules suppressed a manic giggle. Oh, God, she was doing this.

And her brother was going to hate it. Not idly, she wondered how someone else might feel but she quickly boxed that up and dumped it in her brain's attic.

Imagining Jack's reaction checked her glee a little, but she'd worry about that later. "Can we keep it on the downlow for the moment? Somehow I don't think my brother's going to be as cool with it as you are." She placed her palm on the handle of the restroom door and pulled it ajar.

Cara snorted. "Like it's any of his business."

A familiar worry crinkle bisected Lili's brow, but her concern soon morphed into a conspiratorial wink. "Don't worry about Jack. I'll break it to him gently later on."

Smiling her thanks, Jules opened the door wider and— *bollocks*—found her brother standing scarily still with head cocked and brow as dark as an Atlantic storm.

Of course.

"Break what to me gently?"

CHAPTER TWO

If you want to find out the worth of a
man, put a woman in front of him.

—Italian proverb

Starting out on the back foot was *so* not how she wanted this conversation to go down. No one said a word as the air, already shimmering with tension, was sucked into the vortex of Jack's disapproval.

"Is someone going to explain what needs to be broken to me gently?" Her brother threaded his arms across his chest in one of those I'm-not-budging moves.

Jules tried to match him with her best unimpressed shrug. "I'm going to start dating."

Jack's green-gold eyes, the one physical feature they had both inherited from their late mother, narrowed to slits. "And you thought I wouldn't handle it well?" He looked over her shoulder to add Lili and Cara to the cozy circle of glaring. "You all thought that?"

Jules imagined she could hear the heavy, creaking nods

of the girls behind her and she nodded herself, feeling curiously hopeful.

"Well, you were right," her brother barked. "Is this why you moved out? So you could bring dates back to your flat?"

So he was still pissed about that. Jack's reaction when she'd told him she was moving out was the perfect example of why she had wanted to keep this dating idea to herself for a while. He worried about her constantly. He was crazy as a loon about Evan. But she needed to stand on her own two feet.

"I moved out so I could have some privacy but I won't be bringing any dates back." There was no way she would do anything like that with Evan around, and that Jack thought so hacked her off royally. Irritation dogging her every step, she skirted him and marched back to the bar. In her wake, she heard Jack's heavy tread followed by the lighter footfalls of the girls.

She scooped Evan from Tad's arms and held him close.

"Jules, are you all right?" Tad's brow furrowed like a corduroy swatch as he gauged her dark mood.

"Juliet Kilroy, wait just a second." Jack. Still, Jack. Her brother scrubbed his fingers through his hair, a gesture he made when he was annoyed as hell. Considering some of the stunts she had pulled, it was a wonder he had any hair left. "Where are you going to meet people? Are you going to be hanging out in bars? Are you going to be picking up men in bars?" This was said like it rhymed with "dirty old prozzie."

Fury stifled any effort to speak, not that Jack seemed to expect a response. He was too busy answering his own questions in his head.

He turned to Lili. "Help me out here, sweetheart."

"Oh, you're doing just fine by yourself," she said with an eyebrow lift that would have made Jules laugh if her heart wasn't thundering so hard against her rib cage. There was a time when she'd had no compunction about picking up a guy in a pub and letting him buy her a few drinks. She hadn't thought so highly of herself then. Telling herself she was using them just as much as they were using her was the mantra of tough, broken girls everywhere.

Serenity, bloody well, now. "I was thinking of doing it more systematically. Online dating."

"You're going to start dating?" Shane gave her a crooked smile of solidarity. "Good on ya, Jules."

She thanked him with her eyes before letting them wander to Tad.

Who opened his mouth to say something, but like some kooky ventriloquist's trick out came the voice of Jack instead.

"Don't encourage her," he sniped at Shane.

Okay, it was time to bring out the big guns. "Jack, you're happy. Shane's happy. You're all so happy." She whipped her gaze by Tad, who was happy as long as there were untapped sources of women in the Chicagoland metro area. "I want to meet a nice guy. Find that something that everyone I know already has." She held her brother's gaze and aimed for the jugular. "Is that so wrong?"

"No, of course not," he said with a mix of exasperation and what sounded like guilt. It might be a low blow, but she could always rely on Jack's nagging doubts about whether she was content to get the job done.

"I want you to be happy. We all do," he went on. "I'm just not seeing how you can *decide* to date. Typically that's not how these things work. Usually, love hits you when you least expect it."

"Literally," said Lili, a nod to how she and Jack had met, when her frying pan connected with his big, arrogant head.

She rubbed her husband's arm soothingly. "It worked out for us, Jack, but it doesn't have to be left to chance. Or the possibility of a concussion."

Jules could feel Tad's heated gaze on her cheeks, but when she met those sharp DeLuca blues, his face lifted in a grin.

"Practicing?" he mouthed, and she repressed her natural impulse to roll her eyes. So she had dug for her inner flirt with the repair guy and it had worked. Well, when that part came in, she would know it worked.

Jack was still muttering his discontent. "We need to talk about this some more. I only agreed to let you move out because you would be living in the flat I own across from Shane and he could watch out for you."

Let her move out? A growling sound came from deep in Jules's throat. Deeper than that, even. From her gut where a bitter-tasting pool of frustration simmered.

"Jack, this isn't your decision to make. I'd appreciate your support but with or without your blessing, I will be dating."

Her brother looked like he'd sucked down an entire lemon tree. She didn't care. Improving the forward momentum of her life demanded that she do something—anything—to get out of her rut. She had no talents, no skills, no special gifts. All she had was her family, her bonny baby boy, and a need to be loved burning a hole in her chest.

The determination in her voice seemed to catch everyone by surprise, but she couldn't be sure about Tad who had yet to offer an opinion aloud. His arms were crossed—those sexy, tanned, hairy forearms—over his broad chest. The one she had laid her head against countless evenings as he talked her through another hormonal meltdown.

When she caught his eye again, he wore his patented amused, sardonic expression. That about confirmed it. They were good friends.

Just as it should be.

* * *

Tad unlocked the front door to his parents' house and pushed inside. *His parents' house.* Almost ten years gone and he still thought of his home that way. It would always be Vivi and Rafe DeLuca's home—and he would always be the tres-passer. On cue, his phone buzzed and this time he answered because he could no longer put off the dreaded conversation with his sister Gina.

"Hey, G, how's Flo-Rida?"

"Still filled with hot young Cubans and wrinkly old geezers."

She had moved to sunnier climes with her husband David last year when he got a job as a manager at the Ritz in Miami, and despite the fact she was annoying as hell, he missed her.

"We have to talk about the house. I know it's tough but we need the money—and so do you."

Now he remembered that he didn't miss her so much after all. She had inherited half the house after Mom and Dad died, and he couldn't afford to buy her out, so that was that. She wouldn't force him to sell, but it didn't stop her from nagging about it on every call.

There were days he agreed with her, usually around the time of the anniversary when his memories and his guilt threatened to drown him. But he was learning how to cope—a few days away and several hangovers later, he would come out the other side, determined that this next year would be better. Giving up the house, the last connection he had to them, smacked of failure.

A splash of paint, some modern furniture to replace the heavy, oak pieces his mother had inherited from her mother—he'd had those put in storage before Gina got her knickers in a knot—and a judicious pruning of the family photos, and it had become bearable. He wasn't trying to excise his parents from his life, just make the place less of a ghost town. He could rent it out and live elsewhere, but honestly, it was convenient to live here. Vivi's was a short walk, as was O'Casey's Tap, his local. He was just a few blocks from Jack and Lili, close to Cara and Shane, and within touching distance of Jules.

The house felt stuffy so he opened the back door to let some air in, sighing at the sight of the run-down yard. Weeds sprung up between the patio tiles, fighting to escape the piss-colored lawn grass that was clearly on life support. Each year, he threatened to bring his mother's overgrown herb garden to life and each spring passed with no result.

"When the bar takes off, I'll be able to get a mortgage to cover your half. Just a few months." Of course, the bar might not take off. The reviews might be bad. He might not be able to find a decent chef or ever serve food. Jack's investment had to be settled before Tad could even consider taking his share.

His sister hummed in his ear. "We want to have a baby soon and we could really do with the cash. David doesn't earn that much money and it's not cheap to live here."

Maybe she should quit going out every night and acting like she was still a wine cooler–swilling teenager. Marriage was supposed to calm her down but his sister had always been a par-tay girl.

Feeling hungry and knowing there was nothing in the

fridge, he wrenched open cupboard doors, but too late remembered why the cabinet closest to the fridge was off-limits. With a bitter swallow, he shut the door on the bottle of Bordeaux he had forgotten was sequestered there. His father's last gift.

Gina sighed into the silence. "Have you ever thought that maybe it would be...you know...healthier to move out?"

He paused to give the question the consideration she felt it deserved, all the while knowing the answer would be the same. "Just give me some time, okay?"

They chitchatted about this and that, and he hung up with a promise to visit her in the coming months *(unlikely)* and to keep her posted on when that mortgage would be happening *(no time soon)*.

The crappy food situation had him phoning in an order for an Italian salad and a slice. He'd been eating too much pasta at DeLuca's Ristorante, his uncle Tony's place, which made the gym workouts more punishing than they had to be. Next time he hit the treadmill, he was going to have to turn the dial up a notch. Maybe the workout endorphins would help cushion the blow of Jules's sure-as-shit announcement.

So she wanted to date. Well, it was no skin off his nose.

Why then did he have an urge to pick up a chair and throw it through the plate glass window of his brand-new wine cellar? She was his friend and he was supposed to be happy for her.

Because there were weirdos out there, psychopaths trawling online looking for unsuspecting women who were tired of the bar scene. Maybe if she was putting herself on one of those Christian dating sites, there was a chance the guy might have more than murder or getting in her knickers on his mind. Though even that prospect was dim, because a woman like Jules would tempt the pope to forget his vows.

Either way, her heart would be open for any guy to come in and bat it around the outfield for a while before bringing his dick home.

For once in his life, Tad found himself on the same side of the divide with Jack as far as Jules was concerned. If she met someone in the natural course of things, that was one thing, but this online dating idea seemed so dangerous. The men answering her ad or whatever they called it would pick up on how defenseless she was.

Jules gave off a scent of vulnerability and such goddamn sweetness that every creep out there would be able to smell it through their laptops. They'd be queuing up in droves to get their hands on that gorgeous honey pie.

She needed his protection. After all, what were friends for?

He picked up the phone and dialed. It took her a few rings, usually because Evan had her hair in a stranglehold.

"Hiya," she answered breathlessly.

"Hey," he said, a little breathless himself though he had no excuse. *Gotta get to the gym.* "Did I catch you in the middle of something?"

"Just finishing up bath time for the demon formerly known as Evan. I think he's feeling a bit strange because the flat is new. He's the one who has an early bedtime, but I'm the one who's worn out."

"Nothing a glass of wine won't sort out," he said.

"Oh, so tell me, master sommelier, which works better on a devil child—a nice Cab or a fruity Pinot Gris?"

"The Cab, but if you give it to Evan, it's considered child abuse so be sure to drink it all yourself. Afterward, all his antics will take on a nice rosy hue."

He could hear her smile. "So, what's up?"

You're about to start fucking dating, that's what's up. "How come you didn't tell me about the dating thing?"

There was enough of a hesitation for him to doubt the truth of what came out of her mouth. "It was spur of the moment. I was just running it by the girls when Jack overheard and got his boxers in a twist. Why? Do I need to get your okay?"

Yes. "You don't want me to be your wingman?" he asked, all light and airy, hating with the heat of a thousand suns that things had changed between them in the last year.

She harrumphed. "You'd scare any decent guy off with all your macho posturing. Whenever we used to go for a drink or dancing, no one came near me because the Tad force field of fuck off was always locked in place."

So she'd noticed. "It was for your protection. As long as you were with me, they thought you were mine."

The word hung between them, weighty and full. He covered the receiver to mask his hard swallow.

"Is this really why you called? To nose around in my nonexistent love life like my brother?"

And nonexistent it would stay. "Actually, I'm calling to find out what you're doing tomorrow around lunchtime." Far too soon for her to have found a date, he was sure of it.

"I was going to go to the gym. Frankie offered to look after his highness for a couple of hours." She sounded a little uncomfortable, and he suspected it was because she felt she had baby weight to lose. He thought she looked more than fine but that was the kind of argument a man can't win, especially when that man should not be appreciating the fine figure of his friend.

"Skip it."

"What?"

"Skip it and come into the bar. You said you wanted to learn more about wine and I need to practice my spiel." Weak, but whatever.

"Playbook getting overused, is it? Need to craft some new chat up lines?"

"My wine spiel, wiseass." He licked his lips, feeling unaccountably nervous. If she couldn't make it, she couldn't make it. No big deal.

He heard her hesitation. "I can't drink much. I'm such a lightweight these days."

"You won't get tipsy. We'll treat it like a professional tasting and I'll let you spit."

She laughed, warm and husky. The sound stroked his spine. "Bloody hell, I hope your spiel is better than that. Okay, it's a date."

CHAPTER THREE

To a quick question, give a slow answer.

—Italian proverb

First, we have to come up with your profile."

Cara opened a binder, which allowed Jules a moment to catch Lili's eye. As she suspected, Lili was halfway between an eye roll and a brow hitch. Notorious for her organizing skills, Cara never began a project without a binder and an unhealthy supply of office products, and everyone enjoyed ragging on her for it.

They were slumped at a table in the juice bar at Wicker Park Fitness, trying to catch their breaths after a Zumba class that had left Jules reeling. Cara had urged Jules to get to date weight (*just a touch-up and tone!*). Jules had let the comment slide because she knew that not being able to indulge in her usual exercise regimen while pregnant was tough on a woman who had once defined herself by her D/s relationship with her Stairmaster. Since acknowledging her complicated relationship with her body as she recovered from anorexia, Cara had eased up on herself but she still loved hanging at the gym. Using the mother ship as her HQ for organizing Operation Get Jules Hooked Up was like comfort food for her.

"I have the muscle tone of an eight-year-old child," Lili said sadly, pulling on the soft skin under her upper arm.

Every similarly toneless muscle in Jules's thighs and arse throbbed, and not in a sexy way. She lay her head down over crossed arms, ready to be taken by a higher power.

"Kill me now."

"Oh, quit the dramatics," said Cara, drama queen extraordinaire. "There's work to be done."

Jules grunted, which Cara took as her cue.

"So I've done a little research." She skipped over a frighteningly complex-looking spreadsheet, complete with multicolored pie charts, and cracked open a section about a quarter of the way in. "And there are certain commonalities to the most successful profiles."

"Such as?" Jules asked, raising her heavy head.

"Blondes have it best."

"Already ahead of the curve. Good thing Lili's off the market, bless her heart." She smiled at her sister-in-law, who ran a hand through her cloud of unruly dark hair, made even wilder by her Zumba exertions.

Cara gave a sly grin. Blondes of the world unite.

"The best profiles use words like 'fun,' 'easygoing,' and 'travel.' There's a shockingly huge love of travel in the online dating community."

"It's a wonder anyone gets time to date if they're always out of town," Lili commented dryly before dissolving into a coughing fit. She took a sip of Cara's muddy green protein shake and made a face.

Ignoring her, Cara attacked her laptop's keyboard with

gusto. "Fun-loving girl who lives to laugh, travel, and squeeze every drop out of life."

"Sounds painful," Jules muttered.

Tappity-tap. "I'm looking for the guy to light my fire," Cara plowed on, ignoring the smart arse commentary, "and make me smolder."

"Arsonists should bring their own gasoline and matches," Lili said, drawing a laugh from Jules and a glare from Cara.

"It's important to be fearless," Cara said primly. "Ask for what you want."

"How do you know all this?" Cara seemed awfully prepared considering Jules had only made her announcement yesterday.

"I was going to start the manhunt online last year but I ran into an Irish brick wall first." She smiled shyly.

"So you don't recommend a drunken marriage to a total stranger in Sin City?"

"It worked out," she said, touching her stomach reverently like she was the Virgin Bloody Mary, "but that's a one-in-a-billion thing." Cara had turned into quite the softy since she'd met Shane and fell in love with him on their way to an annulment.

Cara completed the vital statistics section quickly while Jules peered around the monitor. As usual, the words on the screen shifted and changed before her eyes, so it was a good thing she trusted her friends to write this up. Numbers weren't a problem, though. Twenty-five years old, zip code 60622...

"You put me in as five-five. I'm five-eight if I'm an inch." Closer to five-nine. It was always a nightmare to find men who were taller.

"Not online you're not. Guys are intimidated by tall women. Start as you mean to go on."

"By lying?"

"Everyone fudges the truth. You're painting a picture of you on your best day—"

"Or the day when you're at your shortest," Lili chimed in.

"We all create faces," Cara went on, undeterred and clearly speaking from experience. "You can't show what's inside up front, not in a forum like this. You have to craft something first and play your cards close. Then when you've got him on the hook, reel him in, and let him know a bit more about you. It's a delicate balance but we'll be there with you. Daily reports."

It sounded so complicated and just a little bit deceitful, though the line about creating faces hit the mark. There had been a lot of that in London. Bad Girl Jules was a pro at never letting the bastards see the real you.

"What about the talent here?" Lili cast an assessing gaze around the gym, seeking out potential guinea pigs for Jules's Big Dating Experiment. "Oh, there's Tad."

Yup. There he was.

The Italian hunk lay stretched out on a bench at the back, pumping weights like they were matchsticks. Holy Channing Tatum, look at those forearms! Not to mention his strong, muscular thighs as they strained against the hem of his shorts with every smooth motion. The sight of his glistening olive skin and the touchable thatch peeking above the neckline of his tank completed the unwholesome image and boosted her pulse precipitously.

One look at Tad DeLuca: cardio without moving your fat arse.

A perky gym bunny—a two-percenter in the body fat department—approached and settled in for the show. Within seconds, she was joined by another. And another. It was as if they were breeding. As Tad set down the weights, there was a minor scuffle over who should hand him his towel.

"See anything you like?" Lili asked with a smirk.

"Catfights are always entertaining," Jules said, ignoring Lili's insinuation. After wiping down the bench like a good gym citizen, Tad generously allowed his horseshoe of admirers to pay homage for a few before he swaggered off to the showers.

Swallowing a green lump of envy shot through with want, Jules turned back to Cara, who was clicking through menu options with nimble-fingered expertise.

"Now, what do you want in a guy?"

This was more like it. She had given her requirements some thought. "All his own teeth. No rugs. No aspiring anything like actor or poet. Maybe somebody who works with his hands."

"Okay, starting low," Cara said suspiciously. "An auto mechanic? A carpenter? Do you want to date Jesus?"

She'd take an emotionally intelligent and sensitive guy over a hot shot lawyer or brain surgeon any day of the week. Smart guys always freaked her out.

"What are you looking for?" Cara continued. "Companionship, friendship, marriage?"

"I'm supposed to come out and say that? I thought we were fudging the truth."

"Not about this," Cara said gravely. "The whole physical profile is one thing, but the expectations going into the relationship are important. You want to be on the same page with potential matches about where the dates are going. If you want a commitment, you don't want to be with a guy who's looking to play the field."

Since becoming pregnant with Evan, she had been the good girl. No reckless behavior like stripping to her undies at a party on a dare or pulling a guy she had just met into an alley to play doctor. No self-destructive indulging her need to make her body feel good because it compensated for her lack in the brain department. Bad Girl Jules was a thing of the past.

Her little monkey would always be number one, but wouldn't it be nice to have someone to talk to where there was a potential for a little more? A chance to dress up, be admired in flickering candlelight. Jules suspected she looked wonderful by candlelight. She wasn't expecting the great love story the girls had with Jack and Shane. Like Cara said, that was a one-in-a-billion thing and she'd already fulfilled her quota of wild passion when she'd fallen flat on her face for Evan's father.

Simon had been her great love and look where that got her. Evan, yes, and she wouldn't swap a single day, but it had also landed her a heaping load of heartbreak. The kind that no amount of cookies and ice cream could fix.

Most of all, she needed to get over this crush on her friend. What a cliché. The lonely single mother hankering after Chicago's most eligible bachelor. Tad was a bona fide bad boy, hottie, and heartbreaker in one sizzling package. Paeans were written to his beauty and his skills with a cocktail shaker. Women loved him, men wanted to punch him. And during her moment of weakness—the Incident—he had told her in no uncertain terms that he would never, ever, not in a million years think of her *that* way.

Dating would open her mind to a non-Tad, non-Simon world. Things were fairly insular right now. She spent all her time with family and that lip-licking fantasy of her dreams was always there, not so much holding her back but making her wishful for things. She needed to expose herself to new people and new men.

"Just companionship at first. A nice guy who I can talk to—"

"Who's good with his hands," Lili finished.

Cara's suspicious tone waylaid her expression. "Why don't we add, lives in his mother's basement? Works the line at Mickey D's? Dungeons and Dragons one hundredth level wizard?"

"They only go to twenty," Lili said, and when they looked at her curiously she added, "I dated a gamer in college. And those guys are smart, too."

"Hmm," Cara said, not convinced. "You don't want some idiot who can barely put his pants on in the morning. You want someone gainfully employed, nicely groomed, who can afford to take you out to dinner."

"Or can make you a nice dinner," Lili said. "We know lots of chefs."

"No chefs," Jules said so sharply that the girls looked taken aback. After her experience with Simon, she was done with chefs. "It'd be nice to date a guy who was around at nighttime." That left handsome, Lothario wine bar owners out of the running.

The girls sighed in recognition. Both had chosen to make their lives with chefs who had insane working hours, but they came from a restaurant-owning family so they knew the score.

"No chefs," Cara said, her eye snagging Lili's.

"No chefs," Lili repeated.

* * *

"So I guess the days of restaurant critics wearing disguises to make sure they get the genuine service experience are long gone," Tad said with a smile at the woman sitting before him. Not so much sitting as perching on the edge of the leather sofa in his office.

She had already given an oh-so-surprised lip tilt when he didn't sit down beside her, but instead chose to put an appropriate distance between them by plunking down in the swivel chair three feet off. Definitely close enough to conduct an interview with Monica Grayson, food critic for *Tasty Chicago*.

She smiled back, her teeth radioactively bright against her porcelain skin. Her sharply angled bob framed a strong jaw and stubborn chin.

"It's usually enough to reserve under a fake name," she said in the flat vowels that signaled her origins as being East Coast, probably New York. "I'll come by two, maybe three times before I write the review. But really, I'd like to do a more extended profile."

"Well, anything that brings us positive attention." A profile was so much more than he'd expected when *Tasty Chicago*'s top food journo had called to say she wanted to meet with him ahead of his opening.

"So Tad...I can call you Tad, right?"

"Sure."

Glancing down at her phone, she tapped a couple of times and scrolled. "But your full name is Taddeo?"

"Only my aunts call me Taddeo. Everyone calls me Tad."

She gave what he imagined would be a very winning smile for the right audience. He was curiously unmoved. "And the name for the wine bar? Where does that come from?"

"Vivi was my mother's name." He had said her name a million times while preparing for the opening, but there was something about "Vivi" and "was" in the same sentence that called up an achingly familiar lurch in his chest.

Monica made a note and he was grateful for the few seconds to get his emotions under tether.

"You were voted one of the top ten mixologists in

Chicago last year, and I wonder how many of those votes came from your female fans." Squinting, she consulted her notebook. "The Hot Taddies, they call themselves."

He had wondered how long it would take to get around to that stupid AssBook page. Her comment was iced with condescension, as though it were a fact she was unfortunate to have in her possession but, by God, the readers of *Tasty Chicago* must be informed.

"It's nice to be appreciated, I suppose," he said evenly.

"More than nice. The Facebook page your fans created has close to thirty thousand likes. Your name is a regular in all the 'Hot Bartender' lists." She paused and eyed him from under her dark lashes. "Things really took off for you when Jack Kilroy picked your family's restaurant to be on his TV show a couple of years ago. And now he's an investor in your new venture."

"Jack brought a lot of attention to DeLuca's Ristorante, but the quality product has always been there. There's only so far an association with someone like Jack can take you and I intend to prove it at Vivi's."

"Right. Talent is key as well," she said with a smirk he didn't enjoy.

He waited for whatever dig she had at the ready, but she retracted her claws.

"So what makes your wine bar different?"

"Well, small plates are a lately popular trend and that's not going away. I'd like to bring the Italian *enoteca* concept to Chicago where the emphasis is on shareable meals. In Italy, the core elements of traditional *enotecas* are small plates of simple, authentic, delicious food, plus plenty of affordable wines."

She looked unimpressed but then he supposed that was her job. Practiced indifference. "And the wine?"

"We want to keep it accessible. Everything on the fifty-six-bottle wine list will be available in three-ounce and six-ounce measures, as well as in full bottles. We mean to be generous with the food portions and the pours."

"You're fairly well-known for your generous dating policy."

He coughed, unsure he'd heard that right. "Excuse me?"

"You have a lot of exes, though they all seem to rave about you. No one has a bad word."

He shifted in his seat. "I thought you were here to interview me about my opening in two weeks. My private life couldn't possibly be of interest to the readers of *Tasty Chicago*."

"You'd be surprised. These days, the cult of the celebrity chef, bar owner, entrepreneur—"

She waved a hand that he supposed encompassed the type of businessman she was forced to lower her standards to deal with.

"—extends beyond New York and L.A. People are always interested in what inspires people, what impassions them, what turns them on. People are always interested in sex, don't you think?"

Huh. That was pretty balls-out. While he had no problem with a woman openly expressing her interest in him, there was a professional line of ethics here he wasn't willing to cross. Neither was he sure she was genuinely interested. He felt a little like a mouse being batted about by a predatory kitten.

He tried to bring it back to the reason they were here. "Well, sharing a full, lush Pinot over a mouthwatering plate of crostini in the right venue can be a sexy experience in itself."

"Fantasizing about the handsome sommelier might work

wonders for a date as well," she said, eyes sparking in challenge.

"Fantasies cost nothing," lied the guy who spent his nights, and increasingly his days, playing a sensual loop in his head about a particular person. Those fantasies cost him sleep, peace of mind, and untold supplies of lotion. He should get stock in Jergens.

Monica had the bit between her teeth now. "Your reputation as a guy who knows his way around a woman's body precedes you. It's like the equivalent of 'for a good time, call this number' on the bathroom stall wall. Lisa Delaney said you were just the ticket after her divorce."

Lisa Delaney… Lisa Delaney. Ah, yes. Lovely Lisa with the legs that stretched miles past eternity and a penchant for licking whipped cream off his body. That had been over a year ago, long before he had made a vow to keep his dick in his pants. The moment Jules's soft, lush lips touched his, interest in other women had waned to nothing. He still dated, if you could call it dating. He tried to get excited about a pretty face and a nice pair of breasts but as soon as he got to that crunch moment, it all fell flat. Literally.

His smile felt stitched-on. "How is Lisa these days?"

"Oh, fine. Still *whipping* herself into a frenzy over any cute guy that comes along." She laughed at her joke, and Tad's body clenched into tight fists. At what point should he stand up and throw a hissy fit about how insulted he was? If the roles were reversed, the feministas would be out in full force.

So he had a reputation—past tense. *Need to dust off those cobwebs? I know a guy who'll tune you up real good. Gone through a rough breakup and looking to climb back up on the horse? Call this guy. He's got moves you've never seen.*

He was good at making a woman feel good and keeping

expectations to a minimum. He used to be good at other things. Cooking with passion, laughing like he meant it, loving without reservation.

At his stony silence, she stood and adjusted her skirt, pulling it down in an obvious attempt to draw attention to her thighs. Attention drawn and acknowledged. He was infatuated with another woman, not completely dead below the waist. He made to get up and she placed a hand on his shoulder.

"Look, can I be honest here?"

"Sure," he said though he really meant 'no' because nothing good ever followed that question.

"I'm attracted to you and I think you're attracted to me."

For fucking out loud, what the hell was he supposed to say to that? He reached for the professionalism that seemed to have left the room through the air vents about ten minutes back.

"You'll be reviewing my wine bar once it opens. Seems it wouldn't really be appropriate."

She looked down her beautiful Roman nose at him. "Getting a good review in *Tasty Chicago* can make or break a new establishment. I'm sure you've heard the statistics about new restaurants. It applies to wine bars, too. Nine out of ten restaurants fail in the first year."

Those stats were bunk. It was more like one in four.

She ran a nail down his collarbone and unpicked the top-most button of his shirt. For the briefest moment, he considered letting her continue but common sense prevailed.

He placed his hand over hers before she could work her way farther.

"You can write what you want."

The edge in his voice made his position crystal. Standing, he swapped her hand out for the doorknob, attached to the door he wished he hadn't closed. This had now taken on the trappings of a crazily inappropriate situation.

Her laugh was low and sultry as she placed a hand on his chest. "Okay, Tad. Just kidding around."

He felt the door push back against his hand. On the other side stood Jules, her eyes wide with surprise.

CHAPTER FOUR

The best armor is to keep out of range.

—Italian proverb

Thanks for the interview, Tad. I'll be in touch."

The sloe-eyed, raven-haired woman with alabaster skin she must have gotten by bathing in the blood of male virgins slid past with barely a glance. In two brief seconds, she had surmised that Jules was not a threat. Frumpy motherhood was stamped all over her and radiating non-threatening vibes.

Jules's eyes were inexorably drawn to the undone top button of Tad's shirt. The Slinkster had just had her hand in a very proprietorial hold over that button and the tasty man flesh beneath it. Like she had needed to give herself a boost of Tad's body heat for the road.

Jealousy-tinged bile rose in Jules's throat as she watched this piece of work slither off. She was woman enough to admit it. She fancied her friend something rotten and when another woman mauled him, she felt territorial. And then she felt ill.

Tad looked annoyed, like he'd been caught with both hands in the cookie jar. Except in this case the cookies were stunning brunettes with legs that went on foh-evah. A dull flush flagged high on his scimitar-cut cheekbones.

"The new dishwasher seems very nice," Jules said with her cheekiest grin once she was sure her voice wouldn't betray her.

He ran a hand through his hair. "She's a critic who wants to do a profile of me for *Tasty Chicago*."

A critic. Someone clever and intellectual, who probably did Scrabble triple-word plays in her sleep and the *New York Times* crossword in under five minutes.

Silence ruled while they stared at each other. Clearly, he had forgotten his invitation for her to come over and learn about wine.

"We were going to..." she prompted.

"Right, right," he said quickly, scrubbing his hair again. Wow, this woman must have done a number on him. What exactly had they been doing behind that closed door?

"I brought that mushroom bruschetta you said you liked." She held up her Tupperware container, feeling more foolish with every painful, passing second.

He looked at it blankly before breaking out the usual Tad grin. "Awesome. I know just the fruity little number to go with this."

Hesitantly, she followed him into the kitchen, desperately trying to get her inner envy monster under control. This was how it always was with Tad. The guy was a sex magnet—he loved women and they loved him. She shut her mind against the images of that clever bitch running her clever hands all over Tad's body.

Serenity, bloody well now.

She had seen it before, but it still surprised her how

small it was for a professional kitchen. Just two burners, two gleaming chrome prep counters, a fridge, and the brick oven for pizzas.

It was perfect.

"How's the oven coming along?"

He shook his head. "Your boyfriend claims he's coming out with the part tomorrow." He grabbed a loaf of ciabatta and a bread knife, and started to slice it for toasting. "Maybe you should be here to turn on that special charm of yours and make sure the job gets done. Or perhaps you've already found his competition. How's the dating going?"

"Nothing's happened yet," she said, her mind still abuzz with the stunning woman who had just left. She had an Elizabeth Taylor circa *Cleopatra* thing going on that was rather troublesome. "Just getting my profiles up."

"Profiles? Plural?" He looked up, a flash of something flitting over his face before leveling to a blank expression.

"Cara has a strategy. Fling the net wide and watch the fish flail. Her words, not mine."

She tried to smile and cover how awkward it felt to be talking to Tad about this. It was never awkward when he talked about his dates, but now she thought of it, she had been hearing less and less on that score in the past year. Since The Incident.

He popped the bread in the toaster and dug out a corkscrew from his pocket. On the counter, he had put a bottle of red and two large bell-shaped glasses. The bottle's label read "2010" below—she squinted—*Chaka Khan*?

"Funk soul queen Chaka Khan has her own wine now?"

His smile was dangerous with not an ounce of pity. Tad was the first person she had shared her literacy problems with when she came to Chicago and he had never once made her feel any less about herself.

"Close. Chakana. It refers to the Inca cross. Big in South America. This is one of the better known Argentinian Malbecs."

Beneath the name was an image of an animal, a stylized version of a cat with large, dangerous teeth. Not unlike the man before her.

He watched her closely as she absorbed the label. "They call it the *yaguerette* in Spanish. Jaguar." Tad knew what she was doing. He knew more than anyone about her compensation strategies. She put it together as "Chaka-cat."

He popped the cork and poured a small amount of inky-purple wine into the stemware. The air came alive with the aroma of earth and fruit.

Then he leaned in and buried his nose in her neck.

She jumped back, her skin buzzing from crown to toes. That was . . . something.

"What do you think you're doing?"

"Smelling you."

Her gaze flew to the wine, looking to lay the blame on alcohol that no one had yet imbibed. She felt color flaming her cheeks.

"Why?"

Again, he moved in and got all up close and personal. The sheer outrageousness of it kept him safe from a thumping or a ravishing. There had to be a good reason for it—didn't there?

"What's that scent?"

Swallowing hard, she struggled to come up with an answer. Eau de flop sweat or essence of green-eyed gorgon?

"It's a body wash. Orange and oatmeal."

In other news, he smelled pretty incredible. Clean and fresh, one of those grocery store soaps that meshed with hints of his body chemistry and created a brand spanking new male scent that made her weak-kneed.

"Fruity porridge. I like it." He drew back and picked up the glass, all casual-like, as if he hadn't just been sniffing her like a feral tomcat. "Wearing an overpowering cologne or perfume can play havoc with your taste buds."

Ah. That was as good a reason as any for the personal space invasion. Her stomach roiled in disappointment. Nervous and not a little stressed out, she put her mouth to the lip of the glass. She needed a drink real bad.

"Hold up there, Nelly. There's work to be done first." He shook his head slightly and, oh, bloody hell, tutted. "Give it a swirl."

She repressed an eye roll. Whenever she saw people do that, it looked so pretentious.

"Does this get us into wine-tasting mode?"

"It activates the aromatic compounds and gives us a clue about alcohol content." He swirled his own, coating the glass with the dark liquid. Mimicking his motion, she was just getting the hang of it when some precious drops jumped the lip and landed on his shirt.

Oh, crap. With a grimace, her hand flew automatically to his chest, a maternal reflex from days spent cleaning up after Evan. Not that her fingers would do any good in cleaning Tad up and not that her feelings toward Tad resembled anything close to maternal. Before she could withdraw, he placed his hand over hers, oddly legitimizing her grope of his rock-solid muscles.

He felt warm and male, a conclusion that had her feeling ... warm and female.

"This is harder than it looks," she spilled nervously, the words out of her mouth before she realized the innuendo.

"Sure is," he said, hoisting an expressive eyebrow. *Sure is?* What felt like several lifetimes passed before he released her. What felt like several more passed before she could trust her hand to pick up the glass again.

She swirled again, less vigorously this time.

"Now get your nose in there. Just a few sniffs, nothing too deep, but hold it for three to four seconds. It might smell fruity or spicy or earthy."

She did as she was told, then listened as he told her all the things that could go wrong with a wine: excess sulphur, oxidization, corked wine that smells like wet, musty running shoes. The smell she found was . . . well, wine.

That most learned conclusion sent her into an uncontrollable laugh.

He read her mind. "Brat."

She pursed her lips to hide her smile.

"Now you can taste, but don't gulp it, you heathen. Roll it around your tongue and try to hit all the taste receptors."

She took a healthy mouthful and swirled it around her mouth, with better consequences than her swirl around the glass. No spit takes here. All class.

His lips contorted expertly as he moved the wine around his mouth. She tried to do the same, suspecting she looked ridiculous.

"What do you taste?"

Startled by his question, she swallowed. Wow, this shit was good. The fullness felt like a dark chocolate with a cherry finish. Decadence in a glass. "Berry flavors. It tastes bright."

He smiled, clearly pleased with her answer, and her body flushed at his approval. After just two sips, she was feeling a touch light-headed. Blame it on the wine and not the drop-dead delicious hunk of male before her.

"Maybe we should eat something," she said quickly.

"Let's try this bruschetta then."

He pulled out the warm toasted bread, drizzled a little olive oil on it, then spooned the mushroom bruschetta on top. She watched as his sensuous lips closed over the bread. Tad's lips were one of the things she enjoyed most—they could give the forearms a run for Top Tad Body Part—and now she found herself a little obsessed with how they moved while he chewed her food.

Very nice, Bad Girl Jules mused.

Control yourself, Good Girl Jules snapped back.

"Hmm," he hummed in clear satisfaction. The sensual pleasure she took in watching him eat was soon evicted by a different kind of pleasure. The warm glow she felt when someone tasted one of her humble creations.

Whenever she brought an eggplant dip or artichoke spread to Sunday lunch at the DeLucas and watched as they all plowed through it like they did Tony's gnocchi or Jack's focaccia, she felt that zing of victory. She wasn't a professional chef or anywhere close to the same league as the culinary royalty in her family, but she had something. A spark she felt when she was in the kitchen.

"This isn't half bad," Tad said.

"You sound surprised."

He smiled, a little crooked. "Nothing you do surprises me, Jules."

"You sure looked surprised when I said I was going to start dating."

Some unnamed emotion flickered across his handsome features. "I wouldn't say surprised. More like intrigued. Maybe a little worried."

"You don't think I'm ready?"

"I don't think the world is ready for you, Juliet Kilroy." He followed it up with a penetrating stare that made her skin itch. The air in the kitchen felt close, oppressive.

"So what are we going to do about it?" he asked in a low voice.

"About what?" Her heart hammered in her chest.

"This amazing talent of yours." He gestured to the last morsel of the toast and popped it in his mouth. When he'd finished chewing, he spoke again. "What else have you got in your bag of tricks?"

"Salsas, dips…" Things that didn't require her to read a recipe. Things she could figure out as she went along. Wandering the Green City farmers' market, she committed the scents and shapes to memory. She felt the skin of an aubergine, remembered that it was purple—just like Malbec—and focused on the shape of the word so she would know it the next time she came across it. It didn't always work, which was the primary reason why she kept her ambitions to herself. Jack didn't believe in doing anything by half. He would expect her to attend culinary college, and schooling was the worst thing she could imagine.

"I'm so stupid," she would think during primary school as the letters on the page swam before her eyes. She might recognize basic three-letter words—cat, dog, man—and could sound out some others, but reading aloud was a nightmare. Standing in class, all eyes on her, cruel mouths judging and ready with their taunts at the first stumble. After too many soul-sucking pauses, she would be dismissed to her seat by Mrs. Macklin with her sharp, ferret features.

Tad was speaking and she had to work to focus. "What would you say to putting some of it on the menu?"

"Some of what?" she asked, searching for her place in the conversation.

"This bruschetta. We could try it as a special and see how it goes over."

"Are you serious?"

He nodded, a slow burn of a smile lifting his face.

Thrown by his offer, she launched at him and molded her body to his. She could still blame the wine, all two glorious mouthfuls, but really, it was the perfect excuse to touch him, absorb all that heat and musk that improved her day by a factor of ten thousand.

"Tad, do you mean it? You'd put my bruschetta on the menu?"

His arms circled her waist and held her fast. Oh...that was nice. She wasn't quite ready to go so she supposed it was okay to stay here. Hugging her friend. Hugging the hard, hot body of her friend.

"Frankie and Aunt Syl would be happy to look after Evan while you work here."

Screech.

She stepped back but he still held on to her. Caged in his embrace, she tried to form words.

"Work here? But I can't do that."

"Sure you can."

"No, I can just make the food at home and bring it."

He shook his head. "Not unless you want to go up against the City of Chicago. It's illegal to operate a food business out of your home kitchen and it makes more sense to do it here where we're already covered. Liability issues, you know."

That *did* make sense from a business standpoint but from every other angle it was a disaster in the making. She was trying to stay away from him—she knew she shouldn't have come over here—and now he was dangling this lovely brown sugar–glazed carrot in front of her.

Bad Girl Jules laughed softly. Good Girl Jules had nothing.

Forging a path of independence required finding what she

needed to do with her life. She loved to cook and Tad was giving her a chance to do it professionally. For money. That felt good.

His hand made fiery circles on her back.

That felt good as well.

She stepped away from that lethal body and all it promised, but she wasn't going to step away from this opportunity. It was far too good to pass up.

"I can't guarantee I'd be here every day. Don't want to take advantage of Frankie and Sylvia." And she wanted time, no, *needed* time, to get a lunch date in every now and again.

"We'll work something out." He thrust out his hand.

Showing no hesitation, she took it and tried to ignore the zing that rough, callused palm sent through her. She tried to ignore everything except the rush of empowerment surging through her body.

Good luck with that, Jules.

* * *

Jules bounded up the steps of the DeLucas' brownstone in Andersonville on Chicago's north side, feeling light as a fluffy meringue. Just when you think your feet are in cement, along comes a power drill to break you free.

Hmm, was Tad the power drill in that scenario?

She really needed a mind-cleanse to expunge those dirty thoughts from her system and it came in the form of the man emerging through the strong, oak door at the top of the steps: Tony DeLuca, patriarch and father to Lili and Cara, uncle to Tad. Tall, urbane, and imposing, Tony was a man of few words, so every time he spoke to her, it felt like a gift.

"Julietta," he said, leaning in for the Euro double kiss.

She loved that. He always made her feel so Continental with his Italianization of her name and the affectionate greetings.

"Hiya, Tony. How's it going?"

He lifted his shoulder in a half-shrug, more of the Old-World nonchalance that came as natural to him as breathing. Despite his casualness, she knew he wasn't an easygoing man underneath it all. The high expectations for his family made him tough to be around, but he had never once made her feel less than welcome since the DeLucas took her in two years ago.

"It is time you visited the kitchen again, Julietta. You have much to learn."

She had been hanging around the DeLuca restaurant kitchen on a semi-regular basis, watching the chefs making homemade pasta and rich, flavorful gravy as they called the marinara that formed the basis of so many of the veteran establishment's dishes.

"Yes, Yoda. Come to kitchen I will."

Tony looked his usual stone-faced self. She didn't believe it for a second.

"You young people speak a different language," he said gravely.

Laughing, she hugged him, gratified when he softened in her arms. Tony might be a hard arse but he could also be a big, soft, teddy bear.

"Go earn the big bucks," she said to his back as he scooted down the steps on his way to work. Like her brother, he headed into his kingdom by early afternoon to begin prep for the dinner service. No doubt he had been up at the crack of dawn accepting deliveries and his visit home in the middle of the day was to spend a little quality time with his wife, Frankie.

A nooner with his wife. Blimey, even the oldsters were getting more action than she was.

"There's my little monkey," Jules said, picking up Evan from the floor of Francesca's living room as soon as she stepped inside.

"He's been asking for you all day," Francesca said.

Over her son's head, Jules smiled at Francesca, the woman who was the closest thing she had to a mother. When Jules had first showed up in Chicago, Tony and Frankie had taken her in, no questions asked, while she tried to repair her fractured relationship with Jack, who was busy laying siege to their youngest daughter.

"Do you have time to stay and have an espresso with me?" Frankie asked with a smile.

"I always have time to get caffeinated."

Frankie got busy at the espresso machine while Jules settled Evan on her lap. He curled into her neck and breathed deep. She loved when he did that, when he gave these little signs of need. She knew to enjoy it while she could. Like all kids, he'd eventually go through a phase of despising the ground his mother walked on.

As Francesca worked her magic with dexterous fingers, Jules looked around the DeLucas' warm, homey kitchen, which seemed to be steeped in a permanent aroma of just-baked biscotti. Her memory receptors flared—thoughts of those early, terrifying days of her pregnancy flooding her brain. Knocked up, ignored by her aunt and uncle back in London, barely communicating with Jack. Wishing Simon would come charging in on a white steed to whisk her away.

He hadn't come and now she was glad. Finding the inner strength to solve her own problems, even if it meant admitting she needed Jack's help, was a lesson she needed to learn. In this kitchen, she had made her tentative peace with her brother and found a family to love and love her back.

"So how is the party planning going?" Frankie asked.

"Party?"

"Yes, the surprise party for our thirty-fifth wedding anniversary." She bathed Jules with her impish grin. "Did you think I did not know?"

"No idea what you're talking about, lady," Jules threw out with a mischievous grin of her own. The family was planning a great shindig at DeLuca's Ristorante next month, or rather, Cara was planning it with the military precision of D-day and everyone else was following in lockstep. Jules was not going to be the one who officially spilled. Boldly, she held Frankie's stare until the older blonde laughed and returned to her coffee-making task.

Jules's gaze fell to the table and a sheaf of pages held together with spit and string. Handwritten in a curly yet neat script. A little flare of excitement ignited in her stomach. Recipes.

"Is this a family cookbook?" she asked as Frankie put the espresso down in a cute demitasse cup with the twist of lemon on the saucer. Jules dropped the twist in while Frankie grabbed the tin of homemade almond-cranberry biscotti off the counter.

"It belonged to my sister-in-law, Genevieve."

Tad's mother, better known as Vivi, who had died in a car accident with her husband about ten years ago. Tad had been nineteen, his sister Gina a year older. Whenever their names came up, there was no missing that hollow look in his eyes.

"She was a marvelous cook. Better than her husband, Raphael, Tony's brother." She laughed softly, a private tickle of a sound. "Better than Tony, though don't tell him I said that."

"Tad doesn't talk about them."

"It was hard for him when they died," Frankie said, her voice low. She took a sip of her espresso, then dipped a stick of biscotti in the tobacco-colored liquid.

Tad shared stories about Gina, his childhood with Lili and Cara, but not about the people who had raised him. Jules never pressed. Her own upbringing had been marked by a cool sense of obligation on the part of her aunt and uncle. They hadn't been interested enough to know what to do with a girl who failed miserably in school and was destined for a job where intellect was unnecessary. She had fulfilled all their expectations and more—up the duff, careerless, living off the welfare of her brother.

Jackpot.

Which was why Tad's offer had been so enticing in spite of the clear emotional danger. Knowing that her work—oh, that wonderful word, *work*—had the potential of value was worth the few extra cranks to her pulse rate every time she saw her friend. Besides, while she would be in the kitchen, Tad would be off doing wine bar owner things.

"May I look?" Jules asked, her fingers itching.

Francesca nodded sagely.

The pages were worn and dog-eared, no doubt had been used over and over again. There were a ton of stories in here, between the lines, in the margins. Each section began with a folksy Italian proverb. *A woman is not capable of friendship, she knows only how to love*, started the appetizers. Another one pronounced, *If your life at night is good, you think you have everything.* Preach it, sister. Sounded like advice from one bad girl to another. There was even a message addressed to Tad above a chocolate tart recipe: *Taddeo, make sure more chocolate gets in the bowl than in your mouth!* Jules couldn't help her smile. This woman who had meant so much to her friend had put her heart and soul into these pages.

Gingerly, she turned the pages, stopping wherever she recognized a word. *Pasta fagioli.* That was an Italian white bean soup and she recalled seeing it on the menu at DeLuca's. *Arugula. Formaggio.*

"What's this one?" She pointed at the recipe with the familiar words.

"A cheese and onion tartine. Quite a nice antipasto."

Yes, it would be. She could see it on Vivi's bar menu now, a mouthwatering mix of caramelized onion, thyme and oregano, perhaps some piquant red peppers or chili flakes to give it some heat.

"What kind of bread should this go on?"

Francesca's lips curved. "A thinly sliced herbed focaccia. Vivi's focaccia was legendary." She pointed to a section below the words Jules had recognized. "Perhaps you would like to borrow this? I could translate the recipes you are interested in."

Jules's heart hammered triple time. It was only a cookbook but there was something very intoxicating about using one that had all this history and significance. Still, a niggle on the edge of her brain started up.

"Doesn't Tad want it?"

"He doesn't cook."

That was true. He had come up with the menu at Vivi's but as owner, he was expected to be out front, turning on that Tad charm for the guests. He knew a lot about food but everyone around him did the cooking, a fact she had never thought all that odd until now.

"But he used to with Vivi," Frankie answered Jules's unspoken question. "She and Taddeo were very close. Taddeo would have been a great chef—it was what he wanted—but his father wanted him to go to the university. Become an engineer."

"An engineer? Tad?" The words sounded alien on her lips. All the times they had talked and he had never let on. Engineers struck her as logical, intellectual, analytical types—not that Tad wasn't any of these things, but he was emotional and caring as well. Big with it. A profession like that seemed too constricting for his larger than life personality.

"Oh, yes," Francesca said. "He was taking engineering at the University of Chicago. A full scholarship. Vivi and Raphael were so proud of him and how smart he was. That boy has brains to..." She flapped her hand, searching for the word.

"Burn?" Jules prompted.

"Yes, *bruciare*. He could have done anything. Been anything." She downed her espresso in one smooth swallow. "When they died, he dropped out of the university, traveled abroad for a few years."

Her eyes shone bright, remembering sadness of sometime long past. "On his return, he became the bartender for Tony."

"He didn't want to become a chef and take over at DeLuca's?"

"No, the joy left him the day Vivi and Raphael left this earth."

An ice cold shiver frosted over her heart. *The joy left him.* What a strange thing to say about Tad, who radiated good humor and vibrant life.

Frankie visibly regrouped. "Tad was always the sensitive one of all the children. So much compassion and love for everything. Losing his parents was especially hard on him. It hollowed him out, closed him off to possibilities. But he has been better these last couple of years, now that he has found something he enjoys."

Craftily, she eyed Jules, and the corner of her mouth tugged upward.

"Wine. He enjoys wine," Jules said, feeling like a bug under a glass. She and Tad enjoyed each other's company. Obviously so, perhaps. More than once their comfortable laughter had drawn curious looks at DeLuca family lunches, but now Frankie's all-knowing gaze made Jules squirm. Scooped out her brain a touch, too. The woman was thinking.

That was never good.

Evan stirred in her lap and let out a sound of *Feed me.* Saved by the wail. She stood and settled her heavier-by-the-second toddler on her hip.

Frankie closed the cookbook and slid it a couple of inches toward Jules. "Let me know how the *tartine* turns out."

Oh, I know your game, lady. Jules looked down at the package of pages, wishing she knew how to read Italian. Wishing she knew what the hell she was doing.

CHAPTER FIVE

Forbidden fruit is sweetest.

—Italian proverb

Climbing the stairs to Lili's studio at the Flat Iron Arts Building on Milwaukee Avenue, Tad allowed himself a moment to enjoy the glorious sensation coursing through his body.

Victory.

So he had employed a rather sneaky approach to the situation. That Jules was a great cook he didn't doubt, and her bruschetta had been pretty damn good. But he'd had no notion to actually employ her until he'd seen that look pass over her face when he took a bite. The glimmer of joy, one he recognized because he used to feel that way when someone ate something he created, had punched him hard. She craved the encouragement, and while everyone loved the living daylights out of her, no one expected her to amount to much outside of being a great mom. Jules was so much more than everyone gave her credit for.

And that's when the idea came to him.

He was under no illusions that he could keep Jules from swimming in the dating pool completely, but with a job she might take it slower. Dip her toe gently. See how warm it was before submerging completely. Giving her a job cooking would kill several birds stone cold dead—and having her nearby for even a couple of hours a day would keep him sane.

Tad would never forget how scared she had been when she showed up in Chicago almost two years ago. So vulnerable, so alone. Jack was too busy, and Jules was too hurt and proud to ask for his help. It was a watershed moment for them but before they made it over the hump, Tad had been the one who listened. Even after they had reconciled, Tad was still around being her friend.

Her friend. So sometimes a few stray, inappropriate thoughts crossed his mind and stiffened his dick. She was a hot woman and he was a red-blooded American male. And maybe he was in a bit of a funk and *maybe* it coincided with a certain scorching kiss his gal pal had surprised him with a while back.

His mind didn't have far to reach for that particular memory. Eleven months ago, Evan was teething, keeping Jules up all night with his crankiness. Tad had gone over to Jack and Lili's with Pad See Ew and a bubble tea—he thought it tasted like shit but she loved that stuff—and the relief on her face when she saw him had melted his bones.

"I'm so hot for you right now," she had said, barely looking at him as she grabbed the brown paper bag from his hand.

"Hot for my late-night delivery, you mean."

"That's what you give the ladies, right, babe? Hot stud at midnight." She'd danced into the kitchen singing ABBA's "Gimme! Gimme! Gimme!"

This was their way, the joking and bantering, always so easy between them. She was often alone, between Jack pulling late nights at the restaurant and Lili in her artist zone at the studio a couple of blocks away. That night, the food was good, the company was better, and *Game of Thrones* was on TV. Not a bad way to spend an evening.

Until Evan started up again, which wouldn't have been a problem except it sent Jules into a tailspin of doubt.

"I don't know what I'm doing," she said tearily when she finished soothing the infant back to sleep.

He walked her back to the sofa, a big black leather affair that squeaked when they sat. Funny how certain things stuck in your head. Such as how the dark smudges had arced like crescents under her eyes and strands of her honey blond hair had fallen out of her hair-tie thingy. One errant lock curled over her cheek and he brushed it away, unthinking.

Not realizing that even the smallest action has a consequence.

"You're doing just fine, honey. You're a new mom who's overwhelmed but everyone is here to help you."

She closed her eyes just then, shuttered those stunning peepers in the most unusual shade of green he had ever seen. A clear verdant emerald, like that first flush of spring grass on a Tuscan hillside. And he knew that when she opened them again, he would kiss her until she realized she had been kissed.

So he got a jump on that terrible idea and held her tight instead. Wrapped his body around her and whispered words of comfort against her golden hair. Put that smooth mouth he wanted to ravish her with to more benign uses. But it couldn't last, not with this relentless pulse thrumming in every cell, telling him to make her better. And in the harbor of her body, he might finally get some of that elusive peace he had been seeking.

Drawing back, she tilted those weapons up and blinked away a tear. God, she was killing him.

"Tad," she whispered, her voice filled with a longing that scrunched his heart, and he was helpless in the face of her softness. Her Jules-ness. If pressed in a court of law, he couldn't say who kissed whom first. One second turned into three, then five...Her soft, supple lips tasted of bubble tea sweetness with a hint of salt from her tears, the electric fuel that sparked his body to life.

He pulled away before the recharge was complete because if he'd let it get to fifty, even seventy-five percent, there would be no going back.

"Jules, we—we shouldn't do this." They shouldn't get hot and sweaty and dirty. They shouldn't tear off their clothes and twine their limbs and fuck each other stupid. Most of all, they shouldn't comfort each other and lose all sense of reason. Since his parents' death, he was a broken mess, an amalgam of jagged pieces held together by sheer force of will. His need for her in that moment knocked him on his ass, and while he had no doubt she would ease the pain in the short-term, he couldn't reciprocate. He would take and take from this amazing woman, and give her nothing but heartache in return. With her it would be real and raw and there would be no coming back from it.

Her shock at his reaction sent a dread chill to his gut. He continued to compound it with his stupidity because he was a guy and that's what guys did.

"We would be terrible together. Absolutely terrible," he said.

Stupid, absolutely stupid.

"Right." Clipped, British, final. Those beautiful green eyes frosted over.

She slunk to the other end of the sofa and he slunk out

the door, mumbling like an idiot. They barely spoke for two weeks until Evan fell ill, and with Jack and Lili out of town, he stepped up to take them to the emergency room. The little blighter was fine and suddenly, so were they.

Their friendship had survived but his sex life had plummeted into the toilet.

Eleven months. He'd gone eleven months without so much as a whisper across his zipper. It wasn't that he couldn't perform—he had a very satisfying relationship with his right hand that was prepared to suffer a blast of blister burn in the name of self-love. He just couldn't get excited around any of the women he dated. He would drop them home and they'd look up (one looked down, but that was another story) with eyes wide and expectant. Cherry red lips were licked, finely sculpted breasts were heaved. Occasionally, he would kiss those lips, waiting for the click in his dick. That chemical explosion of endorphins or connection or whatever the hell was supposed to happen to move him from first base to home. More often, he just politely went on his way, ignoring the surprise on their faces.

It ain't you, honey, it's all me.

It wasn't as if he saw Jules as soon as he puckered up and went in for the kill. That would be a blessing because at least then he could run with that fantasy to slide all the way home. No, it was worse than that. He saw nothing. Just a void where his libido should be. Only later, lying awake and pondering why he couldn't close the deal, would he allow his hand to take over and relieve all that pent-up frustration. And if thinking about a certain blond beauty got him there faster, then that was between him and his pillow.

Perhaps it would be better if she dated. If she found someone she liked, someone who would be kind to her— preferably a eunuch who was good with kids—then he'd be happy for her. She needed a good guy without a truckload of baggage and a very checkered sexual history. Once she nabbed her frog, and he saw her settled, then he could finally get laid again.

But it would be best if it didn't happen too fast.

The door to Lili's studio was ajar. Shut, it meant Lili was with a photo subject and he shouldn't just saunter in. The women she photographed were usually knockouts—tattooed Goth chicks, hot-to-trot soccer moms, fresh-faced sorority girls, all dying to get naked for Lili's art. He was in the wrong business.

It was a relatively small space that had become more roomy when Lili's studio mate Zander moved out and on to greater things in New York. Jack had offered to build Lili a studio at their town house but she preferred to come to this separate space to work. Tad stole a few enjoyable moments taking in the skin on the walls, but then stilled when he heard Lili's low murmurs of encouragement echoing from the other side of the studio. He pulled up short, ready to retreat. A thick pillar blocked his view.

"Tip your chin up—yeah, just like that." *Click.* "Now lean forward, lemme see those puppies."

"Lili," came the slightly embarrassed reply. *Jules.*

"Come on, don't be shy. You have an amazing figure and—oh, perfect. Hold that." *Click.*

Tad's heart thudded insanely fast. He crept a few inches forward until he had cleared the pillar with his gaze. Lili had her back to him, shielding her subject, but he got a very healthy view of shapely legs inadequately covered by something red and soft-looking.

"You know, if you ever felt comfortable enough to go bare, I'd love to photograph you."

Jules snorted. "I can see Jack's face now."

His cousin laughed. "We could insist he put it up in the dining room at Sarriette. He'd be so torn between wanting to encourage my art and being totally skeeved out."

Girly giggles ensued.

"My wild days are behind me," Jules said on the downside of a laugh. "You wouldn't believe some of the shenanigans I got up to back in London." He heard her breathy sigh of reminiscence and strained to hear what salacious details might follow. This London version of Jules sounded like a woman he'd like to know.

"Oh, yeah? Spill, girl."

"Well, there was one time I jumped in a fountain and stripped down to my—"

"Hey, cuz," Lili said to him, a sly smile quirking one corner of her mouth. "How long have you been there?"

He patted the pillar he had just been leaning against/hiding behind like they were great pals. "Just got here."

Lili's smile turned slyer. "Didn't expect you."

"Do I need an excuse to come see my favorite cousin?" It came out a touch testy.

"Not at all. I just thought you'd be busy stroking your Cabs and Pinots."

"Only do that on Tuesdays and Thursdays. Should I leave?"

"No, we're just finishing up." Lili sat at her iMac and hooked up the camera with a cable.

"All right?" Jules asked, almost shyly, as though they barely knew each other and in a way it felt like he was looking at her anew. The dress she wore was one he hadn't seen before, a cherry-red, draped affair. One of those wraparound deals that separated her breasts and flared over her waist. Not especially sexy but...

In that dress, she looked like she should be running the

PTA, then going down on her husband in the Subaru in the school parking lot. Thankfully, that was years off because Evan was just an ankle biter...unless she hooked up with some lonely widower who already had school-age kids. Damn, that was a real possibility. He bet those websites were crawling with lonely widower fathers.

He was having problems catching his breath, a hitch that extended to his cock, which suddenly needed breathing room. To be perfectly honest, if Lili wasn't there, he would be seriously considering unwrapping that dress and exploring the finely curved gift underneath. Jules stared back, probably wondering why he was ogling her like a just-released convict who hadn't seen a woman during his fifteen and a third in the clink.

"Hey," he said, finally responding to her greeting of about ten minutes back. He diverted his eyes away from her breasts to a good twelve inches north. Women 101. They preferred when you looked at their faces.

"Getting your photo taken?" he mumbled in a clear case of graduating summa cum laude from the School of the Freaking Obvious. His IQ had just dipped a hundred points.

"Uh huh. For my profile." She blushed, and that's when he noticed that she was wearing a lot of eye make-up. The smoky, sexy eyes that you saw on magazine models. She had done something different with her hair, too. It was tousled, fuck-me hair.

"My glamour shot, as Lili calls it," she said with an eye roll. *Can you believe what they're trying to make me do?*

His body clenched and he willed it to relax. *Her glamour shot.* She may as well have painted a sign: Come All Takers, Get Your Hot Mama Here. Lord knew he was trying to stop staring at her but he couldn't tear his eyes away from all those damn curves.

"Is something wrong?" she asked.

"No," he snapped, and then softer, "It's all good."

"I'll just get changed," she muttered, swaying away to the cover of an ornamental screen in the corner.

He blinked to get his brain in the groove and made inane chitchat with Lili about the plans for Tony and Frankie's wedding anniversary party. If his parents had still been here it would have also been their anniversary. The couples had married in a double wedding extravaganza thirty-five years ago. He shoved that to the back of his mind with the rest of the shit he had succeeded in burying.

He was an absolute expert at it by now.

Jules walked out from behind the screen, pulling up the zip of her sweatshirt, but not so fast that he missed the sweet swell of her breasts in something thin and stretchy. *Come on!*

"Could I see how it came out?" she asked Lili as she set a suit bag over a chair.

"Sure." His cousin clickity-clicked her screen.

Tad stole another glance at Jules. He couldn't not look at her. A pearly pink glow had washed her cheeks and she looked so damn fine, he wanted to lick every inch of her. He turned back to the screen and what he saw wasn't much better.

She looked fucking gorgeous.

Well, she always looked gorgeous, whether she was in baggy sweats or a frayed tee that had seen better days. Even when she looked like she was falling asleep on her feet, she never failed to look amazing to him.

Now she looked amazing to the world.

Lili had caught her in a pose that suited her. It was more sensual than sexy, an acknowledgment of how much she had to offer. Her head was cocked to one side, a jaunty tilt that revealed her humorous side. Some guys didn't care how funny a girl was, but Tad liked that in a woman. Jules was one of the funniest people he knew, with a dirty mouth that would shock a trucker.

"Oh, Lili, it's—it's..." Jules turned to Tad with her hand over her mouth, her eyes sparkling like stars.

"Gorgeous," Tad finished for her. Croaked, more like.

"Do you really think so? You don't think it's too much?"

Oh, yes, he thought it was way too much, but he was playing at friend right now. The good friend who supports his gal pal in everything she does even when she created a visual invitation to take her slow and deep until they both collapsed in a sated, sweaty heap.

"So you like it, cuz?" Lili cut into whatever-the-hell-that-was. "Cara's done all this research. Apparently red is supposed to be the color that men find most attractive. Some evolutionary junk about how a woman looks flushed when she's ovulating."

What? Man, he hated Cara's guts right now.

"Yeah, it's great. It's just..."

"It's just what?" Jules asked, concern pitching her voice a couple of octaves higher than normal.

He backpedaled... "It's just that it gives off a certain something." ...into dog shit. "I mean, it just might attract the wrong sort."

"What do you mean *the wrong sort*?" Jules snapped.

Careful. "Guys who are looking for a good time."

So much for careful. That statement cannoned straight from his gut to his mouth without checking in with his brain first.

Lili eyed him shrewdly. Of everyone in the DeLuca menagerie, they were the closest and she always saw right through his bullshit. "Maybe *she's* the one looking for a good time."

"Yeah, maybe I am," Jules said in a huff. She glared at

him for a second before shaking her head in disapproval. He felt her disdain to his toes.

"I've got to go and pick up Evan from Frankie. Thanks a lot, Lili. Maybe we can talk later about how to make it more suitable for *the right sort*." Without saying good-bye to him, she strode quickly out the door, her suit bag flapping over her shoulder like a stiff cape.

Clang went the door.

Lili started a slow clap.

"Oh, shut it."

"Proud of yourself?"

"She has to hear it, Lili. This isn't some indictment on your art. I just think she should have something a bit more wholesome. Guys see that picture and she's going to be fighting them off with a stick. And the kind of guys who use those sites are weirdos. Men who can't get dates in the normal way."

She blinked at his outburst, which had sounded a bit over-cooked. "So is Jules a weirdo for doing this?"

"It's different for women, especially women who don't get a chance to meet people through the usual channels. I can understand why she's doing this." Hated it, but understood it. "The men are bad news. At least, if she looked like—"

"Like a mom?"

"What's wrong with looking like a mom?"

"Nothing, but maybe she'd like to look like a sexy, gorgeous, bangin' mom. A MILF." She wrinkled her nose. "Do they still say that?"

He cleared his throat noisily. "Yeah, they still say that."

"She's beautiful and there's no reason why she shouldn't be allowed to have a little fun."

Not on his watch. "I thought she just wanted to find someone to have dinner or go to a movie with."

Lili looked at him like he was an idiot. "Perhaps she'd like to take a turn around the block a few times with a down 'n dirty pop-pop before she digs into the husband hunt."

His head was building to explode. How the hell was he supposed to get Lili and Cara on his side when the two of them made such a formidable team? He'd said it before and he'd say it again: every single woman in his family was a menace.

"Jack's not going to like that at all."

Lili laughed, a naughty tickle. "I know. He's going to hate it, but he's got to admit his sister is all grown up and she's ready to play." She cocked her head and considered him. *Here it comes.*

"There's nothing to stop you from asking her out yourself."

"She's my friend," he said, not feeling in the least bit friendly toward anyone right now, especially one Juliet Kilroy.

"I know you like her, cuz. What I don't understand is why you won't do anything about it."

"I like her too much to inflict someone like me on her."

"Whatever that means." She stared at him, her grin fading. "God, you're serious, aren't you? You really think you're not good enough for her."

Crap on ciabatta, that had not come out right. Before he could respond, she was out of her seat, looking like...Jesus, like she wanted to hug him or something. That was not how they operated. He was the one who gave the comfort. Always had been.

"You want to talk about it?" she asked, biting her lip.

"About what?"

"The price of olive oil, dummy." She rolled her eyes. "How about how you look at her like she's the only woman in the world or how your eyes light up like Michigan Avenue at Christmas every time you hold Evan."

His heart seized at her words, at the rightness of them. As close as they were, they didn't talk about the important things, or at least about what was important to him. And they were not about to start.

"She's like a sister or cousin to me," he said, getting back to Jules and his brotherly concern. "Annoying, pain-in-my-ass, whatever. I wouldn't be doing my job as an overbearing Italian relative if I didn't have an opinion about this."

His cousin gave him the DeLuca stare down. She'd always been the best at it but he'd always been the best at withstanding it.

When he refused to melt under the weight of her glare, she asked archly, "Just doing your job?"

"Just doing my job."

* * *

Baking focaccia sucked.

Jules loved focaccia, the oily, crunchy chew, and her brother made a truffle oil version that she sometimes considered worthy of her child as payment. But this lump of dense, dry, *dead* bread was nowhere near Jack's level of perfection.

A basic staple, and she couldn't even get that right. She glared at Vivi's recipe, not that it would help. Frankie had written out an English translation on a Post-it note so really she didn't need the original piece of sepia-tinted paper, but Italian mama had insisted she take it home with her all the same. Something about drawing strength from the original words, as though the mere presence of this magical object blessed Jules's entire, dodgy enterprise.

While she'd combined the water, flour, and yeast, and

kneaded the dough—using the stand mixer didn't fit in with the Old World vibe she was cultivating—she had felt close to this woman who had meant so much to Tad. She had even worn a peasant blouse and gauzy ankle-length skirt.

So much for that. All she was left with was a big old rectangular block that not even the layer of olive oil on the bottom of the sheet pan could salvage. Who had she been kidding when she'd thought she could do this?

Failure in the kitchen, failure all round. Damn Taddeo DeLuca.

Who the hell did he think he was to tell her that photo might attract the wrong sort? Who the hell was the wrong sort, exactly? He thought she looked like she was asking for…Lord knew what. Just that it had sounded insulting. Like she was a girl-woman incapable of making her own decisions when it came to her own dating choices. Her own sexuality.

Back in London, she had been determined to own her choices, sexual and otherwise, but as much as she tried not to let it, her reading problems informed so much of her life. She had gone through moments of not feeling worthy, feeling stupid around everyone, self-destructive blue periods where she slept with guys because if she couldn't offer sparkling repartee, she could offer her body. She found herself drawn to macho, pushy guys who got aroused at the thought of ordering for a woman in a restaurant. *You order for me, babe, I'm sure you know what's best,* she'd say with an eyelash flutter over the menu she couldn't read. That small surrender of power would manifest in the heightened flush of red on their cheeks. A flash of something in their eyes that mirrored the shift in their seats to accommodate the hard-on.

Sometimes they didn't even make it home. Her date

would meet her at the restroom, push her back inside and take her there and then. It was funny how this flaw of hers and these little tricks she had for covering it often ended with hot and heavy sexual encounters. They liked that she didn't keep up with the news, though she played a touch dumb there. She watched TV but if she tried to read web pages, she got a headache as she puzzled out the words. They liked the ditzy blonde who was happily unambitious with her menial bar job collecting glasses—she didn't even want to work with the cash register. They liked her until she started talking back, not quite embodying that blond stereotype. There would be a curious narrowing of the eyes, as if they couldn't quite compute what they were hearing. *Oh, you have an opinion on Wall Street bankers or human rights abuses in China?* They'd laugh uncomfortably, like the mannequin had come to life, and then she would realize she'd made a mistake. Shown too much.

Until Simon. Simon St. James with his easy smile and his arctic-blue eyes. The man who understood immediately that her tough dummy act was a well-crafted show of smoke and mirrors. Who called her on it and wanted her all the same.

Oh, God, she didn't want to think about Simon but she had no choice because the man was clearly thinking about her.

Jules wiped her hands on the apron and picked up her phone, all while burning her retinas into the screen, as if she could change what she saw into something that made a lick of sense. It was only a number—the same missed call on her phone over the past couple of weeks—but now it looked like the most ominous string of digits she had ever seen.

Because this time it was accompanied by a voice. A voice mail, to be exact. After more than two years, Simon St. James had knocked her off her feet. Again.

There was a time she would have done anything to hear

from him, especially during those first nights clutching her
pillow in a strange bedroom when she had landed in
Chicago. She had told Jack she couldn't return, that she had
to get out of London. She had acted as though she were on
the run, and in a way, she was. From the memories and the
pain of finding out the man you loved and whose child you
carried saw you as merely an inconvenience. Crying herself
to sleep during those first few lonely weeks at Casa DeLuca,
she had vowed not to return, but a whisper in her heart said
she would cave if he called.

Her weak-as-water resolve was never put to the test because he never did.

Now he was ringing from a new number. Had he lost his
phone? Was that why he couldn't call for two years?

Not. A. Chance.

Jack visited his businesses in London every couple of
months and she often wondered if he ran into Simon, who
was one of his closest friends. Did he mention that his sister
lived with him in Chicago, that her child was a bonny, blond
tyke with shocking blue eyes just like his father's?

Those first couple of calls with no messages left—was he
nervous about what to say? Was he unsure how to bridge the
gap between them after so long?

I'd love to catch up with you, Jules, the message had said.
Detached but friendly. Everything and nothing.

She'd love to bean him with a rock but then we can't all
get what we want, can we?

CHAPTER SIX

*One may have good eyes
and yet see nothing.*

—Italian proverb

Sometimes, I think he misses my kid more than he misses me," Jules said to Lili, not in the least bit bothered that her brother might hear her.

Jack lay in a sprawl on the living room's floor in the townhome he shared with Lili, propelling Evan into the air with ease. Her son whooped and laughed every time Jack faked his ability to maintain such a fat little lump in the air.

"At least I don't have to worry about Evan," Jack threw out between push-ups. "Kid's got more sense than you do."

Jules let go of a sigh. Jack was not coming around to the notion of her dating. He hated that she was out on her own, especially after they had become so close since she sought his help two years ago. A lifetime of not being there for her had transformed him into Mr. Overprotective. She loved how much he cared, except when she didn't.

Lili flipped open her laptop and pulled up the Bonds of

Love dating site. It sounded like a BDSM hook-up thing but Cara insisted it was legit. Her dating mentor thought she should put herself out on a few different ones, but Jules preferred to start with one and get the lay of the land.

"I know I said it before," mused Lili, "but hot damn, you clean up well."

"I think you just have the magic touch with your camera."

It had been yonks since Jules felt anywhere close to sexy and just slipping on that new dress had started something. Lili had applied her make-up, although she insisted she didn't know what she was doing. But she did. Between the dress and the charcoal eyes, Jules looked hot. Possibly smokin'.

Or so she had thought until Tad threw in his piece.

Five hours later and she was still furious.

Not once since she'd become pregnant with Evan had she felt like an attractive woman. She felt tired and worn and stupid and sometimes horny, but never attractive. Until Lili had started clicking and talking in that soothing voice of hers, the one that drew out female power in all her subjects. She had felt it coursing through her as she crossed and uncrossed her legs, leaned forward to show her assets, leaned back to play it cool.

For a brief moment, when Tad said the photo was gorgeous, her heart had soared, then crashed and burned with his qualifying follow-up. Of course he was just being nice when he said it looked good. Tad was her friend and he didn't think of her that way. So proven, time and time again.

"You don't think it's too much?" she asked Lili. Maybe it was a bit come-hither. It was the kind of aura she had given off in London, which was why Tad's comment had struck so hard in her heart. It was all she had to offer, so she had played it to the hilt.

"Forget what Tad said," Lili said, reading Jules's mind. "He's just doing his Italian macho thing. No woman of mine and all that."

"What do you mean? I'm not his woman." *His woman.* It gave her a sensuous thrill to say it.

"I mean the protective streak that all Italian guys feel about any woman in their immediate circle. Tad feels a responsibility to you as a friend and practical relative." Lili considered her. "There was a time I thought..."

"You thought what?"

She shook her head, but Jules knew this trick. She'd seen her work it on Jack, this "oh, never mind, I must have been mistaken" thing, and before Jack knew it, he was confessing some misdemeanor or doing whatever the hell Lili had wanted him to do in the first place.

"What, Lili?"

"I always thought you guys would make a go of it. I know you said once it was a non-starter, but you never really explained why."

Evan's and Jack's noisy laughter provided cover for their conversation, but Jules lowered her voice all the same.

"I made a pass at him and he turned me down."

Lili's DeLuca blue eyes widened. "Oh."

"Yeah, oh. It was almost a year ago, just before you and Jack got married. I was feeling hormonal and lonely and before I knew it Tad was holding me through some ugly sobbing fit and I was laying one on him."

"Yowza. And?"

"And, that's all she wrote. He jumped off the sofa—uh, this sofa, actually—like I was diseased, said it was the worst idea in the history of ideas, and hightailed it out of here as if I had asked him what china pattern we should get for the wedding registry. Later, we talked and he told me that it was for the best, that we're great as friends and he'd hate to ruin a good thing, yadda, yadda. And I agreed. It was a moment of lady weakness and it had been a long time since someone I wasn't related to had held me. He smelled good and I had an attack of the crazies."

Lili looked skeptical. "So how do you feel about him now?"

"He's my friend. One of my closest friends and he was right. It would have been awful if we got together and it fizzled. We'd have to see each other all the time. It's not like we can avoid it." She couldn't bear it if all their meetings were anywhere near as awkward as those first few had been after her smooch attack.

"But what if it hadn't fizzled? What if the two of you are better as something more than friends?"

Too often, she had let her mind wander to how good it would be to have Tad in her life that way. Her lover, her partner, a father for Evan. But they were too entwined in each other's lives with the practically incestuous natures of their respective relatives. The fallout from crossing the line and failing would be devastating.

"It's better this way, but I don't want to be a nun. I'm ready to get out there."

There was a pretty scary place, but she had to do this. For herself, and for Evan, especially now that Simon was hovering on the edges ready to attack.

Lili opened her mouth to respond but luckily, Shane and Cara walked in from the kitchen, having just entered through the back door. After making sure Cara was sitting comfortably, Shane plucked Evan out of Jack's hands and tickled him silly. Evan screamed "Chay," which was what he called his uncle Shane.

Jules had been worried sick when he hadn't spoken by

the time he was fourteen months, but the pediatrician said he was at all the right developmental milestones otherwise and Jules shouldn't be concerned. How could she not be? She knew that her dyslexia had nothing to do with her intelligence but there was still that nagging thought that she had passed on some intellectual deficiency to her son.

The relief when, a month later, he said his first word—*Mummy*—had been so overwhelming she had broken down. Jack found her sitting on this very floor, playing building bricks with her son while the tears streamed down her cheeks. Now at eighteen months, he jabbered constantly and she never got sick of hearing him.

"So how's the profile looking?" Cara asked.

Lili turned the laptop around and Cara whistled. "Holy jalapeño, Mama likey. And you've already got hits!"

"I do?" Jules peered at the screen.

"Yes, that's what this number means in the corner. You have eight messages waiting for you. That was fast."

"Fresh meat," Shane said while he chugged Evan on his hip. "Your mam's this pretty young chicky and all the foxes are sniffing around the hen house."

"Uh, thanks, I think," Jules said, ignoring the scowl Jack sent Shane's way.

Cara clicked open the messages box. "Hmm, not bad. Not bad at all."

"Lemme see." Jules sat beside her while Lili crowded around the other side.

"This one's an architect, but he's an oldster. Fifty-two. Pity, because he has nice teeth." She raised a perfectly plucked eyebrow. "I know how important that is to you."

An architect sounded intimidating. Too smart for her. She would prefer someone who wouldn't expect much in the way of the little grey cells.

Cara opened the next one, who looked like a beach bum. His photo showcased washboard abs, biceps toned from surfing (she assumed), and sun-kissed, Fabio hair.

"Hubba hubba," Lili said into the appreciative pause. That was about as articulate as anyone needed to get for that.

Cara's forehead wrinkled. "We're going to have to make a Fling and a Ring pile. Some of these guys are not worth the trouble of dinner, but they might be useful in other ways."

Jules was just about to ask for details when she felt Jack at her shoulder, doing his glowering bit. With a sharp glance at Evan who was still resting in Shane's arms, he cupped the little guy's ears with his hands.

"So you just want sex?"

Squinting up, she took in her brother's dark disapproval with a side of infinite know-it-all-ness. "I want adult conversation."

"You get plenty of that. We're all adults here."

"That's debatable. But really I'd like an adult conversation that has the potential for sex. So yes, I want sex."

A low growl rumbled from Jack's throat. For a reason known only to him, he subscribed to the view she'd only had sex once, likely an accidental fall onto a stranger's penis that had resulted in Evan.

"Sex, Jack. Your baby sister wants to get rogered," she said just as he released his hands-as-headphones from Evan's ears.

Oops.

"And where is all this sex going to happen?" he snapped, his face a reddening storm. "You can't carry on like that with Evan in the next room."

"I know that. Do you not think I know that?" The temptation to tear out her hair made her fingertips buzz. "There are no end to the places I can get it on. Bathroom stalls, the backseat of a car, a convenient alleyway. Don't worry that big, nosy head of yours about me scandalizing Evan."

Jack threw up his hands in a very Italian gesture and strode into the kitchen, where he proceeded to make his position known in the language of clanking pots and pans. A chef tantrum.

She turned back to the room and the impossibly wide grins of Cara, Lili, and Shane. Even Evan thought it was funny, though he couldn't possibly know why.

"Sex," her son shouted. Fantastic.

The chorus laughed, keeping their amusement soft in case Jack's wobbly in the kitchen whirled into something more threatening.

Jules eyed the computer screen with purpose. "Now, where were we?"

* * *

"She said that?"

Tad had just finished up the day from hell. The wine distributor had messed up the delivery so he'd spent an hour on the phone reaming the guy's ass. The pizza oven was still playing up, refusing to hit the optimum temperature. Two hours on the phone lost to that. Now Shane had just got through telling Tad about Jules's stand-off with Jack and while Tad would normally be taking that kind of thing in his stride, he was more than a touch interested in some of the statements she had made. Particularly the ones about how she wanted sex and the places she was happy to get it in.

"She was very forceful about it, too," Shane said as he lifted a pint of ale to his lips. O'Casey's, the smallest Irish bar in Chicago, was busier than usual with a group of bachelorettes snagging the attention of every guy in the room. In his heyday, Tad would be all over that, tapping the prettiest girl in the group. But now he couldn't muster the interest, not even in the one who brushed her breast against his arm—slow and deliberate, like—as she tried to get the attention of Conor, the owner/bartender.

"Sorry," she said, the sound more wheezy than Marilyn-breathless. A white veil was pinned at a drunken angle on her head. It had been a while since he'd hit on the bride and over the years, he'd raised his standards some.

"No problem," he said, moving aside to give her space.

"I'm Giselle," she said. "Like the supermodel."

Who called their kid Giselle? And who tacked on "like the supermodel" during the overture? *Minus fifty points, honey.*

"Pretty name." He turned back to Shane, not before registering the moue of distaste that crossed her glossy lips.

"Is she really going to let some guy she met online fuck her in the back of his"—Tad carved the air with his hand, reaching for the douchiest car name he could think of—"Lexus?"

Shane gave a smirk of, *that's the best you got?* "I think she was just trying to make a point to Jack." His eyes flicked to the tipsy bride-to-be, then back to meet Tad's with a look of *up-for-it babe at three o'clock,* followed by an eyebrow lift of *what's your problem?*

The guy needed to shut the hell up.

"So she's not dying to get jumped by the first guy who shows her some interest?"

"Who's not dying to get jumped?" Conor had just served Giselle her rum and coke with all the efficiency of a guy who could keep one eye on the Blackhawks game, run a thriving bar, and also put out fires with his work at Engine No. 35 down the street. He leaned over, ready for a gossip.

"Jack's sister, Jules," Shane said. "She's dating."

"She's thinking about it," Tad said sharply.

"More than thinking about it. She's already on one of those dating sites. Getting lots of interest."

"Jules, Jules, Jules," Conor murmured like he was trying to think of who she was. Fucker knew exactly who she was because once seen, Jules was impossible to forget. "Blonde, green eyes, Sprite with a twist?"

Tad frowned his agreement.

"She used to come in with you when she was pregnant," Conor said, his voice taking on a suspiciously dreamy quality. "Haven't seen her in a while. Had her kid?"

"Evan. He's great." He really was. Tad adored that bundle of terror.

"So she's ready to get back in the game? Interesting."

"Don't you have customers to serve?" Tad asked grumpily, waving an arm around the crowded bar.

Conor continued, undeterred. "I always thought you two had a little something."

Tad could feel his body turn to titanium. Just because he looked happy with Jules did not mean they had "a little something."

"You're losing business, *cretino*." Tad gestured to a cranky-looking guy angling for service at the other end of the bar. Just at that moment, the man pounded the bar to get Conor's attention.

Straightening to an intimidating six-feet-four, Conor sent a dagger storm the guy's way. "Do that again and you're barred, asshole."

He turned his back on the chastened customer. "So all those times you were hanging out with her in here, it was one of your plays? Is that Number Twenty-Three? The one where you use the pregnant chick to establish your friend-to-all-women credentials, then you go in for the kill with some other hottie?"

Tad slid a glance in Shane's direction. "Is this guy for real?"

Shane shrugged. "Well, it worked, didn't it?"

"No wonder you have to hold down two jobs," Tad sniped to Conor. "You suck at being a bartender."

Conor gifted them a devilish grin and sauntered off to salvage his customer base.

Tad's neck prickled with the heat of Shane's stare.

"What's going on, dude?"

I don't know. He should be thinking about his opening in a week. About how he should have been nicer to that reviewer from *Tasty Chicago*. About how he should have banged her in the office, made good on the expectation she had the minute she walked in that door.

"Jules is a friend," he said to Shane through gritted teeth.

"And?"

"And," he dragged out, "in another lifetime or if I was a different person, maybe I'd make a play for her."

"If you were a different person? You're sounding a bit sad, man. Do we need to go deeper here?" Shane rubbed an imaginary beard and scrunched up his eyes in mock consideration. "Tell me about your dreams," he said in a terrible German accent.

Christ, give him strength.

"In these dreams, are you wearing dee frocks? Are dee penises involved? Are there women with dee penises?"

"Bite me," Tad said, unable to restrain his laugh, uncomfortable as it was. He took a long slug of his beer and set the bottle down carefully. "I've been with a lot of women, Shane. A lot. I'm hardwired to play the field." Maybe not so much lately, but it would come. Jesus, it had to. "I'm not interested in settling down, and that's what Jules and Evan need. Stability and family."

So what if during those precious moments with her and Evan, the crushing pain he felt over his parents' passing and the shameful part he'd played in it seemed to weigh less? But it would never ease up enough to want to use her as a crutch for the hard times. She deserved a guy who didn't turn everything he touched to shit.

Shane stood up and drained his beer. "From the way she was talking today, she's not so interested in settling down just yet, either."

Alarm streaked through him. "I thought you said she was just saying it to rile Jack up."

"Yeah, but she sure didn't object when my lovely wife put a ton of guys into the Fling pile. Looks like she's going to work on that list first, then move onto the Ring pile."

"The what?"

"You know, a hot hook-up versus finding the one. There's a complex points system in development."

Tad had no idea which was worse: Jules having a meaningless affair or Jules meeting the love of her life. The first one. No, the second one. God *damn it.*

Shane threw a twenty down on the bar, his work as the Grim Reaper of Tad's heart done. "I'm off home. You coming?"

"No," he muttered mutinously.

His so-called friend watched the gaggle of sparkly pink-teed women as they downed shots the other end of the bar. "Looks like you have your pick, playah." He sauntered off to the exit.

Tad picked at the label on the beer bottle, determined to get it off in one piece. It tore a quarter of the way in. Wait a minute . . . *a points system?* He turned but Shane was already out the door.

"Aren't you going to help me celebrate my last night of freedom?"

Giselle, again. Glassy-eyed, sugar-lipped, up-for-it Giselle. The bride, which was usually on his list of no-nos. Maybe he needed to break a rule or two just to get his mojo back.

He reached for his well-worn smile. "You look like a Jagermeister type of girl. Am I right?"

She hooked up the corners of those do-me lips and leaned in close. "You've got my number, handsome."

CHAPTER SEVEN

The man loves a little and often…
the woman a lot and rarely.

—Italian proverb

Jules's phone vibrated on the counter and she flicked a glance.

Bingo. That old saw about never letting the sun set on an argument was something Jack lived by. He was the poster boy for blowing up hot and cooling down fast.

"Hey," she said, holding the phone to her ear while she opened the jar of Nutella as big as her head. Thank God for Costco.

"I was worried you might not pick up."

She smiled at how easy he was making it for her. "I know you're just being your hard arse self, Jack. You're older, and it's tough to effect personality change at this stage of your life."

His indrawn breath was so long she could hear the ten-second count in his head. They had always pushed each other's buttons and because his one hundred percent Irish genes made him more emotional, he usually cracked first. Time with Lili had helped him realize that he should be more conscious of the filter between his brain and his mouth but there were moments he couldn't control his temper. Most of them involving Jules.

"I worry," he said, the two words he had probably said to her more than any other. She loved and hated how much he worried about her.

"I know, but you realize I'm not trying to stick it to you. This is just me looking to get things started. Stand on my own two feet."

The line crackled with an unspoken retort. She was living here rent free and he kept her bank account flush so she was still relying on him. He was within his rights to point out her distinct lack of independence. But this wasn't about money. Until she figured out her life, she wanted to feel something other than tired and inadequate.

She wanted to feel.

"I miss Evan," he said softly.

Her heart keened at his pain. Not only did he miss Evan, but he wanted his own baby with Lili more than anything. They had been trying since the wedding ten months ago with no peep of a bump.

"He asked for you earlier before he went to sleep." She walked into Evan's room, immediately comforted by the breathy sighs that filled the room. In the first months after he was born, she would spend every waking moment playing helicopter mum over his cot, waiting for that catch in his breath that signaled difficulty. Surely something in her genetic make-up—her stupid gene, as she called it— would have a bearing on his ability to be normal. Might cause him to hold his breath or forget to move his head to draw in air, but it never happened.

She held the phone close to Evan's face and on cue, he let out a sleepy murmur of content. Good job, little monkey.

"Hear that?" she said into the phone.

"Uh huh. He went down okay?"

"He was a bit fussy, but he's getting used to his new room." In truth, her golden prince had been a grizzly bear today, getting into a strop as soon as she put him down. She had let him air-punch himself to sleep with his chubby fists. Now, he gave off an angel vibe but no one was fooled.

"That apartment is too small," Jack muttered.

"It has character."

"Another word for small. I lived there with Lili, remember? The shower was a nightmare, especially for two people."

"Ew, TMI!" She laughed. "Speaking of. Shouldn't you be taking out little Jack by now?"

He sighed. "You're never going to find a man with a filthy mouth like that."

"You opened that particular door, bruv."

The dense silence that followed checked her teasing. Jack usually had no problem telling her how he felt, so this hesitancy was new.

"We had a bunch of tests done."

"And?" She held her breath. A pregnant pause, if you will.

"And everything's fine. There's no reason why we can't conceive." He sounded so woebegone she wished she could reach through the line and hug him. She wasn't a hugger by nature but she'd do it for Jack. After Evan, he was her favorite person in the world.

"So you just have to let it take its course. It'll happen."

"If I stop being so impatient, you mean?"

"I know you can't help it, but that kind of tension probably sours the mood." Bleedin' 'ell, was she giving sex advice to her brother? Quickly, she shoved the pin back in the grenade. "What does Lili think?"

"That I'm being my usual pain in the arse who has to have it now. Like everything."

More likely, she was worried about disappointing him. He didn't always realize he was doing it but Jack's expectations of balls-out passion from everyone tended to set him up for discontent. Jules had lived most of her life afraid of not measuring up in Jack's eyes. It had taken an unplanned pregnancy and a transatlantic flit to Chicago before she confessed to him that she couldn't read.

Telling Jack was the hardest thing she had ever done, even harder than telling him she was pregnant or walking away from Simon that day two years ago. But Jack had been perfect. He had gathered her in his arms and told her he loved her more than anything. He took her into his home with Lili, stayed up to help her feed Evan, let her sleep when she needed it. He was also the most overprotective, stifling, pain-in-the-arse brother any girl could want.

"Go sexually harass your lovely wife. 'Night, Jack."

" 'Night, baby girl."

She headed into the bathroom, slipping her robe to the tiled floor as she went, and turned on the tap to fill the bathtub. Cara had given her a set of essential bath oils because she was lately allergic to everything and now, Jules examined them, looking for answers. One claimed to be for stress relief. Another promised purification of body and mind.

No, thanks. Her dirty fantasies were about the only indulgence she had.

Her phone vibrated again, a low buzz that sliced through the steamy whorls and rush of water.

Speaking of dirty fantasies… Tad's sickeningly handsome face popped up on the screen. The temptation to ignore it pinged her briefly but they had left things in a weird spot at Lili's studio and maybe he wanted to clear the air.

Before she answered, she took a deep breath. "Erotic Circus Clown School. Squeeze more than red noses."

"Very tempting." She heard the hitch in his breath. "I'm downstairs. Can I come up?"

Hell to the no. It was far too late for a casual visit. She waited a moment, unsure how to play it.

"I've got salted caramel gelato," he said into the steamy silence.

She didn't want gelato . . . said no one ever. This guy was the devil who knew all her weaknesses.

"Okay, but you can't stay long. I just put Evan down," she answered, more for her own peace of mind. Oh, no, she would never use her child as a human shield.

She turned off the bath tap. Deliberately, she covered her warm, damp skin with the silk robe and stared in the mirror. Hair in a frizz, a lover's flush on her cheeks, nipples standing in a stiff salute as if they knew the general was here for inspection.

It's late and you're alone, Bad Girl Jules cheered.

Child in the next room, Good Girl Jules replied primly.

Her hands flew to her hair in a smoothing motion as she shuffled to the door. Immediately, she pushed them back down to her sides. She didn't need to make herself pretty for her friend.

His heavy tread up the stair had her heart beating a mile a minute. God, she was acting like a complete Muppet. So this was the first time he had visited her at her new place. He had come by plenty of times when she lived at Jack and Lili's, so why should this be any different?

Because you're in your own gal-pad now. Where anything could happen.

Where nothing would happen because he was not interested.

His dark head rose into view and she felt her pulse rise with it. Damn, she did not want to feel hostage to her hormones.

Apparently he was on board with that idea. The flick he gave over her robe-clad body was dismissive, adding further to her feelings of frumpery. A true friend would have lingered a touch on her breasts. What a waste of pouty nipples.

"What's up?" she asked sharply, irritation over her body's reaction and his clear lack of one provoking her surliness.

"I just wanted to stop by and see how you were."

When she lived with Jack and Lili, he had done that a lot. Jack and Lili would be working late, leaving Jules alone with Evan who used to sleep more than he did now. Tad would call and ask her if she wanted him to stop by. Sometimes, she claimed busyness, not because she didn't need the company but just to prove that she could say no. More often she said yes, because the one percent refusal made the acceptance more palatable.

And then one night, she jumped him like a lioness cutting down a baby antelope.

The T-shirt he wore tonight was a plain grey that would have looked, well, plain on any other guy. But not on Tad. Nothing looked plain on his sinfully sexy body. Thin cotton stretched over his well-defined chest muscles and fought a losing battle to cover his biceps. He'd always filled out a pair of jeans nicely, but for some reason, she was so much more aware of him tonight. Putting herself in "dating" mode had forged new neural pathways or something. Or she was just feeling randy after so long without a guy.

He brushed by her into the apartment, his upper arm kissing her shoulder and shiver-shocking her system. The

one with all those newly forged neural pathways that led to
Destination: Unfulfilled.

She shut the door behind her, the definitive click bringing
Jack's words about the size of the apartment back to her in a
rush. Not so much character as claustrophobic. Toasty.

"Where's the gelato?" she asked, removing her heated focus from his muscular body to his empty hands.

"What? Oh...I don't have any." He scanned the living
room, still box-cluttered and messy from her move-in a
month ago. "How are you settling in?"

"Okay. You want to tell me why you're here?" For a moment, she had forgotten that she was mad at him from earlier
and now he had waltzed in like she had nothing better to do
but be at his beck and call. Her sour mood might have had
something to do with the broken promise of salted caramel
gelato.

He rubbed his chin and in the strained silence, she could almost hear the rough bristles under his palm. "Jules, about what
I said earlier at the studio. I'm sorry if it came off as—"

"Paternal? Assholic? Slut-shaming?"

His eyes widened. "I'll gladly own up to paternal and
maybe, ass—"

"—holic," she supplied helpfully.

"Okay," he said, the word dragged out to soothe the
barmy woman in the room, "but slut-shaming is all wrong."

"You pretty much said that photo gave off a vibe. That's
the kind of crap guys come up with when women are attacked and they're making excuses for their gender. She was
asking for it because of what she was wearing. Commonly
known as slut-shaming."

He looked gobsmacked. "That's not what I meant at all. I
worry about you and I don't want you to attract sleazy assholes looking to use you."

She let loose a sigh in the hopes it might relax her anger-taut muscles. She wasn't even sure *why* she was so angry. All she knew was she was cheesed off at all the paternal shit.

"I've already got a big brother, Tad. I don't need another one."

Thoughts chased each other across his face before finally settling on intense. Shocking, thunderstorm intense. "I don't want to be your brother, Jules."

The way he said it—a low rumble of sex—sent a shiver all the way down to her good parts. She opened her mouth to ask more and then closed it because she had nothing. Her mouth was desert dry. The sensitive area between her thighs? Not so much.

He walked into the kitchen, drawing her attention to his loose-limbed gait. She loved how he moved. He grabbed a spoon off the counter, twisted off the lid of the Nutella jar, and scooped some out.

"I heard you're going to get busy with some guy in the back of his Honda Civic." He popped a heaped spoonful of Nutella into his mouth as if that punctuation would keep him from shoving his other foot in his mouth.

Rage boiled up once more. "Been having a nice old gossip with your girlfriend, Shane? You braid each other's hair, too?"

She took the spoon from him and helped herself from the jar of chocolate-hazelnut goodness, careful to keep as much distance from him as possible. Because there was a fair to middling chance she was going to use the spoon to excavate the sensitive area between *his* thighs.

"I thought you wanted to ease into the dating game. Now I hear you're looking to hook up."

She let out an exasperated noise. "And this is your business how?"

"Paternal. Assholic." He held her gaze long enough to make her tingle. "Indulge me."

She dug deep for her casual voice. He was here because he cared about her as a friend, no other reason, and she needed to get on board with that.

"Cara thinks I should play the field a bit. Pick a guy to have a summer fling with. Nothing serious, then start looking for the real deal after I've worked it out of my system."

He cocked an eyebrow. "You've got something to work out of your system?"

"It's been a while, Tad."

"And you think picking some stranger off a website and starting an affair is the way to go about this?"

Of course not. She had no intention of touching that option with a ten-foot pole, but the fact *he* thought so was interesting. Eventually, she wanted to find a nice guy, a man who would treat her right and would love Evan like he was his own.

That Tad loved Evan was a solid gold certainty, but it was easy to be the uncle who handed the toddler back when he got stroppy. The man had already done so much for her, from supporting her through her pregnancy to holding her hand through every push in that delivery room.

He had shown her how to breathe.

But now she had to breathe on her own. Make her way and as much as she'd like Tad to be involved in her life as more than a friend, he was just not into her. The sexual charge she felt in the air between them was all generated on her side, she was sure of it.

Still, the idea of testing the limits here sent a wild pulse through her.

"I just know I'd like to have some fun while I'm still

young. Something short-term and meaningless would be good, I suppose."

It was a universal truth that a Nutella binge could not be enjoyed without leaving evidence. A smudge of chocolate scored Tad's cheek near the corner of his mouth, and she itched to rub her thumb against it.

So she did.

Then she sucked the smear that dotted the side of her thumb.

Slowly.

Tad's burning gaze latched on to her thumb-filled mouth, sending her sex into a heated clench. Warm liquid surged between her thighs and her nipples pebbled against the sensually thin silk of her robe. One look from Tad was like the equivalent of a good forty minutes of foreplay. One look and her body was ready for him.

Crazy, just crazy.

She blinked away her lascivious thoughts and stopped sucking on her thumb. This was completely ridic. Subtle seduction had never been part of her repertoire; old, slutty Jules was direct and to the point. Besides, Tad wasn't interested in her in that way. He'd made that abundantly clear.

Except... something shifted incrementally. That imagined energy between them turned tangible the longer they stood there, staring.

"What about me?" he asked, low and soft.

"What about you what?"

He remained silent, just held her gaze with those unwavering blue eyes the color of a Chicago summer sky over the lake. Just stood there exuding... vibes. Sexual, dangerous, reach-inside-her vibes. While her heart danced a samba against her rib cage, she tried to comprehend what he was saying. Or not saying.

"Tad, this isn't the time to do that dreamy stare you use on your victims."

He took her hand in his, rubbing heated circles with his thumb along the inside of her wrist. "Something short-term and meaningless. That's what you want, right?"

Not really. She wanted someone to hold her and soothe her, but that wasn't what she was hearing here. She was having a hard time computing what exactly she was hearing.

"Are you—are you offering to be my fling?"

"Is that such a bad idea?"

He pulled her thumb to his mouth. For a moment she thought he was going to kiss it but then he surprised her by wrapping his lips around the tip. His tongue lapped at the delicate pad, taking her fingerprint.

Taking her breath.

Words would not form, but who needed words when every cell was roaring with pleasure? And how was she supposed to respond to her friend offering to...what exactly? How was she supposed to respond with his tongue swirling around her thumb in the sexiest contract-negotiating tactic she had ever encountered?

Thoughts were impossible, so she forced herself to dig deep and rely on actions. She yanked out her thumb and stepped away. His eyes fell to her breasts, which played their part in the proceedings by getting their perk on.

"Bloody hell, Tad, are you mental?"

"If all you want is some guy to..." He paused, searching for appropriate words for the most inappropriate conversation. "To get you off, some sort of release, then isn't it better you do it with someone safe, someone you know who you can set the rules with beforehand?"

He was serious. Completely serious. Hotter-than-Hades Taddeo DeLuca was offering his much-vaunted services.

Images of those big, blunt hands all over her body, molding, teasing, pushing her to the limits, flooded her sex-addled brain.

How exactly would that be "safe"?

A nervous laugh spilled out. "Tad, you do know how wacked this sounds. We're friends and if we crossed that line, how would we go back?" A flash of what had happened between them a year ago scorched her soul. She had almost destroyed what they had with her desperate fumble and it had taken months for them to get back on track.

He didn't answer. He just stared in a way that made her feel hot and desired. Ravenous.

"We're practically related," she went on, striving for her most reasonable tone. Someone had to keep their head here. "We're always going to be in each other's lives and to think it would be difficult between us ... or cause problems for everyone else ... that's just not worth it."

Well handled, Good Girl Jules said.

Note we didn't dismiss it out of hand, Bad Girl Jules responded dryly.

A very focused look knotted his face and a vein at his temple jumped, but when he spoke, the contrast astonished her. Deep, low, calm. "I thought we could be adults about it. We scratch an itch and then move on."

"Scratch an itch? I've got an itch"—not that her itch was a Tad itch, but more a general itch than any guy could attend to—"but what's your excuse? You could have anyone. Surely, you haven't run through all the Hot Taddies?"

Ruh-roh. A black curtain descended over his face and that twitch at his temple went nuts. He opened his mouth. Closed it.

"Forget it," he ground out. "It was a stupid idea."

He skirted her, careful not to touch her, and headed for the door.

Nah-ah. He was not walking out just because he didn't like the direction of the conversation. "Tad DeLuca, stop right there."

He halted but didn't turn. His broad back muscles rippled in anger.

"You know what I'm saying. You have your pick of the crop so the only conclusion I can draw here is that you see me as some object of pity. You're not attracted to me. That much I know, so—"

A chink of light creaked open in her brain.

"The photograph? You saw how well I scrubbed up in that photograph and now you want to tap some of what you haven't had? That was just a Lili-crafted illusion. This is it." She carved a shaky hand through the air in front of her baby-ravaged body, feeling suddenly more vulnerable than she had ever felt in his presence. "Half the time, I have corn-flakes in my hair and my clothes are stained and I barely have time to shower."

He turned slowly, deliberately. Statues had nothing on him. His deep blue eyes blazed his annoyance.

"You think I'm that shallow, that I'm only here because you looked good with some make-up on? Jesus, Jules, I thought you knew me better than that."

Oh, but wasn't that the problem? She knew him far too well.

"Tad, I know what kind of women you like and we both know I'm not it."

Hurt flashed across his face. Probably just an ego hit, but what if it wasn't? What if she had truly wounded him? Mouth working furiously, he wrenched open the door.

"Got it," he bit out as he slammed the door behind him.

That went well. She hadn't meant to insult him but really, his offer was a sandwich short of a picnic. Tad as her lover?

It beggared belief. Fantasizing about it was one thing but to have it suddenly presented as a possibility was just crazy cakes.

Wasn't it?

A faint tap on the door pulled her out of her guilt trip. She opened up to find him standing like a raging bull, still scowling.

"Tad, I'm sorry—"

His mouth covered hers, crushing the words and forcing the apology back down her throat. The sweet, chocolate-y taste hit her at the same time as her lips fell apart, the loss of control inevitable. Her muscles quickly followed suit.

Tad was kissing her. This shouldn't feel so good but the possessive claiming thrilled through her, confirming this man's mouth could work miracles. She clutched at his shoulders, molding her body flush to his in recognition that she may never get this chance again. His arms encircled her, one hand tight against her back, the other cupping her arse professionally. The hard ridge of his erection pulsed against her belly.

Oh, wow.

Their tongues mated, tangled, delighted in the dance. His musky body scent, the taste of cocoa and *him*, all combined to send her reeling in a downward spiral of pleasure. It was a movie kiss, the one in the rain, the reunion in the desert. That first, humiliating fumble all those months ago, was finally erased by this most perfect melding of mouths.

He pulled back, breathless, before she could get busy with her hands. A helpless little sound, part lust, part disappointment, emerged involuntarily from her throat. She wasn't proud of it.

"Jules, I've seen you with the Cheerio hair accessories and that Manchester United shirt so ragged you should burn it. Sometimes you look like you just fell out of bed and your hair hasn't seen a brush in forever. All it does is remind me that your focus is your kid and that you're the most unselfish person I've ever met. Seeing you, the real you, turns me on big time. So don't tell me how I feel."

She swallowed, absorbing into her bloodstream what taste she could savor from his lips and those heart-stopping words. Holding on to that taste for dear life. "Okay."

Those flinty blue eyes, more navy than blue now, drilled into her. Unavoidably, she licked her lips to taste him again, drawing a flare of arousal in his eyes and a heated growl. A very erotic sound.

This is actually happening.

"Think about what I said."

Maybe not.

"What you said," she whispered, when really she wanted to scream at him, *Kiss me again,* because thinking was so not what she wanted to do right now.

He uncurled her clawed hands from his shoulders—she had been gripping him tight enough to bruise—and removed himself from her barnacle grip.

"You're right to be worried. There's a lot on the line here so we shouldn't do anything rash, but you need to know that I want nothing more than to get all up in your business, Juliet Kilroy. Let's sleep on it and give it some consideration, okay?"

She nodded.

He smiled.

Oh, mercy, that smile was like a hot lick to her mouth. She had seen that weapon in action. Worse, she had seen the consequences. Understanding his appeal had never been difficult—Good God, the man was sex-in-motion—but in this moment, she finally got why his rejection of her last year was the best thing to ever happen to her. If she were to wake up to that smile, even once, she would be finished.

"Sweet dreams, Jules."

He may as well have said, *Sweet dreams of me, Jules.* Her response died in her mouth. Just as well when all her brain power was dedicated to keeping herself (a) upright and (b) from begging him to stay and audition for the role of Jules's Summer Fling. As he turned to leave, she caught the twitch of his lips. The man knew what she was thinking.

He was her friend after all.

Dazed, she watched as he pounded down the stairs to the rhythm of not just her heart, but something infinitely lower. The guy looked as good going as he did coming. Unavoidably, her mind flew to the contents of her nightstand drawer and her battery situation.

"Everything all right?"

She jolted at the sound of Shane's voice behind her. The door to the apartment he shared with Cara was a few feet down, but he couldn't possibly have seen what just happened...how long ago was it now? She had no idea how much time had passed while she stared at the steps that took Tad away from her. Ten seconds? Ten minutes?

Binding her robe tighter around her overheated body, she turned to Shane. "Fine." Tad had just kissed the stuffing out of her but otherwise, it was all cool.

At Shane's bare feet, his cat Vegas—so named in celebration of the place and crazy circumstances surrounding Cara and Shane's marry-cute—rubbed his owner's legs.

"On walkabout with Vegas?"

Taking the utterance of his name as an invitation, the scrawny, mottled grey bundle of fur moseyed on over to Jules's door and snaked by into her apartment. Since she'd moved in, the cat had scratched at her door at least three times a day trying to get inside his old digs. Shane let him walk about the hallway, trying to wean him off his reliance on his old environment. Spoiled rotten, he was, which didn't bode well for the kids.

"Do you mind if he takes a gander?" Shane asked, resigned but indulgent. Vegas was already padding about in Jules's living room, sniffing the living room rug and rubbing against the side of the sofa.

Shane leaned against the door frame, casually handsome in sweats and a tee. Although not related by blood, they had become close since he'd come into their lives about a year back. He and Jack shared a father; Jules and Jack shared a mother.

His lips scrunched in a grimace. "Can I ask you something?"

"Sure."

"When you were pregnant with Evan, did you get, you know, um…"

"Did I get what?"

"More, you know…" His cheeks flushed brick red and his gaze fell to a fascinating threadbare patch of carpet.

"Out with it, Shanester."

He huffed a breath. "More interested in sex the further along you got?"

Oh, not what she had been expecting at all. They were friendly but not *this* friendly. Had he not heard of the Internet?

"Look, forget I asked." His uncomfortable gaze sought out Vegas. "Come on, fur-bag, time to go."

"No, Shane, it's okay," she said, regrouping. She had a certain level of experience here that she could expound on knowledgeably. "So Cara's insatiable appetites aren't restricted to pickles and Cherry Garcia?"

His grin was shy. "She wants it all the time and while I have no problems giving her what she wants, I'm just worried it'll be harmful for the babies."

There had been moments in the latter stages of Jules's pregnancy when her body was on fire with want, mostly with her inappropriate desire for Tad.

"Hormones can be tricky," she said honestly. "There's an alien being inside sucking the life out of you. There are days you want to eat everything in sight or punch whoever's standing in the way of you eating everything in sight. Then there are other days when other urges take over."

Shane stared, leading Jules to realize her dirty wants were plain to see on her face. Did everybody but Jules have to be having sex?

Time to wrap this up.

"I'm sure it's fine. Cara's a lot tougher than she appears."

Jules knew Tad could give her what she needed. That one night to lose herself in ecstasy and pleasure, and with a man who would know a thing or two about how to please a woman.

"Shane, honey, I need you." Cara's sex-starved voice drifted out into the hallway.

"Looks like you're on deck, stud."

He couldn't help his devilish, Irish smile as he scooped Vegas into his arms. "It's a dirty job..." he murmured. Turning to leave, he threw a parting shot over his shoulder. "You could do worse than Tad, Jules."

He closed his door, leaving Jules to ponder just how much worse it could get.

CHAPTER EIGHT

A woman is not capable of friendship,
she knows only how to love.

—Italian proverb

You're saving my ass big time, man. I can't thank you enough."

Tad liked to think he wasn't scared of anyone but he was fairly sure if he found himself walking down an alley late one night and Derry Jones was coming his way, he might find the side of a Dumpster mesmerizing. Big and burly, with fists that could probably punch through stainless steel, Sarriette's sous chef looked like he'd been hatched from a dragon's egg. His thick arms were covered in wine and cheese label tattoos; his age ranked somewhere between twenty and forty. But the guy was a genius in the kitchen. And Tad needed all the kitchen smarts he could get.

Derry ran a hand over his close-shaved head and stared at the sample menu Tad had come up with. And stared. And stared some more...

"Lamb Merguez and feta sliders, pear and gorgonzola flat

bread, duck rilettes…" Tad recited a few of his suggested favorites, all of which he knew would be child's play for any chef with an ounce of talent. The man before him had pounds to spare.

Derry grunted something unintelligible.

"You could add dishes of your own, of course. I don't want to stifle your creativity. Also, Jules will be making one of the special appetizers each day—"

"Juliet Kilroy?" His expression was pained. The poor guy probably thought his sabbatical from the high-pressure of Sarriette's kitchen meant he was getting a vacation from the family Kilroy.

"Yeah, she's actually good at this," Tad said. Not to mention a few other things. Kissing him senseless, haunting his dreams, driving him wild.

Derry's arched eyebrow said he'd be the judge of that.

"So I can leave it with you?"

The hulk shrugged, extracted a pen from his pocket, and dismissed Tad with a turn of his broad back.

Tad spent the rest of the afternoon performing cellar inventory and trying to parse last night's events.

Was he out of his ever-loving mind?

He had propositioned his friend and when she laughed him out of the room, he had gone back for more. So going back had worked out fairly well. Very well. Even now in the cold, harsh light of day, his body heated in remembrance of those soft lips parting for him, giving up that last token of resistance. A preview of coming attractions. Jules was stubborn and he bet she was like that in bed.

He shouldn't have kissed her, but hell, there was no unringing that bell. Now his brain was tripping on the taste of her lips and the flare of surprise in her eyes when he had taken her in his arms. That by-now familiar tug of desire in his groin turned sharp, but today it felt different. One erection should feel like another, but when images of a blond, green-eyed knockout met memories of how her soft, womanly body had felt against his hard-as-titanium dick, it was easy to see that this particular morning wood had Jules Kilroy's name on it.

He looked at his phone. Too early to call her. Too desperate.

But damn he was dying to hold her again and feel her flush against him. See how her eyes changed color when he entered her and she arched into him, begging him to fill her. Do her like no other guy could.

"So this is it."

Startled out of his fantasy, Tad looked up from the staffing schedule he had been unable to focus on and found his uncle Tony standing in the doorway of Vivi's.

About freakin' time.

He had played this moment out in his head and now it was here, he felt shockingly unprepared.

"This is it," he said.

Tony stepped inside and gave the place a good going over. His flinty blue eyes, the same as Tad's father's, appraised and judged.

"How many bottles?"

"Fifty-six to start; we'll expand later."

For the last two years, while Tad had tended bar at DeLuca's, he had been working toward opening this place. Tony had been ambivalent, to say the least. When Tad had finally broken the news that he would be striking out on his own, his uncle had given a curt nod and returned to stirring the gravy. Talking had never been their strong point.

"You want the tour?"

Over the next ten minutes, Tad did the proud owner impression and tried to ignore his uncle's clear disapproval at seeing Derry making himself at home in the kitchen. As they walked out to the front of house, Tad steeled his lungs for Tony's pronouncement.

"Your father did not want this for you." Leaning against the bar, Tony loosed the sigh of a familial patriarch. The younger generation of DeLucas was nothing but a thorn in the old man's side. "But if you must be doing this, you should be cooking. It is where your talent lies." *At DeLuca's,* he didn't need to add.

"I need to do something for myself. Something separate from the DeLucas."

And cooking was not on that list. Tony needed a successor, given that Lili and Cara wouldn't follow in his footsteps at the restaurant. Lili came close but she'd found photography and Cara was a born event planner, not a chef. Which left Tad, the only male cousin in a family overrun with estrogen. The natural heir to the DeLuca throne.

There was a time when Tad had wanted a life on the line more than anything. Afternoons with Tony, learning the ins and outs of a professional kitchen. Evenings with Vivi, learning how to infuse his food with love. Cooking had been fuel for his soul but all that changed one rainy night. A soul as black as his couldn't be redeemed by the perfect ravioli.

Tony looked thoughtful. "Why would you want to be separate from your family?"

Tad choked back the bitter laugh that scratched the back of his throat. That was about the nicest thing Tony had said to him in the last ten years. Sure beat out the things he hadn't said. Things Tad imagined hovering on his uncle's lips, fighting to find voice.

Your selfishness killed my brother.
Don't think about it. Don't think about how it feels to lose

the two people in the world you care about the most. Don't imagine their mangled bodies twisted up with blood-scored metal or lying in a hospital bed with tubes and electronic heartbeats for company. And the worst of it was that all he could do was imagine.

Because he had been dead to the world in a drunken stupor with not a care.

If he had been somewhere else—if he had been someone else—then his parents would be here today. In their house, cooking and laughing and nagging him about when he was going to settle down and give them chubby little bambinos.

He had robbed his parents of the opportunity to meet Jules and Evan. Given the chance, they would have fallen madly in love with Jules's sunshine grin and Evan's boundless energy. It would be impossible not to.

At Tad's silence, Tony's face softened slightly. "Taddeo, we have not talked properly in a while. If you have time—"

"I'm sort of busy right now." He gestured to the paperwork in front of him on the bar. The last thing he wanted was a lecture from his uncle; there was enough self-recrimination simmering in Tad's gut as it was. "Thanks for stopping by. I hope you can make the opening next week."

"Of course. Your aunt has talked of nothing else."

Tony left, leaving Tad to ponder the old man's question. *Why would you want to be separate from your family?*

If he really wanted to be his own man, he should have stayed away from Chicago for good, but those years in the wilderness after the accident had wound him tight as a spool of wire. He had missed his sister and cousins, and it was time to rejoin the land of the living, even if it was only a half-life. Everywhere there were reminders, but it was preferable that he endure them here with the people he cared about. His family, for better or worse.

Each year he thought it would be better. That time would make his skin looser and his heart less tight. Grief was supposed to pass, or at minimum, mutate into something less sharp. But as he got closer to the anniversary of their death, the same old responses clawed at his internal organs. The need to crawl inside his own body and wait it out with the help of hard liquor. No upscale cellar choices for this bender. Just a prayer that he could control, alt, delete his way into a reboot of his life to get him through the next year.

What a selfish bastard he was. Here he was contemplating a possibly friendship-ending affair with Jules, grasping at the messed-up notion that losing himself in her curves would give him the peace he needed. Last year, when he'd turned her down, he had known his reasons. He couldn't give her what she needed, the long-term commitment that a woman like Jules deserved. He already cared so much about her and Evan. If he let it go any further, if he tore down those guardrails around his heart, he would be a goner. And if something happened to them... if he was to lose them...

No, it was good that Jules would never have to see how low he could go. No one deserved that.

* * *

While working in the garden at Jack and Lili's was one of her favorite pastimes, there was nothing Jules liked more than strolling through Green City Market in Lincoln Park to buy the produce and herbs she couldn't force out of the soil. Beneath a warm May sun set in a storybook blue sky, a sea of white canopies beckoned, each one host to a self-contained world of new tastes. The largest market of its kind in Chicago usually never failed to inspire her. This morning, though, she had a different source of inspiration.

The memory of Tad's soft lips and the taste of his tongue as he licked the corner of her mouth then tangled with hers had kept her awake all night and fueled a less than satisfactory session with her vibrator. Once you've had close to the real thing, battery-operated couldn't cut it.

It was craziness. He was feeling protective. Okay, a weird way to feel protective but perhaps there was something to Lili's theory that Italian men felt territorial even with women who weren't strictly in their sights as a sex object. But that kiss hadn't *felt* protective. It had been possessive and sexy and more than a little friendly.

He was her friend. The friend she had a massive lady boner for.

Sweat trickled between her shoulder blades. *Stop thinking about the lady boner you have for your friend.* Vegetables. Focus on the crisp, fresh vegetables. She loved talking to the farmers about their products, learning how to cook vegetables she had never heard of, and coming up with new recipes in her head. Seeing the raw materials up close, touching them, imagining the possibilities. Parsnips and tomatoes and carrots.

Long, lovely carrots.

Oh, God, she really needed to stop thinking about carrots. Think of anything—anyone—else. Ah, there he was. Farmer Joe.

Of course that wasn't his real name; she didn't know it and the mystery was all the sweeter. He wasn't like any farmer she had ever imagined when she lived in Camden Town where the markets were full of cheap tat and bootleg CDs. Farmer Joe put the brawn in brawny and with his big shoulders and barrel chest—covered in plaid!—he was the kind of guy who made mud-streaked rain boots look good.

Usually, she had Evan in tow, but Cara had offered to look after him this morning so Jules could move faster. Farmer Joe always had a pepper for her toddler. Good for his teeth, he'd say, and Jules would conjure a ridiculous fantasy of wearing wellies and getting up at four in the morning to milk the cows, then crowding round the Aga like something out of a Jamie Oliver cookbook.

"Mornin'."

He wasn't one for small talk, either. He always got straight to the point in that blunt, flat voice of his that made her think he didn't really like her. But the last few visits she'd come home and found a little extra in her bag, such as a bunch of beets or a nice bouquet of kale. Wooing by vegetable.

"I brought you some of the *caponata* I made with the aubergine from last week." She pulled a Mason jar of the sweet and sour side dish out of her cloth shopping bag and handed it over to him.

"Eggplant," he grunted.

"Pardon?"

"Here it's eggplant, not aubergine."

Hmm, the old *two nations separated by a common language* line. Was he flirting with her? Was this how farmers flirted? He scrunched up his face and studied the jar, then put it down on the table. He gave a terse nod of … thanks?

Okay.

"A bunch of cilantro, two of basil …" She scanned the array, stopping to rub the leaves of a plant she didn't recognize between her finger and thumb. It looked like Italian parsley, but the word on the tag whirled before her eyes. "What's this?"

His eyebrow raise signaled his impatience and scuttled her heart to her stomach. *It's right there in front of you, dummy.*

"Chervil," she heard in her ear, as if it were a secret message. "Great over eggs, and with soups and fish."

"You stalking me?" she said to Tad, not turning around. *Playin' it cool.*

"I was just about to ask you the same thing. *I'm* here to visit the prettiest cheese monger in Chicagoland." He thumbed over his shoulder and Jules got an eyeful of impish, red curls framing a heart-shaped face above a spitfire body. Bree—her name was actually Bree—hawked cheeses from a farm in Michigan and Tad had always had a crush on her. He refused to take it further, claiming he didn't want to cross state lines to get his jollies.

"So what's your excuse for being in this neck of the woods?" he asked.

"I don't need an excuse to—"

"Go five miles out of your way to buy herbs you could get at Wicker Park Market?"

"Maybe I like what I see here better."

Tad gave a dismissive glance at the herbs that managed to take in Farmer Joe. Her fantasy boyfriend held up the bunches she'd already chosen.

"I'll take some chervil, too," she said with her brightest smile at Farmer Joe, who still looked grumpy. No heart-shaped beets for her today. She paid up and moved into the path of walkers.

"So what's on our minds this morning?" Tad asked, mockery in his voice.

"I'm thinking of running away to the country with Farmer Joe."

He released a bored sigh. "So, my suit has not found favor then?"

Back to sarcastic, jokey Tad. He had realized what an idiot he had been the night before and had decided to downplay what happened. She tried to convince her heart that disappointment and relief existed side by side on the spectrum.

"Lili says it's a fault of all Italian men. Chest-thumping and amateur dramatics when they see a woman in their immediate circle take charge of her own sexuality. Across the pond, we call that willy waving."

He stopped, evidently expecting her to stop with him and acknowledge his dramatic halt in his tracks. She kept going. His nonsense was not going to sway her.

A few quick steps, and he'd caught up with her. "Are you saying I'm threatened by your sexuality?"

"All men are threatened by a woman's sexuality. They don't like it when she makes clear her needs."

"I offered to take care of your needs," he said loudly.

A couple of people looked at them strangely. Jules hovered at the Jenkins Farmstand and picked up a vine-ripened tomato, eager to feel the heft of something solid. The thud of her heart was so loud she imagined everyone could hear it.

"Yes, but why? Want to know what I think?"

"I've no doubt you're going to tell me."

"I think it's because you're worried about upsetting the status quo. Your Italian insularity can't bear the thought of strangers infiltrating the group and upsetting the fine ecological balance. Lili's with Jack, Cara's with Shane, and according to conventional wisdom, you and I are supposed to be paired off, right?"

He looked at her as if she were mad. Subtle contortions worked over his mouth and a few beats passed before he spoke.

"We are?" Strain underlined his words.

"No, but everyone seems to think so. Frankie, Aunt Sylvia,

the rest," she said, enjoying his discomfort much more than she should have. She didn't really believe a word of what she was saying but it was interesting to see what Tad thought about her cockamamie theory. "We do tend to be drawn together at the parties and the family gatherings"—she smiled serenely—"and the farmers' markets. There's a certain comfort in knowing that I'll have someone to chat with when everyone else is so sickeningly in lurve."

"I suppose so," he said slowly, "but we're friends and that's what friends do."

"A pound of the tomatoes," she said to the farmer in front of her. She waited until he had counted back her singles in change, potently aware of Tad exuding enough tension to split the ground under their feet. It also gave her the time she needed to get her thoughts in order.

"Yes, we're mates, Tad. Really good mates. And I know you think you were being a mate last night when you made your offer, but I'd like to know that after I've had my heart broken by some accountant whose mother hates me or an unemployed stockbroker who's living out of his car and needed to borrow money, that I could still sit with you at Sunday lunch at Casa DeLuca, and that we could still talk about whoever screwed us over last week. Though in your case, it would be whoever you screwed over. I went a little nuts last year, and you put me straight when you told me it was a bad idea. You were right."

He blasted her with a dark look. "I was?"

"Enjoy it, because that might be the only time I ever tell you that."

She had been trying to tease him about his macho need to protect her, but it had turned into something else about halfway through. It wasn't just that she wanted to keep him as a friend; it was that *he* would be the one breaking her heart. He wouldn't do it purposefully—he was too good-natured and guileless to do that—but he would do it all the same.

"Sounds like you have it all worked out," he said, a touch morosely. Men hated when women were the logical ones.

"I do," she said in as chirpy a tone as she could manage. "Bloody hell, protection sex, Tad? That's just crazy."

She was starting to hate that word. *Crazy.* If she emphasized how crazy this was a million more times, it might eventually ring true. *Crazy, crazy, crazy.* There, much better. Why then did her heart contract painfully as her desperation-tinged cheeriness tainted the air? *Because it wasn't so crazy, Jules.* Okay, the "protection" bit was out there on the city limits of Nutsville, but the sex part of the equation? Not so much.

She wanted him. More than ever. Shit.

His unwavering stare twisted a dangerous curl of hope around her heart.

Say it's not crazy. Tell me we can do this. Fight for me, Taddeo DeLuca. Fight for us.

But whatever famed intuition he had in the ways of the opposite sex was off today. He was a man after all. Laughing softly, he shook his head.

"I suppose it was pretty crazy."

Oh, yeah, that word sucked donkey balls.

Shoving her disappointment deep, she gave a mental hitch of her pants, inordinately proud of how adult she had handled this very awkward situation.

"Now tell me all about this cheese monger you've got the hots for."

CHAPTER NINE

Women and motors are
hard on the heart.

—Italian proverb

Most online dates started with e-mails or IMs, but Jules couldn't do that, not unless she wanted to have someone proofread all her messages for her. So she went straight to phone calls. If she was expecting an instant connection, then clearly she needed to calibrate her hopes. Over the years, she had become fairly adept at picking up cues in other people's voices, so the disappointment of how the dates went surprised her.

The first one had ended when the guy got a call from not one, but two exes, then proceeded to ask her advice on their respective merits, complete with supporting documentation that he described as "boudoir shots." The second went all the way through a pleasant, if bland, lunch until she asked why he kept bending down to scratch his foot. That's when he showed her his nice, sparkly ankle bracelet. The flashing green light indicated he was still in monitoring range of the receiver in his apartment above the diner.

As she told Lili and Cara in her reports, if someone had filmed her disastrous dates, all her reaction shots would show gaping mouths and melting faces from variations of Munch's *The Scream*.

Now at Starbucks in Wicker Park, Jules's third first date since she had opened for business, as her brother called it, stretched ominously before her. Bachelor Number Three— Aaron Roberts—had yet to arrive and every swoosh of the front door had her raising her eyes in a brew of anticipation and dread. She had picked him because he owned a rug company, which hinted at safe and secure. Yet her schizophrenic mind had also jumped to sheepskin hearthrugs and cozy evenings by the fire because apparently she wanted a side of romance with her boring entrée.

Pathetic.

The door opened, her head shot up, and *ding, ding, ding*, what have we got here?

Bachelor Number Three wasn't half bad!

He wore pressed khakis, a button-down Oxford, and the air of someone at home in the corporate surroundings of Starbucks. The Michael Bublé soundtrack matched perfectly his smooth, non-threatening entrance. A quick scan, and he strode over, head ducked a little shyly, nice all-American smile spreading wider as he drew closer. His online dating avatar did not do him justice.

"Jules?" he said tentatively.

She nodded. "Wow, you're..." *Shite, where was she going with this?* "...not an ogre." Evan was on a *Shrek* kick right now, so ogres, both real and fictional, were uppermost in her mind.

He laughed, a comforting sound that she could imagine

blanketing her safely while she stretched out lazily on that sheepskin hearthrug. "Neither are you. Good thing we got that out of the way. Could have been awkward." He shot a frown at her empty table. "Think we have a problem, though."

"We do?" she croaked.

"You don't have a coffee and I'm not sure I can break bread with a woman who isn't a coffee addict like myself."

She let loose a nervous giggle that made her sound a touch manic. "Oh, I just haven't ordered yet. Didn't want to get too far ahead in the perk stakes."

"I love that sexy accent of yours," he murmured. "Let me get the drinks in and then you can tell me all about yourself in that posh voice."

Hmm, complimentary without being too forward, and manners to boot. She told him her caffeine requirements and watched unashamedly as he walked away.

Nice ass, Mr. Roberts.

Well, it looked like third time was the charm. Every girl had to kiss a few frogs first to get to her prince. Unable to help herself, she stole another glance in his direction. Aaron shot her an unfroglike grin and she wiggled her toes in a little happy dance under the table.

"Oh, my gawd, he's so adorable!"

Jules's attention switched to the entrance once more. A woman dressed in fluorescent lime workout gear so tight she could probably lose weight standing still gushed loudly as she held the door wide to let in a guy with a stroller. The cutie pie who was the object of Screecher's adoration wore a miniature Cubs cap and a manipulative preen Jules instantly recognized. Her bonny baby boy.

And the guy with the stroller was none other than Tad. Oh, hell, what was *he* doing here? And with Evan, who she had left with Cara not fifteen minutes ago. He couldn't possibly know about her date, not that it would matter if he did. Because they were just friends.

Anxious, she jumped out of her chair as they approached, registering on some deep, feminine level how the female door-opener's blatant admiration had moved higher to Tad's denim-clad ass. Jealousy snaked through Jules's insides—and the irony in ogling her date's ass was not lost on her.

"What's wrong?" she asked Tad, who had bent down to pluck a begging Evan out of his stroller.

"Nothing. I'm getting coffee."

"No, I mean, why do you have Evan?"

"Cara had an emergency meeting with a client, something about an exploding fondue station. The chance to have some one-on-one guy time with my best boy here was too much to resist." Brows angled, Tad hugged Evan to his hip. "You don't mind, do you? I've watched him a million times."

"Of course not. I'm just surprised to see you." She rubbed her little guy's chest, making him giggle and lash out for her hair. Securely stashed on Tad's hip, he looked so happy. In fact, together, they were right there on the corner of picture and perfect.

"Where'd the hat come from?"

Tad grinned, and her heart lifted with the curve of his lips. *Stupid heart.* "I saw it the other day at Wrigley Field. It's time he started to learn about all aspects of his heritage. Italian, British, and baseball."

She returned his smile, and an electric sizzle passed between them. They were both remembering his promise, made on the day of Evan's birth, to teach her son everything he needed to know. A toasty ache blossomed in her chest at the notion Tad spared a thought for Evan while he was out and about on his day to day.

"So why are you here? You look..." His gaze fell to the floral sundress she wore and dipped all the way to the cute strappy sandals that revealed shimmering blue painted toes. A weird expression came over his face. "You're on a date."

Inappropriate guilt pinched her chest and she chased it away with an internal scold. Kissing her until her lady parts turned to jelly did not give Mr. No-Follow-Through any special privileges over her dating choices.

"Yes. He's—"

"Right here," Aaron said, setting the coffee down on the table. "Grande caramel macchiato for the lovely lady."

Tad's eyes flew wide and he paled beneath his dark olive skin at the sight of Aaron in all his emotionally available, preppy perfection.

"Well, well, well, if it isn't Tad DeLuca," Aaron said, eyes lighting up in surprise. "Haven't seen you in what, ten years?" He divided a curious look between Tad and Jules. "You two know each other?"

"Uh huh." Tad clamped his mouth shut and retained all his energy for sizing up Aaron.

This could *not* be happening. Of all the guys in all the world, the first decent one she had met was a friend of Tad's? Though "friend" might be pushing it given how Tad was glowering at Aaron like he had borrowed his rare vinyl recording of the Beatles' *Revolver* and returned it with greasy smudge marks. Along with the DeLuca death stare, Tad seemed to grow a few inches in stature and inch closer to her. Anxiety spun out from her pores. Surely, he wasn't going to pull that protective shit now?

Aaron appeared unfazed. "And who's this little guy? You're a father now, Tad?"

"This is Evan," Jules cut in. Evan gave a gurgly grin at the mention of his name and shouted, "Mummy!" She had discussed with the girls how soon she should broach the subject of her kid. Cara had flattened her lips and recommended caution (*give them a chance to enjoy the show first before you whip out your mom credentials*). Lili had told her that if the guy couldn't handle that, then he was not worth the time.

In dread, her body clenched waiting for Aaron's response. She hated herself for it.

"He's a knockout. So you two..." Aaron looked at Jules and Tad, trying to figure out their connection. Good luck.

"Oh, no!" Jules said, much too vehemently if the sharp look on Tad's face was any indication. Seeing that no one was focused on him, Evan chose that moment to grab at Tad's hair with a chant of "Tad, Tad, Tad." It didn't help that it sounded like "Dad" to Jules's frazzled brain—or that she liked far too much how that sounded.

Her heart pounded in her ears. "He's..."

"The nanny," Tad finished for her.

"The nanny?" Aaron both smirked *and* chuckled. "Thought you were a bartender. Saw you in some magazine at my dentist's office about best cocktails in Chicago." He raised an eyebrow at Jules, inviting her in to the conversation. "Tad and I took a few classes together at U of C. Guy was going places; we all expected great things."

There was an awkward moment of silence as everyone settled into their new roles. Aaron cocked his head, considering. "You got into that bar fight the night we were all celebrating the end of exams and then you disappeared off the face of the planet. What happened, dude?"

Death and loss happened, and apparently a bar fight, which was the first Jules was hearing about it. Not a muscle moved in Tad's face—was he thinking about what might have been if he'd finished his degree, gone on to become an engineer, fulfilled all that promise his family held for him? Or was he thinking about his parents?

"College wasn't really my thing. So what are you up to these days?" Tad's tone was neutral but Jules knew better. She could hear the strain in it. He tightened his grip on Evan, an oddly possessive and protective move over her boy that made her light-headed.

Aaron rocked back on his heels, a little smug, steadily losing the goodwill he'd built up with that entrance and smooth opening overture. "Running my dad's rug company out in the western suburbs. Schaumburg."

"And you can't get a date out there?" Tad asked, still on edge. "Need to come to the city to steal our women?"

"Tad!" Jules gave him a gentle cuff on the bare forearm cradling her son, one of those playful, *Oh, don't mind him, he's just joking* taps that desperate peacemakers use to keep hostilities from escalating during pissing contests. But instead of smoothing over the awkwardness, the touch electrified her body in startling awareness of Tad's towering virility. His arm was so much thicker than Aaron's, and while she was sure Aaron's forearms were adequately qualified to support her son and wrap Jules in safety, she doubted they could fulfill either of those functions quite as well as Tad's. Why, oh, why did every man have to suffer by comparison to Bloody Tad DeLuca?

Annoyance and attraction duked it out in her chest, and she was rooting for the former to come out ahead. A million reasons to be hacked off at Tad bubbled below the surface. The jackass had kissed her in the name of protecting her. He had offered his body, then whipped the rug from under her when he chickened out. Those gems, along with that knuckle-dragging *our women* jibe, should have dimmed her appreciation for his forearms. They really should have.

Aaron smirked again. No, he *smiled*. She needed to stop looking for faults, failing him for not being Tad. Aaron's forearms were in no way scrawny and he clearly had a nice dental plan. So the knife-edge crease down the center of his khakis was troubling, but as long as he didn't expect her to get too friendly with an ironing board, they'd be okay. He was a nice guy who had made himself vulnerable on an on-line dating site. That kind of effort should have sent Aaron soaring in her estimation.

It really should have.

"I'm long past the point where bar-hopping and drunken hook-ups are my thing," Aaron said, making his case. "I'm well established in my career, have a nice house, and I'm ready to take the next step. Schaumburg's a great place to raise a family."

The dig at Tad was unmistakable. The college dropout who tended bar and used his mixology skills to mix things up with the ladies he served in more ways than one.

"Tad's about to open his own wine bar around the corner," Jules chirped up in her friend's defense. "Everyone's so proud of him." She was proud of him.

Apparently it was the wrong thing to say. Tad's face darkened so much she worried Evan might start crying any second, but then he flicked a switch in his brain. Toggled it to good-humored Tad and smiled, first at Evan as if he was trying it on for size, then at Aaron and Jules. In those flinty DeLuca blues, she saw him draw conclusions about what Jules was looking for in a man: a provider, a good bet, a guy who wears khakis. Aaron Roberts had filled out an exhaustive dating profile and announced to the world that he was ready for a commitment. And Jules couldn't wait forever.

Tad might want to get all up in her business but he wouldn't fight for anything real.

Heart crushed in disappointment, she hovered on a ledge, waiting for Tad to move on and let her get on with it. The date would be a struggle now with Tad's ghostly presence imprinted on her messed-up psyche, but she would make the best of it as she always did.

So it was with barely contained surprise that she watched Tad lower his impressive male form to a seat, settle her son in his lap like he belonged there, and take a sip of the coffee that Aaron had so kindly purchased for her.

Well.

"I'd love to catch up properly, *dude*," Tad said with a fuck-you smirk of his own at Aaron. "Sit down and tell me more about the rug business in Schaumburg."

* * *

"And where did you get this one?"

For what felt like the hundredth time, Tad balled his fists and suppressed the budding growl in his throat. Jules lay her soft hand on Derry's arm, questioning the provenance of yet another of his colorful tattoos. The usually brooding mountain certainly didn't show any signs of minding.

"Marseille. Vintage Pinot. Seven hours," Derry said. Anyone who didn't know him would think he was being standoffish, but Tad knew better. Coming from Derry Jones, that was practically a gush.

Jules continued to caress one of the wine labels—which looked faded and could do with a touch-up, Tad thought snarkily—and gazed in awe at Derry's ink.

"Isn't this early for you?" Tad bit out in Derry's direction. He didn't usually show up for prep until 3 p.m. and that he was here at noon rang a million alarm bells.

Derry looked sardonically amused. Dude always looked sardonically amused.

"Nope," he answered, which wasn't much of an answer at all.

Tad resented this cut into his time with Jules. For the last couple of days, once she had finished her prep and got her special on the stove or in the oven, he had been breaking out a nice bottle and completing her education. And then fantasizing about all the other things he could teach her.

A few days had passed since their conversation at the market when he had agreed with her about the crazy-cubed nature of his proposal. *Bloody hell, protection sex, Tad?* Said in that deadpan of hers that sounded even more mocking with that cut crystal accent. And he had laughed along with her when really he wanted to shout to the tops of the farm stands that he had never been more serious about anything in his life. He had meant every word and more. Itches would be scratched. Amazing orgasms would be achieved. Worlds would be rocked.

Worlds would be changed.

He had bailed because relationships were hard and a relationship with Jules—something real with this woman—would be his undoing and hers. But now he was starting to realize he had a bigger problem.

Out in the dating world, Jules was an unstoppable force.

Shane had filled him in on her disappointing dates so far, mostly idiots and guys with shit for brains. But that could not last and Aaron Roberts was probably the first guy who truly looked good on paper—stable, safe, suburban. Tad had nipped that in the bud by sticking around long enough to ensure it was the least romantic first date ever. Evan had played his part by throwing a tantrum and letting the Rugmeister know that this family business took work.

But Tad couldn't be in position with a cranky toddler and a scowl, ready to sabotage every date. There would be others with good jobs and picket fences and no qualms about taking on another guy's kid because Jules and Evan were an amazing package deal. Neither would it be long before she clicked with someone.

Seeing how guys reacted to her now that she was on the market was killing him. First, that farmstand guy at Green City, then Aaron Roberts, and now Tad had to watch her get all handsy with Kitchen Hulk.

"This one. That's..." She scrunched up her face, squinting to figure it out. Tad loved that look on her, how the dawning recognition of a word overcame her frustration at not knowing it immediately.

"Beaujolais Nouveau," Derry said, referring to an intricately drawn ink of a chateau winged by grapes. "Fifteen hours," he added with a grim smile.

Jules turned to Tad, her face bright and open. "Do we have any Beaujolais Nouveau in our cellar?"

Our cellar. That made him warm.

"A new batch is produced every November," Tad said while he sliced some artisan cheddar. "We don't cellar it because it doesn't improve with age and people expect the latest vintage."

Jules shook her head. "I've so much to learn between the vintages and the terms. *Cru, brut, cuvée.* There are so many and that's just the French ones."

"Tricky bastards, the French," Derry said with feeling.

Tad just about managed not to roll his eyes.

After a few more minutes of ink adoration, Derry left to run some errands. *Yes, I am paying you to work here.*

Jules's disappointed gaze followed Derry out, but she covered quickly and returned to the crab with crème fraîche

spread she had been working on before the Derry Jones tattoo slide show had begun.

Huh. So Jules had a crush on a certain hard-boiled chef.

What did Tad expect? She wanted to meet someone and
he wasn't exactly stepping up to offer her anything beyond
a good old-fashioned bang-and-bolt. Derry was a decent
guy. Rumors swirled that he was ex-military, maybe a Navy
SEAL. Not the most sparkling conversationalist but he
seemed dependable and trustworthy. Real husband material.
He'd make a good father to Evan while Tad was barely good
enough to be uncle.

The idea of another guy soothing Evan to sleep or holding
him when he was upset distressed Tad almost as much as the
notion of Jules with someone else. With Derry.

Shit.

"I want to show you something," he said to her back.
"Wait here a sec."

Thirty seconds later, he placed a black binder on the
counter before her.

"It's a guide to all the wines we have in the cellar." *Our
cellar.* "The selection is small enough right now that it can
fit, but we could always add to it. I was creating it as a training tool for the staff and then I thought…" He trailed off,
unsure how to complete that sentence. A pang of discomfort
pinched his chest but it was too late to undo this.

Placing the knife down carefully, she flipped open the
binder, her tight stance a brace against an encyclopedia of
words beyond her understanding.

"It's a picture book," she gasped.

He had printed off images for all the labels and paired
them with a legend for that wine's characteristics. A globe
for "earthy," a lemon for "citrus," a jar for "jammy," and so
on. She had an excellent memory and once she had com-

mitted the key to that quick-as-a-fox brain of hers, he was confident she'd have it down.

"You're a visual person so this method might work better for you." Dyslexics tended to see pictures instead of words and were more likely to perceive with all the senses. They also liked routines, but they got frustrated easily. Becoming a stellar chef like her brothers might seem difficult on the surface but she had innate abilities that just needed to be encouraged. He wanted to be the one to help her realize all that potential.

Not Derry Fucking Jones.

"Tad, I . . ." Eyes shining bright with emotion, she raised a couple of fingers to her mouth and took a harsh breath.

Instinctively he pulled her in his arms, something he had taken pains to avoid since that night a year ago when he had almost lost himself in her. As always, touching her brewed up a storm of sensation that threatened to make landfall and decimate his last defenses. He gasped for air, got a lungful of her. She smelled like heaven, if heaven smelled like oranges and summer and home.

Shut up, brain.

"Jules, I'm sorry. I didn't mean to upset you."

She rested her forehead against his shoulder and it was so perfect that he had to suppress a whimper. Or a grunt, not a whimper. He never whimpered.

"No—no, you haven't upset me. It's perfect. I just thought . . ." She hesitated.

"You thought what, honey?"

"After all the awkwardness, I thought maybe we weren't as good friends anymore. It's been sort of strained between us."

Ya think? He'd noticed but he was trying to power through. Making it work if it killed him.

"Jules, we're going to have our good days and our bad days but I'm never going to stop being your friend. You're my best girl."

He pulled away but she held on tight, whispering, "Not done here."

He chuckled against her temple and let the moment take him somewhere wonderful.

She peeked up and his breath trapped in his lungs at those ethereal green eyes beseeching him. "So, Teach, could I ask a favor while you're feeling all educational?"

"Anything," he breathed, and he meant it. He would give her anything, do anything to make her happy.

Withdrawing from his embrace, she lolled against the counter, her finger tracing a line along the stainless steel edge. "I was going to ask Derry for some tips but he ran out of here."

His body tensed again at the mention of Derry's name. "What kind of tips?"

She picked up an onion from a wire basket on the counter and threw it in the air, catching it easily as it fell. "I wanted to learn how to chop vegetables more quickly. Slice 'n dice."

Panic threaded up from his gut, but he forced it back down his rapidly tightening throat.

It's only an onion, cretino.

"I could probably do that."

* * *

For an awkward moment, she thought she'd made a mistake. Tad looked put out to say the least, but then he reached for something deep inside and his expression smoothed.

"Okay, let's get started," he said with not a trace of his

former hesitation. "First, we need the right music." He punched up a song on the iPod in the corner and the melodic strains of "While My Guitar Gently Weeps" flooded the kitchen. Tad's favorite band was the Beatles, about the only thing he had in common with her brother.

"So today," he said, "we're going to learn not only how to chop an onion but how to do it without turning into a blubbery mess."

"Cute," she said, nodding at the iPod as the significance of his song choice dawned on her. "But not possible. I've heard all the tricks. Refrigeration, using a fan, onion goggles. Nothing works."

He looked smug. "I've got the no fail way."

"Get someone else to do it?"

"Other than that. Here, watch."

With a quick slice, he peeled the onionskin away before she had a chance to see how he did it. Bet he was as quick shucking the clothes of one of his dates.

Holding the shiny white ball aloft, he said, "You leave the root and shoot on. The root is where the tear-making enzymes are located so as long as you don't cut it off and make it bleed, there should be no tears. Capische?"

She nodded.

"Now for the knife. You need to be comfortable holding it, letting the weight do the work. Be one with the knife. We slice it in half"—he halved the onion through the root—"and then we arrange our fingers like so." On the onion's curve, he rested his fingers spaced in a triangle, the middle one in front, the other two behind. He ran his knife along the first knuckle of his middle finger. "Use this knuckle to guide the knife along the onion's flesh."

Flesh. There was something very erotic about that word, or perhaps the lips that formed it. Yes, definitely the lips that formed it. Her body tingled in memory of how marvelous it felt to be held in his arms.

Like a good chef who was respectful of dangerous equipment, Tad kept his eye on the knife as he started to slice through, getting as close to the root as possible without cutting into it and releasing those testy enzymes. Her gaze ping-ponged between his focused concentration and his quick-moving hands. Lips, hands, so versatile and skilled. Good thing she wasn't holding a knife because she probably would have lost several fingers by now in her distracted state.

Turning the onion, he placed two careful horizontal slices through the flesh, then pivoted again and gripped it before launching into the dicing part. So smooth and easy, the knife edged up along his quick-moving knuckle like it was part of his arm. She had never seen anyone so gifted, not even Jack.

"Use the weight of the blade," he murmured, almost to himself. "Then we chop around the root and voila, a diced onion...*senza più lacrime*." Finally, he looked up at her, and for the briefest second he looked surprised to see her. He had gone away for a moment.

"*Senza*...?"

"*Senza più lacrime*," he said. "No tears." But his eyes looked a little shiny all the same.

"Who taught you that?" she asked, knowing the answer but needing to hear him say it.

"My mother." The slight break in his voice sliced through her quicker than the blade through the onion. He returned his gaze to the board. "Vivi taught me everything."

"What was she like?"

In the pause, she thought he was going to ignore her but then he spoke in a low, husky tone. "She was a pain in the

ass. Stubborn, pushy, with a laugh that lit up a room. She
could cook anything, make everyone feel better with a hug.
She was the best person I've ever known."

"And you miss her terribly."

He shrugged, but it was shaky. Pain bracketed his mouth.
"It felt like her life was unfinished, like she had so much
left to accomplish. Some people aren't meant to leave us so
soon." He looked up and the hollowness in his eyes shocked
her to the core. She didn't like that statement or its implica-
tion. That some people *are* meant to leave.

Jules's mother had died when she was two, her father
three years later, and she didn't remember either of them
very well. Jack hadn't been around much and living with her
aunt and uncle, she may as well have been an emancipated
minor. She was used to people leaving, but the last two years
had opened up a new world for her. Being alone was not natural. People were not meant to leave.

"What were they like together? Your parents?"

"Happy. Devoted. Kind of like Tony and Frankie, but
more open about it."

She knew what he meant. Tony and Francesca were one
of those model couples. They had survived Frankie's cancer,
their restaurant almost failing, the pain of their eldest daughter's anorexia, and had come out stronger than any marriage
she knew. But they were quiet about their devotion. It was
one of the things Jules had noticed first about the DeLucas—
how non-stereotypical they were in their Italianness. None
of that "Mamma Mia" and constant hugging that you saw
on TV or in the movies. Even Cara and Lili were more re-
served, sort of like Jules herself. Lili was fond of saying that
Jack was more Italian than any of them, and he didn't have
an Italian bone in his body.

Hearing that Tad's parents were demonstrative was fascinating. Tad was like that, too. He was more tactile than she was used to, unafraid of human contact, but in the last year, he hadn't touched her much since she'd tackled him on her sofa. Probably worried she'd get wicked ideas.

Last week he'd endured her hug when he offered her a job and today, he had let her get close again. Affectionate bookends to that scorching, but far too short, kiss from a few nights ago. She'd forgotten how much that physical closeness meant to her, how the contours of his body seemed to find a worthy match in her soft curves. If only any hard, hot specimen of maleness could do it for her, but with every crappy date, it became increasingly obvious that only one man turned her crank with the simplest touch.

Taddeo Gianni DeLuca.

He might not know it, but he needed it as well. This pulsing desire within her to comfort him, to fill those deep pockets of sadness he wore, pounded through her with a merciless beat. She wanted to draw him out, let him know she could be as strong for him as he had always been for her.

"So your mom taught you how to become handy with a knife. How come—"

"I don't cook?"

She nodded.

The corner of his mouth hooked up but she could see it took effort. "You do realize that practically every DeLuca cooks before they can walk? There's always someone on deck. Except Cara."

Cara could run a kitchen with military precision but put a frying pan in her hand and the room would either burn or starve.

"Just because everyone else cooks doesn't mean you shouldn't. If not professionally, then...for yourself." She wasn't sure why but this exchange had taken on unexpected significance. So he came from a family of mega-talented chefs and he didn't want to cook. No biggie, except her conversation with Frankie about Tad's dream of being a chef and his reaction when his parents died played on a loop in her brain.

The joy left him.

"How about you give it a go?" He slid the chef's knife across the cutting board.

So that wall would remain in place with the "No Trespassing" sign for another day. That was okay. She picked up the knife and let the weight fill her palm.

"Are you thinking 'be one with the knife'?" he asked wryly.

"I'm so one with it you should be wearing armor."

He smiled, just a flash. "Good girl." He placed the other half of the onion in front of her.

Mimicking his finger position on the onion, she started slicing slowly, careful not to cut into the root. Her usual method of chopping an onion—of chopping any vegetable—had always been haphazard. She got frustrated easily and until now, she hadn't wanted to take the time to learn even when it would have saved her countless hours in the long run. Really, she didn't want to ask Jack to teach her because he would see her interest and start expecting things. As a perpetual disappointment to him, she had no desire to set herself up for more failure. Better to stay under the radar.

But with Tad, she didn't want to hide the passion she felt for creating something. Tad wouldn't expect anything of her. Tad would just be...Tad.

She couldn't be sure when exactly it had happened, but she had a sudden wash of his body heat as he leaned in closer to her, his eyes never leaving her hands. Wow, she wished he had that intensity when he looked at her face.

"Make sure you keep your middle finger out front." Her finger slipped—*oops*—and he moved behind her. She shouldn't have done that but she couldn't help herself. And her wicked scheme bore immediate fruit. "Here. Let me show you."

Oh, yes. So she might have played him there.

The kitchen was suddenly very, very snug. Gently, he cupped his big, warm hand over hers. His fingers shaped hers to his liking while his body shaped hers from behind. Strong, hard chest to her tense, rigid back. His breath, hot and sweet, flushed her neck. The urge to relax into his strength almost undid her.

"Now, slice."

She started a tentative chop across the flesh—she couldn't get that word out of her head now—and let him guide her fingers back as the knife inched closer. In her ear, he made a rumbling sound of approval she felt right to the juncture of her thighs.

"Good," he whispered. "Now turn."

Her body twisted and because he stayed in position, her hip brushed the top of his hard thigh. His very hard thigh.

"The onion," he said, amusement warming his voice.

Oh, wow, his forearms. Her dream forearms! They hemmed her in on either side, tanned and coated in crisp, dark hair. Delicious, muscle-corded, Italian forearms that would look so good against her pale, English rose skin. A very illicit thought of their limbs entwined—why not break this fantasy out to legs as well?—and moving in torturous unison against cool, cotton sheets staged a coup in her fogged brain. His dark skin would be gleaming with sweat because she would be giving him a fine, fine workout.

Tad turned the onion. Apparently her brain was far too full with dirty fantasies to send a message to her hand.

"Oh, of course," she said, the words spilling out in a nervy rattle. Was it her imagination or had he moved closer to her? Sweat trickled through every nook and cranny of her heat-saturated body.

Say something. *Anything.* "You must be looking forward to the opening. Your parents would be so happy to see it."

His body stiffened behind her. "I don't know about that. This isn't really what they had in mind."

"Why?"

"My father wanted a lawyer or a doctor. Someone he could be proud of."

The pain in those words made her heartsick. How could anyone not be proud of this man who was always there for his family? For her?

She longed to turn into his arms and soothe him as he had done for her so many times. See if she could be a friend without getting all grabby. Just as she came to that conclusion, he spoke again.

"Vivi would have liked you."

Her breath caught. "How do you know?"

"Because you're stubborn, you're brave, and you never give up. She was a great admirer of doggedness. Of people who went after what they wanted no matter the odds."

Her vision blurred and that earlier urge to lean back against his strong chest finally overwhelmed her. He snaked a gloriously thick arm around her waist and pulled her close. Held her for a few precious moments.

"There are times I think you don't realize how amazing you are. How great a mom you are and how you're going to find your place. Just you wait."

He brushed his soft lips against her temple.

She couldn't speak. She couldn't move.

It's always been you, Tad DeLuca. From the beginning, his faith in her had been nothing but steadfast.

"Jules." He turned her to face him and tipped her chin up when she refused to meet his gaze. "I'm sorry I've been such a big Italian jerk. All that ridiculous stuff about trying to protect you."

"Is that what you were doing yesterday in Starbucks when you muscled in on my coffee date?"

"A guy who runs a rug company, Jules? Come on, I was doing you a favor. I knew as soon as I got him talking about it, you'd see visions of your dinner conversation for the next fifty years. Aaron Roberts would turn your brain to minestrone."

She hmphed, annoyed because he was right. Of course, the mere existence of Tad was enough to turn her entire body to a soupy, gloopy mess.

He brushed the underside of her jaw with his knuckles. "You mean so much to me and the thought of you with some other guy who might not get how great you are pisses me off to no end. You're a fucking queen and you deserve the best."

She had no idea what she deserved but she sure as hell knew what she wanted. This man before her, in the worst way possible.

"That's a lovely thing to say," she whispered, because it was.

"I have my moments." He smiled, heartbreaking and beautiful at once.

"A queen, huh?"

"A *fucking* queen. And don't you forget it."

In the charged space between them, she felt closer to him than ever. Which made what she had to say next exceedingly difficult.

"About the opening tomorrow . . . well, I can't make it."

His face darkened to thunder. "Why not?"

"Usually I can rely on Frankie or Cara to look after Evan, but all the DeLucas will be here to celebrate their golden boy made good."

He shot her a look more black than golden and extracted his phone from his pocket. As usual, she was envious of the phone that got to spend so much quality time next to Tad's lovely assets.

"Sylvia, it's Tad." His dark mood changed to sunny in an instant. "I need a favor."

She backed away, meaning to give him privacy but he hand-shackled her wrist and pulled her toward him. The light pressure from his fingers on her wrist made her tingle everywhere. As if he knew just what an effect that had on her, he rubbed heated circles over her pulse with his thumb, all without paying attention to her face. It was the most erotic thing she had ever experienced and she had plenty of options to call upon from her Tad playlist.

About forty finger pad whirls later, he lifted his eyes to meet hers. She hadn't heard a word of his conversation.

"Aunt Syl can take care of Evan."

"But doesn't she want to go to the opening?"

"I promised her a free meal for her next date with Father Phelan. Guy's an oenophile and his secret is that he uses a nice Bordeaux for the sacramental wine instead of the special kind the Archdiocese ships in by the crate load. I'll wait on the two of them hand and foot if it means you'll be there."

Sylvia was a big fan of the clergy at St. Jude's, or rather one clergyman in particular. The parish priest couldn't actually date, and if he could, it probably wouldn't be a bouffant-crowned widow in her sixties, but trust Tad to know the woman's weakness and exploit it. He seemed to know every one of Jules's.

"You don't have to do that," she said, her voice scratchy.

He clasped her hand. Warm, dry, secure, but not safe. Never that. "It wouldn't be the same without you. Okay?"

"Okay."

CHAPTER TEN

He who eats alone suffocates.

—Italian proverb

The knock on the office door was soft, yet ominous. How a soft tap could be ominous he had no idea. He braced against the onslaught of the people he didn't want to see. Pretty much the lot of them except Jules.

"Your public awaits," he heard in Francesca's sweet soothe.

His public. All waiting to wish him well or tear him down. What in the hell had he been thinking opening his own business? So the myths of restaurant failure were exaggerated but it was still as high as twenty-five percent.

He raised his head from where he had been resting it between his legs while he willed blood to flow to his brain, but she was already inside, hunkered down with her hand on the back of his neck.

"Taddeo, are you unwell? Do you feel faint?"

"I feel like my stomach is going to swallow up my balls and give them an acid bath." Hello, word vomit. "Sorry."

Her lips widened into that puckish smile and he remembered how good she had always been to him. Even during that dark time after the accident when he didn't deserve a kind word.

"Your parents would be very proud of you. It is quite an accomplishment for one so young."

He didn't feel young. He felt like the most beat-up, elderly twenty-nine-year-old who'd ever lived.

"Tony and Dad opened DeLuca's when Dad was twenty-five." Paul McCartney recorded *Abbey Road* when he was twenty-seven. George Harrison was only twenty-six. Besides, all he was doing was opening a wine bar. Not exactly changing lives here. The acid bath churned, threatening to corrode his throat and all the organs in between. "Dad wanted more for me, Frankie."

"Yes, he did but he was hard on you. It is the way of all the DeLuca men." His cousins had borne the brunt of Tony's expectations but managed to come out strong and resilient. "Remember that you are your own man, Taddeo. Not your father's or your uncle's. You have the right to be happy."

Happiness as a right? The pursuit of it, perhaps, or at minimum the pursuit of hedonistic pleasure. Anything beyond that seemed greedy when his parents would never again feel the sun on their cheeks.

"This year, Taddeo...maybe it's time to stop being so hard on yourself."

In his aunt's eyes he saw her worry that he was going to take all that shame and self-loathing and give it an extra twist. Francesca was the only one who knew how bad it got. Every year, he carved out a couple of days away: a friend's cottage in the Upper Peninsula, a flea bag hotel in

Cabo, anywhere he could lay low and drink himself to un-
consciousness. She had tried to talk him through it, but she
also realized he needed it to survive the rest of the year.
Between them was an unspoken understanding that she keep
it from the rest of the family. Doubtless, she was worried
he'd take off on another round-the-world binge and he didn't
exactly discourage that conclusion. In the end, charming Tad
emerged from his drunken cocoon and went back to his daily
business.

Except this year he had an actual business to run and
people who relied on him. He would have to find a way to
manage the pain without it affecting anyone else.

His gaze locked with Frankie's and he tried to draw from
her strength for the hard times ahead. She had made cancer her bitch a couple of years back and he had never met a
more tenacious woman. He opened his mouth to say that and
a million other things but was interrupted by another knock
on the door. Firm this time, but no less ominous.

"Tad," Kennedy, his manager, called from the other side.
"People are asking for you."

"I'll be right there," he called back.

As he stood, Frankie moved up with him, choking the
knot on his tie. He wouldn't have been surprised if she
started wiping nonexistent smudges off his cheeks.

"I'll give you a moment, but do not take too long."

Five minutes and a shot of grappa later, he crossed the
threshold from back to front of house and scanned the bar.
His wine bar, his dream finally come to fruition. Frankie
was right: it *was* an accomplishment. The wood gleamed,
the glass shone, the wine flowed. Derry's bacon-wrapped fig
and thyme appetizers seemed to be a hit with the fashionable
crowd.

No one had spotted him yet so he took a moment to

soak and enjoy before he had to turn on Smiling Host Tad. Practically every DeLuca in the Chicago area was here to support him. Cara had done an excellent job organizing the opening and now she presided over Shane's triple-tiered cupcake creation, shaped to look like a champagne fountain. Clever, clever. Off near the far end of the bar, Jack and Tony stood in companionable conversation. They'd had a rocky start, but Jack had insinuated himself into *la famiglia* remarkably quickly, becoming as good as a son to Tony. Tad couldn't help the thread of jealousy that ran through him whenever he witnessed Tony's easy relationship with his sons-in-law.

But tonight was not a night for petty jealousies. It was *his* night, the start of the rest of his life.

He stepped forward into the room, then stopped cold when his gaze crashed over a blond, green-eyed beauty— and her sharply dressed, very tall, clearly appreciative date.

* * *

"Nice speech," Shane said with a smirk, when Tad finally wended his way back to Cara and Shane. He couldn't remember much about it. Something about wine and coming together and making new friends. And then something else about wine.

"Thanks," Tad muttered, trying to put a good-natured spin on it when really he was ready to punch something. *Take a couple of deep breaths.* Over at the bar, the sharp suit laid a hand oh-so-casually on Jules's arm and Tad's body went into a full-scale lockdown.

"Who's that guy?" he asked Cara, who seemed to be running Operation Get Jules Bedded.

"Darian Fuentes." She let out a breathy giggle. "*Doctor* Darian Fuentes, actually. He's a friend of mine from Lurie Children's Hospital."

Cara did volunteer work at the kids' hospital downtown and it put her in contact with all sorts, including guys that mothers wet-dreamed up for their daughters.

"Congratulations, man. Nice digs." Tad turned to find Conor looking all spruced up in a spiffy suit.

They shook hands. "Thanks, Conor. Glad you could make it."

"You serving beer at this joint?"

Tad snorted and turned back to Jules and Dr. Perfect.

"Just think, our Jules with a doctor." Cara clutched her chest dramatically.

"Kind of jumping the gun, aren't you, LT?" LT was Shane's nickname for Cara, an abbreviation of Lemon Tart, which suited her perfectly.

Cara looked superior. "Well, they seem to be getting along, don't they? He loves kids, is a bit of an Anglophile, has a thing for leggy blondes. I don't think I'm being premature here in saying this is quite the coup. Maybe I should look at getting into this matchmaking business."

Shane laughed and kissed his wife softly. "One more service from DeLuca Doyle Special Events."

"From meet to altar and beyond," Cara said, her eyes bright as sapphires. "Full service events from dating all the way to family planning."

Tad cut in, irked with how this conversation had started and even more irked with where it was going. "What are you going to do? Stand over them on their honeymoon and tell him where to put it?" He could see Cara doing exactly that in some sex clinic somewhere. *There, no, there.* Probably how she treated Shane.

Unfazed by his snappishness, Cara curved her lips. "Some people need the extra push, don't you think?"

As family, Tad was contractually obliged to love Cara, but sometimes he had a hard time liking her. She was so freaking bossy and too damn organized for her own good, and this latest example of interference took the champagne fountain-shaped cake. Since meeting Shane and getting knocked up, she had become even more insufferable. Like all happy people, she wore that air of smugness that made everyone who wasn't in the same boat of puppies and unicorns want to strangle her.

"Big deal," Tad said, getting back to Dr. Perfect. "So he hands out lollipops to kids after they give blood."

Cara gave him the DeLuca stare down. "He's a pediatric oncologist."

"Guy treats kid cancer?" Two cents from Conor.

"Sure does, and he looks damn fine while doing it," Cara said.

The guy who treats kid cancer was currently making Jules laugh so hard her breasts bounced. Tad didn't have to be close to know what her laugh sounded like. She didn't dole it out freely and he remembered every single one she'd gifted him with. Now every smile she gave to this jerk was stolen from the bank she had for him.

From this angle, her profile was all curves, which made him realize that Jules had rarely worn anything figure-hugging or revealing until she had started on this dating business. As if he had wished it, she turned and he got the full picture. More like the whole photo album. Dressed in an emerald green dress that draped over her hips and breasts just perfectly, she looked like a goddess.

From beneath scowling eyebrows, Tad watched her, trying to interpret her body language. At times like this he wished he didn't know her so well. She was stepping away, just an inch or so at a time, but then Dr. Feelgood cupped her elbow and drew her back to him. A very calculated gesture that unfurled her body and eliminated any hesitancy that had existed before in her stance. Was she so starved for contact, so desperate for attention, that the simplest touch was enough to draw her in?

She was a freakin' time bomb.

Her quiet strength and radiant luminosity drew people into her burning orbit. That she was owning her power swelled all sorts of things in him—his heart, his cock, the green lump of jealousy like a foreign object in his chest.

Not so foreign, he supposed. Since Jules had put herself out there, he had been jealous of every man she considered worthy of a first date. And it shamed him to admit it, but he was envious of her bravery. She had made a decision to take the next step and risk her heart; the mere idea scared him shitless.

Jules scared him shitless.

He bet there was a really long-ass German word for what he was feeling right now, but standing here sulking wasn't going to get it done. He shoved a foot a few indignant inches in front of his rigid body, ready to make his move. Just as Jules and the doc parted.

Thank Christ.

She walked a few steps his way and then encountered...

Tad turned to the empty space to his left, not quite believing his eyes. That Conor fucker had slunk away and beelined for Jules.

Blood was in the water and the sharks were circling. Herb farmers, gruff chefs, cancer doctors, barmen firefighters... what next? The entire clergy at St. Jude's?

"You okay, man?" came Shane's soft Irish burr.

"Fine," he gritted out. "I'm going to do the host bit."

"You do that," Shane said. As Tad stalked away with that acid bath traveling from his stomach to his throat, he could have sworn his so-called friend was humming Kiss's "Calling Dr. Love."

* * *

Dr. Darian gave her hand a squeeze before moving off to grab her another glass of wine. Her third.

Oh, dear.

They'd had a nice, innocuous chat about toddler antics and the latest *Iron Man* movie, and she hadn't felt nearly as stupid as usual. Feeling a touch squiffy always helped. That he appreciated her in this dress, which revealed more than it covered, sent a thrill of pleasure through her that somehow managed to mitigate the smallness she felt in the presence of this clearly intelligent man.

Once she had figured out she was never going to win any awards in school, she had compensated by becoming popular with boys. Smile at her, flash a dimple, say her name in a low rumble, and she was a goner. Touch her gently, tell her she was pretty, murmur a kind word, and she was toast. All these things were fuel for her dangerously low self-esteem. Who needed to know she couldn't read when conversations without words were eminently preferable? Who needed to know she wasn't nearly as stupid as she appeared when she was safely cradled in the arms of a guy who didn't care to ask the hard questions?

She suspected Dr. Darian had a decent set of forearms underneath that worsted wool. Probably not Tad DeLuca quality but she bet they would do just fine. She looked over to find the dishy doc chatting with Jack. Knowing her brother, he was giving him the third degree and angling for his social security number so he could run a background check.

A brush against her bare arm diverted her attention from the Gestapo interrogation. She turned to find Conor Garcia going in for the hug.

Jules had always liked him, and it was nice to see a friendly face, especially one so handsome. Half-Irish, half-Cuban, which was a pretty kick-ass genetic combination, he also had chocolate brown curls winging strong cheekbones. His cerulean blue eyes hinted at devilish depths.

He held on to her a couple of seconds longer than necessary, then gave an indolent dip of a gaze over her body. Promising, promising. If she'd had any doubts as to his interest, they were swept away with his words.

"Holy smokes, Jules, you are gorgeous!"

Unable to help herself, she loosed a giggle that smothered her nerves. She didn't look half bad. The dress she wore was a touch tight around her doughy middle but it draped in all the (other) right places. Her Pour La Victoire pumps fulfilled their function as sparkly foot props, lengthening her legs and making her feel sexy. All night, she'd had no shortage of appreciative looks.

She only wished someone else was paying her attention, but Tad had barely glanced at her. Busy schmoozing, he had made no effort to come her way. He cut circles around her, sometimes close to where she stood, but then he was off to talk to someone else.

And the wound got a nice salting with how fit and fine he looked in that suit, like Don Draper had time-traveled to the twenty-first century. The charcoal grey fabric stretched indecently across the tight arse and broad back she saw more and more of as the night wore on.

"So how's tricks, Conor?" she asked, determined to enjoy this handsome man's attention.

He grinned, cocksure as they come. "Not bad. I heard you're on the market. You want to catch a drink some time?"

Blimey! Conor wasn't one for small talk. "Well, I'm starting out low-key. Meeting for coffee, that kind of thing."

"Mine's black with two sugars. And I like my eggs over easy with two strips of bacon." He winked, drawing her smile.

"Cheeky bugger."

"Can't blame a guy for trying. I'm serious about going out on a date, though." He leaned in close, sending his aftershave wafting beneath her nostrils. Something expensive that summoned a flutter in her stomach.

Over at the bar, Tad stood in a cozy huddle with the Queen of the Night, aka the sloe-eyed critic who had been in his office a couple of weeks ago. Something she said made him laugh and his unsubtle eye lock on her acre of boobage was the heifer's reward. Sighing, Jules turned back to Conor, who had somehow managed to close the minuscule gap between them.

"I hear you have a complex points arrangement. How'm I doin'?"

She cocked her head. Ten points for looks, an extra five for that impish look in his eyes. Gainfully employed, owned his own business, hot damn, a firefighter. Ten, twenty, thirty points right there. Sense of humor and a quick wit added on another ten.

"You like kids?"

"They're our future."

"You nice to your mother?"

"Dinner every Sunday." At her mouth twitch, he amended, "Every other Sunday."

Hmm, what was wrong with him? She touched two fingers to her lips, seeking out flaws.

"Longest relationship?"

"Two years." He gave a slight shrug. "She cheated."

Her hand flew to his arm. "Oh, Conor, I'm so sorry."

There was no missing the flash of hurt that crossed his brow, but he speedily dialed up a toothy grin. "It was a while ago. I'm long over it."

Perhaps, but Jules couldn't help feeling for him. Or awarding him extra points for sensitivity. Dr. D had competition.

"So what do you say we go somewhere a little more—?" Frowning, he pulled his phone out of his pocket, its buzz loud above the chatty crowd. "Looks like we'll have to take a rain check. I'm on call at the firehouse. Five alarm on the south side."

"Oh, okay. Be careful," she said, concerned.

With a blink-or-you'd-miss-it incline of his head, he brushed his lips across hers. Warm and dry. No tingles, but not bad. "I'd like to take you out sometime, Jules. Can I give you a ring?"

"Sure," she said, because if something was to happen to him on his call tonight, at least he went off thinking he might have a date in his future. But his viability as the future Mr. Juliet Kilroy had shrunk to a big fat zero. As much as she admired a man who did such important work, the thought of waiting around at home with her heart permanently in her mouth did not sit well.

There she went finding faults again.

With a big smile, he walked away, leaving her to ponder the curious problem of how her dating life had suddenly become very promising, yet she still felt ridiculously hollow inside.

Damn Tad DeLuca.

She didn't need to look over her shoulder to know he was enjoying himself immensely with that food magazine journalist. Perhaps they were making arrangements for a special set of interviews later that involved a shirtless Tad. The woman was smart enough to undo shirt buttons and Jules bet she had graduated with a double first in pulling down zippers.

This should not bother her. He was her friend and yes, she had let her mind wander to wicked, wanton thoughts about her friend, but those were just fantasies. He had to kiss her, didn't he? So what if she had kissed him first all those months ago. They had overcome that. *The Incident.* They had got the train back on track and were doing just fine until he had some sort of brain malfunction and made his offer.

That woman's husky laugh reverberated off her skull, seizing Jules's heart in a vise. Tad must be in fine form tonight. She couldn't listen to him ply his Mediterranean charm on another woman. Not anymore.

She had to get out of here. Tottering like a toddler in her too-high heels, she threaded her way through the hip crowd with the restroom as her goal.

"Hey." Cara lay a slender hand on her arm. "Everything okay?"

"Sure. Just need the little girl's room."

Cara zeroed those ice blue eyes in on her and moved the weapon—her baby bump—into a block. "You'd tell me if there was something wrong, wouldn't you?"

"Of course. Just TBS. Tiny bladder syndrome."

Cara shot her a shadowy look.

"I'm fine," Jules said with a strained patience, every cell poised for a meltdown that might relieve her throat, thick with tears.

Cara waddled aside. Okay, Jules wished she did. Rather, she sidestepped Jules with more grace than a woman with that much baggage should be allowed. Her superpower was to look radiant while carrying fifty extra pounds. Jules finally got to the restroom, crashed in, and locked the door once she had determined she was alone.

This thing with Tad had to stop. She could no longer allow herself the luxury of soul-sucking jealousy. Indulging in negative energy while she imagined him with other women, imagined him doing things to them that she wanted done to her. Time to snap out of it.

Dr. Darian was a viable option and how handy would that be to have a pediatrician in the house? She spent a couple of minutes practicing her game face in the mirror. She had found non-Tad and now she needed to reel him in.

As she left the ladies', her phone chirped and she looked down, expecting to see Sylvia's battle-ax face with an Evan check-in but it was that strange number again. The one from London.

Him.

She couldn't put it off any longer.

"Hello," she said, trying to keep the shake from her voice. She could already feel his vibes through the phone line.

"Hi, Jules."

A million memories rose to the surface, far too many for so short an acquaintance, but of course she had invented ones to fill the gaps. Desperate imaginings of what might have been. The timbre of his voice hadn't changed; if anything, he sounded more lethally dangerous than ever. Needing air, she headed to the back door that exited onto the alley.

"Hiya, Simon," she said in a singsong. She hadn't lost her accent since moving to Chicago, though it had become tempered somewhat. Now, it came out of her mouth strong and clear. *Rule Bloody Britannia.*

She stepped into the alley and tried to catch her breath. The stench of rotting rubbish rose to sting her nostrils like a bad case of smelling salts.

"What do you want?"

"No small talk, Jules?" An ocean between them and he sounded like a gentle whisper in her ear.

"Never our forte, was it?"

"Suppose not. I've been thinking of you a lot lately," he continued. "Wondering how you've been. I heard you moved to Chicago with Jack."

"Yeah, a couple of years now." *What do you want?*

"Things are going well here," he said, though she hadn't asked. "I'm on my third restaurant and I've got a chance at a pilot for a TV show on the BBC."

During their time together, Simon had done a remarkably poor job masking his envy of Jack's success. Even now, she could hear his voice lurching on the edge of bitterness, despite the fact he was doing well for himself. Some people are never satisfied.

If Jack knew who Evan's father was, he would lose the plot in a major way. Knocked up by one of her brother's closest friends back in London—she wasn't sure she'd ever be ready for the greyness that would descend over his face if he knew. He would blame Simon and he would paint Jules as the victim, when that wasn't the case at all.

After all, she had more or less seduced him.

"Why are you calling after such a long time?"

"You were always a cynical one, Jules."

Tears welled behind her eyelids at his accusation. That was so unfair. She might have a smart mouth and a jaded manner about certain things, but she had never been cynical about *them*.

"Maybe I miss you," he said quietly into the pause, so soft that she almost believed him before the words registered fully. Qualifying it with "maybe" was a typical Simon move, especially in their final days together, when he'd parsed out the affection as if he were using a tincture dropper.

"I really need to go," she said, knowing she would break down any moment now if she let him continue his devil whispers in her ear.

"I want to see my son, Jules. You can't keep him from—"

She hung up and slammed the phone against the nearest Dumpster.

CHAPTER ELEVEN

If your life at night is good, you
think you have everything.

—Italian proverb

Aristotle might have labeled man a social animal but Tad was feeling far from it tonight, which made it difficult to be charming with his guests and critics.

"Nice turnout," La Grayson said, her sharp eyes assessing the room before turning sharper still in assessing him. "Very nice."

"Hopefully they come back when the drinks are no longer free."

"A good review can do wonders."

He reached for his good humor, something that seemed to be in short supply these days. "You'll have to visit us for a full meal. When it's not so crazy."

She smiled but it didn't quite reach her astonishing grey eyes. Little crow's feet shot out from the corners and it occurred to him that Monica was probably older than he had first thought. Maybe early forties.

"Perhaps we can open a bottle in private?"

"Smacks of bribery."

"I won't tell if you don't." She sipped on her Prosecco, letting her eyelashes lift provocatively in a flutter over the rim of the glass. Quite the performance.

"I'd best see to my guests."

She lifted a slender shoulder in a half shrug, though it was clear his resistance bugged her.

It felt like it was going well, except for the weird Monica situation. Sexy lounge music flowed like mead from the speakers, the crowd was relaxed, the vibe was brimming with potential. Why then did he feel like his internal organs were in a cage match in his chest and his lungs were taking a pounding?

It might have something to do with the fact Jules was catnip and all the big felines were circling her, looking for a rub.

A quick scan of the room revealed Doctor Dreamboat chatting with Cara and no sign of Jules. At least she wasn't with Conor, who had left on a call to duty. Neither of them were right for her. Sure, he knew dick about the doc and Conor was a decent guy but hell if he was good enough for Jules.

Now he sounded just like Jack, speaking of which.

"Well done," Jack said, sidling up to him. "You didn't screw up once."

"Don't get all mushy, Jack."

They shared a knowing stare down. Jack's crash into their lives a couple of years ago had not exactly been the beginning of a beautiful friendship. While it took Tad less than five minutes to figure out that Jack's intentions toward Lili were honorable, the street didn't run both ways. Jack's protective streak where Jules was concerned was as wide as it was long, with good reason.

Jack watched the bubbling crowd in that lord-of-all-he-surveys way he had. "You seem tense."

"Critics."

"Fuck 'em. I learned a long time ago that you can't please them all so don't even start trying. Just keep doing what you're good at—what you should be doing—and the rest will take care of itself."

Wasn't that the crux of the problem? Tad loved wine and yes, he was good at it but he wasn't sure it was what he *should* be doing. It certainly wasn't what Dad wanted and as for Vivi...he had told Jules that his mother was a great admirer of bravery, yet every day he felt like he was stuck on pause. Too much of a coward to grab what he truly wanted. This was supposed to be his dream, the way back to himself, but he still felt as empty as ever.

He needed air.

A few moments of man-to-man trash talk later, he escaped Jack and the hip-as-shit crowd. Heading for the back office, his gaze snagged on the door to the alley, curiously ajar. Just as he was about to curse one of the staff, the heavy door was wrenched open and Jules stumbled inside.

She looked like he felt. Disheveled, brain-tangled, not quite present.

"Jules, what's wrong?"

Her vacant stare passed right through him. Around her phone, impossibly slender fingers clenched like talons. Something—or someone—had happened to her.

"Is it Evan?" He grasped her shoulders, barely registering the silky slide of her skin above the fact she was cold as ice. A knot of panic unraveled in his chest. "Jules, has something happened to Evan?"

She blinked and came back to him. "No, Evan's fine." And then with determination, "He *will* be fine."

Whatever that meant. Under his touch she shook, instantly belying those resolute words. Gathering her close was the only course of action open to him. He couldn't *not* do it.

"*Mio tesoro*, I'm here." He wrapped her in his arms, sheathed in that stiff armor crafted by Armani, and felt his whole body relax as it found its place in the cradle of hers.

She shuddered against him, finally letting go of whatever she had been holding on to.

"Oh, Tad." Her voice was husky, desperate, and he felt it right in his groin. His body clenched at the possibilities. Frantically, he searched for common sense and a smidgen of whatever decency he might have left. She was upset and she needed him to be her friend, not to paw all over her like some animal.

"Did somebody touch you, Jules? One of those guys in there?"

If Doctor Perfect or that Conor asshole had so much as laid a finger on her—with or without her permission—he was going to deal a heavy dose of deliverance with his hands.

"No—nobody touched me." The words came out wheezy, as if there wasn't enough oxygen to support them. She was rattled about something but he knew her well enough to know she'd need time to get it out.

His gaze dipped to her breasts, her creamy flesh abundantly spilling over her dress's neckline like ripe, golden-white peaches. *Neckline.* A misnomer if ever he'd heard one judging by how distant it was from her actual neck. Up close for the first time this evening, he saw she wasn't wearing a bra. Generous curves pulled against the folds of her dress, mesmerizing him. Last week's kiss had allowed him to get up close and personal with the shockingly soft pillows of flesh but tonight, in his arms, she felt more exposed to him than ever before. Just…more.

Stop ogling her, you damn dirty ape.

"I just needed some air," she said, unaware that he was devouring her like she was his last meal on death row.

The door was still open, the aromatic scent of a Chicago alley stealing into the hallway.

"You've picked the right place for it." He sniffed. "Hints of rotten vegetables and"—he paused, reaching for a word—"eau de pee."

She wanted to smile. He could see the effort in every muscle on her face, but it wouldn't come.

"I need to go home but…" Stepping out of his greedy embrace, she cast a wary glance over his shoulder. He took the hint.

"I'll walk you back." Closing the door behind him, he moved into the alley, the sounds of the bar now replaced with different sounds. City life. His own breathing. And the cogs of Jules's brain as she mulled over whatever had bitten her.

He shucked off his jacket and placed it over her shoulders. "It's gotten cold."

Out of the corner of his eye, he saw blatant relief sketched on her face as the jacket caped her body. She eased up the clawed grip on her phone and returned it to her sequined purse, but not before he saw the jagged gash across the screen.

"What happened to your phone?"

"I dropped it," she mumbled.

She headed toward the street and he lolled beside her. Too close, and not close enough.

"You don't need to walk me home," she said, her voice mechanical, distant. "Your guests need you."

"They can survive," he said tersely. "You're more important."

She stopped and turned to him, a flash of fury in her eyes illuminated by the streetlights overhead. "Haven't you heard the stats? Seventy percent of new restaurants fail in the first year. That probably goes up to ninety where the owner can't be bothered to actually spend time there."

Hello, mood swings. He welcomed her pissiness. Better that than what he had encountered back at the bar. That version of Jules with her soft, vulnerable eyes made him want to wrap her in his arms again and never let her go. But if he gave in to that protective wrestle, he was going to indulge in every filthy urge and make her cry for other reasons. Come-so-hard reasons.

Pissy Jules was the best option all around right now.

"You're not walking home alone," he ground out.

The words sounded almost possessive, so much so that he felt a stir in his groin. The combination of her bad mood, the urge to keep her safe, and how sexy she looked in that dress was arousing him unbearably. *Good job keeping it in check, dickhead.* Once he got her home and away from him—because let's face it, the biggest threat to her right now was his boiling libido—he'd be on his way.

A few pin-drop silent moments later, they came to the front door to her building. She fumbled for her keys, fumbled again with inserting the key into the keyhole, then three-for-three, fumbled with turning the knob.

"Righty-tighty," she muttered. "No, that's for lightbulbs and screws." She continued turning it the wrong way, all while spitting expletives under her breath. "Bugger, bugger."

He splayed his hand over hers and opened it. The touch was enough to make her stumble through the now-open door, and he caught her forearm.

"Careful," he said, more to himself than to her.

With her eyes averted, she shrugged off his jacket and handed it over. "Thanks."

"I'll walk you up," he said, slipping his jacket on so it was clear to both of them he would be on his way as soon as his chivalrous duty had been performed. Because people put on jackets to, you know, go outside.

"You don't—"

"I do." He tucked his hand under her elbow, the touch electrifying his every cell once more. He didn't let go of her arm as he guided her up to the second flight.

He took the key and opened her door. No problems with the doorknob.

"I've got it from here," she said, still avoiding his eyes. *Good girl, look away.* If she had any sense of self-preservation, she would close the door and send him packing because he was this close to pushing her against the wall and banging her boneless.

"How did your date go tonight?"

Fuck. The self-preservation thing goes both ways, *bischero.*

There was that flare of anger again. He wished she'd come right out and say what she was mad about.

"I didn't know Cara was going to bring Darian."

"So, a pleasant surprise. A doctor." *Merda,* that came out sarcastic, which, to be honest, he meant it to be. Judging by the freeze-his-nuts stare she aimed his way, she took it in that same spirit.

"Think I don't have it in me to date someone smart like that?"

"Don't use that card, Jules. You have it in you to get anyone you want. I just don't think that guy's right for you."

"Why?"

Because he's not me.

None of those idiots understood the first thing about her. Tad did, though. He knew that sometimes she felt dumb because the words on the page refused to cooperate for her. He knew that she had spent her childhood wishing that someone, anyone, would see her. He knew she had fought like a tigress to get here so she could provide the best life possible for Evan.

Tad had been there from the beginning, shoulder at the ready for her tears, hand outstretched so she could crush it while delivering Evan. Fancy diplomas, fat bank balances, a McMansion in Schaumburg—none of these things qualified them for shit where this woman was concerned.

"He's just looking for a housewife to support him and pump out his kids while he does his important job."

"Wow, you got all this from watching me flirt with him?"

He could feel his teeth mashed together like a trash compactor and he spat out the next words with trouble. "Conor's no good for you, either, so you can forget about that."

"What's his problem, then? He owns his own bar, saves people from burning buildings...Oh, is that it?" She kicked off her shoes, an angry smirk crinkling the corner of her mouth as one of the heels hit the leg of her coffee table with a satisfying thud. "You don't think guys who save lives are good enough for me. You're not exactly saving any lives when you pair that silky Pinot with the aged manchego."

As insults go, it was pretty tame, but the sharpness in his chest registered the unintended blow. Saving lives was the last thing he was qualified for.

"I'm just trying to look out for you, Jules."

"That's a neat trick. You move your lips and Jack's words come out. I've already told you I don't need another brother."

She might not need a brother but she needed a protector. Someone who could be with her through the tough times, who understood the meaning of sacrifice and family. Someone not like him.

But he could be her friend. "What happened to get you so upset tonight?"

Her brows drew together over eyes sparkling with determination. "I realized I have to take what I need and fight for what's mine."

Whoa, if he wasn't turned on before, he sure as hell was now. *Mine.* He loved how that sounded on her lips, even though he had no idea what she was yammering on about. She was grabbing something by the balls—her destiny, perhaps, and he was man enough to say, she had him by the balls as well.

The smoky lines around eyes dark with emotion hit him like a shot of moonshine. Every hair, and more, stood to attention at the sight of her Cabernet-red lips in that beautiful bow shape that would look so perfect trailing scorching kisses across his chest and beyond. Warmth washed through his veins. The edge of desire rose up to meet him and he embraced it fully.

He was only human.

She padded toward him, showcasing the sultry sway of her hips even without the sparkly fuck-me heels. Her eyes turned to shadowy emeralds like the pupils had swallowed the usual sea-green brightness. He recognized that look. He had seen it the other night in the wake of his kiss. Except for one difference: Juliet Kilroy, his friend, hot MILF, was now seducing him.

She brushed by him and closed her fist over the doorknob. Looked like her difficulties with the open/close thing were a thing of the past. Drawing the door ajar a few inches, she speared him with a look that might have flattened a lesser man.

"I'm giving you a choice. You can walk out this door and pretend there isn't something happening between us or you can stay and give me what I need."

His cock thickened and grew achy. "What do you need, Jules?"

"You. Inside me. All night."

Oh, sweet Jesus.

He held her green tilty gaze, aiming to infuse his next words with cut-the-bull clarity. "I'm not like the others, those men you've been dating, the ones who slobbered all over you tonight. I'm not boyfriend material."

"That's not what you offered, though, was it?"

Leaning past her shoulder, he pressed the door shut, the snick short and final.

Inevitable.

"That's not what I offered."

* * *

That's not what I offered.

So much to unpack in that. He was making it clear that anything he gave would be on his terms and could not possibly lead to something more permanent between them. She was supposed to be okay with that, but the fact he was so okay with it gave her pause.

But wasn't this what she wanted from him? One night to lose herself in the pleasure of his kiss, the ecstasy of his touch, the oblivion of his body. Tonight she didn't want to talk or think or dwell on her problems.

Her world was about to crash and burn in a fiery wreck. All her lies and evasions were coming home to roost because Simon wanted to see Evan. Yet her mind was filled with desperate thoughts of one man's strong arms, the hair on his body raising every hair on hers, the sensation of him as he buried inside her that hard length she had felt pressed against her belly a week ago. Guiding her through this storm in her head and tumult in her soul. Not just any man but her friend who stood before her like a Roman god of sex, offering the comfort she so urgently needed.

Take him! Bad Girl Jules screamed, *That body is made to love you tonight.*

He's going to break your heart, Good Girl Jules said sadly. That bitch was such a downer.

"What about the bar?" she asked, darting her tongue over parched lips.

"Kennedy can manage. Unless you've changed your mind and are trying to get rid of me?" He brushed his knuckles against the swell of her breasts. Greedily, they strained to meet his glancing touch—a clear answer to his question about her supposed turnabout.

His lips twitched in understanding.

"Tell me everything you want," he said, slow and edgy as if every word took colossal effort.

Surely he knew what she wanted, what a night in his embrace would mean to her. *Love me, Tad. Love me like you love all the others.*

"For one night, I want you to look at me like I'm your world."

It was all the invitation he needed. Whip fast, he pushed her back against the door, pinning her completely with all six-feet-two inches of hot Italian male. His unyielding firmness moved against her soft body, no rhythm, no rhyme, just primal got-to-touch you. All she could feel was heat, his breath on her neck, his hot solidity shaping her, his body imprinted on hers.

Feeling bad had never felt so good.

His raw moan in her ear shot straight to the fork of her legs.

"Jules."

She had heard him say her name so many times—sometimes amused, oftentimes with affection, even in exasperation when she called him to task about how he had treated some poor girl he dated, but never had it sounded like this. Needful, desperate, as if it was the only word in his vocabulary.

As if it meant everything.

Heat roared over her body. Pleasure howled through her. There was a decent chance she was going to explode any minute if he didn't ki—His mouth found hers and claimed it for his own.

Those sensuous lips should have been familiar to her from chaste pecks and the not-so-chaste kiss a week ago, but tonight everything felt new and fresh. Some kisses needed a build to get to the heat, not this one. It ignited the second they touched, so much so Jules wondered how it could possibly improve. There should have been nowhere to go but down. Instead it spiraled up, plateaued for a moment to catch a breath, and then rose higher still to find new ways to blow her mind. He tasted of wine and male, a combination that all but destroyed her.

Her fingers raking his hair drew him away from her with a subtle pressure. In his hooded eyes, she saw his warm gaze stoke to flame as he admired her cleavage. Her breath caught in her lungs at the intensity in his expression.

"You're not wearing a bra," he said.

"Observant," she said dryly.

"Yes, I am. And so was every other guy tonight." He brushed his thumb over the stiff nipple that poked through the sensual fabric of her skimpy dress. At the throaty sound she made, he pushed the fabric aside and frowned.

"What's wrong?"

His eyes flashed in anger. "Anyone could have done that all night. Every guy in my bar was thinking about getting their filthy hands on you and I wanted to punch every last one of them."

His voice was husky, the beast of a growl straining at the leash. Along with the snarl, she felt his body tense and coil. Against her hip, his curled palm flexed, as if testing his willpower. He was a gleaming, dangerous predator and she was prey.

She wanted to be taken down.

"You're the only one I want touching me. I need your hands, your mouth, your everything on me."

"I'm not going to last if you keep talking like that." Slowly, his fingers moved sensual circles around her exposed breast, ruching her nipples, driving her wild. No one was going to last.

"*Così bella,*" he whispered, followed by a stream of Italian she didn't understand and didn't need to. It sent arrows of want to her sex.

Her fingers got busy with his belt, deftly separating the buckle and pin.

"Not so fast," he said, pushing her hands away.

"Yes, fast. I want you now."

Before she could re-apply her avaricious fingers to his zipper, he yanked up her dress, hoisted her up and around his hips, and strode to the bedroom. The sheer manliness of it thrilled and annoyed her equally.

"Against the door was fine," she said impatiently.

"Nope."

"Then the kitchen table."

"Not a chance."

She bit back a horny girl's sigh. "Sofa?"

"First time's in a bed."

The bed was unmade. "Only time."

"We'll see."

"Stop being so cocky."

"Stop being so stubborn." He fitted his mouth over hers and backed her against the wall just outside her bedroom. She felt every inch of his hardness grind into her softness. He wanted her to know how much he wanted her.

She liked that. No mind games, just lust in its most concentrated form.

"Don't fight me on this," he said after he let her come up for air. "I'll always win."

"God, your lines are terrible."

"Brat."

That drew her smile. She loved how he took everything she gave him without taking offense. Tad was comfortable enough in his own skin to recognize that a woman with desires and needs was not a threat to his masculinity.

No wonder he was popular.

"Grab the light," he muttered between brain-melting kisses as they crashed into her bedroom.

She reached for it, glad that it turned on the more atmospheric lamps rather than the garish overhead. He placed her on the floor near the end of the bed, which had not magically made itself in the last two minutes. What must he think of her?

He's about to get lucky. He's not worried about the slatternly bed linens.

With a practiced motion, he unzipped, and her dress fell

away in one fluid drop. It puddled at her feet, and she stepped out of it, feeling like Venus emerging from the shell. She would let him take care of her already soaked panties.

Now for the dreaded appraisal. She wasn't the kind of woman who was overly conscious of her body but dinosaurs had been roaming the earth the last time a man had seen her naked. Her hands went instantly to her stomach, over those last few pounds of pregnancy weight clinging like accordion folds to her bones. She could probably fit a baby joey in there but at least she had the girls to compensate. Since breastfeeding, she had gone up a full cup size; they weren't so pert anymore but the way that muscle at the corner of Tad's mouth twitched told her that wouldn't be a problem.

From under her lashes, she assessed him as he undressed. Was there anything sexier than a guy pulling off his tie?

Slowly—so bloody slowly—he slipped off his jacket and unbuttoned his shirt to reveal that dark pelt of hair. *Gimme, gimme, gimme.* She clamped her lips shut. There would be no begging words coming from the mouth that was suddenly as dry as the Sahara.

"You need help?" Not begging, just moving things along.

"Just stay right where you are, baby." He said it low, but with an unmistakable edge. It surprised her. It also surprised her how much it turned her on.

She squirmed, sending her breasts into a jiggle. His reaction? Slow his fingers to a snail's pace. Add a smirk for good measure. She was probably going to kill him before the night was through.

"You're absolutely gorgeous, you know that?" he whispered as he undid the last button on the shirt placket.

Feeling skittish, she moved her hands over her stomach. "You don't have to give me compliments, Tad. I'm a sure thing."

"Don't do that."

"What?"

"Turn this into a transaction. It's not. There is nowhere I would rather be and no one I would rather be with right now."

She swallowed past the lump in her throat as big as hope. Those words touched a pristine part of her, vibrating through to start a web of cracks across the surface of her heart. He really shouldn't talk like that.

He shucked his shirt, still slow as cold honey, still never taking his eyes off her. "I've thought about you, Jules. About how it would feel to fill you with my cock. How good your sweet lips would look wrapped around me while I hold your head just right. What kind of sounds you'd make while I take you slow and hard. I've used it to bring me home more times than I care to admit."

She let out a gasp. It was one thing to be caught up in the moment but surely he couldn't mean...

"You could say that my spank bank contains only one kind of currency. Minted in the treasury of one Juliet Kilroy."

Not a gasp this time, more like a raspy moan of want. He had thought about her, probably not as much as she had thought about him, but still. Maybe she wasn't such a horny-deviled freakazoid after all.

She launched herself at him, immediately proving *that* conclusion wrong.

"Jules, I told you to wait," he said indulgently.

"And I need to touch you." She wrapped her arms around his neck and rubbed her sensitive breasts against all that soft chest hair and steely flesh. So, so good. "I can't help it, I'm excited. You know, long time. Itch to scratch."

He sighed. "You're going to be difficult, aren't you?"

"Would you have me any other way?"

He filled his big, wide palm with her arse cheek and pulled her flush to his erection.

Best. Meet. Ever.

"I wouldn't change a thing about you. You're perfect in every way, even when you get all mouthy. I love how you talk back to me and never let me get away with anything."

She loved that, too, but right now she wanted to know more about what he had been thinking, and if it bore any similarities to what she had been thinking.

"Tell me about these fantasies of yours. I need details. The dirtier the better."

He tipped her chin up, his eyes midnight blue magnets. "I've imagined burying my nose in your neck, getting that first hint of the pleasure to come. I've imagined taking your nipple in my mouth, my tongue coating your skin, my throat tasting the wine between your thighs. I've imagined experiencing something so good there might be no coming back from it. I've imagined my ruin."

Oxygen was suddenly at a premium, and she felt light-headed with relief and desire. Those things he said, they battered her breathless.

"Now I know you're impatient for me to get you off, but as this is going to be the culmination of my fantasies, I'd like to take a few moments delaying the gratification. You got a problem with that?"

"No, no, please carry on." She backed up until her legs hit the messy bed. Laid out, she stretched her body like a satisfied cat and lay there, waiting. She could hear her chest rising and falling, her pulse quickening, life charging through her.

Life *changing* with every beat of her heart.

He pulled down his pants' zipper about halfway, then gave a short tug. It got stuck and he made a face.

"Taaaad . . ."

"Just foolin'." There it was, that devilish smile that had been rocking her pulse for the last two years. How he could move from that take-charge guy to the insouciant charmer astonished her. Playing parts, that's what he was doing, and it struck her that in giving her the full Tad DeLuca experience, he might be playing her. Fulfilling that special request to make her the center of his world for this one special night.

You know what else struck her? *She didn't care.*

He removed his pants and well, that was worth the wait. Black, silky boxers above marvelously sturdy and erotically hairy thighs. She'd had glimpses of his calves when he wore board shorts during the summer but the thighs *au naturel* were something else. Tree trunks to match his matted arms, thick as oak branches. An impressively weighty erection strained the dark fabric.

Yum.

She crooked her finger. *Come and get me, babe.* His eyes darkened to night, consuming all that soft blue. The predator was back; her heart thudded at an alarming rate.

He leaned over her, his hand cupping her jaw. The spread of his fingers against her neck felt gentle, possessive, and unbelievably sensual. The moment held, suspended on a taut string between them. He drew back, sending the pulse at the base of her throat into a fluttering panic against his thumb pad.

"It's okay, honey," he soothed, like he had done so a million times before. "Just let me look at you."

She thought he meant her body, so when he maintained his single-minded focus on her eyes, she almost turned away. That familiar gaze seared her soul and reached into a private place.

He shuttered his eyes, and her imagination strayed to

the fanciful notion he might be committing this moment to memory for unpacking later during long, lonely nights.

She closed her eyes and did the same.

"Last chance," he whispered.

Did he think she could back out now while she was this close to heaven? A cavalcade of clowns rolling through the bedroom wouldn't be able to stop this. She was too far gone and from the dark, smoky lust in his eyes, so was he, but they needed to tick the boxes. Agree to the terms and conditions.

Only one requirement for this job.

"If you're not inside me in the next ten seconds, Tad DeLuca, we'll have words."

"Right answer." That dangerous grin, the one she might never recover from, lit up his handsome face. With an abundance of care, he peeled down her panties, his eyes still focused on her with an intensity she would never have expected.

"So do you typically orgasm more than once per session? Or is one your limit?"

"Wh-what?"

"I need to know how far I can push you, baby. If you can handle what I can give you."

"You arrogant piece of sh—*oh!*"

He slipped two fingers inside her and she groaned at the pleasurable invasion. *This. This. This.* Slowly he pumped through her warm, slick heat. With his free hand, he cupped her bum and pulled her roughly to the edge of the bed, then pushed her to the erotic edge with a brush of his thumb over her throbbing clit.

"Show me how you like it, *mia bella.*" He grasped her hand and placed it over his. She guided his fingers to the tempo she needed. A little faster, a little rougher. Inexorable spirals of pleasure uncoiled throughout her belly while his dynamic digits worked wonders.

"Open your eyes, Jules. I want to see those beautiful eyes of yours when you come for me."

The eyes she hadn't realized she'd closed fluttered open and met his too-intimate gaze. Its intense focus thrummed through her. The pleasure was already too much. Too, too much.

"Kiss me," she begged.

He did, slowly, his tongue exploring her mouth with the same rhythm as his fingers. Those electric blue eyes never wavered from hers. *Hold on,* she thought, *make it last,* just as her orgasm crashed through her so hard she saw tweety-bird stars.

"Oh, my God," she muttered against the sensual curve of his lips.

"Just Tad, babe." And then he added the so-help-her-Tad smile, melting her bones and heart and soul into soup.

"You need some time?"

She blinked a few times to focus on what he was saying. Coming back to herself after an orgasm had never been this labored before. That was...she had no words for what that was.

"Time for what?"

He rubbed his sandpapery jaw against her cheek. "Time until your next orgasm."

Blimey, were they on a schedule here?

It took a moment but she reached for a calm she never knew she possessed. "I think I can handle whatever you can give me...*baby.*"

His eyebrow scooted up in challenge as only Tad's eyebrow could, before he lowered his head to her breast and suckled her expertly with an unbearably arousing suction that drove her senseless with pleasure. Then the other got his expert ministrations, the perfect combination of nip and suck, rough and soft. Too soon, he moved his lips on a sexy trail south. Just as her reached her navel with a whisper of a kiss across her overheated skin, he looked up.

"Touch your breasts, Jules. Slowly."

Orders! Oh, she liked that very much. In her fantasies, he took charge but it was so different from the Tad she knew that it had never occurred to her he might actually *be* dominant in the bedroom.

She brushed the underside of her breast, luxuriating in the tease. Hesitantly, she hovered with her hands, partly to torment but mostly because her limbs felt heavy and pleasure-drunk. Her nipples had remained in sensitive peaks from his torturous manipulations.

"Baby, don't try my patience. I said to touch your beautiful tits. Squeeze those pretty pink nipples."

She could do better than that. She dragged a hand along her stomach then dipped it between her legs. With fingers glistening from her own dewy sex, she massaged slow circles around her nipples. The dark flush flagging his cheeks signaled his approval.

He shot to his feet. "Don't hate me but I can't wait another second, Jules." Quickly, he stripped.

Please let him be big. Please, pretty please.

She gasped at the sight of his huge erection, full and proud with a slight lean to the left.

High five, universe.

Her thighs fell apart and her sensitive folds swelled in anticipation, ready to accept that incredibly arousing example of masculine glory.

"Hurry, I need you," she whispered, not caring that she sounded a hundred miles past desperate.

Two seconds later, he had a condom on, covering a hard-on as big as a jeroboam. He seated his powerful hips between her thighs and rubbed against her sensitive, blood-flushed sex. This was the best moment right here, soaking with possibility.

"Baby, I'm usually able to hold out longer than this, I swear—"

"Cock. In. Now." *Inner slut, come on down!*

"So damn bossy," he murmured as he slid into her in one fluid stroke. It felt so bloody brilliant she cried out at its perfection. She had missed this so much. The bloom of heat. The spark of connection. A strong man inside her.

"Your muscles are so…" Whatever they were got swallowed in his deep groan, but she could finish that sentence. They were greedy like her hands and her eyes and her heart.

He never stopped staring at her with all that heart-wrenching intensity. Did he produce it at the same level as his testosterone? Did he not realize how dangerous that was and how close she was to falling for him?

Switching to shallow, teasing thrusts, he tested the limits of her patience. She grasped his gorgeous arse to encourage him deeper.

"More. Please, more."

"Think you can handle it?"

She dug her nails into his tightly loomed butt muscles. "I'm going to murder you if you don't fuck me properly. Stop holding back and give it to me hard."

Thunderstorms swirled in his dark, blue eyes, heralding the relentless strokes he now impaled her with. Each thrust became more punishing than the last. Each one broke her apart and put her back together again.

"You feel…Jules…You feel so much better than I imagined." An invisible line ran from his voice to her sex and it stroked her along with each one of his long, hard thrusts. His hand moved to where their bodies met and pressed against her clit.

She screamed as the pleasure raked over her and his fingers rubbed another orgasm from her throbbing core. In a glorious crash of noise and sensation, she came. With one final thrust, he met her at the peak and it was beautiful to behold. Those DeLuca blue eyes held her captive while every muscle in his body bunched tight through the final pump of release.

Still hard as granite inside her, he buried his chin in the crook of her neck while his shallow breaths returned to an even, steady draw. Moments of peace passed before he moved up on his elbows and gifted her a long, slow kiss that melted whatever was left of her internal organs.

"If you think that's the only time we're doing that," he murmured against her lips, "you can think again."

CHAPTER TWELVE

*He who is loved by a woman
is fortunate and rich.*

—Italian proverb

Tad DeLuca is in my bed.

She mouthed it again in the dark like a demented mime.

Tad DeLuca is in my bed.

Sleeping soundly, after she had worn the poor guy out ordering him about. So it had been a while for her—a long, lonely while—and she had a guy revered by women throughout the Chicagoland metro area for his beautiful jaw and his well-shaped glutes. She had the guy in her bed for one night only and she planned to get her value.

Boy, did she.

Jules's gaze took in the finest streak of male she had ever seen, illuminated by soft light from the street. The sheet, wrinkled and mussed from their exertions, did a poor job of covering him. The smooth curve of his tight arse peeked above the hem, his strong arms embraced the pillow, and the muscles of his back stretched taut, revealing long striations shading the ladder of his spine. He looked peaceful and pliable, though she knew neither was true.

An hour ago, she had watched as his body twitched through a turbulent dream. After a minute of tossing, she had tried to wake him with no luck. Finally, he rolled over to his front with a murmur of "I'm sorry" and went back to the Land of Nod.

Now she wanted him again. It was 4 a.m. and her one-night stand was snoring softly, and she wanted to feel him inside her. She wanted to grip his cock with her now-sore muscles and imprint him on her body. She wanted his thick hair rubbing against her skin, inducing a delicious state of shiverhood.

How was she ever going to get past this? All those years she had given herself to any guy who smiled at her, who showed her the slightest interest. The brief attention had been reward enough. Even with Simon, her pleasure had been an afterthought. Not so with Tad. He had worshipped her with his body. Every brush of his mouth against her skin felt like an offering. Every thrust of his hips against hers felt like a gift.

And now she was supposed to go back to the murky-as-crap dating pool after that?

"You're thinking," she heard from the pillow beside her.

She was glad the dark masked her smile. "Of course I'm thinking. Sentient being and all that."

"You're thinking really loudly. Loud enough to wake me up." His sleep-softened voice sent another wave of lust crashing over her. Mr. Intuitive must have felt that because he turned over and pulled her into the long, lean heat of his body.

"You okay, *bella*?"

No, she was not. She was teetering on the edge of something, maybe on the edge of *telling* him something. About Simon. About her lies. About what she needed more than anything. Dangerous thoughts that would acquire a raw power if she spoke them aloud.

Keeping her composure here seemed like the best play. She nuzzled his jaw, that rough swatch of stubble.

Because that helps.

"Tell me we'll be fine," she whispered against the beat at the base of his throat.

The words sat between them, solid as heavy objects.

"Do you want us to be?"

She thought about what he meant. Of course she did, didn't she? But maybe she wanted to blow them up. Take what was happening here and throw all her chips on red seven.

"Yes," she whispered because she was a coward.

"Then we will be," he said with all the confidence of a man who had just taken a woman to places previously unknown and knew it. "I need you again. I feel like I've run a marathon but I can't stop myself." His mouth found hers and worked her lips slowly, torturously.

"I know," she said. "My muscles are screaming at me but I'm shutting the little buggers down."

"Stupid muscles."

He leaned his body over hers and slipped his hand between her legs to dispense paradise from his fingers. His face was a canvas of smooth planes and astonishing angles, his dark beauty focused on her for this one moment. On this one perfect night, she was the center of his world and tomorrow could go to hell.

"Any chance you might have some condoms lying around, you hussy? I used up the three I brought."

"Sorry. Despite what my brother thinks, I wasn't planning

to open a brothel as soon as I got the new drapes up." She arched into his hand, ensuring more friction. "We'll have to improvise."

"Shower caps? Sandwich bags? Ziplocs? They'd have to be the gallon size."

"I'm sure snack size would fit just fine." She took him in her hand, palming the impressive measurements that didn't need her verbal approval. Both heads—big and little—were already far too large.

"You sure know how to wound a guy." He pulled her astride him as if she were a rag doll. "I'm going to have to punish you."

His thumbs parted her like he was breaking apart orange segments. Soft strokes pulled on every sensitive nerve, holding off on touching her core.

"What does this punishment involve?"

"Taking you slow. Doing you right. Pushing you to the edge and pulling you back until you're begging me to finish you. I'm going to ruin you for your vibrator, Jules Kilroy."

"I'd like to see you try," she moaned, already gone.

The shadows couldn't hide the light in his eyes. Challenge taken.

"Take a swivel, honey. Let's be efficient and take care of each other."

And they did. For the next hour, he continued in his mission to furrow soul-deep ruts in her body and mind. Every motion, murmur, suck, and kiss spiraled her desire higher until she broke open over and over again.

Ruined, just as he promised.

* * *

The buzz created its own world. Men in uniforms, hands resting casually on the guns at their hips, caressing them like lovers. The buzz up ahead in the corridor, like a fly in a trap. Buzz to let him pass from the bowels of the dank, institutional building into the grey hallway with peeling paint. Buzz again as he climbed higher to the interview rooms of the CPD Seventh District. The door opened and—

He jerked awake.

Full consciousness crept up on him slowly. The dream was always more vivid at this time of year, as if his circadian rhythms could tell cherry blossoms were on the branches and the girls would start wearing short skirts any day now. More likely, his conscience was on a timer and the ticking to zero hour was running the show. He had thought that after what happened last night, the dream might stay hidden in a dark corner of his mind. A mind-blowing lay can do a lot of things but apparently it can't perform miracles.

He flicked a glance to his left at the clock that read 6:15 a.m. Flicked another glance to the right and frowned. He added a testing hand to find warm, sex-ruffled bed sheets, but no warm, sex-ruffled woman.

Damn.

Off in the direction of the kitchen, the soft clinks of crockery meshed with a bass line beat from the radio, announcing the start of the day in Chicago. Before he'd moved to Hyde Park during his freshman year, those domestic sounds had eased him into the morning. Vivi liked to make her presence known downstairs, creating as much noise as possible because she knew it annoyed the fuck out of him.

Oh, did I wake you, Taddeo? Well, you're up now. Come make the coffee.

For the first time in forever, that memory didn't split his heart into icy shards. He stretched and crossed his arms behind his neck, thinking about the new memories he had created a few hours ago. God, he felt good. His body was sore, understandable given how long it had been since he'd had sex, or sex that strenuous. Hot, dirty, no-holds-barred sex. The complete opposite to how a casual friends-with-benefits scenario was supposed to play out. No, this wasn't how he had imagined sex with his sweet, girl-next-door friend.

It was a million times better.

With Jules.

He whispered the secret words, barely loud enough to take up a puff of air in the room. "With Jules." Sounded good. Sounded better than good.

They had fit so well together, not that he'd had any real doubts, but sometimes you build something up in your head and the reality cheats the fantasy. Not here, though. The reality was infinity times better.

She wasn't afraid to ask for what she wanted, either, and he liked to think she had built up a few ideas in her head as well. A highlight reel of what they had done last night re-played in his head. When she came back in here, he was going to get her to do that thing with her—

Later. He needed to take a leak and not be such a horn dog first thing in the morning. From the sounds of it, Jules was making breakfast, though he doubted any food or beverage could possibly match the burst of energy he'd get just by seeing her sunshine grin. After taking care of business, he sauntered toward the kitchen, ready to start a little somethin'-somethin'. His dick was wide awake and zeroing like a homing pigeon in on its destination.

"Mornin', *bella,* you ready for me?"

"Taddeo Gianni DeLuca, where did you spring from?"

Aw, shit.

His aunt Sylvia filled a seat at the kitchen table, her eyes bugging out over her coffee cup. Thank Christ he had put on his briefs but still, this was his aunt they were talking about.

Buon giorno, de-rection.

Jules had frozen with a spoonful of what looked like mashed-up banana and Nutella halfway to Evan's mouth. Her mouth dropped open, but it didn't stop her perusal of his barely clad body. Some things just can't be ignored. However, she beat him silly in the hot-morning-after stakes with a scrap of fabric that barely passed for shorts and gorgeous braless breasts that strained at a gossamer-thin tank.

"Sylvia dropped Evan over on her way to Mass," she said with a deep breath that moved those breasts in a way that had to be illegal. *And you're standing there half-naked,* she accused with those iridescent green eyes.

"You never said you had company," Sylvia cut in, her gossipy glee impossible to disguise. "This is great news. I've had my eye on you two for a while."

"No news, Syl." Jules handed Tad a dishtowel, then changed her mind and switched it out for an apron. He gave her a look of, *what the fuck am I supposed to do with this?* She gave him a look of infinite patience.

"Tad overindulged at the opening so he stayed over after he walked me home."

Sylvia curved her gaze past him to the living room, her towering bouffant swaying precipitously. The kids liked to joke that it housed boozy Smurfs.

"I don't see any bed linens on the sofa."

Jules returned to feeding Evan, who was talking baby babble about bananas. "Funny story there. I know everyone has been expecting Tad and I to get together and last night..."

Sylvia leaned forward.

"I was all primed and ready..."

Sylvia nodded several times in encouragement.

"But he couldn't, well, you know..." Jules shaded her mouth with one hand and said in a stage whisper, "Perform."

He wrenched his head so quickly he winced.

"Excuse me?"

"You don't remember, babe, but you were pretty bladdered. The spirit was willing but the flesh was oh so weak." She made an up-down gesture with her hand that seemed to indicate... "Flaccid."

That was *not* the word he was going for.

Sylvia's eyes were on stalks.

"So he's all talk and—?"

"Small, useless appendage."

Sylvia tutted and walloped him in the side. He didn't even flinch because that was her standard manner of showing affection.

"You have a beautiful woman, ready and willing, and what do you do? Let the DeLuca name down and can't fulfill your end of the bargain."

Oh, for fuck's sake. The bargain had been fulfilled, over and over again. All night, she had been right there with him, alternating between satisfying his starving cock and begging him to feast on her honeyed heat. No part of his anatomy had even flirted with "flaccid."

"Now hold up a second. I am more than capable—"

Jules waved a hand, countermanding his defense.

"Tad, love, nobody thinks any less of you for it. I'm sure these things happen all the time. I mean, it's the first time *I've* encountered it, but I'm sure once you sober up it'll be fine."

Sylvia's face lit up. "Betsey Corrigan's boy just got out of a messy divorce. No kids, *grazie di Dio*. Taddeo, you remember Johnny Corrigan from your days as an altar boy?

Don't you think he'd like to meet a *bella donna* like Juli-etta?"

Tad scoffed. "That guy was such a Goody Two-shoes. Little pussy was afraid to get toasted on the communion wine with the rest of the crew."

A quirk of amusement crossed Jules's lips. "Communion wine?"

"Had to start my love for the grape somewhere."

Their gazes locked. Held. Turned to heat and smoke that curled through his blood.

Jules blinked owl-like and nodded to the kitchen clock hanging above the counter. "Bet Cassie Shaughnessy is go-ing all out with her walker to get into the front pew, Syl."

His aunt dropped her coffee cup as if it were coated in killer African bees and shot out of her seat. "I had no idea it was so late!"

Sylvia and the Widow Shaughnessy were engaged in what could best be described as a to-the-death battle for the soul of Father Phelan. The prime real estate of the front pew at St. Jude's was Ground Zero.

Before his aunt left, she appraised him with a shake of her head. "You must do better, Taddeo. Someone will snap her up."

"Yes, Aunt Sylvia," he said, suitably admonished, and gave her a kiss on the cheek.

"Must. Do. Better," Jules said, poking his chest for em-phasis before walking his meddling aunt out.

Tad picked up the plate of banana-chocolate mush and helped himself. Not bad. Evan's face lit up at the prospect of someone new to play with and Tad's heart lifted right with it. The kid had a great personality. Playful, smart, and always reaching for the stars with his chubby fists. Not unlike his beautiful, bangin' mom.

"Tad!" Evan shouted. "Banana banana."

"That's right, buddy. Time to eat it all up."

Not for the first time, Tad considered Evan's father. It was the one area of his relationship with Jules that was out of bounds. She never talked about him, and the fact she had concealed his identity from Jack pissed off her brother royally. Frankly, anything that pissed off Jack was A-okay with him, but her secrecy had Tad curious. The asshole must have bailed when he found out about Evan. What a fucking dick.

Tad knew in his heart that, despite having enough baggage to fill multiple 747 cargo holds, he would never abandon a woman who gave birth to his child. He'd want to be part of his kid's life: the baseball games, the algebra, the awkward sex talk, the works. In a way, he was glad this duty-shirker was out of the picture because Tad didn't like to share. He'd heard Evan's first cry. He'd seen his girl's face when she met her son for the first time. He'd felt the love of instant connection with a brand new human being.

Those memories belonged to him and him alone. He wanted to create more just like them with this woman and her beautiful kid, who more often than not felt like *his* beautiful kid.

With Tad off in la-la land, Evan grabbed at the spoon and got his hands filled with mush for his trouble. Soaking a washcloth under the faucet, Tad took a moment to appreciate how Jules had made the kitchen her own. Culinary-themed engravings and woodcuts dotted the walls above counters bordered with colorful cookie jars and kitchen utensils. A few well-worn cookbooks claimed space in the corner by the stove. This place had a good aura. Lili and Jack had fallen in love here, followed by Shane and Cara while they played kissing neighbors with each other across the hall. Now Jules was here, forging ahead with her life and taking charge of her destiny. The vision of her blazing expression last night as she announced her plan to take what she needed and fight for what was hers grabbed him by the throat. No one had ever telegraphed her passion quite like Jules.

This woman was the real deal.

The last thing he expected to see arrested his gaze and sent his pulse into a dangerous spike. Slotted among a block of books on the counter behind Evan's high chair, it looked surprisingly at home.

Vivi's recipe book.

He had assumed Gina had it, but he realized that Frankie or Lili must have been keeping it safe all these years. Now it was in this place with the one person who could appreciate it and fulfill all the promise within those precious pages. His chest felt too full, his blood surged with the rightness of it. His mom was here, mentoring another budding chef.

He swallowed away the rock of emotion and wiped Evan's sticky pudding hands. Looking up, he found Jules in the doorway with a pensive expression on her face that morphed into a smart ass grin.

"Your mom thinks she's hilarious, Evs. Did you enjoy raking my hard-won reputation over the coals, you minx?"

"Immensely. Serves you right for waltzing in here in all your glory and giving her an eyeful."

All his glory. Hell, that made a man feel good.

"She's seen it all before," he said. "She used to give me baths when I was a kid. Very thorough."

Her grin turned impossibly wider, chasing away the last shreds of any remaining reservation. He felt that smile down to his toes. Stepping in close, she took over cleaning duties for Evan, Tad absorbed the scent of their happy little triumvirate into his bloodstream, something unique that the three of them created together.

This was happening.

"And there I was thinking the morning after might be awkward," he said, testing.

"You don't think your aunt showing up is awkward enough?"

"Nah, we made her matchmaking dream come to life. If only for a few magical seconds." Their gazes tangled for a moment until Evan squealed because the adults weren't focused on him.

Jules sighed. "Time to get you cleaned up, monkey. And that goes for you as well, Taddeo Gianni DeLuca."

He tried to steal a kiss but she ah-ah'ed him with a significant glance at Evan.

"Let's keep it PG."

"Impossible with you in the room. My head is filled with Triple X."

"Boy, those lines don't improve the next day."

He nipped her shoulder. "You're the mint in my mojito, the honey to my bee..."

"Oh, hush." But she was smiling as she said it.

As he headed back to the bedroom to dress, he mused on how terribly that could have gone. It was a risk he had been willing to take because his reptile brain had taken over and he was a greedy motherfucker. He wanted her and he had decided that the prospect of not having her body was worse than the prospect of not having her as a friend.

But there was more to this than friendship-risking lust. Frankie's words echoed in his Jules-addled brain: *You have a right to be happy, Taddeo.*

Jules made him happy and he suspected the feeling might be mutual. Stepping out of the shadows and choosing life had never felt so right. And with Vivi's cookbook in the house, it felt like his mom was looking down, giving her blessing.

Five minutes later, he was following her hot little tail as it swished in those skimpy shorts all the way to the front door. Last night, he'd grasped that curvaceous ass of hers, molded it, owned it. He wanted to do it again, but for now he settled for grasping with his eyes.

"Well..." she said, her hand on the doorknob.

"Well."

"These situations can be tricky, so it's great that we were able to handle it with such..." She waved her hand, seeking the right word.

"Maturity?" he offered.

"Yes, maturity." She looked at his mouth, and her mouth twitched, and his mouth twitched right back.

He leaned in. She leaned back.

Okaaay.

A thoughtful look came over her. "Sex conjures up all sorts of feelings that sometimes we're not ready to deal with, you know?"

He nodded, content to let her lead. They could take it slow, take it fast, take it up the middle. He didn't care as long as he got the chance to bury his body between those beautiful thighs in the very near future. And he wanted to hang with her and Evan more, maybe share his favorite recipes from his mom's cookbook. Connecting with Jules like they had last night was the perfect amulet against the dark cloud that threatened to engulf him.

"You've no idea how nice it was to get back on the horse in a safe environment. With a friend."

He nodded again before realizing he had jumped the gun. He tried to parse that statement but the words "nice," "horse," "safe," and "friend" jumbled in his brain and refused to compute. A niggle started up somewhere in the vicinity of his lungs.

"Get back on the horse?"

She smiled again, and the niggle turned into a full-scale body nag. "It's been a while. Well, you know that."

Right, because he was her friend. Her nice, safe, horse-providing friend.

"And getting into this dating business, I was seriously worried I'd make a shambles of it."

The surprise on his face must have been obvious because she added, "Make a shambles of sex," as if what they were talking about needed clarification.

"I don't think it was a shambles," he said quietly. Best sex of his life, nothing shambolic about it.

She laughed and it sort of grated. That was a first.

"Oh, no, I don't think it was. In fact, it was a great way to dust off the cobwebs. The last person I was with was Evan's father and since then I haven't always felt at my most attractive. There's always been a spark between us, so it's good we've done it and got it out of our systems."

"I suppose so," he muttered, unbelievably pissed that she had mentioned Evan's father in the same sentence as her brush-off. Because that's exactly what he was getting. The old heave-ho.

In his confused fog, it took him a moment to notice that she had opened the door and stuck her head out for reconnaissance. With her other hand, she pulled him toward the doorway. The electric tingle where she touched his forearm shot through him before short-circuiting in the acid bath of his stomach.

"You really did help, Tad. Now, I can get serious about dating and not worry that the first time in a while will be all fingers and thumbs." She smiled beatifically and pulled the door open wider. "Well, we can hope, right? At least I won't show myself up. Thanks for being a pal."

"Sure," he mumbled. There was a whole lot of mumbling going on. He had no choice but to step across the threshold, feeling a touch raw about the whole situation. Was it his imagination or was the hallway cooler? He turned back to find her closing the door.

"Oh," she said, peeking her angelic head through the quickly evaporating gap.

"Yeah?" Shit, did his voice just break there?

Discomfort brushed across her face. "This isn't going to be awkward, is it? I mean, if you'd rather I didn't work at Vivi's..."

"Of course not. I'll be—we're fine. Just fine." *It's all good, honey. We're just fine.*

She gave a serene smile. "Oh, good. Because I'm enjoying it so much. You've no idea what a world it's opened for me."

"Glad to help." *With your all-round confidence and sexual tune-up.* The bathroom stall doors were right. This was where his talents lay. Easy. Casual. Every muscle in his body strained over his efforts to keep it so damn casual.

"Catch you later, babe," she said, still with the regal smile before shutting the door on his frozen grin.

CHAPTER THIRTEEN

*One can't garden without flowers; one
can't become a woman without love.*

—Italian proverb

The radishes were ripe for the ripping. Jules had planted them only three weeks ago, and now they had matured and were ready to be harvested. The perfect, renewable resource.

Casting about her vegetable garden, pride expanded in her chest and pushed aside more negative emotions. The lettuce and pea seeds she had nurtured indoors just six weeks ago were now showing healthy growth. It may be on her brother's property, but she still considered it her garden and the achievement she felt at having created something from a patch of nothing got her every time. Just a five-minute walk from her flat, she tried to get here at least every other day.

"Want out!" Evan pumped his fist and strained at the straps pinning him back in his stroller.

"Sorry, Demon. If I could trust you not to bash your head on something, I'd let you roam free."

"Want juice!" came his next offer in the negotiation.

More sugar, she could do that. In yet another plug for Worst Mother of the Decade, she placed the sippy cup in his hand and watched as he chugged away merrily. Simple pleasures.

She picked up the trowel and thought about how it might make a nice tool for a lobotomy.

Tad hadn't called.

She was unbelievably annoyed about that, not just because he hadn't called but because her reaction to it was so ridiculous. Waiting for a guy to call was old, desperate Jules. They were friends—he didn't need to call her. She could call him because that's what friends do.

Of course she hadn't given him much reason to call. Two days had gone by since she had practically handed him his Armani suit and told him his sexually therapeutic services had primed her good. Evan had been sick the next day so she hadn't been able to go in to work. In true coward's fashion, she had texted Tad to let him know.

Something she never, ever did.

Texting was her bête noir. She always preferred to call someone but this time, she had dropped a, probably, misspelled sick note to her boss-slash-lover, letting him know she wouldn't be in.

No problem, he texted back. *Let me know if you need anything.* She knew enough to get the gist.

It was exactly what he would have said in the old days, as in two days ago before they moved from friend zone into bone zone, with one shocking difference.

Pre-shag, he would have called right back and insisted she accept his help. Soup, a ride to the doctor, a shoulder to lean on. Not that she needed it, but she craved the assurance that they were still in the same place.

Nice job keeping the status quo, Jules.

"Derry told me but I didn't believe him."

Jules turned from top soil she had been moving around aimlessly to see Jack sauntering over from the back door. Panic flooded her chest. How could Derry have possibly found out about Tad?

"Told you what?" she fronted.

"That you're cooking at Vivi's."

Phew. "It's just an experiment."

Jack hunkered down and unclasped Evan, who looked like all his Christmases and birthdays had come at once. "More than that, I hear you're getting on the menu."

"Not every day. And it's mostly my chutneys and jams." She felt a sudden rush to defend her presence among gleaming steel counters, as if she had been caught playing dress up in her mother's clothes and make-up.

His mouth drew into a pinch. "Why didn't you tell me you wanted to work in a kitchen?"

She shrugged. "I wasn't even sure I did myself until Tad suggested it. He tried my bruschetta and he offered." An uneasy thread wormed through her. "Should he have run it by you first? With you being an investor?"

"No, not at all. Tad can hire whomever he wants. I just...sometimes I'm not sure I know what's going on inside your head. I wish you'd talk to me more."

Oh, God, talking, her other bugbear. She and Jack had been doing a lot better since she moved to the States but years of sealing every hurt inside was a hard habit to break.

When she was five years old and they had gone to live with her aunt and uncle after her father died, Jack had promised to look after her. He would become her guardian when he turned eighteen—*just three more years, baby girl!*—and she had believed him. Not that Daisy and Pete were unkind, they were just stereotypically miserable East Londoners. They didn't like Jack, who was always in trouble, and their care for Jules was tone deaf and obligatory. Once Jack turned eighteen, he was already in Paris for his apprenticeship, and those whispered promises to look after her were forgotten. By the time Jules was eleven, he was putting in eighty hours a week at his new restaurant in Covent Garden. TV and New York would come calling a few short months later. He soared while she plummeted further and further, unable to explain her problems in school with anything other than an insolent shrug.

"I just like cooking. It's fun." Minimizing it was her default position. It had taken a few minutes in a kitchen with Tad for him to understand the uncontainable need to be someone other than Jack's sister and Evan's mother. It had taken a few minutes with her legs coiled around his hips like a python for him to get how raw and dirty she wanted it. How did this guy know her better than her own brother?

Because she wanted him to know her. She wanted to be known.

Jack tilted his head, assessing.

"You could do it properly. Go to culinary school."

"That's not for me." She raised her eyes from the patch of earth she had been weeding with fervor. "I'm not really cut out for school."

She braced herself for the Jack assault of fraternal affection, where he told her she could do anything and be anything. She loved him for it but sometimes it was just too much.

His indrawn breath was deep and pep talk–sapping. *Thank you.* "Well, if you ever want to cook together…"

"And have you breathing down my neck telling me everything I'm doing wrong?"

His smile was filled with compassion. "No, sweetheart. Just cooking. For fun."

"I'm sorry," she said quickly. This Tad business was making her cranky. "I'd love to cook with you sometime."

His grin faded. "So I heard something else odd. I mean, so bizarre that I'm finding a hard time getting my head around it."

She grasped at a particularly pernicious weed that she was sure she had disposed of a few weeks before. Of course, certain problems have a habit of resurfacing just when you think you've made strides to eliminate them. Such as Simon St. James. He hadn't followed up his call but she felt his presence like a sword teetering by a whispering thread.

Simon might want to be a part of his son's life, but what good would that do? Seeing his father twice a year, or whatever Simon would think was appropriate, would confuse Evan. Any man in her life would have to want her baby, one hundred percent. No uncles-for-a-month or on-again-off-again stepdads. No half measures.

Tad was amazing with Evan and he would continue to be there for her son, assuming their friendship survived the mind-blowing sex. If she pushed for more and things soured between them, everyone would feel the shockwaves. He had made it clear he wasn't boyfriend material and begging for a man to see the real her was no longer her style.

"Are you going to tell me what you heard or are you going to leave me hanging?"

Jack's mouth hardened. "I heard that Tad stayed over."

"Yep, he stayed the night. Nothing happened. End of."

"I know. Sylvia said there were performance problems."

They might have just got done with the latest episode of *Super Fun Bonding Time with Jack and Jules,* but they weren't going there. "Tad and I were kidding around, putting on a show for Sylvia. He's my friend and we're not a couple."

"Music to my ears. He's not good enough for you." He bounced Evan on his hip to her toddler's delighted squeal.

"No one's good enough for me, according to you."

"True, but especially him." The disgust in his tone surprised her.

She put down the trowel and leaned back on her haunches, luxuriating in the stretch to her back muscles. Between the gym (all right, one time at the gym), gardening, and her acrobatic sexploits with Tad, her muscles were singing songs that were usually out of their tonal range.

"What is with you and Tad? You've invested in his business and you always seem to be civil to each other, but there's this weird vibe between you."

Jack sighed. "I invested because he's good at what he does, which is the ability to sell anything and charm anyone. Those are good skills in food retail and getting skirt but I don't see much else beyond the surface."

She suspected Tad was as adept as she at putting on faces. Sometimes, she caught him off in another world at the DeLuca family lunches, his face straining for smoothness whenever his parents came up in the conversation. When they spent time together at Vivi's kitchen, she saw how he went inside himself to a place filled with painful memories.

The joy left him.

"He's my friend, Jack, and I think you're wrong."

"I'm not saying he isn't a nice guy, Jules. We get along just fine and he and Lili are close, so I recognize that he's not all bad. But I don't see much depth there. He was a bartender forever before he decided to break out on his own. He plows through women like a Frenchman guzzles cheap table wine. Everything is a game to him."

He held her gaze boldly. "And deep down, I think you know that because so far, you've had the common sense not to fall for him. Your spidey senses recognize he's bad news and no good for the long term. He's not what you need."

Bad news, no good, shallow-as-a-spatula Tad. Jack's words made sense but it didn't stop her from musing on what might have been, much to Good Girl Jules's annoyance. Bad Girl Jules was always on board where Tad DeLuca was concerned.

Uncertain if she was annoyed with Jack, Tad, or herself, she turned back to her lovely radishes and used her frustration to dig a big, deep, unnecessary hole.

* * *

"So, guys, thanks for coming in early for a spot of staff training." Tad arced his gaze around half of Team Vivi, his bright young staff members, who sorely needed an education about the finer things.

"You're paying us to drink on the job, boss," Kennedy said, a petite redhead who was permanently "on" in that way actresses had. He had been leery of hiring her as his manager, worried she'd bail as soon as she got a juicy stage role, but they'd hit it off during the interview so he gave her a shot.

"Everyone got their Vivi bibles?" With not a small amount of satisfaction, he watched as Kennedy lay her collection of laminated cheat sheets on the bar. It had been Jules's suggestion to turn the binder into something brief, portable, and—most importantly—spill proof. Now, he was using it as a training tool for the staff.

"Hmm, I forgot mine." Bella, his hostess, wouldn't be serving but it was important that she be able to converse intelligently about the bar's lifeblood. Unfortunately this might be a problem because she was not the brightest bulb—more like halogen. During her interview she had detailed her disappointment that Cupcake Vineyards Red Velvet had *not* tasted like red velvet cupcakes. But she had an easy way with her that the customers seemed to appreciate.

He passed her a spare bible from behind the bar.

"Oh, hey Julia." Another annoying thing about Bella was that she insisted on calling Jules "Julia."

"Hiya, Bella." Jules looked a little flushed—and as beautiful as ever—as she strode quickly from the kitchen with a plate of crostini, her contribution to tonight's menu. "Tonight's special appetizer. Goat cheese, bacon, and onion finger-panini with amatriciana jam."

"Thank God, I'm starving." Kennedy scooped up a slice and shoved it in her mouth before catching Tad's eye. "Um, this was for us, right?"

Tad sighed. "Yep. We should all try the special." Usually amatriciana was a standard sauce with bucatini, but Jules had used it as base for her panini. He loved how she wasn't afraid to try new things. He also loved that she was using some of Vivi's recipes and adapting them as her own, though they had yet to discuss it.

"Mother of Mary, this is fantastic," Kennedy said around bites of the toasted goodness. "Great job, *Julia*." She added a conspiratorial wink.

Jules's expression jumped from hesitancy to relief to a particular brand of smugness that chefs had a patent on. Every cook Tad knew lived for the moment someone went into an orgasmic meltdown on tasting his food. Turning someone onto wine was gratifying in its own way, but not quite as much as cooking.

"So, see you tomorrow then," Jules said after she had taken a moment to absorb Kennedy's clear appreciation.

"Want to stick around for a few minutes and taste with us?" he asked.

Jules narrowed her eyes at the bottle of Chablis, the label facing away from her. "Is it Chardonnay?"

"No," he lied. Chablis used the Chardonnay grape but Jules hadn't reached that part of her education yet. She did have a particularly virulent hatred for the oaky, overly-toasted flavors typical of American and Australian chards but Chablis with its subtle flavors of green apple and pear had escaped the bad rap.

She took a seat at the bar. "Pour away."

Like good little wine tasters, they all tipped, swirled, and buried their noses in the aroma of crisp Chablis.

"What do you smell?" he prompted.

"It smells fresh." This learned conclusion came from Bella, who went on to take a healthy slug despite his previous efforts to instill in her patience.

"Citrusy," muttered Kennedy, then eyeballed her phone that had just chirped urgently. Probably an audition.

He turned to Jules for support. *Don't let me down, honey.*

"Tuscan summer breezes…no, wait." She sniffed again. "*Autumnal* breezes. More specifically, Florentine."

Right continent, wrong country. Though she was completely off base, he waved her on because he had a sneaky suspicion he was about to be thoroughly entertained.

"I think there might have been a herd of Chianina cattle the next field over. I'm definitely picking up hints of barnyard mixed with earthy. Am I close?"

"Uncanny." Tad was having a tough time keeping his lips in a straight line.

Considering the glass, she continued with a touch of a finger to her chin. "Now the taste…" Taking a healthy sip, she sloshed it around her mouth, making sure to hit all the receptors. Just like he had taught her.

"Fruit-forward, attention-seeking, grabs you by the nuts and holds on until you scream 'uncle'…how'm I doing?"

"The Court of Master Sommeliers better make room. There's a new sheriff in town."

"Well, with a palate as refined as mine, they could do a lot worse." She laughed, warm and husky, and he felt like he had swallowed the sun.

He took a sip, then…just chugged. So much for his second level sommelier training. "Tastes good."

Jules's face bore all the strains of incredulity. "That's the best you can do? Tastes good?"

"You've used up all the good adjectives, smart ass."

Cue brazen Jules grin. *Holy shit.* He flicked a glance to see if anyone else was knocked flat by that molten ball of light. Only him? Alrighty then.

The phone at the hostess podium rang, drawing Bella away. Kennedy texted violently. She was prone to dramatics with her ne'er-do-well boyfriend and Tad suspected he was on the receiving end of that killer thumb tirade.

"Maybe I can come up with some exciting adjectives for your special sauce." The sauce was supposed to be peppery-sweet with heat from the chili flakes. He slipped a bite past his lips and chewed. Robust flavors, a good kick, but something was missing…

"Did you use guanciale?"

"No, pancetta. I couldn't find it at the store and Frankie said it was practically the same thing."

He frowned. Frankie ought to know better.

"It's not the same. Guanciale is cured pork jowl and it can be hard to find, but not impossible."

His heart wrenched at how miserable she looked. "So it's no good…"

Quickly, he backpedaled. "Are you kidding me? It's fantastic, but let's try it with guanciale next time. I'll get you some and you'll see the difference."

The guanciale is key, Taddeo. It brings the dish together.

"My mother used to cure her own, you know." Now what in the hell inspired him to share that nugget?

Jules's eyes widened. "Really?"

"Yeah, she even slaughtered a pig once. When I was a kid, she kept it in the backyard and I'd go to pet it. She'd tell me, 'No, Taddeo. Don't get attached. He's for the butcher's block soon.'"

Sadness crossed her brow. "That's awful!"

It was, but then as a kid, he had been a sensitive soul. He went into a funk when he lost at soccer. Girls were more likely to break his heart than the other way around. And that damn pig had plucked on every heartstring.

"I thought so, too. I ran away with him. Got as far as Tony and Frankie's, but Cara turned fink when he ate one of her shoes."

"Cara," she muttered, shaking her head in sympathy.

"A week later we were eating bacon morning, noon, and night. Poor Ulysses." At her arched eyebrow, he added, "I was on a James Joyce kick."

"A pig in the backyard and no mercy. Sounds like your mom was quite the woman."

"She was."

Somewhere along the way, he had leaned on the bar and she had stepped in closer. Every time he opened up to Jules about his mom, another layer of the mortar cemented around his heart seemed to melt away. It still hurt, but not quite as much.

"So…" *How are your dates going? Have you found the love of your life yet? Do you miss me even half as much as I miss you?*

"So," she said, backing away from what he now realized was a hot-enough-to-scorch stare. "I'd better get going. I have to relieve Frankie from Demon Watch."

Her parting look was an "are we okay here?" and he returned it with a confirming smile. His face ached with how okay they were.

"Maybe we could do a movie and pizza one night," he said as she walked away.

Her shrug cheered him by degrees. "Sure, you know where to find me." And then she was gone, taking the scent of oranges and happy and Jules with her. Taking some piece of his chest as well.

It took him a moment to realize that Kennedy was waving a hand in front of his gormless face.

"Earth to Tad."

"What?" he snapped, tearing his gaze away from the door.

"Just do each other already, would you?"

If only it were that easy. Doing each other was no longer going to cut it.

CHAPTER FOURTEEN

The kiss is to love as
lightning is to thunder.

—Italian proverb

Jules was in a killing mood, and Cara DeLuca was first on her list. Next would be her online dating profile because that needed to die a quick death. Frustrated at what Cara perceived as Jules's distinct lack of progress in the dating arena, the bloody busybody had set her up on a date.

Dan runs his own construction business, Cara had said. *But he doesn't get his hands dirty; he orders people around.* She had a glint in her eye when she said that, as if Jules was supposed to get all stirred up at the thought of a guy ordering people around. Bet he's bossy in the bedroom, her innuendo made clear.

Worst of all was the location for the date: Vivi's. That was Cara's idea, too—or Cara posing as Jules. She sent an e-mail trying to cancel to Construction Dan but he didn't respond and now she didn't want to leave him hanging. She would pop her head into Vivi's at zero hour, or 6:30 p.m.—rather early for a date, perhaps he was used to eating with his elderly mother—and tell him it had all been a dreadful mistake or she had a headache or her cat had died.

Then she would strangle Cara slowly and gleefully.

Thankfully, Tad wouldn't be there until 7 p.m. He was taking part in a wine tasting event on the other side of town, so she could slip in and out, take care of business, and move on without muss or fuss.

Bella smiled a little dimly at her when she came in, still no lightbulb of recognition. Either she wasn't the sharpest tool in the shed or it was a calculated move to dismiss the competition. Not that Jules was competition for anyone, but she had seen how the girl looked at Tad. It was the same way all women looked at Tad—a cross between wet-your-panties lust and something more feral, where the likelihood of fangs-bearing increased with every second.

"Hey, B," Jules said, enjoying immensely how Bella's eyes narrowed at the faux intimacy. Jules scanned the room quickly. Three of the fifteen tables were occupied with couples and the bar was lousy with overdone, underdressed women. Charter members of the Hot Taddies club, by the looks of it. They were making do with bartender Reuben who, while handsome in a blank sort of way, was in no way a legitimate substitute for the owner. Early eating Dan had yet to arrive.

"How many?" Bella asked, still with that vacant look where Jules couldn't be sure if she had connected the dots.

"Zero," Jules replied, her eyes drawn to Kennedy, who had just exited the kitchen. Her body language spoke to extreme agitation, or perhaps it was the fact that she whipped off her apron and beelined right for Jules.

"Thank God you're here," she said to Jules with a toss of her auburn fall of hair, her blue eyes wide with worry.

"What's up?" Jules asked.

"Come with me. Now." Kennedy was already steering her through the tables toward the kitchen.

"What's going on?" Jules urged again. The actress in Kennedy was in full throttle, shaking her head dramatically without actually parting with any information. "Kennedy, you need to spill."

The spitfire threw open the swing door to the kitchen and pointed. "That's what's going on."

The kitchen was small enough that she could take the details in with a single glance and a slight sniff: half-finished prep at the counter, a plume of smoke wafting from the troublesome pizza oven, and one big bear of a chef slumped over the sink, losing enough blood to make him as pale as his starched chef whites.

"Derry!" She raced to his side and turned over his huge hand to reveal an ugly gash bisecting his palm.

"Fine," he muttered. "First-aid kit."

Kennedy produced the red box and rummaged around in it, removing a couple of scrappy bandages that would barely cover this man's pinkie.

"We've only got these small ones."

The slice looked deep enough to have damaged a tendon or some nerves.

"You need to get to the emergency room," Jules said, grabbing a clean kitchen towel and wrapping it around his hand. "I'll take you."

Derry grunted. She knew enough about his flavor of guttural communication to discern that was disagreement.

"I've already told him that," Kennedy said in exasperation. "The big oaf won't budge."

Jules held his cloudy gaze squarely. "That hand is your livelihood, Derry. Even if you could stop the bleeding, there might be permanent damage."

She shared a glance with Kennedy, who shook her head solemnly.

"Need—a chef," he ground out.

Around his tree-trunk forearm—her fondness for fore-arms didn't quite extend to Derry's—Jules's gaze curved to the prep station, where colorful yellow peppers were dotted incongruously with drops of blood. It was a sanitation nightmare.

Her mind searched frantically for a solution. "I'll call Jack and get him to send someone over."

"You could do it," Kennedy said blithely as she unpeeled a finger bandage from its wrapper and held it over Derry's hand. Her forehead crimped in annoyance; she tried another one. "I'll take him to the ER. It's so dead out there that you should be able to manage until Tad gets here in thirty."

"I—I can't," Jules said, bobbing between Derry and Kennedy, neither of whom seemed to grasp the gravity of the situation. Derry was bleeding out, Kennedy was planning to leave them server-less, and Jules Kilroy was the one to save them all?

Ignoring Jules's clear distress, Kennedy tucked a guiding hand under Derry's elbow. "All right, Dare-Bear, do you need me to carry you or do you think you can walk to my car without fainting like a little girl?"

Derry's grunt this time sounded slightly less disapproving. The bastard was going to leave her.

"We'll go out back," Kennedy said, steering him toward the alley door. "Don't want to make the customers gag on their Chardonnay. Well, no more than usual, right, *Julia*?"

Talons of panic clawed at Jules's innards. "Seriously, you guys, I don't think I can do this."

Kennedy was already shoving Derry out the door. "It won't get busy for another hour so Bella can serve in between seating guests. I'll text Brooke and Tad on the way to the ER and tell them to get their tushes over here lickety-split."

Derry spoke out of the side of his mouth. "You're ready, Jules."

The door closed behind them with a condemning whoosh.

Shit.

She whipped out her phone, still cracked from when she'd smashed it after Simon called. It worked just fine, but immediately she questioned whether a call to Jack or Tony would actually save the day. By the time anyone arrived, customers would be fainting with hunger and composing their nasty reviews on Yelp.

This was important to Tad.

It was important to *her*.

She had wanted to do this and now was her chance. Through the window to the dining room, like a porthole onto another world, she surveyed the restaurant that needed feeding. Bella had just seated a table of four and another party hovered at the hostess podium. Who the hell were these people and why were they eating so early?

She looked down at the hands that fed her son, rubbed his tummy when he was ill, soothed him when he was teething. She was more than a mom, a sister, a friend. One day, she would be a chef and it looked like that one day was now.

Time to brief her staff on the new world order. She was headed to the front of house to tell Bella who was running tonight's show when in walked her date.

Bollocks.

* * *

Jules was actually enjoying herself. The menu was so small that she knew it by heart. Food was getting out in a somewhat timely fashion and nothing had been sent back. Bella was struggling but Jules was usually on hand to recommend a cheese or charcuterie and wine pairing.

She had installed Dan at the bar and asked Reuben to give him whatever he wanted. Having to work at the last minute was actually the perfect excuse to send him on his way, but he had seemed so forlorn when she started in on her story about the scheduling snafu that she didn't have the heart to cut the night short.

Besides, he looked no more than twelve and was sporting a bow tie. That indicated a certain level of sadness that she didn't want to pile onto.

Ten minutes to go before Tad got here and rescued her, except she realized that she didn't need rescuing. She had always thought that she had, from the moment she stood in class to read and felt the cruel stares of the other children before she had opened her mouth. They had all known what was coming. The stuttering, coughing delivery of an imbecilic schoolgirl, light years behind her peers. She had wanted the cheap linoleum tile of her classroom to open up and swallow her because rescue was inconceivable. It had taken the life-changing event of Evan for her to meet Jack halfway. To let him rescue her. And he had been doing it ever since.

Well, no more.

Blimey, what a great night! Except for Derry losing five pints of blood, that is.

Bella popped into the kitchen to pick up the cheese and charcuterie for Table 3. Jules had suggested a nice creamy Camembert and a smoky duck prosciutto that she was very fond of. It went so well with that medium-bodied Chilean Pinot Tad had introduced her to last week.

"I think it's her," Bella said as she picked up the plates. She could only manage two at a time, bless her.

"You think it's who?" Jules asked absently. She smeared golden-toasted ciabatta slices with her artichoke and mortadella spread. Pride swelled her chest. *My food is on the menu.*

"*Her.* You know."

"Going to need more deets, B."

Bella put one of the plates down, then picked it up again, getting a better grip. "The woman from *Tasty Chicago.* I just seated her at Table eight."

Jules bounded over to the kitchen window on a cloud of panic and verified her worst nightmare. Monica Grayson, über-critic, was in the house.

It was now 7:15 and no sign of Tad. Dread curled around every positive thought and choked it dead, not unlike the malicious weeds that tried to steal the life from her garden's produce. But it didn't have to be that way. Jules knew the menu—maybe not the wine menu as extensively as a knowledgeable server would, but she knew it better than Bella.

"Bella, go check on your tables."

"But, what about—?"

"I'll handle this," Jules said with steel in her tone. Ooh, she liked how that sounded.

Bella's usually blank face registered surprise, but she merely nodded and went back out front.

She's just a critic. A sharp, all-knowing, intimidating critic. *Imagine her naked.* Imagine her soft, porcelain skin…and soft, porcelain hands tracing Tad's lean musculature.

Maybe don't imagine her naked.

Untying her apron, she hauled an edifying breath and walked out to Monica Grayson's table.

"Hullo, how are you this evening?" she asked, only to be ignored by Monica, whose sharp, asymmetrical sweep of hair made her jaw jut ominously.

Her male companion looked up, then down again. "Perrier for now. You do have Perrier, don't you?"

She had no idea. "I'll check. Will another brand of H-two-O suffice if we don't?"

That garnered her a pointed look from Monica. Perhaps the words had been tinged with sarcasm.

"The owner not here tonight?"

"He'll be in later. I'll give you a couple of moments to look over the menu while I get your water."

At the bar, Reuben was unmoved by her plea for the natural spring water of the Gauls. They had San Pellegrino.

"It's water," he said in the same ironic tone she would have used if it suddenly hadn't taken on far more importance than it should. She knew how crucial it was that Monica Grayson's review reflect Vivi's at its best. Tad had worked so hard and he needed this night to go without a hitch.

Back to the table she went with the bottles and glasses filled with ice. *(We didn't ask for ice.)*

"Do you have any questions about the menu?" Jules asked after her return trip minus ice cubes.

Two sets of eyes snapped to hers. Monica's bore all the hallmarks of a lioness about to take down her prey while her companion's shone with amusement. Clearly, Monica's evisceration of servers was a familiar spectator sport for her eating buddies.

"What can you tell me about the Chakana?"

Chaka-cat! It must be a sign.

"Well, like all the Argentinian Malbecs, it's robust and earthy with a nice acidity. Goes great with the meatier smears on the menu and the harder cheeses. The Wisconsin reserve cheddar is a good match."

Monica looked unimpressed while her friend radiated disappointment. He leveled Monica with a gaze of, *Try again, dear.*

She flipped a few of the pages, cutting brutally through the French reds, viciously past the Italians, before coming to rest on...agh...the Germans.

"How about the—?" She tossed off something unrecognizable.

A cold shiver of sweat trickled down Jules's spine. "Sorry, the...?"

"This one," Monica pointed impatiently at the menu with a sharpened claw.

"I'm afraid I'm not as familiar with the German wines. I could ask Reuben at the bar."

Monica raised an eyebrow so far it threatened to unhitch her scalp. "It's Greek."

Jules's heart sank to the hardwood floor. "G" was one of her favorite letters because it started off some of her favorite words: Gorgeous (Tad). Gape, gawk, gawp (all things she liked to do at Tad). Gelato (Tad substitute). She had made out the "G" on the wine menu page but the rest of it was well... Greek to her.

There was still time to salvage this. "If you have particular food items in mind, it might be easier to recommend a wine."

"I'd prefer to choose the wine first. This is a wine bar, is it not?"

No argument from Jules there, just that swamp of dread in her stomach at being found out for the fraud she was.

"If you told me what you'd like, perhaps I can come up with a few options." Something jammy, perhaps, that Jules would happily jam down this bitch's throat.

"What about this? Or this?" Monica pointed at a Lord-knew-what entry and the words blurred, not because they were incomprehensible but because Jules's eyes were filling. What had she been thinking? It was like trying to teach a pig the clarinet.

Don't cry, idiot.

Monica made a sound of exasperation. "Good grief, it's right there. The Pinot."

"Monica, lovely to see you. How are you this evening?"

Jules cranked her neck a few inches, not that she needed a visual to verify Tad's arrival. All that male spice and testosterone transmitted directly to every hair on her body, now standing on end.

"I'm surprised, Tad. I'd expect your staff to be better trained," Monica said sharply. "Hard to get good help, I suppose."

"We had an emergency and Jules stepped in, but she's more than capable." He turned to her with a smile, his blue eyes glittering his gratitude and affection. "Thank you."

Jules nodded dumbly. Tad placed a hand at the small of her back, a gesture at once intimate and possessive, and not lost on Ms. Grayson, whose gaze widened at how close Tad was standing to the help.

"Now what can we get you?" he asked politely.

"Just a waitron who can rub two brain cells together."

Jules felt Tad's body turn rigid beside her. "I hope you're not insulting my staff, Ms. Grayson. They work too hard to be on the receiving end of that sharp tongue of yours."

Her grey eyes tilted up. "To succeed in this business, you have to have at minimum a staff who can understand what they're trying to sell to the customers. She's pretty, I'll grant you, but not a lot going on upstairs."

Jules's heart sank to the floor, and not just because Monica's words struck hard in her breast. Mostly, she felt awful because she had let Tad down when he needed her and now he had to cover for her ineptitude.

"Monica, Monica, Monica." His voice was soft and persuasive, and while normally she loved that sexy tone, the fact he was using it to appease Monica killed her. She knew why he had to do it, she just hated that she came out of it the loser.

He continued. "I recognize that all your visits to Vivi's have ended in profound dissatisfaction, so I'll assume that's your disappointment showing its ugly. I wouldn't sleep with you and now you're feeling frustrated. I have that effect on women."

Oh, snap.

Monica's companion had been in the middle of a sip of his San Pellegrino, but started coughing hard when it went down the wrong way. Tad gave him a healthy slap on the back, propelling the guy so far forward his nose almost dipped in the olive oil saucer. An ugly shade of red bloomed from Monica's half-exposed chest all the way to the tops of her cheekbones.

"I'd be very careful about how you finish this conversation, Tad."

"Only one way to finish it, Ms. Grayson. The management reserves the right to throw your bony ass out on the street. And your little dog, too."

"Tad," Jules warned, though it was too late and her heart was cheering like the Cubbies had won the World Series.

He turned his back on Monica's furious expression and any chance he had of getting a good review in *Tasty Chicago*. Smoothly, he steered Jules in the direction of the kitchen.

"You just shot yourself in the arse, Tad DeLuca."

"Never mind that. Tell me how your night has been," he said, his eyes sparkling like beautiful blue jewels. Not a moment's regret lived in their depths.

"Except for Derry having the worst meet-cute with a chef's knife, the pizza oven being on the blink again, and you just screwing yourself over, not bad. Not bad at all." She shook her head. "You didn't have to do that. I can defend myself just fine. In fact, I'd just been congratulating myself all night on how I didn't need rescuing."

"I know, but that's what friends do." He inclined his head and whispered, "I've missed you."

Oh. "I'm right here."

He ran a finger along her jaw. "But for how long?"

Lost in the emotion of what he had just done for her and what he was now doing to her, all she could do was stare into his handsome face.

"Speechless, Jules? That's not like you. Gonna have to take advantage."

He lowered his mouth to hers and kissed her softly, tugging on her lips in a way that was not in the least bit friendly.

He finished the kiss with a smile. "I didn't have to do that, either, but it's just one of those nights."

* * *

Like champs, they got through the rest of the night and sent the throng home happy.

After Tad had returned from walking Bella to her car a block over, he took a moment to enjoy the sight of his savior wiping down the stainless steel counter in the kitchen. Daft Punk's "Get Lucky" was on the iPod and the fluid back-and-forth swiping motion rolled her hips in a sexy sway.

A fun memory snuck up on him. "Remember when we used to go dancing?"

Stopping her body rock—so not his intention at all—she turned and smiled that disgracefully sexy grin. "*I* used to go dancing. *You* used to go into some sort of body fit."

"I'm an excellent dancer. Unique."

She cocked her shapely hip, then tilted her head in the other direction like that could even it up. "You had a tendency to blind people within a ten-foot radius with your flailing. I do miss it, though. The dancing, that is."

He missed it, too, and he had a not-so-sudden urge to get down with her again. In every way. It took him a lust-dazed moment to realize she was saying something.

"Uh, what's that now?"

"Derry'll live. Kennedy called to say he had to get seventeen stitches but there was no nerve damage."

He nodded, hoping it might cover the green tinge of jealousy that was likely shading his cheeks.

"Glad to hear it. Derry's a good guy." So his knife skills weren't quite up to the level Tad would expect from a chef of his stature, but he was solid and dependable and—

"So you really like him, don't you?"

Surprise at his directness crimped her brow. "Sure. Talking to him is like conversing with your dodgy pizza oven sometimes but he's a decent bloke."

"Have you introduced him to Evan yet?" He swallowed, feeling like an idiot but needing to know. "I mean, officially."

She stared at him for a few heart-pounding seconds before breaking into a raucous laugh.

"Oh, Tad, you are too much."

"I am?"

She covered her mouth, then decided it was pointless and let rip with another boisterous laugh.

"I am not interested in Derry and even if I was, he would not be interested in me."

Relief flooded him. "You're not? He wouldn't?"

She shook her head slowly, pulling her grin wider with every return. "Derry's gay."

"No fuckin' way." Derry Jones? *The* Derry Jones? "How do you know?"

She threw a wet towel at him. "I know."

"Does *he* know?"

"He's not shouting it from the rooftops but he knows what he is."

Well, well, well. He had never been so thrilled to hear about the sexual orientation of another human being. Weird, but it had been a weird few weeks.

"I owe you a drink for all you did tonight," he said, unable to keep a grin from conquering his face. Brilliant. Get her smashed.

His little head was trying to call the shots as usual. Showing it who's boss, he took a leisurely stroll out of the kitchen toward the bar. So leisurely he should be whistling.

She followed, her lush sway undulating in his wake, or that's how he imagined it with those gluttonous eyes in the back of his head. He didn't need eyesight to know the glorious line of those hips or how the swell of her breasts filled her blouse. Lucky him! He had memories.

This leisurely thing wasn't cutting it so he removed himself behind the bar where the evidence of his raging attraction to her could be shielded.

"Forget the drink, you owe me a bottle," she said.

"Okay, take your pick."

Her eyes widened. He may as well have offered her the world.

"Anything?"

"If it's on the menu, we'll open it."

"Boo."

"Boo?"

"Boo. Hiss. I know there's better stuff *off* the menu. Secret bottles in the cellar." She nodded to the wall of glass behind him—the window on the world of wine.

He felt the beginnings of a smile. "And how would you know that?"

She leaned over the bar, her breasts settling like lush pillows on the cherrywood. *Madre di Dio.*

"The list you gave me doesn't tally, my friend. There are strange things afoot in there." She looked around as though she didn't want anyone to hear her. "Bumps in the night. Clanging chains. Very suspect."

Mirroring her, he did the fake shifty thing. "So, I keep a couple of special bottles there. It's no big deal. I can stop anytime."

She grinned and he felt an odd lurch in his chest.

"I've been meaning to build a cellar at home but I haven't gotten around to it. Which means, I need to cellar my own stuff here."

"What's so special about these bottles, then? Are they worth a lot of money?"

"Come on, I'll show you."

He led the way to the Cavern, the name he had christened the cellar in honor of the Beatles' first big club venue back in Liverpool. Better than calling it Bob, he supposed. With a name like that, the space should have been dank and dreary but that was so not the case. Encased in glass, it displayed his stock to perfection and made a stunning counterpoint to all the dark wood in the bar. The temperature controls were state of the art and the walls were pocked with bottles that formed a pleasing, logical grid. In here, he could see everything happening out in the bar and farther into the street.

Gently, he removed one of the bottles: a Chateau Pavie Bordeaux from 2000. One hundred points—the maximum—from *Wine Spectator*. Unlike the others, it was sheened with eleven years of dust though the streaks told him it had been drawn out of the nest lately.

"My father knew a lot about wine and he gave me this when I got my offer from the University of Chicago."

A wash of guilt softened her face. "Oh, I'm sorry. You can probably tell I looked at it. I was nosing around last week."

"It's fine. I was supposed to open it when I graduated."

"You have. You've done all this." She waved her hands around the cellar.

"This isn't really what he had in mind." He looked around the wine racks he had built from scratch. "I'd always liked building things so engineering was a logical choice for me. He would have preferred doctor or lawyer, but he was willing to compromise there." About the only thing the old man would compromise on. Opening the bar would have pleased Vivi, but not his father.

"Frankie said you got a full ride. That you're some sort of genius."

From anyone else, it might have sounded snarky but Jules's voice held an unwelcome reverence. He preferred her bite. Sliding the bottle back into its slot, he raised his eyes to hers.

"You know me pretty well. Do you think I'm a genius?"

"Let me see." She held up a hand and touched the tips of her fingers in a count. "You date zombified bimbos, you drive that bike far too fast, and you have an unhealthy appreciation for Jason Statham." Her devastating grin fell away.

"And I happen to think you're a whole lot smarter than you let on."

"That makes two of us."

Her pupils flared in acknowledgment. As far as he was concerned, she was on the money. Smart as he was, he didn't want a challenge when it came to his sex life. He preferred the simplicity of turning off his overactive brain and sliding inside a woman who had no expectations. Hooking up with someone he might actually be interested in on an intellectual or emotional level would be skating a little too close to the drop.

Hell, he had been tottering on that edge since the moment he laid eyes on one Juliet Kilroy. Making love to her was the most real thing he had experienced since his parents had died. So real he sometimes felt he might die if he didn't hold her in his arms one more time.

But he needed to be her friend. And as much as he hated the fact she was dating, he hated even more how she was going about it.

"Speaking of dating below our level, Lili said you wanted certain types of guys. Guys who didn't seem too well endowed"—he arched an eyebrow—"in the brain department."

She blinked rapidly and her swallow was pronounced. "I promised Cara that Cinders would be home by eleven p.m. She's probably got a search party out already."

Arresting her move to the exit, he reached out and gentled her back against the glass. The shimmer from the low-lit bar candles reflected off the transparent wall, giving her a halo effect.

"Why are you shooting so low, Jules?"

"I'm not."

He crowded her, interrogated her with his body. It felt

good to wrap himself around her. To own the space between them for these brief moments.

"Boring, unimaginative guys. Guys who can't possibly appreciate you."

Discomfort darkened her pale beauty. "I'm not exactly the sharpest knife in the drawer. Just ask Monica Grayson."

"Oh, but you are." He cupped her chin, surprised even now at how the softness of her skin electrified and soothed him at once. Touching her was his drug, wanting her was his addiction.

"You're so sharp, it hurts to be around you sometimes. You have the quickest wit of anyone I know and I come from a family of smart mouths. Don't ever think you're not good enough, honey."

What he saw in her eyes devastated him and suddenly he got it. How could he have been so stupid?

"Maybe you'll find this boring paragon you can walk all over, who bores you to tears, and makes sure you never feel what you must have felt for Evan's father. Because that's what this is about, isn't it? Whoever this guy was, he hurt you so badly that you'd rather hook up with a corpse than feel again."

"You don't know a thing about it," she said through trembling lips.

"I know you and believe it or not, I know me. I've been there, Jules. Loving someone and losing them. Hurting so much that it's easier to block out the possibilities that are staring you right in the face." This wasn't the time to indulge in a pity party wankfest, but he needed her to know she was not alone.

Her eyes shone like glossy green buttons. She splayed a hand over his heart, which jumped in acknowledgment of the imminent threat. "Is that what you've been doing since they died, Tad? Every year, adding another row of bricks around your heart? Looking for solace in sex?"

See? Smart as a whip. He was supposed to be making her feel better about this lousy ex situation and here she was cutting to the heart of him with her razor-sharp insight.

"We were talking about you."

"You were. This sharing business works both ways. Tell me why it still hurts so much, Tad. Why you haven't cooked since they died. Why the mention of your parents sends you to a place I can't reach you."

She rubbed his chest, comforting him like he imagined she did with Evan when he was cranky. Those hands of hers were lethal and healing at once.

He sucked air through his lips, making a hissing sound. "I had a fight with my father the night they died. One of those fights where you say things you can't take back, even if he was around to hear it."

Her eyes flew wide. "What was it about?"

"What it was always about. School, what I wanted to do with the rest of my life. It was the end of freshman year and I told him I wouldn't be going back in the fall. I wanted to go to Italy and apprentice with a butcher in Fiesole. That's where the DeLucas came from. He was furious. He told me I wouldn't be welcome in his house if I gave up that scholarship and—" He held her gaze with more boldness than he felt, challenging her to judge him. "I told him to go to hell."

She cupped his jaw and he resisted the urge to fold into her hand. "That was the last time you spoke to him?"

He nodded the head that felt too heavy for his neck. His father's rage still felt like a tangible thing and Tad had internalized it and made it his own. A messed up way of honoring his memory.

"The accident happened later that night and I never got to fix it. You don't know what I'd do to have one more minute with them. One more moment to tell them how much I love them."

This was just the original sin, the foundation brick in the wall. Telling her the rest might break him and he would rather die than face the disappointment in her eyes should the entire sorry tale come out.

"We all carry regrets around with us, Tad, wishes that we had played the cards differently. Keeping it inside and letting it eat away at you isn't healthy. Don't hide from me. From the beginning, it's always been you and me. Simpatico."

The truth of that punched a hole in that wall.

"From the first moment, it's been"—she placed her hand over his stomach—"in here."

"A gut thing," he rasped.

She watched him with those green eyes that cut through all his crap.

"A gut thing. A connection from the beginning. No matter what happens between us, we'll always be in each other's gut. I'll find my safe, boring husband and you'll keep screwing your way through Chicago. But at the end of the day, this connection between us will still be here. Gut connection. You and me."

Another few bricks collapsed, exposing his heart for all to see. She could reach inside and grasp it. Hold it close or stomp it. It was hers to own and he didn't care what she did with it.

"Gut connection," he whispered.

"You and me," she said, tilting moist green eyes up to his.

She shrank against the glass, still with her hand on his side. The movement caused her fingertips to slide down to his belt and brought him close enough to share her sweet breath. Hooking a finger behind the buckle, she traced the metal slowly.

Kiss her, every part of him urged.

So he did.

Just a tickle at first because he wanted to give her a chance to move away. He needn't have worried. Immediately, her hands clutched at his shirt collar and pulled him close. The inch of space separating them was too much. His blood surged. His balls flamed. The heaven of her mouth claimed him.

He was going with his gut and every other body part cheered in agreement. She unclasped his belt. He peeled off her shirt. Next went her skirt, landing in a puddle at her feet. They played catch-up with the rest of his clothes, both of them desperate to get each other naked. He tore at her panties, just ripped them from her body. No finesse, no seduction. Just what it was.

Gut connection.

Soul connection.

She fell back against the cellar's glass wall, the low bar light shimmering behind her and framing her with a honey-tinged corona. Those perfect, creamy breasts drew his gaze, which he followed down to the soft curve of her belly and the thatch of dark blond hair between her thighs. He would never tire of the beautiful lines of her body.

He nudged her feet apart and ran a finger through her gloriously slick heat. Ready for him. Always ready for him.

"You're so wet."

"All night," she moaned. "From the minute you told that bitch off."

Stroking through the swelling folds of her pussy, he punctuated with a brush of his finger over her nerve-strung clit. She sighed her pleasure and pushed back against his hand.

"You're turned on when I protect you," he murmured, not a little turned on by that idea himself.

"I'm turned on when you breathe."

He curled his palm behind her head and crushed his mouth to hers, plundering her with possessive thrusts of his tongue that matched the finger-strokes through her saturated heat. Her moans were loud and throaty, and he swallowed them greedily. She was already close but he knew he could make it better for her.

"Turn around."

"What?" It came out in a sexy quiver.

"I want you to watch the street while I make you come. I want you to know anyone could see you while you're screaming my name."

Without hesitation, she turned toward the transparent cellar wall, and that obedience turned him to granite.

"Feel how cool the glass is against your nipples, *mia bella*."

Covering her with his body, he pushed her flush against the smooth glass, leaving just enough room to slip his hand into the slippery nirvana between her legs.

She moaned, the sound reverberating off the glass, the bottles, his groin. He stroked again over her nerve-packed flesh, gratified when she jerked against his hand. She rocked against him, sawing her body, controlling her pleasure. Her back arched as she pushed back and took what she needed.

It was the hottest thing he had ever seen.

His dick throbbed, pushing against the cleft of her gorgeous ass like it knew what it needed. Like it knew what *he* needed. The heat and musk of her arousal amplified his own, hiking it to a sharp ache. Over her shoulder, the streetlights shone arcs of light against the windows of the bar, illuminating the odd passerby. A curious glance their way would reveal quite the show.

Wild and uninhibited, she rubbed her breasts against the cellar's glass. Low-lit pools reflected off the transparent wall, bathing her features in soft, ethereal light. She was lost in her own world, a world where she was Goddess.

Worship her. Over and over those words echoed in his Jules-fried brain. The message was received by his knees, which jackknifed and sent him to the ground.

Where he belonged.

Roughly, he pulled her hips toward him and delved between her legs with first his fingers, and then his mouth. She tasted...oh, Christ, he would need to invent a whole new profile for how good she tasted. Spice, sweet, pepper.

Jules, Jules, Jules.

Again, she bowed her back and spread her thighs to allow him to suck deeper. Her moans echoed through the Cavern, ricocheting off the dick that was about ready to blow.

"Tad," she screamed just as her thighs clenched and her body juddered in orgasm.

Standing like a drunk who couldn't hold his liquor, he used her hips as his anchor, only breaking the connection to roll on a condom. Thankfully, she understood what was coming next and she turned to face him.

"Please. Now." Hot, desperate, and all for him.

He lifted her off the ground and slid into her, hard and fast. How could she be so wet, yet snug enough to wrap him in this torturous, velvet tightness? Holding her in place against the glass, he watched his glistening cock drive into her deeper.

"Look, *mia bella.* Look what you do to me."

Her lust-stoked gaze fell to where their bodies joined and she made a rough sound in the back of her throat.

"That's so—oh, Tad. You feel so good inside me."

He withdrew, every inch outside her body killing him, but honing his desire. Hers, too. No doubt about it. She grasped at his shoulders, and her thighs tensed. Her satin muscles gripped his slick erection.

"Don't stop," she moaned. "Don't ever stop."

Never. In this moment, there was only the two of them. There was only this time. This room. This everything. The moment bloomed to clarity. He saw clearly for the first time.

He'd always given short shrift to those loved-up idiots who said sex was a million times better when you had a deeper connection with a woman. Sex was sex. There were degrees, for sure, but it was no great mystery. He happily admitted that sex with Jules was the best he'd ever had.

Everything with Jules was the best he'd ever had. Somehow, losing himself in her felt like the surest way of finding his way back.

Biting his lip, he watched as he slid in and out, in and out. Heaven at the Cavern. He continued to thrust until he felt her clutch and compress. Heard her scream his name, again and again. Then his own orgasm exploded, but not in a single burst of relief. This was more like a rolling blackout that hit different parts of his body microseconds apart and ended with a power surge that knocked out the grid that used to be his brain.

* * *

"So here we are," she said, coming to a stop outside her apartment building.

"Here. We. Are." Tad squeezed her hand and it gave her just as much of a thrill as what they had done back at Vivi's.

She never imagined he could be so sweet after taking her so hard and raw.

On the five-minute walk home, they had been unusually quiet, both lost in their thoughts. Was he regretting how he'd opened up about his father and what it had led to or was he contemplating how they could figure out what was happening between them?

Reluctantly, she let go of his warm, male grip to fumble in her big-ass purse for her keys. Purse law said they were hiding at the bottom.

"Thanks for seeing me home."

"Well, I'm not sure your date would have been allowed to stay out this late."

Her date. She had forgotten all about Bowtie Dan with cheeks as smooth as a baby's bottom. He had left with one of Tad's fans about an hour before closing. She wasn't sorry.

She silently prayed she wouldn't be sorry for the next words out of her mouth.

"Okay, here's how it's going to work. For as long as we have this whatever's-happening-between-us, we'll act on it. As soon as one of us wants to move on, we stop. As soon as our bloody families find out, we stop because I am not dealing with the special brand of crazy sauce that rains down on my head when Jack and Shane get involved. To be honest, I'm not sure that handsome face of yours could withstand Jack's rearrangement of it."

The longer she spoke, the squeakier her voice got until by the end, she was rocking Alvin & The Chipmunks decibel levels and standing nose to chin with him. A burn of a grin spread slowly over his face but she was so desperate to get the words out in one breathy gush that she didn't thump him the good one he deserved.

"What's so funny?"

"I love when you get all up in my face, Juliet Kilroy."

She splayed a hand across his chest. The erotically charged memory of where his face had been thirty minutes ago sent her hormones into overdrive. "You wish I was all up in your face."

He growled and pulled her in for a kiss that would have knocked her off her feet if he wasn't also ravaging her arse with his hands.

"So, should I sneak in like a horny teenager now or after you've picked up Evan from Cara?"

She poked him in his rock-hard chest. "No overnight stays and no hanky-panky when Evan's around. And nobody else while we're doing this." She had been about to say "together," but it sounded wrong in the back of her throat. Too needy. Too permanent.

"Same for you. I'm imposing a moratorium on your dates."

Thanks be to God. She'd have to come up with some excuse to keep the girls at bay; she'd gladly do it.

Tearing herself away from the warmth of his body was so hard but it had to be done. Tad was the kind of treat that had to be rationed. Unlike the last time she had tried to open her door with this perfect specimen by her side, she was able to manage the lock with a minimum of fuss.

"I'll call you when I get home," he said, his voice husky in her ear.

"Think I'm worried about you, Tad DeLuca?"

"No, but I'm going to need to hear your voice while I get off. Only way I'll be able to sleep." He sucked on her ear lobe, inducing the most delicious shivers.

Tonight as he'd told her about his last conversation with his dad, a new window onto their relationship had opened. Before, he was the strong one with those broad shoulders made for leaning and those sure hands made to catch her when she fell. Now the subtle shift had revealed new depths to this amazing man and how much he needed this sensual comfort. Neither of them had said it outright, but their bodies knew the score. They could do for each other what no one else could, if only for a short time.

"One more rule," she said, turning to face him.

"Uh huh." He nipped at the soft spot where her shoulder met her neck. *Stay strong.*

"You can't fall in love with me, Tad. This is just us fulfilling a temporary need for each other."

Pride in her businesslike tone summoned the usual internal chatter.

Nicely done, said Good Girl Jules.

Bad Girl Jules remained eerily silent.

The look he gave her was strangely intense, but then his expression unfurled with a smile.

"I'll do my best."

CHAPTER FIFTEEN

My home, my woman, bread
and garlic, my life.

—Italian proverb

Jules grabbed her gym bag and headed for the door. Her phone chirped, and then she chirped because he was calling. Her lover.

She really shouldn't answer. It had been two weeks since she had actually attended the gym, as in physically instead of pretending to. She wouldn't put it past Cara to casually walk Jules to a scale the next time she picked up Evan. Jules could hear the tutting and *tsk*ing already. *Do I need to come with you to make sure you're doing it right?*

If Cara knew exactly what Jules was doing, she might be tempted to point out what she was doing wrong there, too. She was having a hot affair with her best friend and she was enjoying every minute of it. Quickies in the office at the bar, glorious nooners at his place, afternoon delight wherever they could find it.

"Lady Penelope's Love Shack. No request too weird," she answered.

"Why aren't you here?"

"Who *is* this?"

Tad's laugh enveloped her like a warm, sexy blanket and sent her pulse soaring. "You know very well who it is."

"No, I don't. In a feminist pique, I switched out all the male non-relatives on my phone for something more generic. You're showing up as Stud Number Four. It could apply to any anonymous chunk of man flesh."

He sighed patiently. "You need to get your sweet ass over here. The pizza oven guy is in the kitchen, so I had to go home before I lost my shit on him. Now I'm all tense."

"Go for a run. When I get tense, that's what I do." So that was an out and out lie.

She heard a disgruntled noise. "Jules, I know you have a couple of hours set aside for gym time."

"Exactly. Gym time. I'm turning into a giant *gnocchi* with each passing day."

"The singular is *gnoccho*."

"The end result is the same. A pillowy blob with feet."

He chuckled. "Come over here and burn some calories with me, baby."

"Lines. Terrible." *Baby.* How did he get away with it?

"You know I'll take care of you."

That's how. Her body melted like hot butter in a pan and Bad Girl Jules came out to play.

* * *

Tad pulled her inside and smothered her with a kiss, sending her shopping bags to the floor in a thud. She loved his way

of saying hello. She was sure going to miss his special greetings when all this was done.

A warm ache bloomed in her chest.

With strong, clever hands, he tore at her clothes. The zipper of her workout top got stuck but that didn't stop him. He
just peeled it off roughly, almost taking her head with it.

She should have swapped out her cotton-practical and
plain bra for something sexy, but it felt as if they'd moved on
from that. They knew each other too well. The foibles and
quirks. The lickable parts and the imperfections *(hers, not
his. The man had zero)*. They didn't need to gussy it up with
sexy lingerie or high heels. Not that she didn't love the idea
of turning him on like that, but knowing Tad as well as she
did was a whole other level of intimacy.

That ache in her chest expanded. The closeness she
felt with this beautiful man was unlike anything she had
ever felt with another person. It was bound to happen with
their friendship such as it was. She tried to suppress those
wormy niggles of doubt about what the hell she was doing
here.

*It's just a release. Just friends with a platinum benefits
package. Just—*

Her sweatpants were pushed a few inches south. *Rip,*
there went another pair of panties and—ah, yes. All that hot,
hard perfection slid deep and smooth inside her, the assault
all the sweeter because she was knee-cuffed by the sweats
and her thighs kept the passage narrow.

She thrust her fingers in his dark, mussed hair and mussed
it some more. Held his face close to hers so she could look
into those fathomless blue pools. She wanted to remember
this moment when he had wanted her so much he skipped
the pleasantries. When she was the unstinting focus of his
world.

Inside her, he moved in long, fluid strokes, each one more far-reaching and punishing than the last. His hands framed her bum and held her in place for his pleasure. In his eyes, she saw a haze of feral desire, all aimed at her. Being the object of this man's passion was intoxicating.

The moment when that look changed shot through her like a lance. Still a blaze of heat, but tempered with something else.

He stopped.

The tosser stopped and stared with...tenderness.

"Tad." It carried a tone of warning. She didn't want him to look at her this way, not now, not when she felt so dangerously unmoored.

He angled his head to feed kisses down her neck to the pulse at the base of her throat. He teased her with swipes of his tongue and nibbling, soft sucks. His lips nuzzled a sweet trail along her collarbone, punctuating with a nip of her shoulder.

Branding her. Tenderly.

Slowly, he started to move inside her again with an incremental tempo that heated her center to sizzle point. A perfect blend of strength and mastery that built her up again until, with a final thrust, they went over the edge together.

Moments passed as they stood in the hall of his house, still connected in a gnarly embrace. He slid out of her and pulled her sweats up, then his own. She loved how he always took care of her like that. His grin blazed wide, all the tenderness of minutes ago replaced by sexy mischievousness.

"Hi, there," he said, dropping a soft kiss on her nose.

She giggled, feeling foolish for having read so much into those intense looks. "Hi, yourself."

"Thanks for stopping by to let me sex you up."

She looked at the imaginary watch on her wrist. "Hmm,

less than five minutes. If I didn't already have a previous Tad DeLuca experience, I would be severely disappointed in that performance."

"I know you like it fast and raunchy sometimes, *mia bella*. Lie to me and say it wasn't good."

She was good at telling porkies, but not that good. "I'll let Sylvia know you're doing much better."

Grinning, his gaze fell to the floor, where several of the packages she had brought lay strewn on the hallway rug.

"You brought gifts?"

She paused, thinking about what she wanted to say next. "I thought that maybe we could make lunch. Actually, I thought we could cook together."

A curious look came over him, and she worried that she had made another one of her famous miscalculations. *Cook together.* Two small words that weighed a ton. Her heart expanded to fill her chest, pushing against her lungs so she could barely breathe.

"I'd love to cook with you," he whispered.

* * *

"Make sure you don't overfill it," he said as she heaped a spoonful of cooked ground beef, ricotta, and herbs in blobs about an inch apart on the rectangle of pasta dough. "Then fold it over and seal it up with the egg wash."

"Like that?"

He moved in behind her and banded his thick, muscle-corded forearms beneath her breasts. The butterfly kisses he trailed down her neck made her shiver.

"Tight as a nun's knickers. Perfect."

Just like the whole afternoon. Hot sex with a guy she was crazy about, though even that had felt different. More powerful, more consuming. There had always been an underlying streak of want and determination in Tad's love-making, and today when he held her while taking her to paradise, she had opened her eyes and seen it for the first time.

This guy was going to destroy her.

The blabbermouths on her shoulder had nothing.

"The other morning at your place," he said softly against her ear. "I noticed you have Vivi's cookbook."

Her mind fumbled for a defense. "Frankie lent it to me. If you want it back—"

"Don't need a book to remember those recipes. Know them all by heart." His smile against the curve of her neck made her all tingly. "I love that you have it. Feels right. And I love that you're here. That feels right as well."

Forget the tingle; she was two seconds from liquefying in a puddle of want.

"Have you given any more thought to cooking professionally? I know you worry about how much time it takes you away from Evan."

"Not really."

"Hmm, I think you have, *bella*."

She sighed. "I'd like to—well, it's silly, really..."

He gave an encouraging squeeze with his sexy, hairy, thick-as-her-calf forearms. "Tell me."

She gifted him a fatalist shrug, embarrassed by her homely ambitions. "I don't have any special training or skills, but sometimes I think it would be nice to sell my dips and spreads in stores. You know, like Whole Foods."

His silence made her as anxious as a kid on Christmas Day morning. God, she was so stupid to think she could be any more than a hobbyist at the food game.

"It's ridiculous," she said pitchily, thankful he was behind her and couldn't see the panic on her face. "Jack and Shane have worked all their lives to get to where they are so it's stupid to think I can just decide to do this." But she had been deciding a lot of things lately. Taking what she needed and fighting for her and Evan's future.

"You don't have a clue how special you are, do you?" he rumbled in her ear.

Heat flared her cheeks and spread to her toes, and she tried to laugh it off. "Of course I do. Every day I do the daily affirmation thing in the mirror. I tell my reflection how much I like my nose or my ears today. That kind of thing."

"Who's your favorite Beatle, Jules?"

"What?"

"Your favorite Beatle. As in the mop tops from Liverpool, not the multi-legged scurrying kind."

She gave it more consideration than it deserved. Men seemed to think questions like this were very, very important. "I don't have one."

"You have to have one. Everybody has one."

"Okay, Ringo."

"Except Ringo. No one picks Ringo."

She sighed. "I suppose this is where I'm required to ask who your favorite is."

His smile against the curve of her neck felt knowing. "George."

She could feel an eye roll coming on but she suppressed it. "I'll bite. Why?"

"Well, for years he lived in the shadow of arguably the best songwriting duo ever, but when he finally got his chance, he outshone them both. On *Abbey Road*, name the two best songs."

She thought about it for a moment. Jack had played that album constantly when she was pregnant because he wanted to infuse fetal Evan with a musical talent he had no hope of inheriting from his tone-deaf uncle.

"'Here Comes the Sun?'" she offered, not wanting to disappoint him. She did love that song, though. Its breezy and optimistic feel, the idea of crawling out of a long, cold, lonely winter to embrace spring and rebirth.

"Correct, and the other one is 'Something.' Which Frank Sinatra said was the best love song of the twentieth century." He raised an overly expressive eyebrow. "Frank Sinatra, Jules."

"Well, if Frank said it…" Sylvia had pictures of the pope and Frank Sinatra on her living room wall. These crazy Italians…oh, how she loved them all.

"Exactly. Both of those songs were written by George Harrison. Best album by the best band ever, and the best songs were by the quiet Beatle. Sure, he had written songs before that, but with *Abbey Road*, he came into his own. The late bloomer."

Dawning realization crept up on her. In this scenario, her brothers were Lennon and McCartney, and she was the quiet Beatle. The one who took a while to find his stride but then went on to outdo them all.

"I'm not that talented," she mumbled, close to tears. A tremor started up in her hand and she put down the knife she had been about to use to divide the ravioli into little parcels.

"You just don't know it yet. But I do."

Her heart exploded into a million fragments of light. Turning fast, she threw her arms around his neck and crushed her body to the chest that had always been there for her. Where she belonged.

Thank God he couldn't see her lovesick, moony expression, now hidden in the warm crook of his neck. Ducking her head as she turned back to the ravioli, she focused on the backyard with its yellowing turf and unkempt grasses while she desperately tried to keep the tears at bay. Hints of lavender and wild mint wafted through the open window. The things she could do with this space. Tomatoes and peas on the south side, herbs near that back wall, room for a pig.

"Where did Ulysses hang his hat?"

He pointed to the north end near a dilapidated shed. "Over there. We had to keep him separate from the chickens."

His voice washed over her with stories about Vivi and the errant chickens, half of which she didn't hear because she was falling into a hole and scrabbling for purchase on the slippery, muddy slope.

A few minutes later, she scooted out of the danger in his embrace and pinned on a smile. "I should be getting back. This ravioli business took longer than I expected."

He curled a hand to the back of her neck and tilted her head up to his. "You're upset."

"No, not at all." It was completely illogical. He was talking about the bloody Beatles and chickens, for heaven's sake, and now she had the jitters.

Her phone buzzed on the counter and her gaze flew to it on the wings of maternal instinct. At the sight of the number, her heart plummeted to her stomach. *No, no, not now.* She hit "ignore" and took a fortifying sip of the lovely, robust Barolo Tad had opened a half hour ago.

"I need to go."

"So you said." His brows dipped in a chevron as he digested the suddenly weird vibe between them.

The phone buzzed again, cutting loudly through the heavy silence and setting off a flap of panic in her chest. *Fight or flight. Fight or flight. Fight or—*

"Someone wants to get in touch with you badly."

She touched the screen. Took a longer slug of the wine. "Just a telemarketer."

"Answer it and tell them to take you off their list."

She waved it away. "It's easier to ignore it."

The phone screamed again, and this time, Tad grabbed it.

"I'll get rid of them for you—hello, you've reached Sex U Up Productions, how can I help you?"

"Tad, don't!" She tried to grab the phone, but he arched out of her way. It was a good ten seconds before she wrested it from him and hung up on the tinny voice she knew as well as her own. She turned it off altogether.

Rage thundered in his eyes. With those thick forearms, he caged her against the sink and loomed over her, bristling with barely tethered tension.

"That was him, wasn't it?"

Whatever he saw in her eyes confirmed his assumption.

"How long have you been talking to him?"

"He called me a couple of weeks ago. The night of the opening."

Recognition crashed over his face. The night she said she needed him inside her and now the connection between the two was inextricable.

"Why didn't you tell me he'd been in touch?"

Her throat felt rough and scratchy. "Because I've been handling it."

"How? By ignoring his calls?"

Cowardice was a legitimate strategy, and it had been working for her every time Simon called over the last fortnight. She clamped her lips shut. Cowardly.

Fury had sharpened his features to make him almost unrecognizable from the Tad she knew. "What does he want? Is he trying to get back with you?"

"No—no. He wants to see Evan."

"After all this time." His disgust at Simon's supposedly despicable behavior rolled through her. He held her gaze fiercely, all blue determination, before his face softened. "Lili said you won't tell Jack anything about him. Talk to me, honey."

Apparently realizing that his huge, imposing presence in a cross-examining stance might not be especially conducive to a cozy tête-à-tête, he took a couple of steps back and threaded his arms over that blockbuster chest.

Her fingers tensed around the wineglass on the counter. "I wanted him. He didn't want me. Oldest story in the book."

Those clipped words were meant to be conversation-ending, but the look on Tad's face said, *ah, ah.*

"Christ, you are a stubborn pain in my ass. This is not the time to be stoic, Jules. Just let me the fuck in."

Suddenly weary, she sat at the kitchen table. Keeping it all inside for so long was just so bloody tiring. She looked into those deep blue eyes and rallied her strength.

"He's a chef. He runs a very fine restaurant in London and I went there for an interview and left smitten."

"So you worked for him?"

She let out a bitter laugh. "No. I wasn't even good enough to get the job. I bungled the interview. Just one in a long line of interviews for servers or hostesses Jack was always setting me up with because he thought I was wasting my life away working in a pub. I'd blow them off or sabotage them by not making eye contact with the chef, who was usually a good friend of Jack's and only talking to me as a favor to an important culinary genius like my brother. A handshake and a pitying smile later, I'd be out the door. Until Simon."

"Simon," he said, tasting the name and not liking it. He lowered his body to the opposite chair.

"Simon Saint James, chef/owner at Lilac in Islington.

The interview had gone terribly, just like I planned. On the way out, he asked me why I didn't want the job and I said, don't you mean *why* I want the job? He smiled and said, *you know what I mean*, and it was like we had this secret between us. That night, he showed up at the Red Lion, the pub where I worked. He wanted me and—"

She stopped, the humiliation and desperation of it hitting her hard.

"Baby, go on."

She swiped at a ridiculous tear. "I wanted to be wanted. I found myself telling him things I'd told no one else. About my reading problems and Jack and how I felt like I existed on the edges, looking in on this world I couldn't grab hold of. All my life I had been waiting for someone to notice me. My aunt and uncle, my teachers, my brother. And here was this man, pursuing me."

Even now, the intoxicating memory thrilled through her blood. That night he had come to the bar, she had thought it was a coincidence. He was with friends, muckety muck types who brayed too loudly and got handsy with the dogs-body who collected the glasses because she was too terrified to try anything more challenging. She had spotted him at the end of the bar, watching her silently while the noise faded around them. One of those dream moments where time stands still, except it hadn't really. It had just slowed to a pace she could finally reckon with.

He had come to see *her*. Not a coincidence at all.

She headed to the back, knowing he would follow. Through the alley exit, the sound of him echoed behind her, a slow motion chase that sent her blood soaring. He had sought her out and just knowing that he wanted her even when he knew she was an odd, broken duck had taken her over the edge. Within five seconds of the cool air hitting her

face, his hot mouth and body slammed into hers and she
gave it up to him without a word.

More surprising was the fact he wanted to see her again.
He took her home to his flat, one of those fancy lofts on the
South Bank overlooking the river. She had felt as if she had
entered a closed-off world. Jack's world.

Two months it lasted. Fish and chips on the way home
from the pub, scrambled eggs and rashers in bed, mornings
spent tangling up the sheets before he went to work. She was
finally someone else's Number One, the center of another
person's universe, the sun in this man's world.

She swallowed hard and met Tad's steel-eyed gaze. "A
couple months later, I was pregnant and he was back with
his wife. The one he had neglected to mention."

Anger simmered below the surface, finally coming to a
head when he violently shoved back the chair, the scrape like
a scream. He stood over her, the tension in his body fighting
every muscle.

"And he was a friend of Jack's?"

She nodded up at him. "He was the best man at Simon's
wedding. Of course, I only found that juicy morsel out later.
Jack would go nuts."

"This fucker took advantage of you. Of course he's going
to go nuts, but Jack'll have to get in line and hope there's
something left when I'm done with him."

Oh, he didn't understand at all. There was so much wrong
between her and Simon but she was done painting herself in
victim colors. Standing, she placed a calming hand on Tad's
chest and took the measure of his overactive, macho Italian
heart.

Emotion thickened like custard in her throat. "No one
took advantage of me. In London, I was—I was a different
person. I've slept with a lot of guys, Tad, but with every man

I was with, I felt some measure of power. I played the bad girl, the girl who backed up every tease, and I enjoyed it. They used my body but I used them right back."

Saying it aloud rang even more hollow than the mantra in her head. She had given it up easily, and while there were plenty who came back for more, she was under no illusions about what she did for them. Toward the end, even Simon got antsy the moment he had finished shagging her. Checking his phone (she knew why now), telling her he had to get up early to receive the deliveries at the restaurant, inching her to the door and kissing her into a cab.

She pretended it was exactly what she wanted. Intimacy had never appealed to her, or more accurately, she had never appealed for intimacy. That would require some measure of self-respect, some acknowledgment that she was deserving of that kind of human affection.

"Jules," he whispered, and the way he said her name smashed her to the ground.

Tears came hot and fast. "Don't look at me like I need to be hugged. I'm sick of people judging my situation and thinking I'm some victim that needs to be coddled. Jack, Shane, all of you. So my reading sucks, I had an unplanned pregnancy, my brother pays my rent. But I'm not some delicate flower. I'm stronger now than I've ever been and I don't need a man to be my savior."

He pulled her into his arms and it was the best, best place she had ever visited.

"*Tesoro,* I get this guy hurt you and it's okay to be pissed off about that. It doesn't make you a victim, it makes you a survivor. Get angry, honey. Don't hold back."

The anger had passed a long time ago, but the lessons she had learned remained.

"I'm past all that. I was angry at first but not now. Simon

hurt me when I found out he was married, but...he also did me a favor."

"He gave you Evan?" He rubbed her back in tight, heated circles.

"Yes," she whispered against the rough skin at his throat. "But he also helped me realize that I'm drawn to certain types of guys who are no good for me."

Like him. She didn't have to say it. The jerk of his body as he drew back told her he understood.

"Not all guys are assholes," he bit out. "Not all guys will treat you with disrespect or break your heart without a second thought."

"No, some may even be considerate while they do the heart-breaking. How many hearts have you broken, Tad DeLuca? All that charm and those gorgeous blue eyes, then you move on, leaving human rubble in your wake." She tried to soften it with a winsome smile but she suspected she looked like a scarecrow. "The stories you told me made my toes curl. The Brazilian cousins, that bartender at O'Caseys, the hot air balloon. Will I just be another tawdry tale in a couple of months?"

His tone of voice echoed the horrified look on his face. "Jesus, I should never have told you anything. I thought I was cheering you up and yeah, it kind of turned me on to see your reaction. Maybe it was disrespectful to the women I'd been with but, damn it Jules, don't compare this to what I had with anyone else because there is no comparison."

Their friendship might have placed this in a different category but it didn't change the fundamentals. He was the unrepentant bad boy and she was the reformed bad girl and they were supposed to screw each other out of their systems and move on. He back to anything in heels, she onto Mr. Right, Safe, and Boring.

But lately, she was seeing another side to him, or allowing herself to because it had always been there: kind, caring, her best guy, Tad. What was happening between them went above and beyond the hot and dirty playtime she had signed on for.

When he had taken her hard and fast the moment she walked through the door, he had looked at her like she mattered. The beautiful bastard was making her hope. She wanted to hurt him for that.

"I guess talking about Simon brought up some stuff I haven't dealt with." Crediting her upset to her shitty ex seemed best all around here. She had no more tears to shed for Simon St. James, but given a chance, she would have buckets at the ready for Tad DeLuca.

He glowered. Boy, he gave good glower.

"Don't make me a scapegoat for what this guy did." He backed her up against the table and wedged his hard body between her shaking thighs. With both hands, he cradled her face and delivered passionate kisses that burned through her disintegrating defenses.

"This asshole treated you like crap, *bella,* and it's okay to be angry about that. It's okay to rant and rail and go nuts. Punch it out. Cry it out. Screw it out. If you need to deal with this by banging me until we're both cross-eyed, then do it, but don't compare me to him. I know you're strong and you can kick my ass, but that doesn't mean you can't lean on me, too. I'm here for you, Jules. You are my best girl. You are in my gut."

Another kiss punctuated his declaration, more scorching than the last, melting her heart but not the tension in her fists.

She wanted to thump the living daylights out of something, but not because of Simon and the hurt she felt then, but because the sweet, funny, sexy guy in her arms had shown her how perfect it could be. She had owned her choices and come up with a plan to ensure she never made mistakes like that again. And then she met Tad. Dreamed about him. Acted on her greedy fantasy and now she was back to where she had come from. Wishing for things she couldn't have.

"Punish me, Jules. Get it all out," he urged between sucks on her lower lip and hot, open-mouthed kisses along her jawline. He ground his erection into the concave softness of her sex, ripping a heartfelt moan from her throat. Rough-hewn fingers delved below the waistband of her sweats and traced a well-worn path to her center. Oh, she planned to punish him thoroughly; not for the sins of her ex, but for the cardinal sin of making her fall for him.

Making women drop at his feet was part of Tad's skill set, but really it was his *kill set*. He had murdered whatever minuscule chance she'd had of surviving this affair between friends. She didn't want to feel this way. She had tried to be careful but her heart had been half-engaged going in and she was already playing from behind.

She had only gone and fallen arse-over-tit in love with her friend. What a disaster.

He rubbed his blunt fingers against her blooming sex and caught her moan in his mouth.

"You're so ready for me. Like you've been waiting for me."

All her life, she wanted to say. All her life, she'd been waiting for a man like this. She wished...no, she couldn't make wishes for things to have gone differently. Bloody pointless.

But.

Checking out would have been the clever thing to do, but no one had ever called her clever. Besides, she had checked out of her life too many times already. So she told him how hot he made her, how good he felt inside her. She told him to touch her there, to take her harder. She told him everything she could to avoid telling him the one thing she couldn't. She loved a man who could never be hers but she was going to enjoy this precious time if it broke her heart to do it. Another one of those great decisions she was owning.

Only when she had screamed to his satisfaction and come so many times that she almost passed out did she let her mind go back to that forbidden wish. Not that he could be hers for the future, but that he had been hers in the past.

She wished he was Evan's father.

CHAPTER SIXTEEN

Do not talk, kiss me.

—Italian proverb

Surveying Vivi's, Tad tried to take pleasure in the close to ninety percent capacity, but he couldn't get there. Not when it was impossible to shuck what Jules had told him from his mind. The message had been as clear as the stemware racked above his head. Tad didn't make the grade. Adequate for a fling, but not good enough for something real.

If ever there was a time he wished they had not started as friends, it was now. She knew all his faults and flaws. How he had blown through women without a backward glance and now, that knowledge between them was back to bite his ass with a vengeance.

He had thought he was doing her a favor by telling her about his conquests and making her laugh when she was down, but really he was trying to do himself a solid. Sharing all that stuff put her in the friend zone because no decent woman would want a serious shot with a guy like that. It kept her at arms' length. Damned them before they even had a chance.

Every Italian insult he could think of wasn't enough to describe how stupid he was.

Or how lost he felt.

Usually, he'd be bored with a woman and the by-now pedestrian sex, ready to move on to something new and shiny. Boredom didn't even enter the equation with Jules, not when there was so much more of her to explore. He wished he meant the freckle on her shoulder and the heart-shaped birthmark on her hip. Or the sound she made when his tongue stroked her ear and she got really, really excited. But that was just the sparkly top level. He would need a life-time to map her body and a hundred more to figure out what made her tick.

His skin prickled with the need to take action. Before he could second-guess that impulse, he shot off a text, handed the reins to Kennedy, and did the five-minute quick step over to O'Casey's.

Shane saluted him with a long neck beer as he came in. "Pulling me away from my girl this late? Better be good, DeLuca."

"It's only ten p.m., old man."

Conor wasn't on tonight but Shannon, his favorite buxom redhead bartender, slid him a Goose Island IPA, a healthy dose of her cleavage, and a dirty wink. They'd had a brief fling about eighteen months back and he might have men-tioned some of the spicier details to Jules over baked ziti at Casa DeLuca.

While Tad took a slug of his beer, Shane strummed the bar impatiently. Tad took another long draught. The TV above his head showed the Blackhawks getting their asses handed to them by the Red Wings. He felt their pain.

"Unless you start talking soon, I'm going to have to regale you with tales of how hot the sex is with your very pregnant cousin."

"I've been having a thing with Jules," Tad said.

"Tell me something I don't know." Shane shrugged. "No secrets in this family, man."

"So Jack knows?" Not that Tad particularly cared, but he'd like to be prepared.

Shane's mouth twisted in a grimace. "You're still pretty, so that would be a no."

Christ, he wanted to tear this Simon St. James fucker a new one. The ridiculous name said it all. Some arrogant, candy-assed Brit with a Big Ben–sized sense of entitlement, not unlike another Limey he knew. What guy dumps the woman who was carrying his child and then calls up out of the blue looking to slot himself into his kid's life?

Revealing that this douche had been in touch didn't seem wise. They would deal with that later, but he'd give the bare bones for context.

"She opened up to me today about Evan's father."

Shane sat up straighter, his curiosity piqued. Jules's tight-lipped behavior over the identity of her baby's daddy had caused a fair amount of speculation.

"Well, that's good, isn't it?"

"Except she's decided to use it as a representative example of why men can't be trusted. Or more to the point, Italian guys who have a habit of bedding women and moving on quicker than you can say, 'Your ass looks great on the way out my front door.'"

"You've said that to some chick, haven't you?"

"Maybe, but that's not the point." He wasn't sure what the point was, actually. Looking at the beer as though it could provide answers, he pondered today's take home.

He still had his friend in his life.

Could he live with that even if he wanted so much more?

"You two have been skirting each other like snapping alligators for ages now. You finally get together and the minute it gets hard, you throw up your hands and walk? Never took you for a quitter, Tad."

Quitting was where he excelled. Long ago, he had figured out the prescription for a hassle-free, numbed-up life. *Take two blondes, a bottle of bourbon, and call me in the morning.* He had nothing to offer Jules but the port of his body through what he suspected was going to be a tough time now that her ex had reared his no-goodnik head.

And that would have to be enough for now because she had the right of it. She saw deep into his soul and knew exactly what she'd find there.

A gaping void.

* * *

During the five-minute drive to Jack's house for Sunday brunch, Evan continued the tantrum he had started at an ungodly 4 a.m. Teething rings were useless. Rubbing his gums made him antsy. No doubt he was picking up on her weird mood. She hadn't talked to Tad since she left his house yesterday afternoon. Oddly, she had felt closer to him—cooking together, sharing her sad sack story, the off-the-charts sex—yet there had been a tectonic shift. In telling Tad about Simon's legacy of heartbreak, including the pattern he had set for her fragile heart, a timer had been set. Full acknowledgment that their fling had an expiration date.

They had known it would come, but the pain in her chest at the thought of it had been unexpected. Going back to what they had before would be a hard road but it was necessary. Today at Jack and Lili's, they could practice being friends again, and take a step in the right direction. Onward and upward.

"Come on, Demon. Time to be brave."

Her little soldier pushed out his bottom lip in a pout that accessorized wonderfully with his red, puffy eyes. Gently, she stroked his tear-ravaged cheek and buried her nose in his shock of blond hair.

"I love you, Evan," she whispered. "You're going to help me get through these next few months. You're going to mend my heart."

Evan sighed and then launched into a fit when she un-hooked him from the car seat. It took her ten minutes to get him out of the car because he had lost his dino-giraffe and was inconsolable until she extracted it from under the front seat. Between that and wrangling the bag of necessities she carried around with her constantly, it took a while to regis-ter the voice coming from the backyard at Jack's house. A shiver coursed through her body, like someone had danced across her grave.

It couldn't be.

Fleeing was a viable option. She had done it once and while her brain acknowledged she wouldn't get far, her heart was already in the minivan. But Lili had seen her and it was too late.

She stared, unblinking, at the man who had broken her. Two years and he looked no different except for a slight hardness around the mouth. Tall with a leonine mane, he wore the casual air of arseholes everywhere.

He laughed at something Jack said, but it sounded false. A brittle, rusty sound.

"Hey, Jules, let me take that." Lili grabbed the bag that had slipped from Jules's jellied grip.

Simon's cold blue eyes scanned Jules briefly before shift-

ing to Evan, who was playing squirmy monkey in her flagging arms. The gaze turned hungry, but there was also the
hint of performance in it—the man more sinned against than
sinning. He dragged his eyes away slowly and sharpened
them on her.

"Hullo, Jules. Long time."

"I'd forgotten you two had met," Jack said, his tone curious.

"Why are you here?" she asked Simon, ignoring Jack,
whose eyes darkened in awareness.

"You know why."

Moments passed as the emotional landscape was rear-
ranged.

"Jules?" Jack's voice sounded muffled and distant while
Evan's cries grew louder, echoing Mummy's distress. Had
she fallen over? She felt like she should be on the ground.
Just as that thought formed and her knees weakened to make
it a reality, a strong arm circled her waist.

"I've got you, honey," he whispered in her ear.

Thank Tad.

She turned into him, drawing strength from the big hand
curled possessively around her hip. Evan felt unbearably
heavy but luckily, Tad scooped her precious out of her arms
with a, "Hey, buddy." Her son—her beautiful, perfect son—
stopped his needy wail and blinked at Tad, who drew a
bright giggle from him with a well-placed tickle.

She turned to Simon and girded her loins for battle.

Nobody moved until Simon stepped forward and Jules
instinctively filled the gap, her claws sharpening under her
skin. She could deny it, pretend he wasn't the father, but one
look at Jack told her it was too late. Her brother's jaw had
tensed to the point that she suspected he might be losing
teeth in that grim-set mouth of his.

"Jules," Jack said. Not a question now. Not even a plea

for confirmation, just an acknowledgment that she had been found out.

For once in his life, Simon didn't look all-knowing or smug. Evan had that effect on people. His rambunctious sunniness turned everyone into a melty goo of obeisance and adoration.

"He's healthy?" he asked, no longer with the sharpness of before.

"He's healthy," she confirmed, parsing the words out like precious commodities. She knew what he was asking. Was he a dummy like her or had he inherited his father's smarts? It was much too early to know for sure if her son was dyslexic and it wouldn't matter if he was. He was perfect. Her heart thundered, her cheeks burned.

Simon turned to Jack. "I know I should have said something when I called but I didn't want to risk her doing another runner. She never told me she was pregnant."

"Because you had a wife!" Jules exploded in fury. "A wife you kept mum about the whole time we were together."

Good thing Lili had moved in close to Jack because her hand on his arm was the only thing stopping her brother from doing some major violence to Simon. Evan made a sound of clear discontent in the wake of Mummy's raised voice. She turned to take him from Tad's arms, but he held on.

"How about Jack takes Evan inside with everyone else while we sit down and talk about this?" Tad's expression was hard and she realized in that moment, her friend saw her differently and everything had changed.

"I'm not going anywhere," Jack bit out.

"Evan doesn't need the negative energy and Jules shouldn't be left alone with..." Tad jerked his chin over Evan's head at Simon.

Her two favorite men in the world were squaring off

over the right to champion her. Sweet, but so not the time, boys.

"Tad, could you take Evan into the house and give him some crackers?" She fished in her bag for a baggie of snacks, thankful for the moment to bury her hand and allay the tremble. "Jack, I'd like to speak with Simon. Alone."

"Not happening." The muscle tic that was one of his anger tells jumped like the clappers in his jaw.

"Jack," she pleaded.

Lili rubbed her husband's arm and he straightened. "Better make the most of it, Saint James, because it's going to be your last fucking conversation."

"Jack, please. Not now."

Tad leaned in and the scent of him almost undid her. "You going to be okay? I could stay."

She gave a slight nod and steeled her spine to a titanium rod. She needed to ride this wave solo. With one last blade of a look, Jack walked into the house followed by Tad with Evan, leaving her alone with her ex, who wasn't really her ex. Looking back, she knew she had never been his girlfriend, just a shameful booty call. Maybe she wasn't the kind of girl who inspired devotion.

He gestured to a seat at the large picnic table, already laden with the brunch fixings of juice and champagne for Mimosas. She hid her grim smile at how easily he slotted into the role of host. Your master of ceremonies for the most awkward chat of the century—Simon St. James, ladies and gentlemen!

She took a seat and smoothed her clammy hands on her thighs. The silence circled like a vulture above them.

The last time she'd seen him had been the day she went to tell him about Evan. Well, Evan was no bigger than a fingernail at that point—he wasn't her Evan just yet—but he was inside her, sucking up nutrients and making her ill and basically ensuring he was the Demon before he had even arrived. She had kept her pregnancy to herself for more than two weeks, mainly because Simon's attitude to her had changed of late. He had been calling her less, making excuses not to see her, easing her out of his life. She recognized that now. When he had ignored her messages for two days straight, she had bitten the bullet and gone to see him.

Walking through his restaurant, one of those warehouse bistros in Islington, with her hand over her still-flat belly, excitement had trumped her fear. Sure it was too soon and Simon hadn't promised anything, but he would make it better. Soothe and hold her and cook her something that wouldn't make her want to barf every ten minutes. He would be the guy to save her.

The woman she encountered in his office was stunning, the kind of beauty that poets write about. Alabaster skin, raven hair, confidence borne of breeding. Before Jules could utter a word, Simon was jumping forward, his hand on her elbow to introduce his wife, Magda.

His very pregnant wife.

Jules is Jack's sister, Magda, he had said. *She's looking for a job.*

In ten words, he diminished her to nothing but an unfortunate job-seeker who needed to rely on her brother for employment.

Next thing, he steered her out of the office, explaining as he went. The strain of his hours at the restaurant and her job flying transatlantic twice a week had been unbearable. They had been on a break so he was completely blameless in his actions with Jules, but it was a delicate situation, don't you see? The slightest hint of impropriety—*impropriety!*—

would ruin everything, especially as Magda's first pregnancy two years ago had been so difficult.

He already had a child and now another one on the way with his beautiful, aristocratic wife.

And Jules loved him enough to give him every opportunity to make his marriage work and hated herself for being so stupid as to think he understood her. He hoped they could be friends—not just yet, but later when things were on a more solid footing with Magda—and she had smiled that distant smile she turned on with previous lovers. The man who had known her so well didn't know the difference.

Now he was here at her brother's home, rocking her world all over again.

"How did you find out?"

"A few weeks ago, the *Times* ran an interview with Jack about how he's adjusted to life after giving up the fame game." There was a tinge of jealousy in his tone, so nothing new there. "He talked about his family. You, his wife, his nephew. I went to see your old flatmate and she confirmed you were pregnant when you left London a couple of years ago. I Googled you and found a picture of you with the kid at a wedding a few months ago. The resemblance...well, there was no doubt."

"You should have called to say you were coming."

He looked at her like she was mad. "I called to give you a chance to come clean, to do the right thing, Jules, but no. And I've been leaving messages for the last two weeks." He moderated his voice but it didn't moderate the fury etched on his features. "You were always such a brat. Whining because Jack wouldn't visit more often, because you'd had it so rough. Little girl lost with her rich and famous brother, working that crappy job in that dive bar, trying to prove a point. You were so bloody stubborn, so it doesn't surprise me that you'd use this. What did you do? Come crying to Jack when it didn't work out between us?"

His words flattened her. "I came to tell you, you fucking prick, and you were with your wife. Should I have announced it in the middle of your cozy little reunion? Should I have told Magda that the child she was carrying would have a little brother or sister soon?"

Conveniently, he ignored that. "You had no right to keep this from me, Jules. That's my flesh and blood in there." His gaze bored through the back door's wood, seeking out his son. *His son.* The words sickened her. "If you had acted like an adult instead of a spoiled brat, we could have come up with some suitable arrangement."

"I don't need your money. Evan doesn't need a thing from you."

"A boy needs his father. And I plan to be in his life."

The space around her heart contracted. Her entire body took that as its cue, pulling her inside herself, making her feel small and insignificant.

Desperately, she clawed for the higher moral ground here. "What about Magda? Your other child?"

"We're divorced." For the first time since he had arrived, he looked uncomfortable. She cheered a mental home run that collided with pettiness in her chest. "She has custody of all three kids."

Three children. The blessings went on and on. "You don't see your regular family, so you want a piece of mine."

"I want a piece of mine, Jules." He said it with finality, chopping through the air. "We can talk about this till the cows come home but we both know there's only one end here. You kept this a secret from me, and that kind of behavior doesn't play well in front of a judge. Fathers' rights are all the rage now. Your brother can throw his money and weight around all he likes but he can't deny me access to my son."

He stood quickly, rocking the table so orange juice splashed over the lip of a jug. "Time to grow up, little girl, and come out from behind Jack's apron. I'll be in town until Friday."

CHAPTER SEVENTEEN

*It is all one whether you die
of sickness or love.*

—Italian proverb

So what's the plan?" Shane asked, unease in his voice. "There is a plan, right?"

Everyone had crowded around the island in Jack and Lili's kitchen as soon as Simon flounced out. Jack crossed his arms, uncrossed them, crossed them again. Jules recognized that look. He was primed to explode.

"We're going to make sure he never lays a finger on Evan," Jack said icily.

"Jules, is that what he wants?" Lili asked.

"Why else is he here?" Cara threw out. She sat in an armchair with Evan noodled in the crook of her arm. "I mean, he's had all this time to make his presence known—"

"He didn't know about Evan," Jules said quietly, fire rushing to her cheeks. Not once had she regretted her decision to keep Evan from Simon but she could see how it might look. Jules, the home-wrecker. Jules, the liar. "I had my reasons."

"You should have told me who it was, Jules," Jack said so low the whole room felt its chill. "He's married, with kids and responsibilities."

"I didn't know that when we were together," she said defensively, and then more softly, "It was a bad time for me."

Cara made a sound of disgust. "What a dick!"

Too late, she realized that Evan could hear that. She made a brief gesture to cover his ears, then waved her hand at the futility of trying to cocoon Evan from the swirl of negativity. The situation sucked. "He's married and he took advantage of you."

"He didn't take advantage of me," Jules said, thrilled at her sister's support but needing to make clear the circumstances. "Sure, he deceived me about being married but I was just as responsible for what happened. Two of us made Evan."

"Well, he's not going anywhere near him," Shane said, looking at Jack for confirmation. Her brother nodded curtly, his jaw so tight Jules imagined the softest touch might shatter it.

Tad hadn't spoken a word or looked at her since he had come to her rescue moments before. From beneath heavy-lidded eyes, he watched not her or Evan, but Jack. Anger rolled off him in waves.

Jack plucked his phone from his jeans pocket and looked at Cara expectantly. "Cara, what's the name of the lawyer who handled your annulment?"

"What are you doing?" Jules asked.

"Getting a restraining order."

"Jack," Lili said soothingly. "You need to let Jules decide."

Her brother looked exasperated. "This is what you want, isn't it, Jules? That piece of crap doesn't get to have any say in how Evan is raised, what he eats, where he goes to school. He doesn't get *anything*."

Jules's body threatened to shut down. That was true, she didn't want this man dictating anything about Evan but he could make things so difficult for them. What if he was right and the law was on his side? What if he tried to take Evan away from her? She needed a moment to think, away from the grinding chatter.

"I suppose so." Looking up, she found Tad staring at her intently. "Tad, what do you think?"

"It's your decision." Each word was said with brute force.

"I know, but I'd like your opinion."

Intensity clenched his handsome face. "I don't think you do."

"Tell me."

"I think he's the father of your kid and he has every right to see him."

The quietness in his voice was harshness of a kind. She just stared as the dissenting voices washed over her.

"Even after how he treated me."

"Lots of guys are assholes, but that doesn't mean they should be denied the opportunity to see their own kid. Especially when they weren't in the loop." The rebuke in his tone was unmistakable.

"So I should have told him?" Had she not been clear about what a jackass he was? She hadn't shared the uglier details but Tad knew enough to understand how broken Simon had left her.

"You didn't tell him and you can't change that, but you can make it right now."

He stared at her in a way that completely unnerved her. It felt like it was just the two of them, locked together in this battle of wills. All the competing voices faded out as Tad's flinty eyes bored into her.

"Make it right? Why is it up to me to make it right? He

dumped me like rubbish." She knew in her bones what Simon's reaction to the news of her pregnancy would have been, especially in the light of his marital situation. *Get rid of it, Jules.* That's what he would have told her.

"This isn't about who you were back then or what he did. This is about what's best for Evan."

Jack was livid, his color roaring high. "And a guy who cheats on his pregnant wife…this scum deserves to have the red carpet rolled out and welcomed into this family? Over my dead body. And anyone who thinks different knows where to take his opinion."

"Jack," Lili warned. "Jules asked him. He's entitled to his say."

"And I'm entitled to decide who I welcome into my home."

Tad shot up, ignoring the hostility arrowing from Jack's direction. He walked to the door, turning when he got there. "You might not like it, Jules, but blood should out here. And I don't mean Jack."

She jumped up and followed him, shutting the door behind her to give them privacy.

"So I should forgive him?" The slow, sick spin in her stomach took her back to that office and Simon's casual dismissal of her. She had known that telling him about the baby would have made no difference, not when he was trying so hard to reconcile with his wife. Why couldn't her friend, the man who knew her inside and out, understand that?

He cupped her face in his big hands, sending warmth flooding through her. She hadn't realized how cold she was until he touched her.

"Some things are unforgivable, Jules. Decisions are made that can't be undone. Believe me, I know." The hollowness in his eyes ripped through her. "But it doesn't have to be that way here. Only you can decide where your line is, but I think you know what's right."

Tears stung her eyelids and clotted her throat. She could barely get the next words out. "I thought you cared about me. About Evan. How could you want this?"

His hands fell away from her face.

"I don't want this. I'm crazy about you and Evan—don't ever think I'm not—but if someone tried to keep me from my kid, I would do everything in my power to change that. He hurt you and now you want to hurt him. I get that, but you said you're not a victim, that you take responsibility for all the choices you've made. The good and the bad. You can't let Jack or anyone else decide this. It's too important."

He sounded just like Simon, albeit in Tad's clear, commonsense way. It didn't make it any more palatable. What happened to this special connection they had? What happened to being in each other's gut?

"I need you to be on my side here, Tad. I need you to be my friend."

"I'll always be your friend, but this isn't about sides. It's about Evan. It's about stepping up."

On that, he left while the wave of voices rose behind her to fill the void.

* * *

Tad usually enjoyed the morning quiet of an empty restaurant, whether it was DeLuca's or Vivi's. But this morning, his thoughts bounced around his skull, duking it out and making a whole lot of noise.

He had gone three days without talking to Jules, probably the longest stretch since he'd known her. It just seemed easier to give her some space while she figured out what was best for her and Evan, but it killed him not to talk to her. Soothe her through this tough time. Hold her like she was his.

It would have been so easy to jump on board that band-wagon of hate with Jack at the helm. Do the clan thing and vow to protect. Well, he'd never been very good at the family business and his latest actions just went to prove that.

No way would he be party to a plan to cut some guy out of his kid's life. St. James might be a jerk but he was Evan's father and that had to count for something. Tad knew all about the perils of poor decision-making. To make the man pay for that by denying him a chance to see his son? That didn't sit so well with him.

He clicked through some spreadsheets on the laptop and assessed what he saw. Numbers for Vivi's were good and he might even be able to talk to the bank about that mortgage to buy out his sister. The only reason he wasn't breaking out the Prosecco was found in the e-mail he'd received fifteen minutes ago.

Tasty Chicago had blown Vivi's back to the Stone Age. The latest issue hadn't hit the newsstands yet, but Tad knew someone at their offices who had slipped him a copy of the review. If pressed, he could have recited it word for word.

No different than any hip establishment in the by now passé Wicker Park neighborhood, Vivi's does what one would never expect from a bar brought to you by Taddeo DeLuca, famous purveyor of the Bourbon Bomb and the Ab-alicious Gimlet, two of the top cock-tails on last year's Chicago Mixologists List: it makes wine boring. The bar has all the usual trappings— a young staff that prance about like they're on the catwalk, decor straight out of Pan-Asian Home & Gardens, and a passable list—but without the in-house knowledge to determine Greek from German (they still make maps, don't they?), this oenophile was left with a sour, funky taste in her mouth. On my first visit, I tried and failed to enjoy the nostalgia of been there-done that-got the T-shirt. On the second, I had barely a moment to consider the menu before the owner's divo-esque behavior signaled a premature end to my meal. Mr. DeLuca may be banking on his much-vaunted social media popularity and his connections with a certain celebrity chef to keep him afloat but true wine lovers will want to go elsewhere. The bar's one saving grace? The flavorful red pepper, caramelized onion, and cilantro appetizer prepared by Derry Jones, on loan from Jack Kilroy's bizarrely successful joint, Sarriette. Unfortunately, Mr. DeLuca can't rely on borrowed chefs and the Kilroy name to turn this stinker into a winner.

The appetizer didn't even belong to Derry; it was Jules's all the way. And Monica was relatively kind about the rude owner, so that was a bonus. It would go out tomorrow. How fitting—the day he had planned to lay low and sink lower. The anniversary of his parents' death.

At the sound of footsteps, he turned to find Jack swaggering in from the street, his expression grim. He took a seat at the bar and lay this week's issue of *Tasty Chicago* on the glowing wood. Must have his own connection.

"I've already seen it."

"I thought you were good at this. Working your charm. Keeping the fairer sex happy."

"She didn't get the experience she expected. Not everyone is going to leave satisfied." Tad folded his arms across his chest, knowing the move gave off defensive but not caring one whit. "Why don't you say what you really want to say? Isn't this the 'what are your intentions toward my sister' talk?"

Jack inhaled deep. "She's never had the best taste in men."

"And you've never liked me."

"I've liked you just fine, Tad. But when it comes to my sister, you've never given me any reason to think you're a good bet. You make her laugh and she gets all doe-eyed when she looks at you, but being there for her? I don't see it. You had a chance to step up and protect her. Instead you take the side of the guy who fucked her over. What was that?"

Blood raged beneath Tad's skin. "You know it's the right thing to do."

"Right doesn't mean best. That guy has already abandoned his wife and kids, and now he's looking for a substitute to make him feel like his balls are still intact. Once he gets bored, he'll be gone. Or maybe he'll show up every few years, confusing the hell out of Evan. You really think that's for the best?"

"We don't know what the future is going to hold, Jack. All I know is that Jules needed to make that decision on her own without you and Cara and Shane coming down on her like a brickhouse. Yeah, maybe he'll be a sucktacular father, but he needs to be given the chance to get it right."

Jack scowled. "So is Jules your shot at getting it right? You've spent years screwing anything that moves and now you're looking for the one thing—the one person—that'll make you feel better about yourself."

That struck hard. If Tad didn't know better he would think Jack knew the ugly truth, but while the man had many faults, deliberate cruelty wasn't one of them. Vivi's walls, glass, stone, and wood, pressed in on him.

He plastered on a grin. So what if it hurt to do it.

"We're men, Jack. We're never good enough for the women we want. Isn't that the standard viewpoint?"

Back in the day, Tad had been skeptical about Jack's interest in Lili until the first time they had talked, right after a very public kiss between the newly minted couple went video viral and catapulted their relationship into the online hate-asphere. Just one conversation with Jack had been all it took to see the man had fallen ass-over-nuts for Lili. That Jack wasn't astute enough to give Tad the benefit of the doubt really got on his tits.

Jack's expression remained unmoved. "I'm not going to be so heavy-handed as to tell you to stay away from her, but as you're such a fan of what's right, then you'll put your money where your mouth is."

Jules needed someone…anyone who could give her a hundred percent. Meaning anyone but Tad. What man is worthy of the woman he's crazy about? It's like universal man-law.

Thou shalt not be in the league of the woman you want with every breath of your raggedy ass self.

Maybe he had been wrong to encourage her to make up with St. James. The guy was a Grade A douche and yeah, he was probably bad news but no one knew better than Tad the pain of wanting that second chance. Needing someone to see the potential and the possibility. He was being kinder to St. James than he was to himself.

Jack tilted his head, waiting for Tad to agree with him.

Fight for her. Tell everyone she's yours.

But she wasn't and she never could be. She had made it clear that finding a way past his wham-bam ways was a bridge too far and now with this St. James business, he might have screwed up their friendship forever.

"You don't have to worry about me, Jack. Your perfect family won't be contaminated." Hell, he was tempted to wink.

Jack's mouth pulled at the corners. Ah, don't say his Lordship felt bad.

"It's not personal. It's about Jules," he said, less belligerently now. Easy to cop that attitude when you've won. "After what she's been through, I just have to look out for her. You understand?"

There were a million things Tad could have countered with, starting with how Jack's neglect was part of the reason why she had gone through a shitty time in the first place and ending with how he had thrown her at St. James like a sheep to the slaughter. But it was easier to check out of the conversation, and easy was his default setting. His mind was already walking—taking the simplest road to the front door, the street, the rest of his miserable life.

There was a bottle of scotch with his name on it back at his parents' house and a couple of days' shore leave to get through it.

"Got it."

CHAPTER EIGHTEEN

Love without pain is very rare.

—Italian proverb

Food was the only thing that could soothe Jules's soul.

She preserved mangoes and lemons until she ran out of jars. She conjured up ricotta ravioli using Vivi's recipe. She made a dog's dinner out of another batch of focaccia.

She wanted to talk to her bestie, spend an afternoon lying in his strong arms while he assured her she had done the right thing, but she knew his position. She had failed some test she didn't even know she had been sitting.

Three days since Simon's show-stopping arrival, and she had turned off her phone. The well-meaning prattle from everyone threatened to drive her insane. She and her bonny baby boy needed to take a breath, spend some time together so she could work through this. Letting Simon into Evan's life—into *her* life, because that's what it amounted to—was the last thing she wanted, and when Jack took charge she had felt nothing but relief that the decision would be seized from her hands. Someone else could deal with it. Jack could deal with it. After all, he owed her.

Except that was a pit she had been trying to climb out of. Denying her problems. Running away. Taking the easy way out.

But silent phones produced uninvited pop-ins. Now the girls were here to talk her off the ledge they assumed she was balancing on.

"You can put him in the cage, if you want," Jules said, gesturing to the playpen in the living room of her flat. It always amazed her how someone as fastidious as Cara enjoyed her dirty little monkey. Cara tore her gaze away from Evan, who was making fists out of her no-longer-perfect hair while he climbed all over her.

"No, he's fine," Cara said, tightening her grip on the slippery bundle. "You're fine, aren't you, Evs?"

"Here, give him to me," Lili said. "You're going to overdo it. If I have to listen to your husband whine one more time about how you don't know when to stop, I'll punch something." She plucked Evan out of her sister's lap and got him settled in her own. "Has Simon been in touch?" she asked Jules, slicing to the heart of why they were here.

Jules shook her head. "He flounced out with his ultimatum and said he'd be in town until Friday. Not a peep."

She didn't need him to call because he'd already said enough. *Poor rich girl.* Always whining because Jack wouldn't visit her, and that had been true. She had known Simon had an oddly competitive relationship with Jack, and that he admired and despised him in equal measure. He had listened to her complaining when Jack said he couldn't make it back to London some weekend because he was too busy putting out fires at his restaurant in Miami or training his new commis chef in New York. He had played up the friction between she and Jack and she had played the part of Moaning Myrtle because Jack couldn't read her mind.

But her brother had made up for his neglect in spades and their relationship had never been better. And now he wanted to make Simon pay for his sheer nerve at daring to touch the great Jack Kilroy's sister.

Was she ready to do this? Was she ready to cut this man off at the knees? He had made her feel worse than the kitchen grease behind the burners at Vivi's when he practically shoved her into the street.

But she hadn't helped her case much. She could have stood up for herself. She could have demanded he treat her with respect and do the right thing by their child. Instead she took the coward's way out. She scarpered like a mouse and took cover behind Jack.

"I'm more worried about how Jack's going to adapt if I bring Simon into the fold."

Lili sat up straighter, her eyes glinting. "Okay, you know I'm crazy about Jack but the best thing you ever did was move out of the house. And then the next best thing you did was announce your intention to find a man."

"Testify," said Cara.

"Of course, if you'd just told us that you were planning to do the dirty with my cousin, you could have saved us all a crap load of time." She held up her hand to forestall Jules's admittedly weak defense. "We'll discuss Tad later over a bottle of something fruity and liquory. As for your brother, the ego management is practically a full-time job and he needs to be checked every now and then. I'm not saying Tad's right, but he was right about you making this decision for yourself and for Evan. We're never going to judge you and no one can say they wouldn't have done the same in your situation, but Jack should not have any say in this. *Capische*?"

Jules was starting to realize that. She didn't need Jack to make this decision for her. She didn't need Tad to make it, either. The decision about how Simon should figure in Evan's life would be made by the people who mattered.

His parents.

Because the little monkey had two. Simon St. James was a prick but he was also the sperm that had contributed to the creation of her beautiful son, and for that she was grateful. He had given her a gift—an unintentional one, but a gift all the same. She needed to make it right.

"So how is my delightful brother these days?"

Lili sighed. "You know how he hates it when he's not in control of a situation. Between this Simon business and us not being knocked up, he's feeling sort of spinny."

Jules caught Cara's eye, both of them waiting for Lili to elaborate. She tended to keep her problems under wraps so pushing her to share was not an option.

"What's that look for?" Lili asked.

"Nothing," Cara and Jules said together.

"Jack and I are doing fine," Lili said, not altogether convincingly.

"So the S-E-X hasn't turned into a chore yet?" Cara asked. "Ovulation calendars and scheduled hook-ups can do that."

"Like you'd know. What did it take? Three tries and you were picking out nursery colors." Lili buried her pout in Evan's hair. "I'm sorry. I don't mean to be snarky."

Cara did her best not to look smug. She could be such a pain in the arse, sometimes.

"The S-E-X is still smokin' and I'm still hot for my husband," Lili said. "End of story."

That sent a shudder through Jules. "Ew, can we not talk about my brother in that way?"

"Right, let's talk about Tad instead," Lili said with a gleam in her eye. "Much better."

Jules sent her a dark look. "Maybe we should make a rule not to talk about S-E-X with any male carrying the last name DeLuca or Kilroy."

Cara leaned over to Lili and covered Evan's ears. "So that leaves Shane. Who is still taking my hoo-ha to funky town."

"Gah...shut up, would you?" Jules squeaked out. "Shane's practically my brother and I really don't want to hear about how magical his wang is."

That sent them into a bout of bawdy laughter.

"So, our scorching hot sex lives—never thought I'd be saying that in plural—are off limits for now," Lili said around a bite of toast with mango and mint chutney. "Uh, this is awesome. You need to can and sell this stuff."

What she needed was to figure out her next move. She couldn't work at Vivi's anymore and she needed to get a plan in place.

"So have you talked to Tad—in a non-sexy way?" asked Cara in that mind-reading way she had. "I can't believe you were able to keep that under wraps. Gym, my ass."

Jules gusted a sigh. "We had that fight and now it's like we can't get back to how it was between us. He won't answer my calls."

"He probably could have handled it better but I think it was more about Jack," Cara said. "There's always been tension between them because of you, and when Tad saw you caving to everything Jack said, it triggered something."

Lili looked upset. Tad and she were as close as siblings, and it hurt her that the two guys she loved most in the world didn't see eye to eye.

"What are you making over there?" Lili asked, her hungry gaze falling on Jules's work in a not-so-subtle change of subject.

Jules held up the recipe she had extracted carefully from Vivi's book and placed in a protective plastic sheet. She felt a curious closeness to this woman she had never met and sadness that she would never get a chance to.

"It's a recipe for *braciole*." She had tried making it last week with disastrous results but today she would not be denied.

"It looks old. Did you get it from Dad?"

"It's your aunt Vivi's. Frankie let me borrow her cookbook." Her throat worked over a swallow. "What was she like?"

"Her name said it all," Cara said wistfully. "She was the soul of the party, always laughing and joking with everyone. The room always felt more alive with her in it, like Prosecco bubbles fizzing away. When she left, there was a bit of deflation, you know?"

Jules nodded, surprised at Cara's rather poetic gush, which was so not her. She understood what she was saying. She felt it whenever Tad left the room or if she hadn't seen him for a while. She felt it now.

"I know Tad was close to her, but what about his dad?"

"You think Tony's a hard ass," Lili said with feeling. "Uncle Rafe was King of the Hard Asses."

Cara nodded her agreement. "Rafe was a chef just like Dad. They ran DeLuca's together and he wanted more for his kids. He wanted Tad to go to college, fulfill all that immigrant American dream crap. I mean there was nothing stopping him from being a chef but Tad has a huge respect for family. Blood means a lot to him and his father's ambitions for him trumped everything."

Jules understood that about him more and more. The thought that a man could be denied access to his son had upset him greatly, enough for him to swim upstream and fight the prevailing views of the DeLuca-Kilroy mob. She had never thought of the word "honorable" when it came to Tad but now she realized it described him perfectly.

"He spent all his afternoons at DeLuca's. Tony encouraged Tad because he wanted someone to take over, but Rafe was adamant it wouldn't be his son. Tad was going to make everyone proud and be something important. A lawyer or an architect. They used to fight about it all the time, but then Vivi stepped in and convinced Tad to at least get his degree. When he was done, he could decide what he wanted but at least he'd have the qualification. Then they had the accident and he..."

The space between Cara's dark blond eyebrows knit into a frown.

"He what?" Jules looked at Lili, who had turned a curious gaze on Cara.

"He lost himself for a few years. We weren't all that close back then but I remember he came to visit me in New York after he had been traveling for about a year and a half after they died. He had been in Thailand, Laos, Vietnam, a ton of other places. I didn't recognize him when he showed up at my dorm room at Columbia. Thin as a rail, with skin and a beard so dark it looked like he had escaped from a deserted island. Like Tom Hanks in that movie."

Concern marred Lili's face. "I didn't know that. He used to call me every few months but I didn't know he came to see you."

"Yeah. I put him up for a couple of days and skipped classes to hang with him, but he didn't want to talk much. He shaved, bought some clothes, and hopped a flight to Italy. He worked at a butcher's in Tuscany, did seasonal work picking grapes. Learned all about wine."

Jules could see him under that blameless blue sky, shielding his eyes from the sun while he stripped a vine of its fruit. Looking for a peace he still hadn't found.

"He told me that he had a fight with his father the night of the accident. He said things and didn't get a chance to take them back. They must have known he loved them, though. I wish he could believe that, no matter what he said to his dad."

Cara looked uncomfortable. "There's more to it."

"What do you mean?"

Lili broke in. "He blamed himself."

A cold gush crashed over Jules's heart. "But why? He wasn't even there."

Cara's swallow made her slender throat bulge. "They were on their way to pick him up. He'd been arrested for getting into a fight."

Jules's legs turned to water and she white-knuckled the edge of the sink. Realizing she needed a seat, she lowered her body to a chair at the kitchen table.

"What happened?"

"He was doing so well," Cara continued. "Getting good grades and making honors' rolls. You wouldn't believe how sick I was at all the comparisons. Well, he finished the first year with flying colors and I guess he needed to let off steam. He got into a bar fight with some kid who was the son of a cop—knowing Tad it was probably over a girl—and before we knew it he was at a police station on the south side, and Vivi and Rafe were on their way to pick him up."

Jules's heart squeezed. She suspected that fight stemmed more from his soul-crushing argument with his father than the typical end-of-school-year cutting loose.

"And then it happened," Jules finished.

"It was so random," Lili said, her eyes glossy. "Some guy ran a red light. Vivi was killed instantly; Uncle Rafe was on life support for a few hours and Dad had to make the decision to let him go. Everyone was destroyed. Gina, Dad, everyone. But no one felt it more than Tad."

Imagine loving someone so much your life stopped when their hearts did. If something happened to Evan or Jack, she would feel that way. Part of her would sink into the ground with them. She shoved that horrible thought away.

"But surely he knows it wasn't his fault. I mean, everyone told him that, right?"

Cara opened her mouth. Closed it. Looked squirrelly.

"Of course we did," Lili chimed in a beat too late. "He knows. I mean, I've tried…"

"Yeah, but did anyone actually say that to him? Tell him that they loved him." That no matter what happened, they loved him.

Lili chewed on her lip. "He had a big fight with Tony right after it happened. Things were said. There was almost a brawl at the funeral, but he came back to us eventually." She shared a guilty glance with her sister. "He's family, he knows what we think. How much we love him."

"Jesus, you guys suck donkey balls at being Italian."

Cara's smile was brief. "I know. We've never been the most demonstrative types. It's all about food and family and knowing that underneath it all, blood is all that matters. We don't need to say it. It's right here." She touched two fingertips to her chest. A few inches higher than her heart but Jules got the gist.

But he didn't cook anymore, and the light in his eyes dimmed whenever his mother's name was mentioned. He was still stuck in a broke-down place where peace and acceptance was impossible.

He needed a friend, but more than that, he needed her heart.

CHAPTER NINETEEN

It hurts more to be slapped by a woman,
than to lose ten years of one's life.

—Italian proverb

He wasn't at Vivi's and he wasn't picking up his phone. Kennedy said he'd made it clear he'd be out of calling range the night before and all problems should be taken to Derry.

The house looked shut-in and lifeless. She knocked. No answer. Standing back, she assessed her options and thought she saw a twitch at one of the blind slats.

She knocked again and again until her knuckles turned raw.

"Tad, I need to talk to you."

Nothing but dead silence.

From her purse, she plucked the key Frankie had given to her thirty minutes ago with a nod and no questions. Righty-open, inside she went, the light behind her casting a wedge of brightness in the dark hallway where he had taken her so possessively just a few days before.

The door to the living room cracked open.

"Why are you here?" He sounded rusty, as if it was the first time he had spoken in days.

She inched closer and got a waft of booze fumes for her trouble. Giving the door a gentle push, she was relieved to see it give way.

"It's so dark," she said, her fingers moving automatically to the light switch.

"Leave it," he rasped. There was just enough light to make out a bottle on the table, a couple of pizza boxes, and a sheet on the sofa. She didn't need it to make out the lines of his body, which she knew better than any recipe.

His silence combined with the dark gave her a chance to examine him, but she decided quickly that she didn't want to talk to him in the shadows. She moved to the window and pulled on the blind cord. Slatted light filled the room, bathing it in buttery stripes.

Illuminating the matter was an iced water shock. He hadn't slept; that much was clear. His eyes were bloodshot and raw, two days of stubble gave him a pirate's jaw. His whole appearance was one of someone haunted.

She sat beside him, close enough to touch but she held off although every cell in her body fizzed at being so near to him. Would she always feel this way? Probably. Definitely.

"Is Evan okay?" he asked in a whiskey-rough voice.

"He's fine."

He curled his fist into her hair gently and pulled her close. "I'm sorry that bastard ever hurt you and then I just rolled back over you. I'm going to make sure no one ever hurts you again." He released her with a gentle stroke of her cheek. "Including me."

Alarm bolted through her. "Tad, tell me what's going on."

"I need you to leave, Jules. I have to be alone."

"No, you don't."

He rubbed his hand across his mouth and gave her an eviscerating look. She had seen that look before from men who wanted to get rid of her. Guys with whom she had out-stayed her welcome.

She didn't care.

He could glower and glare and give her what-for but she wasn't leaving. He loved her. She knew he loved her. He was the only person brave enough to call her on her cowardice in how she handled Simon. He risked destroying their friendship by going against the grain and if that wasn't love, what was? Jack might think he was acting for the best and everyone took their lead from her brother, the alpha of the pack, but not Tad. He marched to the beat of his own drum.

"You can't be here, Jules. I don't want you here."

"Cara and Lili told me what happened that night."

The look he shot her with was a mixture of disdain and heart-rending pain. "I..." He shook his head. "I can't do this, Jules. In a couple of days, maybe. When I'm through it."

"No, now. I'm here now, ready to be whatever you need." She was ready to provide this man, who had pulled her through so many times, all the help he needed.

"I know it hurts like a bitch," she said. "I know you miss them."

He raised his bleary eyes to hers. "I do but that's not even it anymore."

"What is it?"

"It's so selfish. I can't even..."

Her heart hurt so much for him. "What, love? Tell me."

"I miss me. Who I used to be before. Sometimes I see snatches of that guy when I'm joking around with Lili or out for a drink with Shane, but mostly he comes out around you. With you"—he threaded his fingers through her hair again and pulled her close—"I feel whole and good. You're so beautiful, Jules. So perfect. I could fall into you, get lost in you, use you to make me feel right again for a short while. Take and take and take."

Her throat thickened with tears. "Then do it. Whatever you need, take it. I'm here."

He looked at her with eyes the color of regret and for a moment she thought he was going to shut down. Just close her out completely. But he inclined his head until their foreheads touched, apparently needing that skin-to-skin connection to help form the words.

"He thought I did it on purpose. Getting into that fight after the argument we had. Rebelling against him because he wanted me to be a success, to vindicate all the sacrifices he made for us."

She rubbed his back, encouraging him to let it out.

"I expected my mother to come pick me up but no one came after an hour. Then two. By that time, I'd fallen asleep with my head on the shoulder of some bum and when I woke up, they led me into the interview room. Up all these stairs, through countless doors. I thought they were going to throw the book at me because that big mouth and his South side Irish cop father had already threatened to make my life hell. But I got inside and Tony was there sitting at the table. His face—I'll never forget his face, Jules. You hear that word "ashen" but I never knew what it meant until I saw Tony that day. Then he told me they were dead."

He heaved a deep breath, but it broke up about halfway through. The effort was too much for him and for a moment, she worried it might be too much for her. But it wouldn't be. This man needed her and she had to be strong for him.

"Tad, you know it was an accident. You're smart enough to know this isn't your fault."

He buried his head in his hands. Painful, soul-destroying seconds ticked by.

"My heart says different. It knows what I did and I see it when Tony looks at me. I was responsible for his brother's death. I couldn't face him after that. I couldn't face any of them for a long time. At the funeral, Tony and I had a fight. He said I was a disappointment. He said—"

"He was grieving." She didn't have to hear what else he said. She knew Tony well enough to imagine.

"When I came back, Frankie made him give me a job at DeLuca's, tending bar. I didn't want a job where I had to think."

"Why didn't you work somewhere else?"

"I said I didn't want to think but really I didn't want to forget. I needed the pain to remind me every day that I was the screw-up my father thought I was, that Tony thought I was. Working at DeLuca's, seeing Tony who looks like my father, even hearing the clank in the kitchen, I needed all that to keep me sane. The pain has kept me sane. Every year, it would build to a point where if I didn't take off on some sort of bender I would explode. I'd go somewhere no one knew me and hole up for a few days like some animal going through a transformation. Sometimes, I banged some chick until I couldn't feel a thing. I wasn't fit for company and those few days allowed me to get sane again until the next year. But this year, I have the bar and I had to stay home. Here."

Her soul shattered in the face of all this pain. "Tad, you can't go on like this."

"Are you going to tell me to get therapy, Jules? To talk it out with someone?" He huffed out a weary breath. "I did when I came back to Chicago. And I know I should feel differently, but that doesn't mean I can. What it does mean is that I can't be what you need."

"You're already what *I* need."

He shook his head, his shoulders sagged, his hand fell away from her hair.

"I'm not the kind of guy who can be there for you. I can barely hold my own life together. You and Evan need someone stable and strong like Jack and Shane and Tony. A provider, a protector." He palmed his forehead. "I'm just a fucking ghost."

"All Evan needs are the people around him to love him unconditionally. I don't need a man to provide for us—yes, I've always behaved as if a man could solve my problems but I realize now that I can solve my problems. I can take care of my son. What we need from you is all you've ever given us. Your heart, your love, just you."

She smoothed her thumb over his jaw and he groaned under her touch. She followed up with her lips, working her way from his stubble-rough chin and back over to his mouth.

"Jules, please," he groaned, so deep she felt it in every nerve. Please stop or please go on?

Making an executive decision, she took the groan as an invitation to suck on his bottom lip, to chase his tongue with her own, to kiss him deep. He shouldn't have tasted good: all that booze should have soured him but this was Tad and the chemistry between them was undeniable. It no longer felt like stealing, it felt like taking what was hers.

Taddeo DeLuca belonged to her, and her alone.

She pushed him back on the sofa and straddled him, taking the lead, pulling out her inner bad girl. This wasn't slow and tortured. This was her way. Fast and urgent and *get inside me now before I die from the want.* She ground her body against his erection and peeled his sweatpants down past those lovely hip indents that she knew like the back of her hand. His beauty awed her.

With an animal growl, he got on board and pushed up her skirt.

Rip. There went another pair of panties. All for a good cause. And then he was inside her, pumping his thighs up to meet her downstroke as she took what was her right. Tad's body, his quick mind, the only man who got her. This was what she needed—not a man to take care of her, but a man who would be her partner in all things. Cooking, laughing, loving. Working together to make each other happy. The push and pull of two people who understood each other like no one else.

As they moved together, finding that sensuous rhythm, she kissed him again. She needed the connection that came from touching him everywhere she could. Their mouths, their chests, where their bodies fused as one. He moved his thumb to stroke between her legs, the pleasure so sharp she moaned into his mouth.

"Oh, God."

"Just Tad," he whispered, making her laugh so hard she almost lost her tempo. It felt like he had come back to her with that one little interjection. Even now, with his heart in shreds, he was thinking of how to please her.

No more than a few seconds later, the build of pleasure became so unbearable she had to pull away, but he had other ideas. He turned and flipped her onto her back, and drove into her deep and fast with one long, consuming stroke after another. He curled his fist in her hair and with his other hand pushed one thigh farther apart to heighten the angle of penetration.

The orgasm ripped through her, cresting in an explosion of heat that radiated through every nerve ending. It went on and on and on, no end in sight, no mercy or quarter given. Naked want finding its fullest expression.

Bad girls had it best.

"I love you," she said as the violence shuddered to diminishing aftershocks. Not a whisper, but strong and directly to his face. There would be no doubt that she loved him. He needed to be told, often, and in the clearest terms. He had been revealed to her, laugh by laugh and stroke by stroke. She had peeled away to the man inside and he was all she could ever want.

She could feel his entire body shaking though she knew he hadn't come yet. Still inside her, he stopped his powerful thrusts and plundered her mouth with a long, possessive kiss. He tasted of man and home and salt. He tasted of... tears.

"I love you," she said again.

He shook his head vehemently. "No, Jules. Don't say it—you can't."

"Yes." She could and she would. Forever.

She swiped away his liquid pain with her thumbs. "I love you, I love you, I love you." Over and over she said it as she kissed every inch of his face. She loved this sinful mouth, this strong nose. She loved every last whisker of stubble, every laugh line around his eyes.

She loved this man.

The honesty of the moment ratcheted up her need again. It shouldn't have been possible, but then Tad made the impossible happen. With that inexorable climb, he took her over again with words so faint she thought she must be mistaken.

"I'm sorry," he said against her mouth before he roared his release.

He buried his face in her shoulder while their breathing returned to normal. Just their breathing, though. Nothing else would be normal again.

Slowly he withdrew from her, pulled up his sweatpants, and left the room.

Bollocks.

Before she had time to process it, he was back with a wet washcloth. He pushed aside her torn underwear and gently washed between her thighs, every warm stroke like heaven in contrast to the chill emanating from his body.

"You owe me another pair of expensive knickers," she teased.

"Put it on my tab," he said gravely.

"Tad—"

"Is there a chance you could get pregnant?"

The words, said with a flat indifference, pinned her back. She shouldn't have been surprised. It was a reasonable question to ask but usually...hell, she didn't know what usually happened in these situations.

"I'm on the pill." After what happened with Simon, she treated it with the respect it deserved. Alarms, Post-it notes, you name it, she did it to make sure she didn't repeat that mistake.

He stopped what he was doing and looked up with frost in his eyes. "Weren't you on the pill before?"

"Yes, but I'm more careful now."

"I hope so."

She bolted upright, pulling her skirt down as she went. "Don't do this." *I'm sorry,* he had said right before he exploded inside her. Was he already planning his exit strategy while he made love to her?

"Jules," he said patiently, like he was about to explain something difficult. "What just happened was a moment of craziness. This whole thing between us has been one long series of crazy moments. We were geographically convenient but now it's over."

"Yes, the friends with benefits thing is over, Tad, but we're not. This is real and we're just beginning." She rubbed the back of his neck, easing away the knots of stress. "I know you're hurting now but my heart is strong enough to beat for two until yours can beat again. I've already gone through a lot of pain with Jack, Simon, how stupid I feel. I gave birth, for Christ's sake. If I can bring a life into this world, I can bring you back into it as well. Let me help you."

The look he gave her was cutting. "You can't help me. Jesus, I told you not to get attached. I told you I couldn't follow through and give you what you needed."

Feeling gangly and weakened, she stood and balled her fists at her side. The temptation to clip him around the ear was so strong she almost collapsed under the weight of it. Instead, she took a step away—for his safety and her sanity.

"No, you didn't."

"No, I didn't what?"

"No, you didn't tell me not to get attached. In fact, I distinctly remember telling *you* not to fall in love with *me*." She fanned her hips with both hands and dug one of her flip-flops into the carpet. The other one had gone AWOL during the pounding she just got on the sofa. "And now you have fallen in love with me, you poor sod, so you're going to have to man up and deal with it."

He stared up at her through bloodshot eyes filled with disbelief. "You're crazy."

"Tell me you don't love me."

He settled back on the sofa in an indolent pose, his body straining for the lie. "You know I love you, Jules. It's impossible not to love you. I just don't have it in me to love you the way you need."

She made a very unladylike noise. "Now you're just splitting hairs."

"We're not doing this, Jules. You can't nag or logic me into giving you what you want. We made this clear weeks ago. You're going to find some stand-up guy to keep you safe and secure and I'll do whatever I need to keep on rolling."

"So those chicks you banged during your previous benders? Are you trying to tell me that's what happened here? That I'm just the comfort lay to get you through the tough times?"

He picked up her wayward flip-flop and tossed it to her. She caught it reflexively.

"If the shoe fits."

She could hear the stress in those casual words, the lack of conviction in their casual cruelty. After the pain of Simon she knew she had it in her to be one half—one third, if she counted Evan—of a soul-deep love, but everyone had to play their part. She could carry him for a while through his hurt but she needed a sign that he wanted this as much as she did.

"I thought I wanted safe and secure, so I could avoid the heartache of falling too deeply, but it happened anyway. With you. I know what that feels like. I feel that with you—"

"Jules, honey." More soothe-the-crazy-woman.

She threw her flip-flop at his head. It glanced off the side of his cheek, drawing his shocked expression.

"Jules!"

"Shut. Up. I feel that with you and I know I have it in me to feel it again with someone else. I have a lot of love to give. It's inside me, ready and ripe for the right person. The person who can handle it. You will never meet another woman who understands you like I do, Tad DeLuca. I am the best bloody thing to happen to you but I'm not going to beg."

Above flaring nostrils, those dark blue eyes seared her but when he spoke again, he was as calm as the stultifying air in the room.

"I know you won't beg. You've never begged for anything in your life. You're the strongest person I know and
you'll get over me. They always do."

She had hit a wall. There was only so much she could do
and she had already debased herself too many times with too
many guys. She deserved to be fought over, to be wooed, to
be the center of a man's world. And until Tad learned to love
himself, he wouldn't be able to give her the all-consuming
love she merited.

Convincing herself there was a smidgen of truth running
through her brave speech was the only thing that kept her
from crumpling to the floor. This fountain of love inside her
couldn't be all for naught. She wasn't supposed to waste it
on undeserving men.

You talk a good game, Bad Girl Jules said wryly.

She sure does, Good Girl Jules concurred.

It would stun her senseless for a while but she would get
over him eventually. Seeing him at every family gathering
would help to wean her off that bone-melting smile. Famil-
iarity would breed indifference.

On her way out, she tried to think of some witty comment
to see her through, but none was forthcoming. In the hallway, she took a moment to do what was needed, then closed
the front door behind her quietly.

CHAPTER TWENTY

Beautiful women are always in the right.

—Italian proverb

He crawled into the shower and scrubbed his skin until it felt as raw as he felt on the inside.

A little hurt now—okay, a lot of hurt—was the only way to help her move forward. With every story about his conquests, he had warned her what he was capable of, but she hadn't listened. Hell, *he* hadn't even listened. He was bad to the bone. An out-and-out asshole.

He fisted his hands against the tile and let the hot water strip away his sins. A vivid image of Jules writhing on top of him took over his mind and he jerked that thought aside, only to replace it with Jules writhing beneath him. This was okay. This was just a return to how it was before. Fantasizing about Jules. Running his hands all over his body and pumping his dick to the image of her sweet lips, that pink flash of tongue, her breasts straining at the buttons of her blouse.

But now a raft of other images joined the mix. Jules laughing while he made love to her, that wicked smart mouth when she wanted to put him in his place, how soft her face got when he told her she could do anything. How she kissed away his pain and told him she loved him, every declaration ripping the walls to stony fragments. How crazy in love he was with her and how making a family with her and Evan— not just existing on the fringes—but a real family, was something he craved more than anything.

Shit, and now she would do that with someone else. He had broken her heart but she would recover. She had already started her rebound as she swaggered out the door. He wasn't worth the tears and she would find a doctor or fireman or rug salesman who could keep her safe. New guy would never love her as much as Tad did but it would be a safe love, a lasting love.

Pity he felt heartsick about it.

Ten minutes later, he headed downstairs to eat leftover pizza and something caught his eye. No, it...it couldn't be.

Vivi's cookbook lay on the hallway table, looking as weathered as his heart. The string holding it together was frayed, the pages dog-eared and yellowing. The last time he had seen it in Jules's kitchen, its presence had buoyed him into thinking he had a chance with her. Look how that turned out.

He took it in his hand and contemplated the ceiling, waiting to be struck down for his audacity.

"I've fucked up big time, Vivi."

Nothing, just a small electric fizz through his blood. He sniffed the pages...vanilla and cloves and Mom. His knees were close to buckling, so he lowered his body to the bottom rung of the stair and stared at it a while. Turned it over. Stared some more.

A piece of paper fell out, folded over to make a card. On the front, a child's drawing captured Mommy, Daddy, and Baby makes three.

The oh-so-fertile Simon St. James.

With trembling fingers, he pulled apart the paper's edges. Inside was a note.

He read it and broke into laughter, a long cathartic burst that loosened something in his chest. His black, iced-over heart perhaps. This woman of his had done a number on him all right.

Don't mess with your best friend. The words should be tattooed on his forehead because messing with her had messed them both up good. After a moment, he turned his attention back to the cookbook and began to read.

* * *

Gilt-edged sconces hung beneath old-world imitation moldings in the lobby of the Peninsula hotel on Michigan Avenue. Jules had been here once before for high tea after a brutal shopping slog with the girls. They'd made fun of Cara's pretensions while poor Cara rolled her eyes patiently and commented that they didn't deserve nice things.

Simon sat at the bar, and she took a moment to watch him covertly, checking her body for signs of treachery. None surfaced but that didn't mean they weren't there, waiting to strike.

He turned as she approached. "Hullo, Jules. You look well. In all the craziness of the other day, I never got a chance to say that."

She waited for her body to react with pleasure to that, but nothing happened. At long last, immunity had kicked in.

"Thanks." She took a seat, drying her humid hands and smoothing her floral print dress as she went.

"Can I get you a drink?"

She glanced at the wine by the glass menu, making her connections. "A glass of Chablis," she told the bartender.

Is it Chardonnay?

No, Tad had lied with that killer smile.

She missed him so much.

"Looks like things have changed since I saw you last." Simon gave her one of his thoughtful looks. Once she had caught him practicing it in the mirror, and now she wondered how she had ever let her guard down for this.

"Yep, lots of changes. I'm a real, live girl."

"That quick lip of yours hasn't changed, though." He grimaced, cranking up regretful. "I'm sorry. I'm glad you came. I can only assume that because you're here *sans* your attack dogs, that we might be able to come to an arrangement."

"Evan has to live with me and I'm not moving back to London."

He didn't argue. "I understand that. I just want to be part of his life, Jules. You don't know what it's like to be cut out."

She did, but she wasn't going to lay out her tale of woe. Today, she'd let Simon have his day basking in the sun of self-pity. The bartender set her Chablis down before her, beads of condensation already forming on the glass's surface like fat tears ready to fall. The tasting ritual gave her the time she needed. *Swirl, sniff, savor.* Ditzy Bella was right. Fresh was a good word for it.

"So what happened with your wife?"

"It's always been..." He waved a hand, filling in some blank in his mind. "She has a lot of passion. Hungarians are known for it."

She couldn't help her smirk. "So she clocked you good, then?"

Those arctic blue eyes narrowed. "I'm not blameless. I'm sorry you felt you couldn't tell me about Evan. I realize now that you wanted to but circumstances overtook us."

She stared at him long and hard until he dropped his gaze in embarrassment. "All right, you wanted to tell me but I didn't let you."

While the honesty was flowing, it was time to do her part and pull on her big girl panties. "If I'd had any guts, I would have insisted you know but I wasn't as strong then as I am now. It was easier to run."

"It always is." A glimmer of recognition passed between them. She tried to resent it but couldn't summon the energy. Anyway, she had come here to make peace.

"I'm sorry for keeping him from you. I was filled with so much pain when you threw me away. Hurting you—even though you might never know how much—was the only weapon I had."

Powerless people grasp at any chance to feel in control. Powerless people are often the most dangerous people of all.

"Thanks, Jules. You don't know how much this means to me." Emotion pulled at his mouth and he rubbed it away with a shaky hand. There had been too much wrong already. Today it ended.

She took out her phone and dialed up one of the photo albums of her little ball of sun. The center of her world.

"Prepare to be bored out of your mind."

* * *

The blaring music from Sarriette's kitchen clued her in that now might actually be a good time to talk to Jack. Usually, her brother played dictator deejay in his kitchen, but The Undertones' "Teenage Kicks" meant Shane was likely in charge of the iPod—and Jack was in a pliable enough mood to allow it.

Every little bit would help.

"Hiya," she said loudly so she could be heard above the din of Fergal Sharkey and the clanging of a busy kitchen. The crew was getting ready for family meal, the sit-down dinner that brought the cooks and servers together before service. Jack looked up from a stockpot of something fragrant and grinned broadly.

"Hey, baby girl. Come to see how a real kitchen works?"

Shane left off kneading some dough at the pastry station to hug her. He worked at Sarriette the days he wasn't baking drop-dead gorgeous creations for DeLuca Doyle Special Events.

"You're getting flour all over my clothes, you Irish clod."

He continued to rub powdered hands in circles on her back. "It's how pastry chefs show affection, sis."

Her heart cranked a couple of extra beats at the endearment. Shane had never called her that before.

Jack sauntered over, wiping his hands dry on a towel. "Everything okay, love?"

"I was hoping I could have a word with you. With both of you."

The boys shared a concerned glance.

"It's good news. Well, you might not see it that way, but I think it is."

"Now you've really got me worried," Jack said. He tossed off an order to one of his team to keep an eye on the bouillabaisse and jerked a chin in the direction of the dining room. "Let's have a seat."

Once they had settled in, she told them about her meeting with Simon. To keep it all above board, they had decided to set up a family custody agreement. Jules would visit London twice a year and Simon could come whenever he wanted as long as he gave sufficient notice. There would be Skyping and regular updates as well as discussion about the important decisions: schooling, child support, health care. It would take some time to ease into a routine but she was confident they could do it and the support of the men in front of her would be crucial.

Silence reigned for a few moments after her explanation.

"I wish you had come to us about this first, Juliet," Jack said sternly. *Juliet.* Uh oh.

"You would have tried to browbeat me into submission, Jack. I needed to make this decision myself."

"Did Tad help?" His disgust was so palpable it felt like another person at the table.

"Jack, hear her out," Shane said, ever the voice of reason. In the past year, he had umpired several brouhahas between the two of them.

"I haven't spoken to Tad about this but he did help me realize that this was my decision and mine alone. In the past, I've never been good at that. It was always easier *not* to make a decision, let events act on me instead of the other way around. With my reading, I covered it up instead of taking control and asking for help. Even with Simon, I didn't make a decision to be in a relationship, I just let it happen. Getting pregnant with Evan was the first time I had to face the consequences of my actions and act for my future and the future of my child."

She reached for Jack's hand and squeezed it.

"For the future of us, Jack. But in coming here to Chicago, I was running away from what I'd done and I risked falling into that pattern again, of letting other people decide the big stuff. Moving into my own place, deciding to date, getting a job—these are all ways I've taken control of my life these last few months."

Falling in love with Tad was part of that, too. She had lowered the fence around her heart and let Tad in, and though it had spiraled out of control quickly, she had no regrets, only precious memories.

Jack squeezed her hand back. "This is what you want? Simon to be in Evan's life?"

She shrugged. "Not really, but I have to take responsibility for what happened, Jack. I had unprotected sex with an unreliable guy and had a baby. That baby has a father with rights." She divided a look between her brothers. "If it had happened to either of you, how would you feel if Tony went all Vito Corleone and ran you out of town?"

"You know she's right," Shane said out of the corner of his mouth.

"Of course I know that," Jack snapped. "I just hate that she is."

"Shane, you're my witness. Jack just said I'm right."

On Jack's grunt, Shane threw back his head and laughed. "Wouldn't have believed it if I hadn't heard it with my own ears. Next, he'll be saying you can date whomever you want." Shane gave her a conspiratorial wink.

"Hold your horses, Shane. I'm just getting used to my baby sister acting more maturely than me." Jack leaned in and kissed her forehead. "I'm not going to be nice to Saint James, Jules. You might be an adult capable of making your own decisions but there's a code here and he broke it. I definitely won't be extending an invitation for him to join us on the family vacay to Tuscany."

"Tuscany, bro?" Shane's face lit up. "Hypothetical or for real?"

"I'm looking into it," Jack said with a grin. "Thought we should buy a villa for the girls."

"Suh-weet."

They high-fived each other while Jules looked on indulgently. How lucky was she to have such cool elders in her corner?

"Now, as for the dating," Jack said, directing his hard fraternal gaze back at her. "Sweetheart, no one's good enough for you but if you find someone who makes you happy and he's not a complete pillock, then I suppose I'll have to get on board."

She ducked her head to look under the table, then picked up a frosted glass candle holder and turned it over. "What have you done with my brother?"

He chuckled. "Look, you're an adult and you have to make your own way. You were always an amazing girl, but since you've come to Chicago I've watched you grow into an amazing mother and woman. And I know you hate how in touch I am with my feminine side"—he slid a withering glance at Shane who had laugh-snorted at that—"but I'm not going to apologize for loving the crap out of my sister. And loving you means having to respect that you might be able to make your own decisions. In all things."

She swallowed past a lump as large as a side of beef in her throat. "So you're not going to go all Cro-Mag when I bring home the ex-con with a latex fetish and mommy issues?"

Her brother slid a dark look to Shane, then wheeled it back to her.

"You *would* do that to piss me off, you cheeky mare."

The sound of their laughter covered her too-fast heartbeat.

Shane raised an astute eyebrow. "What about Tad? Isn't he the guy you want to bring home, Jules?"

She hoped her swallow didn't sound as loud as it felt in her throat. True, the only guy she wanted to bring home was the one who was the very definition of home. He had been since the moment she stepped into the kitchen at DeLuca's Ristorante and made the first decision to change her life for the better.

With Tad, she had found a soul connection that should have been strong enough to break free of all that held them back. But sometimes we come to enjoy the cozy confines of the cages we've spent so long building. Tad's faith in her had given her wings; she only wished he could let her do the same for him.

"Tad and I aren't going to work out. We're better as friends."

Concern furrowed Jack's brow. "Did he hurt you, Jules?"

"No," she lied. "He just hurt himself."

CHAPTER TWENTY-ONE

*"At the table with good friends and
family you do not become old."*

—Italian proverb

Tad pulled up outside Casa DeLuca on the Harley, his stomach rumbling with what he wished was hunger but what was more likely a case of sour grapes. Lili had warned him but he had to see for himself.

Quietly, he let himself in the front door and made for the kitchen, but instead of heading outside, he watched the gathering around the big picnic table through the window that faced the backyard. They had a full house today, all the usual suspects and one special guest.

Simon St. Fucking James.

He was one of a cozy pair of bookends with Jules on the other side and Evan in the middle. The wily little prick said something over Evan's head and her soft, musical laugh wafted over the unseasonably warm May breeze through the open window. Tad felt it like a chef's knife to his heart.

Demon threw his dino-giraffe on the ground and Jules

stood up to retrieve it, giving him the full picture. She had
pulled her hair into a top knot like you might see on a dolled-
up poodle. Her oversized tee hung off one perfectly round
shoulder, a streak of something pea-green—probably peas—
cutting a path across one breast. Peeking below the shirt's
hem were the white ravels of cut-off denim shorts, frayed
over her creamy thighs. The whole image should have been
fairly nondescript, but in Tad's eyes, she was so fucking
beautiful.

He lifted his hand in a wave but Evan chose that moment
to screech for the damn toy and she turned back to the table
without seeing his greeting. For the briefest moment, he
questioned if he was even here. He felt oddly insubstantial,
strangely transparent. Talk and chatter continued, all that vi-
tality moving on and around him. His life for the last ten
years had been like this—an ebb and flow, where he would
sometimes pull up to the shore only to have his progress
ripped from under him by the greedy surf.

Simon now bounced Evan on his knee, making the kid
giggle while Jules looked on indulgently. Tad recognized
that look. She was happy—cautiously so, but happy all the
same. They had created a bundle of life together, and no matter the guy's sins, he was still Evan's father. An unbreakable
bond of blood and genetics. And Tad was still his parents'
son.

Doing the right thing had never felt so wrong.

Frankie bustled in, barely looking at him, and wrenched
the fridge door open. She pulled out a large ceramic bowl of
zabaglione.

She pushed a plate of washed strawberries toward him
with a knife. It was a move she tried every now and then,
as if his hands would start chopping involuntarily, somehow
possessed by muscle memory. Every time she did it, he ig-

nored it, and every time he did that, she sighed deeply like the Italian mama she was.

"How is business?"

He curled his hand around the butt of the chef's knife and started to bisect the ruby-pink fruit. *Watch your fingers, Taddeo.*

"The *Tasty Chicago* review is going to be bad but we'll survive it."

She nodded her understanding. As the wife of a restaurateur, she'd suffered her fair share of poor reviews over the years. Nothing was so bad they couldn't bounce back from it.

"How did you spend the day?"

He focused on his knife work. *Be one with the knife.* It kept him from shaking.

"The usual." *Got wasted, screwed the girl he was crazy about, broke her heart.*

"Ten years is a long time, Taddeo."

Common sense acknowledged that but in his heart, ten years still felt like ten minutes. Every detail was as sharp now as the day he lived it. His thumping head, the hard bench in the cell, the unyielding expression on Tony's face when Tad stepped into that interview room at the CPD Third District after a dreamless night.

For one brief glittering moment while he made pasta with his beautiful girl, he had thought he might not need to go on that bender this year. Something—or someone—would be here to distract him. Keep him sane. The dead part of him flickered to life every time he saw Jules and Evan, though it had no right to get so excited.

"I hear you helped Jules through this business with Evan's father."

Through the window, Jules and Simon were focused on their son and at that moment they chose to share the con-

nection with one of those Hallmark eye-locks that seemed
to spark the air around them. *Look at what we have created.*
Envy formed a rock in his stomach, a lump of green desire
that threatened to consume everything around it.

He turned to find Frankie looking at him curiously, perhaps wondering why he would do something so clearly
against his self-interest.

"She lets Jack push her around. He's Evan's family and
that's important."

"Yes, it is. But that man will never love Evan as much as
we do."

Something crumbled inside his chest, probably one of
those stupid fucking bricks Tad the engineer had become so
adept at building. Next thing he knew, his feet had moved his
body out back to stand behind St. James. The conversation
petered out as awareness of Tad's presence stole across the
group.

Jules looked up at him, her sparkling eyes big as the platters on the table. He had no idea if his argument had helped
her come to this decision but one look was enough to know
she didn't hate him. He held on to that while he waited. *One,
two...*

St. James turned around and arched a supercilious eyebrow. He thrust out his hand.

"Tad, isn't it? We haven't met officially. Simon Saint
James."

Tad ignored the hand. Sure it was a dick move, which was
okay because right this minute, Tad DeLuca was the biggest
dick who ever lived.

"I'd like a word with you in private."

He could feel the stares of his family like a nasty kitchen
burn, particularly Tony, whose expression registered concern. Shane shook his head slightly in warning while Jack's

eyes narrowed to slits. Ignoring them, he turned and walked to the gable of the house and waited.

Thirty seconds passed before St. James rounded the corner.

"How can I help you?" he asked, his nervousness not quite covered by that swanky accent.

"By not fucking up."

"I don't plan to. This means a lot to me."

Tad scanned Simon's face for signs of insincerity and came up empty. No matter, the road to hell and all that.

"Jules is part of this family and we'll protect her and Evan against all comers. You'll get to do the father thing, but Evan's going to grow up a DeLuca."

A bomb of emotion went off in his chest, blowing those bricks to kingdom come. *Evan would grow up a DeLuca.* He meant that Evan was a part of *la famiglia,* but Tad wanted so much more than that. He wanted Jules and Evan to have *his—Tad's—*name.

"Hold up there, tough guy," Simon said, his hands raised in mock defense. "I get that you Italians are a clannish bunch but there's no need to get shirty. As long as I get to see my son, we'll get along just dandy."

The urge to punch this idiot took root in his core, but Tad never lost his temper. Years ago, he had learned to control his anger because the one time he had whaled on a guy had set in motion a chain of events that ended with his parents' lying six feet under. But if ever he was ready to pound a guy into the wall, it was now. How did a douche like this get to have a beautiful kid like Evan? Where was the justice in that?

With the last remaining threads of his control straining to breaking point, Tad willed his body and voice to calm. He had a good four inches on this guy. Time to use it.

He stepped in close. "You'll get to see him. You'll get

to call him son. You'll get to hear him say 'Daddy.' But if I hear of one single instance of you forgetting to call when you should, or canceling that visit on his birthday at the last minute, or doing a single thing to piss off my girl, you'd better hope you're on good terms with the saint in your stupid fucking ass name because you'll need him when I get through with you. We clear?"

St. James swallowed and nodded.

"Everything all right here?"

Over St. James's shoulder, Tad locked eyes with Jack.

St. James moved aside and divided a look between them. "No problem. Just getting acquainted." His superior smile looked like it might cause him an injury. "I should get back to my son."

Got it. You have the luckiest sperm on the planet. Tad watched his retreat, rage nuking every cell.

"You need to hit something?" Jack asked.

"Will you hold still or should I get Shane out here?"

Jack sighed. "Perhaps I was a little hasty when I spoke the other day. I don't like what's happening here but I understand now that you had Jules's best interests at heart."

"Always."

A flicker of understanding ignited between them that felt like the beginnings of mutual respect. Nice, but Jack's quasi-acceptance didn't change a thing between Tad and Jules. Her interests would be best served if he stayed the hell away from her.

The pause stretched from uncomfortable to...well, comfortable, if he was being honest.

"Time to eat," Jack said, evidently trying to be the bigger person here.

"I'm not hungry," Tad said, turning away to the street. He wasn't sure he'd ever be hungry again.

* * *

"How come Jack's not here getting his hands dirty?"

Using the heel of his work boot, Tad pushed the pitch fork into the densely packed earth to its hilt. Once secured in the ground, he joined Shane on the patio. His friend passed him a cold one and took a long slug from the bottle in his own hand.

"Don't want to mess up Lord Kilroy's lily white hands. You know how he feels about anyone contaminating the air he breathes." When Shane raised a disapproving eyebrow, Tad went on. "Look, I know he's your brother but he's not my favorite person right now, so he doesn't get invited to partake in the fun."

He gestured to the "fun" with a wave. The yard hadn't improved much since he'd started tearing it apart three days ago. Rolled up grass sod lay to the side, the herb and vegetable garden was at best "distressed," and the earth was in various stages of upturn like the *Caddyshack* gopher had paid a visit. He could have hired people to do it but the work's weight was about the only thing keeping him from smashing somebody's face in.

"I'm touched you thought of me when you needed free labor," Shane mumbled.

"There's beer and pizza in it for you. Besides, I know you can't stay long with Cara needing you to keep her satisfied every minute of the day."

Shane gave a sly smile. "Can I help it if my hot wife can't keep her hands off me?" He took a long draught and leaned his elbows on his knees. "So the beef between you and Jack. Still Jules, I assume?"

"He's just trying to protect her," Tad said, resigned. He lowered himself to the bleach-weathered Adirondack chair and crossed an ankle over his knee.

"Yup, because she really needs protecting. Are you still going with the not-good-enough-for-her play? Or have you moved on to some other crappy excuse? Lean back there and tell me all about it."

Tad groaned. "You missed your calling, Irish. Wasted making cakes. Absolutely wasted."

"I would have thought this business with Evan's father would have focused you. Made you see what you've been missing."

Ignoring him, Tad picked at the label on his beer bottle.

"Or the fact that she started dating. Sure, that woke you up, didn't it? Made you realize you're crazy about her?"

The label tore. He used to be able to get it off in one smooth peel.

"The fuck, man." A combination of awe and disgust thickened Shane's voice.

Tad dragged his eyes up from the bottle, knowing they would reveal everything he had been hiding for two long and painful years, and no longer caring.

Shane's glare was incredulous. "You've been in love with Jules from the beginning."

The final brick in that fortress around his heart fell away. Not admitting it, even to himself, was another one of those brilliant strategies he had for keeping sane. It was up there with avoiding kitchens and liking his women loose and drinking himself into a stupor once a year. Absolutely brilliant.

"Tad, I'm not asking you, I'm telling you that you'd better come clean or I'm calling Cara and Lili in to get it done."

Gripping the bottle tighter, Tad drew a deep breath to fuel what he had to say next.

"It was the night Jack was taping his show at DeLuca's. She waltzed in like the world owed her a living, all bravado and hair and attitude. I turned to Lili and asked who the shit was that and next thing I knew this blond spitfire was marching into the kitchen on a mission. The second I saw her, I knew that was it for me."

Colpo di fulmine. The thunderbolt had struck him to his knees.

"Two minutes later, she announces she's pregnant to Jack and the crew, but for that two minutes, Shane..."

He paused, his heart too full with the emotion of it. That perfect 120 seconds when he watched her take that first step to becoming so strong. He had known she was special then and every second with her since confirmed it—and confirmed he wasn't worthy.

"For that two minutes, everything was stripped away and all that was left was possibility." *And hope.* "But then, boom, she's Jack's sister, and boom, she's pregnant, and boom, she needs a friend, not some horn dog who wanted in her pants."

Shane studied his beer, then pointed it at Tad for emphasis. "And boom, you're still not doing anything about it. You are such a pussy."

Should have known better than to expect a smidge of sympathy from his so-called friend. The bubble of rage in his chest threatened to rise up and choke his throat.

"This from the guy who knew Jack Kilroy was his brother for twelve years before he decided to show his smug-as-all-get-out, pointy-ass, Irish face."

That just got Tad a shake of that smug-as-all-get-out, pointy-ass, Irish head.

"We're not talking about me and my now-perfect life. We're figuring out how a guy who has been in love with a woman since the first day he laid eyes on her still can't get his head out of his Italian arse and work it out. But if you want to go there, be my guest. I let a million things get in the way of connecting with Jack. I built up the barriers in my head—he didn't want to know, he hated our father so he was going to hate me, he was doing just fine without another hanger-on. Etcetera, etcetera. All my life, I wanted a family. Jack, Cara, you guys. I wasted a shitload of time and if I could do it differently, I'd have called Jack the day I found out he was my brother and told him I wanted to see him."

Tad downed his beer, praying for the cool liquid to take the edge off. Shane had excellent reasons for not reaching out to Jack sooner, the primary one being their violent, abusive father who'd beat Shane senseless when he was a kid. Feeling worthless is usually a perfectly adequate reason not to take the next step.

"Well, it all worked out in the end. You got Cara and Jack and soon, you'll have your kids. And you got a cool cousin-in-law in the form of Yours Truly." The guy had nothing to complain about.

They both took long draughts of their beers, the swallows cool and satisfying in the muggy heat.

"Swing set would look nice over there," Shane said after an extended beat.

"Real subtle, asshole."

Shane laughed and pulled out his buzzing phone. "Hey, gorgeous. What's up?" His expression turned to granite as he listened to whatever Cara was saying. "I'll be right there."

He bolted out of his seat. "Come on, Cara's at the hospital."

* * *

Thwack.

Tad turned the corner on his way to the emergency room waiting area and found his uncle dealing a deathblow to an uncooperative vending machine.

"How's Cara?" Shane had jumped out of the car and raced inside while Tad parked.

"No news yet. Shane is with her now."

Thwack.

"What happened?"

"She was meeting with a client, the big one who is the son of the mayor, when she started getting cramps. Of course, she carried on with the meeting. When she left, she headed here and then called Shane."

"Jesus." He knew Cara was a workaholic and the consummate professional but that took the cake. Assuming she made it out of this okay, Shane was going to kill her.

Tony shook his head disapprovingly. "Now we must wait and see."

Wait and see. Well, that just blows.

"Need some help?" he asked, nodding to the candy bar that wouldn't budge.

"It is hanging on the edge right there." Tony's glare was usually quite persuasive but the recalcitrant KitKat gamely withstood Il Duce's pressure.

"You don't eat candy. What's going on?"

"Your aunt is a sugar fiend." His uncle shrugged in that lazy Continental way of his. "Not unlike your father. He had quite the sweet tooth."

Tad felt a smile tugging at his lips. "Junior Mints were his weakness. He said it was the best thing about going to the movies."

A couple of moments ticked by, not uncomfortably. Tad could feel a space opening up in the air around him, a welcoming gap he could step through to a place where everything wasn't quite so skewed.

"I went to the cemetery last week," Tony said. "There were fresh white roses. Your mother's favorite."

Tad had driven out there the day after he sobered up. Rosehill Cemetery was just a few miles as the crow flies, but he had never seen the appeal in fixating on a slash of earth and a lump of stone. Better to internalize the pain and fixate on their memory.

"I hadn't been there since the funeral," Tad said. "Seemed it was time."

"That day was hard for everyone." Tony met Tad's gaze, his blue eyes tinged with regret and distant memory. "I didn't make it easier."

"Easy would have been worse. I needed it to be hard."

The truth of that carved out a cavity in his chest. He had needed it to be hard because that was the only way he could get through it. Tony's disapprobation had hurt but it had worked to keep his guilt tangible, just the way Tad liked it.

His uncle let go of a world-weary sigh. Tad would have sworn the old man was carrying Jesus's cross on the way to Calvary.

"I was never so glad as the day Cara called to tell me you had come to visit her in New York after all that time away. I should have come to see you but I thought you would not want people to crowd you."

This was the first he'd heard that Cara had called home or that Tony had known. Though to be fair, after numbing his brain dead with drugs, drink, and pussy halfway around the world, he didn't remember much from that trip.

"I was only there a couple of days before heading out to Italy. Seeing you might have sent me back to Asia." Instantly he regretted his flippancy. "Sorry, bad joke."

Tony looked thoughtful. "I should have apologized to you properly for how I acted. Two years later you were home, back where you belonged, working at DeLuca's. Not in the kitchen like I hoped, but I expected that would come. I thought that was enough. We have never needed a lot of words."

"I would have liked to hear them all the same," Tad said around the lump in his throat. "I didn't drive the car or run that light but I'm the reason they were out that night. I know what I did was wrong but damn, I needed you to tell me that, even as fucked up as I was, you still saw me as family. As a DeLuca."

Tony's eyes flashed. "That has never been in question. It was an accident. I was wrong to react the way I did and even more wrong not to put things straight between us."

Tad fought to get a leash on his emotions. *Thwack.* He gave the vending machine a slap, drawing a curious look from some punk ass kid off in the corner.

"Taddeo, tell me you have not imagined you were not a part of this family…" He trailed off, focusing once more on that freakin' KitKat bar. Seemed it was much easier for them both to look elsewhere.

"I don't know. I hated myself, Tony, and maybe it was easier for me to think you were still bitter. Every time you looked at me, I saw Dad. I saw his disappointment, I saw his dreams for me go up in flames and the life he wouldn't have. And every time I looked at you, I remembered that I was closer to you than my own father and that just made me feel a different level of guilt. In the kitchen, you and Vivi taught me everything, and when you barely spoke to me when I came home, it cracked me in half."

Aw, crap, the old man looked like he was going to cry and if he lost it, Tad knew he might not be far behind. It had been a shitty week.

Tony drew a deep breath that seemed to stave off the threatened waterworks. "You had changed, Taddeo. You were so closed off and I thought you needed more time.

When I asked you to cook with me, you refused. One year turned into two and…" He waved his hand to fill in the rest.

Something loosened in Tad's chest, a rigidity turning wobbly and warm. Could he really have forgotten that Tony made overtures of peace all those years ago? Every time Tony had spoken to him, Tad had braced himself for a lecture, built a wall to shut it out before it found traction. He didn't want to cook and whenever Tony mentioned it, Tad took it as a veiled criticism of Tad's choices. Just another example of letting down Vivi.

Memory could be selectively cruel, especially when you're so determined to play the martyr. Vivi had always told him he wanted too deeply, felt too acutely, loved too much. Of course he was going to give this martyr business 110 percent.

Your heart may break many times, Taddeo, but when you find the right one… it will be perfetto.

Tad had let his pain blind him to Tony's peace offerings over the years. Neither of them were good with words.

"Tony, I'm sorry."

His uncle looked horrified. "Taddeo, you have nothing to be—"

"Not about the accident. I can't carry that weight anymore, but I am sorry about how it hardened me. About how I let it take over and used it to push people away. Especially you."

Tony's lips turned up in the barest smile. "We are always here for you, Taddeo. This family doesn't always tell each other these things but there is no shortage of love." He patted Tad's arm awkwardly.

Tad's throat was too thick with emotion to respond. A few moments passed. The KitKat still teetered on the edge.

"Now that we are on better terms," Tony continued after

a minute spent staring at the vending machine, "I feel I can ask you this."

"Shoot," Tad croaked.

"Do you have a dollar to spare? It seems I will have to pay again for this chocolate bar."

Good one, Tony. Tad felt as though an elephant had taken a step off his chest and oxygen was now rushing to make his anemic blood strong. Filling in all those transparent gaps, making him solid again.

"There you are," he heard Lili's soft voice behind him.

"How is she?" Tony barked.

"She's okay. It was Braxton Hicks contractions but they wanted to be sure, hence the delay. She's already asking for her chocolate fountains binder. Shane's trying to decide how much rope he's going to need to keep her on bed rest."

Tad sighed. The women in this family tended to have this effect, even the ones who were related by marriage.

"*Grazie de Dio.*" Tony grasped Tad's arm in a friendly way, his relief palpable, then gave him the eyebrow. "Now you must take care of this business with Julietta."

Merda, that didn't take long.

Lili folded her arms and stared at him, using less of the DeLuca stink eye and more...Christ Almighty, was that compassion?

"You okay? You didn't answer any of my calls or texts. Or the door."

"Yeah, I'm fine. I just needed some time."

"You know I love you, right?" She sniffed, as if that could somehow temper the sudden bout of schmaltz. "I don't tell you but you've always been there for me. In high school when I had it rough, and then again with all that online stuff when I met Jack, you've always been like a brother. I don't think you realize how much I care about you. How much we all do."

"Where the hell is this coming from?" he snapped, instantly regretting it because he knew everyone was feeling raw.

She stroked his forearm, easing him out of his ill humor. "We need to tell each other these things more. Maybe Jack's sensitivity is rubbing off me."

He laughed nervously. Lili often joked that Jack, for all his stiff upper lip Britishness, was more Italian than the entire DeLuca clan put together. But that wasn't strictly true. Vivi had been emotional, and Tad used to be like that as well. These days, he felt like a walking open wound and a certain green-eyed girl was the only one with the right-sized suture kit.

"I love you, too," he said gruffly.

"Then you're probably not going to like what I have to say next." She peered up at him, her shining blue eyes determined. "You're, in my husband's vernacular, acting like a total arse. I know you love her."

"Language, Liliana," Tony warned.

"Sorry, Dad."

"Did you guys have a freaking intervention without me?" Her brow furrowed. "What?"

"Nothing." Tad split his gaze between them and inhaled deeply. "I messed up with Jules. Things got hard and I messed up."

Tony considered him. "No one said love was easy. When your aunt had cancer, it was a difficult time for this family, but loving her during that time was never hard. The hard part is the times she will not rest when I ask her to or she refuses to add the extra spoonful of Marsala to the *zabaglione* or acknowledge that I am right when it is clear as day."

Lili laughed. "So she's hard to love when she won't co-operate with you."

"No, I am the one who's hard to love. The DeLuca men never know what is best for them but we must learn from our women."

"Amen," Lili said.

Tad thought back to Jules's determined words as she told him she was the best thing to happen to him. Undoubtedly, she would move on and get over him but as every single one of his female relatives was fond of telling him, men were the weaker sex.

Tad didn't have that kind of strength. He would never get over her.

He sure as hell didn't want to and he sure as hell didn't plan to. Jules was the kind of woman you worshipped on your knees, you walked over burning coals to get to, you went to hell and back for. He had been there and he didn't like the décor. Clawing back his life needed a goal. Not the bar, not cooking, not even that jungle in his backyard.

Just Jules.

If he had her and Evan, then he just might make it.

CHAPTER TWENTY-TWO

*Love is like a shadow—no matter how
hard you try to escape, it will chase you.*

—Italian proverb

Jules's heart thudded wildly as she knocked on the front door of DeLuca's Ristorante. It was usually closed on Monday, but today was the very special occasion of Tony and Frankie's anniversary dinner party, and she was going to help with the decorations. And try not to collapse in a heap around Tad.

The door crept open to reveal Lili, who dragged her inside with shifty looks left and right.

"Can't be too careful."

"Frankie knows already. You can't keep anything from her."

Lili smiled, and Jules's heart gave a solid kick to her ribs at how that smile reminded her of Tad.

"So true. She always knew when I'd been sneaking out as a young 'un. Never missed a trick. But I'm pretty sure Dad's still in the dark."

Jules took another couple of steps inside and was immediately transported. DeLuca's was a wonderfully appointed restaurant with a long cherrywood bar and a frescoed ceiling, but today it was like something out of an old-world fairy tale. Cara had spun her magic with indoor landscaping, working to bring a vineyard vibe indoors, and transformed it into a re-creation of the spot where Tony and Francesca had said their original vows in a joint union with Tad's parents. Empty wine casks, similar to the ones at Vivi's, framed the space while twinkling fairy lights sparkled overhead, shining off the sky-cloud ceiling. A couple of working casks had been set up at one end of the bar, with spigots at the ready to satisfy the influx of DeLuca relatives now waiting at their hotels for the signal to swarm.

It took a moment to realize that Lili was speaking. "So, are you okay? I know it's been a rough few days. Sometimes I just want to shake that cousin of mine."

"The queue forms right here." Jules pinned on a smile, aiming to put her sister-in-law at ease. This was exactly what she had wanted to avoid, the domino effect that failing with Tad would have on the rest of the family. "I knew the risks going in and while it sucks to be me this minute, it won't always."

Her heart felt like a piece of pulverized meat, but eventually she would heal. If she had learned anything over the last two years, it was that resilience suited her.

Cara came bustling out and Jules took a moment's satisfaction in the fact that she waddled. *About time.* Two days ago she was terrifying the bejesus out of her family with her hospital visit. Now she glared at one of her staff who was hanging a banner and generally making a hash of it. Just as she parted her lips to unleash, Shane emerged from the kitchen, pushing a humungous cake on a rolling cart.

"LT, shut that gorgeous mouth down now," he said before Cara could get a word out. "You heard what the doctor said about blood pressure."

Cara growled and rolled her eyes at Jules. "The only risk to my blood pressure is your fussing, Shane Doyle."

Shane stroked her cheek. "Just indulge me. Give our kids a chance to grow some hair on their heads before we meet them."

Cara visibly relaxed under his touch. Satisfied his words had made an impact, Shane turned to Jules.

"Hey, sis, Jack's looking for you. He's in the kitchen."

As much fun as Jules had had running the show at Vivi's during Derry's medical emergency, she knew she didn't want to work in a busy restaurant kitchen. As for what she wanted to do...well, things were a little topsy-turvy right now and she needed to refocus on her little boy. The last few weeks had been confusing for him and she hadn't been shepherding him through the changes very well. One day, she would get back to that goal of carving out her place but for now Evan was her heart—that was all she needed.

Good on ya, the girls whispered in her ear. They had been gentle with her lately.

Of course, they knew what was coming. Tonight, she had to sit at a table with the man she loved and pretend everything was hunky dory.

Could they go back to what they'd had?

Probably not.

Had it been worth it?

Damn straight.

Her confidence in that statement took a nosedive as soon as she walked into the DeLuca kitchen.

She had expected Jack, and there he was, owning the

space as he always did, but that's not where her covetous eyes fell.

Tad.

Tad was here in DeLuca's kitchen, wearing chef whites and testosterone, and making her world crash.

All. Over. Again.

Her brother spoke over his shoulder. "Hey, you're late."

"Your wife kept me gabbing," she said mechanically, her gaze focused on the knife that seemed to be a natural extension of Tad's hand. She coughed and, with great difficulty, turned to Jack. "What's going on?"

"Tad's in charge."

"He is?" Tad was cooking the meal that would celebrate one marriage and would plunge him into painful memories of another. Stranger still, he was working with Jack and the knives were still being used for their original purposes.

He turned and just the sight of him sent a sharp zing humming through her. It was a painful pleasure to run her eyes over all that beauty.

"You ready?" Tad asked her.

"For what?"

"His big fat grovel," Jack said, removing a pan from a burner.

"I don't think so," she said, unsure if she meant her reaction to whatever Tad was about to unload or the fact that her brother seemed intent on remaining as referee.

Tad tapped his knife in an insistent tattoo on the cutting board. "Jack, I need you to take your interfering, know-it-all, Limey ass out of this kitchen and give us some space."

Unfazed by Tad's bite, a relaxed smile came over her brother's face. He looked at her squarely. "Is this what you want?"

"Making my own decisions, remember?"

He held up his hands. "All right, all right. Got it." He kissed her cheek on the way out of the kitchen. "I'll be outside."

She swallowed into the silence, this wedge of awful, bruising space that stretched between them like a cavernous maw. She held on to it for a couple of moments while they assessed each other for...she didn't know what.

"How's Evan?" he asked.

"Fine. Sylvia's bringing him by later." She forced her lungs to cooperate. "Do you have something to say to me?"

He stared at her in a way that made her supremely uncomfortable. That stare coated every nerve and set up a high-frequency vibration through her body. Nervous as hell, she ran a finger over the nearest stainless steel counter. Still, he wouldn't speak.

"How come you're here? In the kitchen?"

"Today isn't just about Tony and Frankie."

It was also about Rafe and Vivi. She loved that he was facing it head on, but she pinned on her game face all the same.

"And it isn't just about my parents. It's about honoring who they were and making them proud and that means making a move forward. I don't think they'd be all that proud of how I've lived my life since they died. I think they'd be pretty pissed off at me."

Her heart turned over, revealing the soft, defenseless underside. "You were twisted up inside. It's hard to get untwisted if it suits you better to be that way."

He looked like he was mentally trying that on for size. A sly smile, directed more at himself than her, quirked his lips.

"Yeah, that's about it. You know, a very wise person once told me that I deserved to be happy. I didn't really know what that meant until a few weeks ago, when we went from friends to so much more. I thought I was too selfish to give myself to another person. To two people, you and Evan. This mistake I made came with its own accessories: a hair shirt, a bucket of mortar in my heart, a black cloud following me around. I let it take over and make decisions for me. I let it turn me into a selfish bastard. But no more."

Riveted by his words, all Jules could do was stare at him.

"Remember that night you told me not to fall in love with you?"

Tears pricked the backs of her eyelids. "Yes."

"Well, I didn't."

Her breath trapped in her lungs and she scrabbled for air. "Bully for you."

"I didn't fall in love with you then or the next day or the day after that."

Crikey, why ever did Jack think this guy could sell anything? "You have my admiration for holding out."

Those DeLuca electric blues trapped her in their beam. "Because I was already in love with you. I had been since the day I met you, maybe before I met you. Only with you, Jules, do I feel all these broken pieces of me fall into place."

Unwavering in his gaze, he walked toward her. Slow and purposeful, with no hesitation. Not wanting to feel at a disadvantage, she held her ground and looked him straight in the eye. New Jules, stronger than ever. But all that girl power went to the dogs the closer he got.

He loved her.

Well, she knew *that.* But any woman who told you she didn't need to hear her man say it out loud was a lousy, rotten liar.

Mere inches away, he burrowed in his pocket and took out a piece of paper. As he unfolded it, she realized what she was looking at. Shit on a shingle.

"Evan wrote that," she bit out pre-emptively.

"Liar."

She couldn't help her smile. It had been a long shot.

"You left this for me the last time you were at my house."

The words she had written came back to her in a jumbled haze. As soon as she saw how far gone he was that awful day, the silly note was forgotten.

He smoothed it out on the scuffed-up, stainless steel counter.

Jules + Evan miss Tad (ez too spel!!) + luv him vary much.

"My heart was breaking and you pulled this manipulative crap on me?" He turned the makeshift card over to reveal the rest of it.

I am not adove using my kid to get wot I want. Luv Jules.

Helpless to control her reaction, she let loose a laugh. It was pretty funny, misspellings and all, but she needed to be strong here. She needed to be sure.

"That was then," she said shakily, as if a week could have possibly changed one iota of her love for him.

"True, but let's go back a little further than that, shall we? How about the moment you marched into this restaurant and made your knocked-up announcement? Do you remember that, Jules? How it all started? Because I do. You stole the show and you've been stealing stuff ever since—my sleep, my peace of mind, my fucking heart." He grasped her hand and put it over his navel, then moved it dangerously low and close to her favorite Tad part. Yes, even above the forearms. She tried to pull away, but he held her fast. Emotion welled in her throat, choking and freeing at once.

"Here."

He drew her covered hand from the belt buckle higher over his abs.

"Here."

He dragged it flush to his warm chest, now vibrating with the *thumpety-thump* of his heart through his double-breasted chef jacket. His next words were a strangled whisper.

"And here."

Her throat burned. With her free hand, she swiped at the tears rolling down her cheeks.

"It's the Holy Trinity of how I feel about you. I want you, need you, love you. There will never be anyone else for me, Juliet Kilroy. The day my parents died, I thought that was the end of me but it wasn't. My heart went into stasis. Some kind of suspended animation waiting for you to jump-start it to life. I've wondered why I couldn't move on and the only possible conclusion is that it was waiting for you. This wonky heart of mine only works when you're in the room. It only beats when you're beside me. It only exists to love you."

The tears kept coming and so did his words, relentless in their assault on her heart.

"A week ago, you made me an offer. You said you'd help carry me through the pain. You assured me your heart was strong enough to beat for two. You promised to bring me back into this life. It was the kindest, sweetest, best offer I've ever had and I screwed up when I turned you down. I can't go another day without you. My heart needs what only you can give, so Jules, put me out of my misery and tell me I haven't ruined the best thing that's ever happened to me. Because it's always been you."

"Oh, Tad." She threaded her hand from his heart to cup his strong jaw. Shockingly, that rock-solid model of manliness quivered under her touch. "I've been waiting for you to see me."

"Jules, there's never been a moment I didn't see you. Never a moment I didn't want you. You're the—"

"Air I breathe?" she offered.

There it was. That outrageously sexy smile that killed mutiple brain cells every time. She might never recover from it.

She might never need to.

He went on. "You're the—"

"Blood to my heart?"

His lips twitched. "The sentence I haven't finished."

"The thought I haven't formed yet."

He kissed her softly, licking the tears that painted her lips. "Your lines are terrible."

"I know," she whispered around a sobby hitch in her throat. "Blimey, I know. What if we screw up?"

"What if we don't?" He touched his forehead to hers. "Jules, we crossed the line weeks ago, maybe months before that. We always knew it would be tough to go back."

"So that's your reasoning. It's easier to move forward than to go back?"

His smile was grimly beautiful. "Forward is never easier. It's terrifying. But I know that we already have an amazing foundation here. We're friends, we're family, we're very hot, attractive people. If we don't make a go of this, the terrorists win."

"You're barmy."

"I'm in love."

His warm, rich laugh reached inside her and unfurled every tight bud of pain and every fist of doubt. She couldn't speak or smile or move a muscle of her face while she worked on not breaking down completely.

At her silence, his laughter died and gravity took root on his handsome face. "Is it the women I've been with? Because I haven't...not since..."

Her neck felt all tingly, as if she were getting a premonition. "You haven't what?"

Raw emotion worked the muscles around his mouth. "That night you went cuckoo and jumped me changed everything. I haven't so much as copped a feel with another woman since."

Not until he placed a fingertip under her chin and pushed it closed did she realize that her jaw must have fallen slack.

"Say something, Jules. Don't fail me now."

Thought shards refused to bond. Tad hadn't touched another woman in the last year. *A year.* Every second she imagined him with someone else had just been more wasted energy. After a moment, she finally managed to put something together.

"Those three seconds of horror—it made you gay?"

He pursed his lips, his mouth working for a suitable response. *Smartass* or *brat* or something equally appropriate.

"It confirmed what I already knew. It made me yours."

Yours. With quite possibly the worst kiss in the history of seduction, she had somehow won this man. And here she thought he was the one rescuing her. Truth was they were saving each other and there was no one else she could imagine sharing her life with.

Make hers a bad boy.

She looped her arms around his neck and kissed him like there was no tomorrow—or like all her tomorrows would be with him. A blast of consuming, possessive heat to let him know just how crazy she was about him. *Crazy.* How had she ever hated that perfect word? When they finally parted, he looked as stunned as she felt.

"Oh, crap, we're really doing this, aren't we?" she husked out.

Tad's smile was as wicked as they come. "Yes, *mia bella.* We are."

Swinging big. Going all in. Living balls-out.

"I've got something else for you." He extracted another piece of paper from his pocket and handed it to her.

With shaky hands, she unfolded it. The logo for Green City Market topped the page followed by her name. The rest blurred through her tears.

"Is this what I think it is?"

He grinned. So, so sexy. "If you think it's an approval to get your own stand at Green City Market, then yes, it is what you think it is. You're going to sell all those amazing bruschettas and salsas and dips. We'll also offer them for sale at Vivi's and see about getting them into gourmet stores throughout the city. I have a few contacts in the food business, you know."

Her mind flailed at how much faith this man had in her abilities. From the beginning, that had never wavered. The faith in them had taken longer, but it was worth the wait.

"About time," Lili said, bounding in.

Following, Cara swiped at her eyes. Cara DeLuca Doyle was crying. Now Jules knew the apocalypse was truly upon them.

"Yeah, we were getting really tired of hooking you up with losers when the answer was staring you both right in the face," Cara said.

"The smug marrieds always know best," Tad said, shaking his head.

"Yes, we do," Cara confirmed. "And we also know that it's time to get this party underway or risk the wrath of DeLucas far and wide."

"We should leave you to it," Jules said, kissing her man. *Her man.* The words and the man tasted so right. Her chest felt full to exploding, like the gooey cheesey center of the perfect *arancini*. She didn't want to leave, not when they had just found each other, but she had to let him get on with it.

She pulled away but he held her close. Hmm, that was nice.

"Where do you think you're going?"

"I thought the chefs would like to get to work."

"Yes, they would. Maybe you should show her what she'll be wearing," Tad said to some point over her shoulder, a devilish smile shading his lips.

She turned to find Jack and Shane standing behind her.

"We got you something." Jack held up a chef's jacket covered in plastic. Above the breast, her name was embroidered in tight black stitching. More tears leaked down her face. This was too, too much.

Jack put an arm around her shoulders and kissed her temple. "There's no crying in cooking, baby girl."

"Nicely done, Jules," Shane said with a wink.

"I told him the jacket doesn't make the chef, *mia bella*, but I know you Brits," Tad said. "You're all about the pomp and circumstance." His gorgeous mouth curled up at the corner. "You ready to cook with us?"

Oh, yes.

* * *

By the time 1 a.m. rolled around, relatives and friends had been sent packing and only core revelers remained at DeLuca's Ristorante. The food—all recipes from Vivi's repertoire—had been a rousing success and now Tad was moonlighting in his other, but no less important job: holding a sleeping Evan in his arms. Every muscle was stiff as a board but he wouldn't swap that numbness for anything.

His eyes locked with Jules's again. All night they had been staring at each other in wide-eyed wonder, not only because they had finally found each other but also because they could now gawk without restraint. No more hiding; love in the open.

"Okay, more toasts," Cara said, raising her wineglass filled with water. "They say it's bad luck to toast with a water glass, but the DeLucas have always made their own luck. To Tony and Frankie, on thirty-five years. *Salute.*"

All clinked their wineglasses for that, except Lili and Jack who had lifted water glasses like Cara.

A fact that didn't go unnoticed by Jules. She shared a knowing glance with Tad, then looked back at her brother.

"Wait a second..." Everyone stared at Jack, who actually managed to look more smug than usual. Yes, it *was* possible.

"Why aren't you drinking? In fact, you haven't been drinking all night," Jules accused Jack.

Tad knew Lili had cut out alcohol while she tried to get pregnant, but for both of them to be sticking to *l'acqua* meant something very significant.

"Are you guys pregnant?" Cara blurted.

Jack and Lili shared one of their well-known hot looks mixed with something else. Lili's shrug did nothing to mitigate her beam. "It's sort of early to be announcing that kind of thing but..."

"Yes," Jack whispered, his voice laden with emotion. "I figured if Lili has to suffer without wine for the next eight months, I can do it with her."

Lili rolled her eyes. "As sweet as that is, I'd rather you drank so I can live off the secondhand residuals every time you kiss me."

Everyone swarmed on yet another happy couple.

"How far gone—"

"Give her some space—"

"I think Jack's going to faint—"

Francesca and Tony looked like they might explode with

joy. Well, his uncle had both eyebrows raised, which was his version of happiness till the end of time.

Jules hugged her brother. "So you took my advice. Lit some candles, threw Barry White on the decks, dug out the sex toys from the back of the closet..."

"Watch it, you cheeky mare."

"You're a brave man to go without alcohol for the entire pregnancy," Shane muttered around his wide grin. "I couldn't do it."

"Hey," Cara said, nudging him gently in the ribs. "You've been well-compensated during this particular pregnancy, Riverdance."

"Congratulations, Jack," Tad said, shaking his cousin-in-law's hand.

Jack nodded his thanks and another brick in that bridge they had been building fell into place. It would probably take a while to prove himself to Jules's big brother but he had all the time in the world.

After giving everyone a few moments to soak up the great news, Tad cleared his throat and stood, feeling taller than he had in some time. "So I'd like to say a few words."

Everyone groaned affectionately. A balled-up napkin was thrust from Shane's direction and landed on Tad's bread plate.

"I'll be short, I promise." He took a deep breath and glanced at his sister, Gina, who gave a short nod of encouragement. "Tonight, we celebrate Tony and Frankie but also Rafe and Vivi. A week ago was the anniversary of our parents' death. Ten years gone and ten years of wondering what might have been. I'll never stop missing them, but I know that wherever they are, they're probably proud of us and—"

"Wondering when you're going to give them grandbabies of their own," Sylvia finished to a chorus of laughter.

His gaze found his best friend, who looked as stunning as he'd ever seen her. Hair in a messy bunch-up, face happily shiny from her exertion in the kitchen, her new chef's jacket streaked with pesto. His at last and absolutely perfect.

"Think I should get my feet wet with this one first," he said with a brush of his lips across Demon's head. "Right now, I'd like to toast us all with a special wine I set aside a while back."

With Evan still curled into his shoulder, he reached to the sideboard behind him and grabbed the 2000 Chateau Pavie Bordeaux, given to him by his father all those years ago. The twinkling lights in the indoor trees caught the now dustless bottle just right, making it shine like a beacon.

Like a blessing.

"So, you may have heard that I've made the Top Ten Mixologists in Chicago list for two years running—"

"Show off," said Lili.

He grinned. "I have a thriving wine bar, an unreliable pizza oven, and the privilege of a terrible review from *Tasty Chicago*—"

"Effen critics," Shane piped up in solidarity.

"Thanks, man. And I'm a second-level sommelier, but for the life of me, I have never figured out how to open a bottle of wine with one hand." Putting down the precious cargo napping peacefully in his arms was not an option. "*Mia bella*, do you mind?"

Jules was already at his side with a corkscrew. "You better put those hot hands to work later, babe," she murmured so only he could hear.

That would not be a problem.

Within five seconds, his nimble-fingered protégé had that bottle uncorked and ready for pouring. Glasses magically appeared and he filled them with a toasting portion for everyone.

He raised a glass to his family.

"*Salute e cent'anni.*" Good health for a hundred years. He added a silent cheer to his parents and filled in the hoped-for benediction from above.

Happy graduation, son.

Leaning in, Jules kissed him tenderly above their beautiful boy's blond head, and he greedily took advantage and deepened the connection. All the chatter fell away until it was just Jules's green-gold gaze and soft lips holding him enthralled. Two years ago, this woman had walked into this restaurant and seized him by the throat, heart, and other parts of his anatomy that should be handled with care.

The twitch of her lips and light in her eyes asked the age-old question, *You okay?*

The same question they had asked each other a million times at a million family gatherings since she had found her home with the DeLucas.

Their people.

His woman.

He could feel a smile conquering his face, one that put every other smile to shame. No one had ever been this happy. With a sleeping demon in one arm and the girl of his dreams on the other, okay didn't cut it. More like perfect.

They were his at last, and he was never letting go.

Instead of getting an MFA,
Lili DeLuca works at her family's
Italian restaurant. When she runs into
celebrity chef Jack Kilroy, can he
convince her to follow her dream...
or is this a recipe for disaster?

Please see the next page
for an excerpt from *Feel the Heat*

CHAPTER ONE

She should have been safely ensconced in the apartment above her family's restaurant, scarfing down leftover pasta and catching up on the reality show glut bursting her DVR. Instead, Lili DeLuca was considering a 3 a.m. stealth mission down a dark alley, wearing shiny, blue Lycra hot pants and a star-bangled bustier. As ideas went, this one was as smart as bait.

Peeling off her Vespa helmet, she sent a longing look up to her bedroom window, then peered once more into the alley leading to the kitchen entrance of DeLuca's Ristorante. The door was still propped open. Light still streamed out into the night. Brightness had never looked so wrong.

A busy Damen Avenue could usually be relied upon to assure an unaccompanied woman that she was not alone. Wicker Park, formerly a low-income haven for underfed artists and actors-slash-baristas, had grown into a dense jungle of expensive lofts, chic eateries, and shi-shi wine bars. Between those, O'Casey's Tap on the corner, and the regular influx of suburbanite good-timers, the streets were always full and safe.

But not tonight.

The bars had dribbled out their last drunks an hour ago and by now, the 708ers were snoring soundly on their sleep number beds back in the 'burbs. Despite the stifling ninety-degree June heat, her neighborhood had never appeared so stark and cold. Living so close to work might have its perks, such as a thirty-second commute and the best Italian food in Chicago, but it was hard to see the upside in the face of that damn kitchen door, open like a gaping maw.

Maybe it was Marco. Her ex liked to use her family's business as his personal playpen, adamant that his investment accorded him certain privileges. A bottle of expensive Brunello here. A venue for an after-hours poker game there. Even a chance to impress, with his miserable culinary skills, the latest lithe blonde he was wearing. He'd cooked for Lili once. His linguine had been as limp as his...

Sloughing off those memories, she refocused on her current problem. Six hours ago, the Annual Superhero Extravaganza had seemed like a harmless way to rehabilitate her social life and get out there (oh, how she hated *there*). Guilting her into living was a favorite pastime of Gina's, and her cousin had persuaded her to attend with honeyed words.

Time to get back in the game, Lili. No, your thighs don't look like sides of beef in those shorts. The Batman with the wandering digits? He's not fat, he's just husky.

A husky Batman might come in handy right about now.

Leaving behind the safe hum of traffic, she crept toward the door. The garbage stench stung her nostrils. Something furry scurried behind one of the dumpsters. A raucous riff from the Rolling Stones' "Brown Sugar" swelled and filled the space around her. Insanity had its own soundtrack.

You might be dressed like Wonder Woman, but that doesn't mean you should play the hero. Just take a look, then call someone.

She sneaked a peek around the door. Expensive kitchen equipment—*her* equipment—lay strewn with serving dishes, pots, and pans on the countertops. Renewed alarm streaked through her. This didn't look like the handiwork of Marco, who thought a *bain marie* was the name of a girl he'd like to date.

So much for the plausible explanation. Some shithead was burglarizing her restaurant to the strains of Jagger and Richards.

The next move should have been obvious, but her cinder block feet and racing brain warred all the same. Call someone. *Anyone.* Her father. Her cousin. That cute chocolate-eyed cop who stopped in for takeout on Fridays and insisted she give him a buzz at the first scent of trouble. She swallowed hard, desperate to stop her heart from escaping through her throat. It settled for careening around her chest like a pinball.

A cautious sniff returned an astringent blast of bleach that competed with the lingering basil aroma of Friday night's dinner service. Trembling, she nestled her camera, an eight-hundred-dollar Leica, inside her Vespa helmet, then squeezed her phone out of the tight pouch at the side of her shorts. She started to dial. *Nine. One-*

Her twitchy finger paused on hearing something more eerie than heart-stopping. From inside the walk-in fridge, a voice bounced off the stainless steel interior. High-pitched. Indeterminate gender. Singing at the top of its lungs. It was also completely out of tune.

She pulled open the screen door and quietly stepped inside. Damn feet had never known what was good for them.

Frantically, she searched for a weapon, and her gaze fell gratefully on the cast iron frying pan resting on the butcher's block. She swapped it out for her helmet, appreciating how the new heft almost worked to stop her hand from shaking. Almost. Her blurred and frankly ridiculous reflection in the fridge's stainless steel should have given her pause; instead it emboldened her. She was dressed for action. She could do this.

Rounding the walk-in's door, she took stock of the enemy in a millisecond. Built like a tank, his back was turned to her as he reached up to the top shelf for a container of her father's *ragu*. For the briefest of seconds, the incongruity gnawed at her gut. A tone deaf, *ragu*-stealing brigand? So it didn't exactly gel, but he was in her restaurant.

In the middle of the night.

Any hesitancy to act was wiped away by his stutter-step backward and the corresponding spike in her adrenaline. She hurled the pan and allowed herself a gratifying instant to confirm his head got the full brunt. Wolfish howl, check. Then she slammed the door shut on his thieving ass.

It had been quite a nice ass, too.

Good grief, where had that come from? It must be relief because a drooling appreciation of criminal hot stuff was so not appropriate. She loosed a nervous giggle, then covered her mouth like she could smother that wicked thought along with her chuckle. Naughty, naughty.

Now what, shiny shorts? Time to call in the cavalry, but as she pulled out her phone, another thought pierced her veil of giddy triumph. By now, Fridge Bandit should have been making a fuss or bargaining for his freedom, yet a full minute had passed with not a peep.

Confident that the broken safety release on the walk-in's interior would keep him at bay, she laid her head and hands flush to the cool fridge door. Somewhere behind her, the music's boom-boom bassline meshed with the walk-in's mechanical hum. Both now vibrated through her body while the thump-thump of her heart tripped out a ragged beat.

Still nothing from within that cold prison. New horror descended over her.

She had killed him.

Fortunately or perhaps, unfortunately, the panic of that dread conclusion was dislodged by the fridge door's sudden jerk outward, sending Lili into a rather graceless meet-cute with the kitchen floor. Butt first, of course.

So someone had fixed that safety lock, then.

Her former comrade, the frying pan, emerged like a mutant hand puppet, soon followed by a wrist and a hairy arm before the whole package materialized. Vaguely, something big, bad, and dangerous registered in her mind. He held the pan aloft to ward off any imminent attack, but he needn't have worried. Still grounded, super powers severely diminished, she blinked and focused. Then she wished she hadn't bothered as the tight knot of fear unraveled to a cold flood of embarrassment.

"Jesus Christ, you could have bloody killed—" Fridge Bandit said. His mouth dropped open. Scantily clad superheroes flat on their butts often have that effect.

Thick, black hair, green eyes flecked with gold, and a face straight out of a Renaissance painting were his most obvious assets. Lili postponed the full body browse because she knew she was in trouble. Big trouble.

It was *him*.

He touched the back of his head, a not-so-subtle reminder of her transgression, and placed the pan down with all the care of someone disposing of a loaded weapon. His casual wave at the countertop behind her cut the music abruptly.

Probably a skill he had acquired during an apprenticeship with the dark side of the Force.

"You all right, sweetheart?" he asked in the casual tone of one who doesn't really care for the answer. He pocketed an iPod remote and made a half-hearted move toward her. She held up the okay-hand. *Too late, buster.*

Lowering her eyes to check the girls, she exhaled in relief. No nip slips. She jumped to her feet, surreptitiously rubbed her sore rump, then cast a glance down to her red, knee-high Sandro boots for inspiration. Nothing doing.

You're wearing a Wonder Woman costume and you just went all-out ninja on one of the most famous guys in the Western hemisphere.

At last, she raised her eyes to his face, now creased in a frown.

"I'm Jack."

"I know who you are."

Lili figured anyone sporting a painted-on outfit like she was probably had, oh, a ten-second ogle coming her way. Her ego might have taken a shot along with her behind, but she knew she had started the evening looking pretty darn good. Hell, four out of five flabby-muscled Supermen at the party had thought so. With her overweight teens firmly in the past, she'd since embraced her size fourteen figure, and on the days she felt less than attractive—for every woman suffered days like those—she had enough friends telling her to own it, girl, revel in those curves.

So here she stood, owning and reveling, while simultaneously forging a somewhat unorthodox path for feminism with her own leering appraisal.

Jack Kilroy's extraordinarily handsome mug was already branded into her brain. Not because she was a fan, heaven forbid, but because her sister, Cara, was constantly babbling about its perfection, usually while nagging everyone she knew to watch the cooking show she produced for him, *Kilroy's Kitchen*. *(Monday nights at seven on the Cooking Channel—don't forget, Lili!)* A hot-as-a-griddle Brit, his star had risen in the last year, first with his TV show, then with his bestseller, *French Cooking for the Rest of Us*. And when not assailing the public with the sight of his chiseled good looks on food and lifestyle magazines, he could invariably be found plying his particular brand of brash foodie charm on the daytime talk show circuit. He wasn't just smokin' in the kitchen, either. Recently, a contentious break-up with a soap star and a paparazzi punch-up had provided delicious fodder for the tabloids and cable news outlets alike.

The camera might add ten pounds but in the flesh, Jack Kilroy was packing the sexy into a lean six-and-change frame. The matching set of broad shoulders didn't surprise her, but apparently the tribal tattoo on his right bicep did, judging by the shiver dancing a jig down her spine. It seemed so not British and just a little bit dangerous. Her gaze was drawn to his Black Sabbath T-shirt, which strained to contain what looked like extremely hard, and eminently touchable, chest muscles. Sculpted by years of lugging heavy-duty stockpots, no doubt. A pair of long legs, wrapped in blue jeans that looked like old friends, completed the very pleasant image.

Jack Kilroy was proof there was a God—and she was a woman.

"Is that your usual M.O.? Frying pan first, questions later?" he asked after giving her the anticipated once-over. He had used up his ten seconds while she had stretched her assessment to fifteen. Small victories. "Should I hold still and let you use your lasso to extract the truth from me?" He gestured to the coil of gold-colored rope hanging through a loop on her hip. If he expected her to act impressed by his knowledge of the Wonder Woman mythology, he'd be a long time waiting.

Maybe she was a little impressed.

"I thought you were stealing. I was about to call the police."

"You're telling me there's something worth stealing around here?"

Her body heated in outrage at his dismissive tone, though it could just as easily be down to the way his dark emerald eyes held hers. Bold and unwavering.

"Are you kidding? Some of this equipment has been in my family for generations." Right now, most of it had been pulled out from under the counters and was scattered willy-nilly on every available surface. "Like my *nonna's* pasta maker." She pointed to it, sitting all by its dusty lonesome on a countertop behind a rack of spices.

"That rusty old thing in the corner?"

"That's not rusty, it's vintage. I thought you Brits appreciated antiques."

"Sure, but my appreciation doesn't extend to food-poisoning hazards."

A protest died on her lips. Her father hadn't used that pasta maker in over ten years, so a zealous defense was probably unnecessary.

"So either I'm being punked or you're Cara's sister. Lilah, right?"

"Yes, Cara's sister," she confirmed, "and it's Lil—"

"I thought you were the hostess," he cut in. "Are frying pans the new meet-n-greet in Italian restaurants?"

It's three in the morning, she almost screamed. Clearly, the blow to his skull had impacted his short-term memory.

On cue, he rubbed his head, then gripped the side of the countertop with such knuckle-whitening intensity that she worried he might pass out.

"I'm the restaurant's manager, actually, and I wasn't expecting you. If I'd known *Le Kilroy* would be gracing us with his exalted presence, I would have rolled out the red carpet we keep on hand for foreign dignitaries."

She sashayed over to the ice cabinet and glanced back in time to catch him, his gaze fixed to her butt like he was in some sort of trance. Oh, brother, not even a whack to the head could throw this guy off his game. With a couple of twists, she crafted an ice pack with a napkin, and handed it to him. "How's your head?"

"Fine. How's your—?" He motioned in the direction of her rear with one hand while gingerly applying the ice pack with the other.

"Fine," she snapped back.

"I'll say," he said, adding a smirk for good measure. *Oh, for crying out loud.*

"Is that *your* usual M.O.? I can't believe you have so much success with the ladies." The gossip mags devoted pages to his revolving door dating style. Only Hollywood fembots and half-starved models need apply. They clearly weren't in it for the food.

For her insolence, she got a blade of a look, one of those condescending ones they teach in English private schools, which for some ridiculous reason they called public schools.

"I've had no complaints."

She folded her arms in an effort to project a modicum of gravitas, which was mighty difficult considering what she was wearing. It didn't help that every breath took effort in her sweat-bonded costume. "So, care to explain?"

"What? Why I've had no complaints?"

"I mean, what you're doing in my family's restaurant at this ungodly hour."

"Oh, up to no good. Underhanded misdoings. Waiting for a superhero to take me down."

Okay, ten points for cute. She battled a smile. Lost the fight. Palms up, she indicated he should continue and it had better be good.

"I'm doing prep and inventory for the show. Didn't Cara tell you?"

Of course she hadn't told her. That's why she was asking, dunderhead. "I haven't checked my messages," she lied, trying to cover that she had and her sister hadn't deigned to fill her in. "I was busy all evening."

"Saving cats from trees and leaping tall buildings in a single bound, I suppose."

"Wrong superhero, dummy," she said, still ticked off that Cara had left her out of the loop. "You haven't explained why you're doing this prep and inventory *here*." It seemed pointless to remind him of the lateness of the hour.

"Because this is where we'll be taping the show, sweetheart. Jack Kilroy is going to put your little restaurant on the map."

* * *

Good thing Laurent had stepped out because if he'd caught Jack referring to himself in the third person, he'd laugh his *derrière* off. That shit needed to stop. It was worth it, though, just to get this reaction. Wonder Woman's mouth fell open, giving her the appearance of an oxygen-deprived goldfish.

"Here? Why would you want to tape your stupid show here?"

Jack let the comment slide, though the snarky dig about his success with women had been irksome enough. Rather hypocritical, too, considering all that hip-swaying and lady leering in his general direction.

"Believe me, it's not by choice. This place is far too small and some of the equipment is much too...*vintage* for what I need."

Contrary to his comment about the size and age of the kitchen, Jack felt a fondness bordering on nostalgia. The nearest stainless steel counter was scuffed and cloudy with wear, the brushed patina a testament to the restaurant's many successful years. He loved these old places. There was something innately comforting about using countertops that had seen so much action.

Returning his gaze to Cara's sister, he speculated on how enjoyable it might be to hoist her up on the counter and start a little action right here and now. That costume she was poured into had cinched her waist and boosted her breasts like some comic-book feat of structural engineering, creating an hourglass figure the likes of which one usually didn't see outside of a sixties-style burlesque show. A well-packaged, fine-figured woman with an arse so sweet he was already setting aside fantasy time for later. His head throbbed, but the lovely sight before him was the perfect salve.

As intended, his "too small" and "vintage" comments set her off on another round of fervent indignation. The wild hand gestures, the hastily sought-for jibes, the churning eyes. Beautiful eyes, too, in a shade of blue not unlike cu-raçao liqueur, and with a humorous glint that had him trying not to smile at her even though he was incredibly pissed off at what she'd done. A woman—a very attractive woman—in an agitated state got him every time.

"This kitchen is not too small. It's perfect." She jabbed her finger at the burners and ovens lining the back wall. "We get through one hundred and fifty covers every Saturday night using this *tiny* kitchen, and we don't need the Kilroy stamp of approval. We're already on the map."

"I never said tiny, but I'm full of admiration for how you've utilized the limited space."

That earned him a response somewhere between a grunt and a snort followed by a surprise move toward a heavy stand mixer. Surely, she wasn't going to start clearing up? He put a placating hand on her arm.

"Hey, don't worry. I'll put everything back the way I found it."

She glanced down at his hand resting on her golden skin. By the time her eyes had made the return trip, she was shooting sparks. *Back off.* Hooking a stray lock behind her ear, she returned to her task—clean up his mess and make him look like an arse. A cloud of unruly, cocoa brown hair pitched forward, obscuring her heart-shaped face and giving her a distinct lunatic vibe.

It would take more than a death stare and a shock of crazy curls to put him off. Teasing her was too much fun. "I'm pretty fast, love, and if you can move with superhero speed, we'd get it done in a jiffy."

Another push back of her hair revealed a pitying smile. "Don't ever claim to be fast, Kilroy. No woman wants to hear that."

Ouch.

Before he could muster a clever retort, the kitchen doors flew open, revealing Cara DeLuca, his producer in full-on strut. Neither the crazy hour nor the mind-melting heat had stopped her from getting dressed to the hilt in a cream-colored suit and heels. Laurent, his sous chef and trusty sidekick, ambled in behind her with his usual indolence and a tray of take-out coffee.

Cara's sister grumbled something that sounded like, "Kill me now."

Sibling drama alert. Unfortunately, with a younger sister determined to drive him around the bend, he was in a position to recognize the signs.

"Lili, what on earth are you wearing?" Cara gave a languid wave. "Oh, never mind."

Lili. He had called her "Lilah." Lili was much better. Lilah sounded like someone's maiden aunt. This woman didn't look like anyone's maiden aunt.

Cara's eyes darted, analyzing the situation. His producer was nothing if not quick, which made her both good at her job and prone to snap judgments. The crew called her Lemon Tart, and not because she was sweet.

"Why are you holding your head like that?"

Jack cast a sideways glance at the sister. He wasn't planning to rat her out, but to her credit, she confessed immediately. In a manner of speaking.

"I thought it was that gang of classic-rock-loving, yet remarkably tuneless, thieves that have been pillaging Italian kitchens all over Chicago, and as I was already dressed for crime-fighting, instinct just took over, and I tried to lock your star in the fridge."

Laughter erupted from deep inside him, although he was fairly positive she had just insulted his beautiful singing voice. A muscle twitched near the corner of her mouth. Not quite a smile, but he still felt the warm buzz of victory.

"Lili, you can't go locking the talent up in a fridge," Cara chided.

"Or hitting it on the head with a frying pan," Jack added.

Cara's head swiveled Exorcist-style back to her sister. "She did what?"

Jack rubbed the back of his head, heightening the drama. "I don't think she broke the skin, but there'll be a bump there later."

Cara caressed his noggin and yelped like a pocketbook pup. "Oh, my God, Lili, do you realize what could have happened if Jack had a concussion and had to go to the emergency room?"

"It might have improved his personality. He could do with a humility transplant," Lili offered, again with that cute muscle twitch that he suddenly wanted to lick.

Laurent had been suspiciously quiet but now he stepped forward, and Jack braced himself for the Gallic charm offensive. As usual, his wingman looked bed-head disheveled, sandy-colored hair sticking out every which way. His bright blue eyes twinkled in his friendly face as he launched into one of his patented gambits.

"*Bonjour*, I am Laurent Benoit. I work with Jack." It tripped off his tongue as "Zhaque," sounding lazy and sexy and French. "You must be Cara's beautiful sister, Lili." He proffered his hand, and Lili hesitantly took it while the corners of Laurent's mouth hitched into a seductive grin. "*Enchantée*," he said, raising her hand to kiss it. This netted a husky laugh, which was a damn sight more than Jack had managed in the five minutes he had been alone with her. Man, that Frenchman was good.

"Now that's an accent I can get down with," Lili murmured.

Jack sighed. While his own British voice accounted for much of his success with American women, over the years he had lost more skirt to that French accent than he'd eaten bowls of *bouillabaisse*. Laurent—brilliant sous chef, occasional best friend, and his most rigorous competition for the fairer sex—was the embodiment of the French lover. As good as he was in the kitchen, his talents would be just as well-suited to tourism commercials. All he needed was a beret, a baguette, and a box of condoms.

Jack's head still hurt and weariness had set in bone-deep. He was sure he had lost consciousness for a few seconds in the fridge and now he battled the dizziness that threatened to engulf him. Coffee. That's what he needed. Coffee and something to focus on. Something that wasn't curvy and soft-looking and radiating man-killer vibes.

"Any chance we can get on with what we were doing?" he sniped at Cara, more brusquely than he'd intended.

"Of course, Jack, babe. We'll let you continue." Dragging her sister by the arm, Cara marched her out of the kitchen with a portentous, "Liliana Sophia DeLuca, a word in the office, if you please."

Laurent stood with arms crossed, staring at the scene of departing female beauty. Jack eyed his friend. *Here it comes.*

"I think I'm in love," Laurent groaned. "Is she not the cutest *chérie* you have ever seen?"

A laugh rumbled in Jack's chest. "That's the fourth time you've fallen in love this year and it's only June."

"But did you not see her cute little nose wrinkle up when I offered her my hand? And that lovely *derrière*. What I wouldn't do for a piece of that."

"She might have 'zee lovely *derrière*,' but she's got a dangerous bowling arm." His fingers returned to the spot where the frying pan had connected. A bump was definitely forming.

Jack followed Laurent's gaze to the swing doors through which Cara and her sister had just exited. A sudden image of brushing his lips against Lili's and watching the pupils of those lovely eyes magnify in passion flitted pleasantly through his mind. It wasn't long before his imagination had wandered to stroking her inner thigh and inching below the hem of those tight, blue, shiny shorts.

Things were just getting interesting when the crash of a dropped serving pan knocked him back to the present. While Laurent muttered his apologies, Jack blinked to quell his overactive brain, the pain in his head briefly forgotten. Maybe he should apply that ice pack to his crotch.

Evie, his dragon-lady agent, had been clear. *Think of the contract, Jack. Keep your head down and your nose clean. And whatever happens, do not engage the local talent.* Right now, that imminent network deal was the rocket that would propel his brand into the stratosphere. No more rinky-dink cable shit. Instead he would spread his message of affordable haute cuisine to as wide an audience as possible and garner fame for all the right reasons.

Which meant grasping women were an unnecessary distraction, even a tasty piece like Cara's sister. He needed to forget about smart-tart birds with eyes and curves that would lead a good man, or one who was trying to be good, off the straight and narrow. After his last disastrous relationship, he wasn't looking to screw around with the help, even if she did have the best *derrière* in the Midwest.

Things are getting hotter...

See the next page for
a preview of *ALL FIRED UP*
by Kate Meader.

CHAPTER ONE

It was the most beautiful wedding cake Cara DeLuca had ever seen. Three architecturally perfect layers of frosted purity designed to make women drool and men feign disinterest as soon as it was rolled out on a wobbly serving cart to the center of the harshly lit ballroom. Undoubtedly, a slice cost thirty, maybe forty-five extra minutes kicking the bag at the gym.

Cara checked that thought to the tune of screeching tires in her head. In a previous lifetime, she had measured every bite in push-ups and treadmill minutes, piling on laps in the pool to punish the slightest infraction. Old Cara would be looking for an excuse to slip out of a wedding reception before the cake so she could work off the chicken-or-fish entrée, and she had several options for how she did that. New Cara—healthy Cara—shouldn't need to count every bite and worry if she had passed over on to the wrong side of the fifteen-hundred calorie border.

But only an amazing cake could tempt her.

Cutting into the slice on the Limoges dessert plate, Cara slipped it past her lips, chewed slowly, and swallowed.

Ugh.

Dry, pedestrian, uninspired. No one knew better than Cara the truth behind that old adage about looks being deceiving. This cake might have been the bride's dream, but a single bite confirmed the suspicions Cara had formed the day she was roped in to salvage her cousin Gina's wedding. About ten minutes after the official planner had finally thrown up her hands in despair and gone running to the nearest sanatorium—read palm tree-lined, sandy beach.

This wedding was cursed.

It wasn't so much her cousin's insistence on the stab-your-eyes-out pink, fishtail-hemmed bridesmaid dresses or her requirement that she must have both a Neil Diamond string quartet for the cocktails *and* an all-girl Neil Diamond tribute band, the Sweet Carolines, for the dancing. Neither did Cara mind organizing last-minute fittings for a wedding party of twelve or a reception for two hundred ravenous Italians. As for corralling the ovary-exploding cute ring-bearers? Child's play, though Father Phelan had drawn the line at chocolate lab pups traipsing down the aisle behind ankle biters who could barely stay upright.

No, all that was manageable and managing was what Cara did best. Where it all went undeniably south was at the joint bachelor-bachelorette party in Las Vegas. This type of thing had become *de rigueur* and as much as Cara would have liked to put down the poker chips and back away slowly, she'd felt it incumbent on herself to manage that, too. A gaggle of drunk-off-their-butts DeLuca women needed her superior wrangling skills to make sure they had a wild and crazy, but safe, time. Unfortunately, her usually sober view had been crusted over by one colossally stupid mistake. A six-foot-tall, amber-eyed, mussed-up-haired mistake.

She should have stayed home in Chicago.

Thinking on those events of one week ago sent renewed fury roiling through her body. She could fix it. She *would* fix it. As soon as she got through this day.

Slowly, she surveyed the room and tried to breathe herself to calm in the face of the happiness onslaught. Her father—Il Duce to his daughters—held court at the elders' table after spending most of the meal bounding in and out of the hotel kitchen. Ensuring his menu was followed to exact specifications, no doubt. His queen, Francesca, rocking regal now that her corn silk blond hair had returned to its pre-cancer glory, wore a familiar upward tilt on her lips as she viewed the dance floor hijinks. Cara tracked her mom's gaze to a flash of flailing arms among the writhing bodies. *Oh, you've got to be kid—*

"I'm beginning to have second thoughts." A crisp, British voice intruded on her internal scold.

Jack Kilroy, her boss and future brother-in-law, wrinkled his patrician nose and lay down his fork primly.

"If you can't even get the cake right, Cara, I'm not sure I should be entrusting you with the most important day of my life," he added with just enough of that divo tone to remind her why she was glad he was marrying her sister Lili in six weeks, and not her. Having worked with Jack as his TV producer when he was *the* Jack Kilroy—ragingly successful restaurateur, cooking show icon, and tabloid meat—and now, as the private events manager for his Chicago restaurant, Sarriette, she was comfortably familiar with his moods and tics. Jack was almost as controlling as Cara, and that type never made it onto her dance card. The one that had turned yellow from disuse. At least until Las Vegas.

"The cake was a done deal before I became involved but don't fret your pretty head," she said, enjoying immensely how his face darkened at her patronizing tone.

Gun. Fish. Barrel.

"You've requested the most spectacular, stylish, knock-'em-dead—"

"Artistic, poetic, avant garde," Lili picked up, a little breathlessly.

Cara smiled up at her sister, newly arrived after cutting a rug on the boards.

"Wedding to end all weddings," Cara finished while Jack pulled his fiancée into his lap despite her whiny protests. It was a cute playact they did that would have turned her stomach at its sheer preciousness if it had been anyone else. The ache she felt in her belly could only be that cardboard cake talking.

"You shall have the wedding you've wanted since you were a little girl, Jack," continued Lili, touching his forehead in the style of a fairy godmother before dropping a kiss on his lips.

"You're so cheeky," Jack said. "Engaged for almost a year and still no joy. I'm told I'm very eligible, you know."

"Been reading your old *Vanity Fair* fluff pieces again, Jack?" Cara asked. There was a time when you couldn't turn around without seeing Jack's handsome mug on a magazine, billboard, or TV screen. Cara wondered if he missed it. Achieving her goal of becoming Chicago's Events Queen depended on him missing it.

"Most women are dying to walk down the aisle…" He coasted a hand along Lili's thigh, clearly appreciative of her va-va-voom figure. Even in the bridesmaid dress from Hades, Lili looked like an advertisement for real women with those generous curves.

Thin women are just as real, Cara's inner therapist whispered.

"But this one has no interest in the fairy tale," Jack went on. "Complete with Prince Charming."

Lili rolled her eyes affectionately. "I'm happy to go quietly to city hall, but if you insist, I'll indulge you."

"Sweetheart, indulge me a little now," Jack said and pulled her in for a kiss.

Cara loosed a sigh and tried to reel in her envy at how Lili and Jack stared at each other to the exclusion of anyone else, the secret messages that needed no words, and their unmistakable joy at being in each other's company. Just seeing how much Jack loved her sister made Cara's cynical heart grow larger. Not three times, but maybe one and a half.

If anyone deserved the fairy tale, it was Lili. Her younger sister had carried the weight of family obligations during their mother's battle with breast cancer while Cara had folded up like a Pinto in a head-on collision with a semi. Cara owed Lili, and she was going to repay a fraction of that debt by planning her dream wedding down to the finest detail—even if her sister didn't know she wanted it yet.

"How's the cake?" Lili asked Cara once Jack let her come up for air. Her gaze slid to the slice, lying listlessly on the scallop-edged dessert plate.

"Not so great," Cara said. "Don't worry. We'll have something much better for your big day." She already had an artiste in mind and if he was good enough for Oprah's farewell do—

"Cake's sorted," Jack announced.

"What?" Cara asked, but the tingle she felt as the word spilled out told her she should be asking, "Who?" She didn't even have to hear his name, her traitorous body was already on board.

"My secret weapon." Jack chuckled and nodded to the dance floor.

Cara followed his gaze and by some Moses-like miracle, the tangle of bodies parted to reveal the weapon himself.

Shane Doyle. He of the Irish eyes, devastating dimple, and incredibly dorky dance moves.

The Sweet Carolines were playing the eponymous tune and Shane was waving his hands in the air, alternating between an interpretive dance featuring a tree and the old mime-trapped-in-a-box routine. Maisey, one of the servers at Sarriette and Shane's dance partner, was holding tight to her side because apparently Shane wasn't just bustin' moves, he was bustin' guts as well. From twenty feet away, Cara could hear him hollering about how good times never seemed so good.

The well of anger bubbled in her chest again. He shouldn't even be here, but after just a couple weeks in Chicago, he had made himself right at home and finagled an invitation to the wedding as Maisey's plus one. Well, she could have him.

Cara was gearing up to drag her eyes away—any moment now—when a rather daring pivot landed him in a face-off with their table. One eyebrow arched. He held her stare. And then he winked. Which he had no damn right to do after what had happened between them a week ago in Sin-Freaking-City.

"No," she said firmly, turning away from those chocolate drop eyes set in that ridiculously fine face. Not just fine, but friendly and cheerful and oh, hell, mostly fine.

"No, what?" asked Jack.

"No, we can't use Shane." When Jack's expression turned curious, she hastily added, "He's too new and he's got far too much on his plate trying to get up to speed at the restaurant.

Let me remind you that you've given me a very tight time-line here. Less than two months to plan the kind of shindig you want means I can't leave anything to chance."

Though Jack and Lili had been engaged for close to a year, Lili had only recently pulled the trigger on the wedding planning now that she was settled into her MFA program at the School of the Art Institute. Jack was champing at the bit to make Lili "Mrs. Jack Kilroy," but her sister refused to be pushed. That summed up their relationship in a nutshell.

Jack and Lili shared a meaningful glance. Cara hated when they did that. .

"Something happened in Vegas and it clearly hasn't stayed there," Lili said. "We all know you slept with him."

Recrimination simmered in her gut. If only it were that simple. Not that sex was ever simple but at least they could put that in the ancient history column and move on.

"I didn't know." Jack's brow knitted furiously. "Cara, tell me it's not true."

"It's not true," Cara repeated, sort of truthfully. She hadn't slept with anyone in too-long-to-recall and even then, she, or he, never stayed overnight. It was one of her rules, or it had been until a week ago when she woke up with a screaming hangover and a big lug of an Irishman twined around her body.

"You destroyed my last pastry chef," Jack said. "Shane's been here only a couple of weeks and you've already got your hooks into him."

"Now, now, Jack," Lili soothed. "You can't tell your employees who they can and can't be with."

"Oh, yes I can. She made Jeremy cry. The poor guy left because Cara stomped all over him."

Cara bristled, then covered with a languid wave. Everyone's impression of her was of a woman who took no prisoners when it came to life and love—an impression she did little to dispel.

"Don't be ridiculous. Jeremy and I went on one date and it didn't work out. Can I help it if you employ weak-willed, mewling kittens just so you can surround yourself with yes men who'll bow down and kiss your ring?"

The man *had* cried, though, the wuss.

Lili's unearthly blue eyes zeroed in on Cara, making her shiver with their perspicacity. "So if you didn't do the deed with Shane, what happened? You hightailed out of that Vegas hotel like you were auditioning for Girl Being Chased Number Two."

"Nothing happened. We just had a few drinks and that's it. Nobody got stomped on." Much. She felt her head cant slightly in Shane's direction. It completely sucked to have no control over her body.

And then as if she had summoned him out of thin air, he was there. The distance from dance floor to table should have given her a decent interval to adjust but Shane had bounded over like a big Irish setter, throwing Cara off kilter. Any farther and she'd be listing like the *Titanic* in its final moments. His hip-shot loll against the table's edge made his ancient-looking jeans cleave fondly to his thighs, prompting Cara's own thigh muscles to some involuntary flexing of their own.

Who wears jeans to a wedding? While everyone else wore tuxes and dark suits, Shane was embracing the American Dream with button-fly Levi's, weathered cowboy boots, and a sports jacket that stretched a little too tight over his annoyingly broad shoulders. Only after that snide thought had formed did it occur to her he had probably borrowed the jacket, likely from one of the other chefs.

Unavoidably, her eyes inched up, up, up, taking in over-long, mink-brown hair that just begged to be raked. The melty mocha eyes with a hazelnut corona ringing the iris. The jaw scruff that hadn't made acquaintance with a razor in a couple of days. The...oh, she could go on and on.

So she did. Down, down, down she traveled that granite-hard body, before resting her gaze on his large hands, not that she needed visual verification of their size. She distinctly remembered how big they were because she had awoken with one spread possessively across her stomach a week ago. She knew just how devastatingly erotic Shane's hand felt on her bare skin.

"Sure, I'm looking for a new dance partner," Shane said with that Irish musical lilt that did wondrous things to large segments of the American female population. Cara liked to think she was immunized against all that *faith and begorrah* malarkey, but she reluctantly acknowledged Shane's accent was one of his most appealing features. Like the guy needed more help to sell the goods.

Shaking off her appreciation, she tried to draw on all the reasons she was mad at him. "What happened to your last one?" She looked to see where the cast-off Maisey had landed but the poor girl was nowhere to be found. "Did you make her ill with all that jumping around?"

"Ah, I'm just too much for one woman," Shane said, exploding into that cheeky smile that had caught her attention the moment she'd entered the bar at the Paris hotel in Las Vegas. A patchwork memory of numerous drinking establishments flashed through her querulous mind. In every one, the guys had got there before the girls. And in every one, Shane Doyle had been first on his feet, motioning to his seat as soon as the lady mob arrived to meet up with the bachelor's posse for the tandem shenanigans.

A nice mama's boy, she had decided. Polite and mannered, the kind of guy she usually liked to date because they let her call the shots. Where to go, what to do, how to please her. A few tears might be shed when they parted—not by her, of course—but so far it had worked out swimmingly.

How had she messed up so spectacularly with Shane?

The band took a break and the music switched to DJ-determined wedding classics. First up, the oom-pah booms of the *Chicken Dance*, and Cara found herself a tiny bit curious to see Shane's interpretation.

"We were talking about the cake," Jack said, defaulting to his one-track mind. Marriage to Lili or bust. In telepathic communication, both chefs' gazes slipped to the slice of maligned cake now insulting everyone by its mere presence on the table.

Shane scoffed. "Whoever made this rubbish should be shot for crimes against pastries."

That pulled a deep laugh out of Jack and a juvenile eye roll out of Cara. Ah, chef humor.

"So I'll expect something amazing for my wedding." He squeezed Lili's waist. "We both will. You up for it?"

A weird look passed over Shane's face, clearing his cheer. If Cara didn't know better, she would have thought he was annoyed, even angry. Which made no sense considering what an honor it was to have Jack choose the new guy for such an important commission.

"I would think you'd want to bring Marguerite in from Thyme," Shane said, his voice as tight as the set of his mouth. "She's your best pâtissier."

Thyme on Forty-Seventh, Jack's New York outpost and Shane's stomping ground until two weeks ago when he transferred to Chicago, sported any number of culinary stars, and Marguerite was the brightest of them all. Cara was in full agreement with Shane. It wouldn't have surprised her in the least if Jack wanted to fly the talented Frenchwoman in for the occasion.

Shane's mood change appeared to have passed unnoticed by Jack. "Yeah, she's great, but I want you. You're a wizard with desserts and after chasing me around for months trying to get a job, I think you're ready for the big leagues."

Shane smiled but it was as if the effort might result in the death of a puppy. There *was* something. "We could do angel food and pistachio cream, or maybe a rosemary-lemon to keep the Italian theme."

"I like how you think," Jack said, smiling broadly. "Keep it up and we'll talk next week."

"Sure," Shane said with a dimple blast in Cara's direction. A return to charming, sunny Shane.

Flustered, she felt her hand move to the still-full champagne flute she had been shunning since the toasts, but before her fingers made contact, he cocked his head. One of those, *Need a chaser of impaired judgment with that bubbly?* head tilts that decelerated her brain. Damn the man and his caramel-hued eyes, now narrowed and holding her captive.

"Back to the dancing," he said.

Cara had important things to say to Shane. Very important things. And avoiding him wasn't going to get it done. After years of unhealthy denial, she had vowed to meet her problems head on, so she wasn't entirely sure why she had let a whole week go by without pulling Shane aside and telling him how it was. How it will be. She'd put it down to how busy she was ensuring Gina's wedding wouldn't be a complete debacle. Declining to examine that closely was about the only thing preventing her from losing her ever-loving mind.

Before she went off on him, it might be easier to soften him up on the dance floor. Besides, there was something just so adorkable about his enthusiasm. She uncrossed her legs and flexed a perfectly pedied foot clad in a Jimmy Choo peep toe. Her feet looked stunning in fuchsia.

Shane's gaze brushed fire across Cara's skin as he reached for her sister. "Lili, would you do me the honor?"

Lili slid out of Jack's lap and Cara's heart slid into her stomach.

"That's if you don't mind, Jack," Shane added.

"Oh, you wouldn't catch Jack dead on the dance floor," Lili said. "He's much too image conscious."

"I'm not afraid of looking foolish. You've heard me sing," Jack said blithely. "I draw the line at the *Chicken Dance*, though."

"It's ironic," Cara said, aiming for levity after being snubbed by Shane because there was no doubt that's what had happened here.

"Ironically stupid," Jack replied. "Just make sure I see daylight between you two."

Laughing, Shane led a willing Lili out onto the dance floor and jumped into flapping his arms with gusto. Lili fanned her hips with both hands, then moseyed into the fray with jerky hitches more appropriate to a Taser victim.

Cara's heart boomed at ten times the beat of the music as she fought to recover her aplomb. It was easy to see why Shane would prefer to dance with Lili, who was never afraid to get into the spirit of things. Unlike stuck-up, no-fun Cara, who needed to drink her weight in vodka to go a little bit wild.

A buzz of her phone alarm reminded her that the next wedding planner task was imminent and that she had more important things to worry about than the mistake that had followed her home from Vegas. She would deal with Shane Doyle later.

Fall in Love with Forever Romance

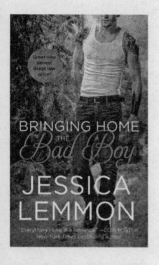

BRINGING HOME THE BAD BOY
by Jessica Lemmon

The boys are back in town! Welcome to Evergreen Cove and the first book in Jessica Lemmon's Second Chance series, sure to appeal to fans of Jaci Burton. These bad boys will leave you weak in the knees and begging for more.

HOT AND BOTHERED
by Kate Meader

Just when you thought it couldn't get any hotter! Best friends Tad and Jules have vowed not to ruin their perfect friendship with romance, but fate has other plans...Fans of Jill Shalvis won't be able to resist the attraction of Kate Meader's Hot in the Kitchen series.

Fall in Love with Forever Romance

FOR KEEPS
by Rachel Lacey

Merry Atwater would do anything to save her dog rescue—even work with the stubborn and sexy TJ Jameson. But can he turn their sparks into something more? Fans of Jill Shalvis and Kristan Higgins will fall in love with the next book in the Love to the Rescue series!

BLIND FAITH
by Rebecca Zanetti

The third book in *New York Times* bestseller Rebecca Zanetti's sexy romantic suspense series features a ruthless, genetically engineered soldier with an expiration date who's determined to save himself and his brothers. But there's only one person who can help them: the very woman who broke his heart years ago...

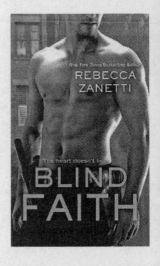

Fall in Love with Forever Romance

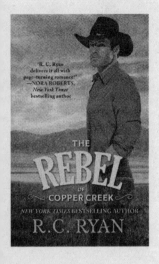

THE REBEL OF COPPER CREEK
by R. C. Ryan

Fans of *New York Times* best-selling authors Linda Lael Miller and Diana Palmer will love this second book in R. C. Ryan's western trilogy about a young widow whose hands are full until she meets a sexy and rebellious cowboy. If there's anything she's learned, it's that love only leads to heartbreak, but can she resist him?

NEVER SURRENDER TO A SCOUNDREL
by Lily Dalton

Fans of *New York Times* best-sellers Sabrina Jeffries, Nicole Jordan, and Jillian Hunter will want to check out the newest from Lily Dalton, a novel about a lady who has engaged in a reckless indiscretion leaving her with two choices: ruin her family with the scandal of the season, or marry the notorious scoundrel mistaken as her lover.

VISIT US ONLINE AT

WWW.HACHETTEBOOKGROUP.COM

FEATURES:

OPENBOOK BROWSE AND
SEARCH EXCERPTS
•
AUDIOBOOK EXCERPTS AND PODCASTS
•
AUTHOR ARTICLES AND INTERVIEWS
•
BESTSELLER AND PUBLISHING
GROUP NEWS
•
SIGN UP FOR E-NEWSLETTERS
•
AUTHOR APPEARANCES AND TOUR
INFORMATION
•
SOCIAL MEDIA FEEDS AND WIDGETS
•
DOWNLOAD FREE APPS

BOOKMARK HACHETTE BOOK GROUP
@ WWW.HACHETTEBOOKGROUP.COM